A Dog For Easy Company

David R. Oakes

Copyright © 2023 David R. Oakes

All rights reserved.

No part of this book may be reproduced in any form or by electronic or mechanical means, including information storage and retrieval systems, without written permission from the author, except for the use of brief quotations in a book review.

ISBN: 9798850745325

Cover Art by Athena Carroll

DEDICATION

This book is dedicated to all the men and women who served or are serving in our armed forces.

And to Betsy, Rufus, Sallie, Bear, and Barney. I will see you all again in the place where rabbits and squirrels are aplenty, but you just miss catching them.

"The 101st Airborne Division has no history, but it has... a rendezvous with destiny."
- *Major General W.C. "Bill" Lee, father of the Airborne, General Orders No. 5, Headquarters 101st Airborne Division, August 19, 1942.*

CONTENTS

	Prologue	Pg 1
1	Dogs For Defense	Pg 7
2	Train, Train, Train!	Pg 21
3	Currahee	Pg 35
4	Jump Wings	Pg 54
5	Training For War	Pg 74
6	Training in England	Pg 97
7	Normandy	Pg 110
8	March, Fight, March, Fight	Pg 134
9	Aldbourne and Holland	Pg 153
10	Healing Wounds	Pg 192
11	Bastogne	Pg 219
12	Darkness	Pg 248
13	Learning to Walk	Pg 265
14	Home	Pg 275
	Epilogue	Pg 289
	Sources	Pg 292
	Acknowledgments	Pg 294

PROLOGUE

The morning Sun shone through the upstairs window of the sprawling, two-story farmhouse. A young girl, barely ten years old, began stirring under her blankets but enjoying the warmth of her bed in the cold of winter. Suddenly, she sat up, her green eyes large and wide. "My puppies!" she cried, jumped from her bed to the cold floor, grabbed her house coat and threw it on over her pajamas. She dashed down the stairs, her mess of long red hair flaring behind her. She ran through the kitchen, past her mother, and into the mudroom.

"Penny! Put on shoes before you go traipsing outside!"

Penny stopped in the mudroom with a 'hmmph' but slipped on an oversized pair of rubber boots. She looked at her mother, a grownup mirror image of herself, pleading to go on.

"Go see your puppies, but just for a few minutes. You need to feed the chickens and goats, then come eat breakfast and get ready for church."

Penny's mother, Marilyn, 38 years old with beautiful red hair matching her young daughter, loved being a farmer's wife. Tall and slim, she worked as hard as her husband, cooking, canning vegetables, and tending to goats, chickens, ducks, and geese. Washing clothes and cleaning the house was a continuous battle to keep the farm outside of the house. But she did it by hard and fast rules- no boots or shoes on inside past the kitchen.

She watched her only daughter run awkwardly to the barn and disappear inside. *That girl loves those babies so much*, she thought with a smile. Jim's hunting dog, Sallie, a three-year-old bluetick hound and the best hunting dog he had ever owned, was probably one of the best hunters in the state. She had a truly profound sense of smell, hearing, and vision. Sallie could smell a raccoon a mile away and spot a squirrel moving through branches so far away that Jim initially thought she was a lyin' coonhound. But he soon learned to trust her and came home with more raccoons, rabbits, and squirrels than ever before. Jim's oldest, James Junior., or Jimmy, would take her hunting and was becoming a good shot, too.

Normally, Sallie stayed inside the farmhouse, but with eight puppies, it was too much disorder, so off she went to the barn. Penny helped set up a clean, warm bed for her to tend to her puppies. That was where Penny was heading now. Sallie was bedded down in a corner of a stall, nestled in straw. Her litter of eight puppies was eight weeks old and ready to leave the nest, though they still suckled on their mother. Eight puppies, all scrounging for a teat, all cute but in an unusual way.

Seven of the pups looked like the father—a full-blooded German Shepherd from a mile or so down the road—except for one thing; floppy ears, which added to the cuteness already bestowed on all puppies. The last one, Jim knew, would never find a home. He was the funniest looking dog he'd ever seen. It had a German Shepherd body and head, floppy ears like his siblings, but then "bluetick" spots mixed into the thick German Shepherd fur. They would find out later that it also had his mother's bluetick hound rumbly bay that was loud and strong.

Penny wanted one of the puppies so awfully bad she would do anything to keep one. "Daddy, can I please, please keep a puppy? I promise to take care of it, I promise! And you can take it hunting with you and Sallie! You know it will be a good huntin' dog because it's Sallie's baby!"

Jim wasn't sure about that. He figured a few from the litter would be good hunting dogs, but others probably would turn out to be nothing more than family pets (not that there's anything wrong with that). Even so, he considered his daughter's request. It was almost December, so maybe a pup would be an early Christmas present.

"Okay, you have a deal," he said not unkindly. "But you must find homes for seven other pups before you can keep the last one. Deal?"

She considered her father's requirement for only a split second before squealing, "Thank you Daddy!" and rushed to his arms. Jim picked her up and swung her around while she laughed.

"Now Penny, the deal is you take care of the dog. You feed it, clean it, train it, and clean up his messes. Understand?" Penny wriggled out of her dad's embrace and ran over to the litter, staring lovingly at them before replying.

"I don't care which one is last, I love them all," she said honestly and full of love.

***

Two weeks later, all the pups except one were gone to new homes. The funny-looking pup was the last one left. Penny didn't care; she had her puppy. "What are you going to name him?" her mother asked. The puppy turned out to be funny, goofy, and full of energy. The day before, the dog had gotten out of the barn and discovered Jim's potato patch. Though long since harvested, there were still potato plants in the garden, and the pup dug them all up and dragged them around the yard.

"That's about the goofiest dog I've ever seen," Jim exclaimed, laughing.

"He sure is a Goofus Rufus," Marilyn said laughingly. Penny remembered the stir it caused with her father, thankful that the garden was through for the winter. Still, it was not a good beginning. Then she thought of a good name. "That's his name! Goofus Rufus! Good ole Rufus!"

Breakfast was waiting on the kitchen table. "Penny, time to come in and get ready for church. And leave Rufus outside!"

***

A year later, Rufus had certainly lived up to his name. Jim attempted to train him to hunt, but even though the dog had an extremely good nose, he couldn't stay on a scent, leaving the trail for whatever attracted him. But Rufus was fearless. He certainly wasn't gun shy, running toward wherever Jim aimed and shot, sometimes returning with a duck or rabbit, but most times not. Sallie always brought game back unless Rufus beat her to it, but that was rare. After several weeks of working with Rufus, he gave up and just allowed the dog to accompany him and the best hunting dog in 5 counties.

As they returned from a Sunday morning hunt in early December, Penny and Rufus met them at the back porch, with coffee for her father and bowls of warm mush for Sallie and Rufus. Marilyn and Jim watched as Penny later led Rufus to the barn to feed the goats. Jim supposed he made the right decision in letting Penny keep the dog. Even so, as he walked into the kitchen that Sunday morning, he stated matter-of-factly, "That dog ain't never gonna amount to nothing."

Boy, was he wrong, on that Sunday morning, December 7, 1941.

***

December 7, 1941
Greensburg, Tennessee

Jackson walked quietly through the dense, tree-covered valley, his dog Beau leading the way. Beau, short for Beauregard, was a 5-year-old English Setter with long, soft white fur covered with mottled black markings. Though Jackson carried a shotgun, he rarely used it. He enjoyed being in the country behind his family's farm, away from everyone and everything, especially school.

As Beau walked alongside him toward their home, Jackson couldn't keep troubled thoughts from invading the early morning hunt. He was a sophomore at Mississippi State College, in Starkville, Mississippi, enrolled in the College of Agriculture and Animal Sciences. He loved living on a farm, raising crops and animals. But he struggled in his classes, mainly economics and chemistry. *Why do I need to take these stupid courses anyway?* He wondered. As many students discovered, there was so much more to Agriculture Sciences than first believed. His courses were tougher than he assumed – chemistry, biology, even biochemistry. He wanted to learn as much as possible and use his skills to make his family farm more profitable, but now it looked like he may not get much more education.

Tall and trim, with thick black hair cut short, Jackson was in excellent physical condition. He played football and basketball for his high school varsity teams and ran the mile in track. While he wasn't the star on any team, he was a hustler and made few mistakes. He continued to go on long runs at school to stay in shape and work off the stress of his studies. He didn't really date many girls, not because they weren't attracted to him – he was a good-looking kid with an honest smile – but he was shy around the girls and tended to stay in his room studying (not that it helped his grades).

They arrived home just in time for a hot breakfast. His mother, Faye, was a good cook and always had a large Sunday breakfast ready when her boys were home. Jackson's older brother, Eugene, was home from Cookeville, Tennessee, where he studied mechanical engineering at Tennessee Polytechnic Institute. A little over three years older than Jackson, Eugene was in his senior year and expected to graduate in Spring 1942. Unlike his younger brother, Eugene swept through his courses with ease, earning all As or Bs. Eugene was a bigger version of Jackson, a little taller, a little thicker in the shoulders and chest, with the same short, cropped head of black hair. Unlike Jackson, he was hardly shy of girls and had many fruitful dates.

The boys attended church with their mother and father whenever they were home. Faye had always believed that raising her boys in a Christian home was one of her most important duties as a mother, and the brothers had thrived under their mother's upbringing. Gene, their father, was a farmer, old-fashioned, worked every day from dawn to dusk, and left the upbringing to his wife. He only got involved when there was trouble, or someone needed a belt across their backside. (It had been many years since he had to use a belt on one of the boys since they were both upstanding young men.)

After church, they returned home for Sunday dinner. Faye went about fixing a few things in the kitchen while the boys sat in the den with Gene, listening to news of the war in Europe. Soon, dinner was ready, and they moved into the dining room. Cornbread, black-eyed peas, butter beans, mashed potatoes, and a large roast awaited them with sweet potato pie for dessert.

The boys cleaned up the table and helped their mother with the dishes before sitting in the den again with their father. Gene had changed the radio to a CBS station broadcasting from Nashville.

It was a little before 1:30 p.m. when the show was interrupted by a news flash. "We interrupt this broadcast to bring you an important bulletin from the United Press. FLASH! Washington, the White House announces Japanese attack on Pearl Harbor."

The U.S. was going to war. The Imperial Japanese Navy had attacked Pearl Harbor. No one said a word while the broadcaster told of the terrible destruction and loss of lives. The attack had started just before 8:00a.m. Honolulu time.

The first to speak was Jackson. "Does anyone know where Pearl Harbor is?" he said quietly. Gene knew. He had served in the U.S. Navy as a young man during World War I.

Eugene and Jackson left their parents and went outside to talk. They both knew what the future held. A draft, boot camp, then off to war. Eugene had already decided he was enlisting in the Army. Jackson had similar thoughts and decided to enlist as well. They figured they would be in the Army fighting by June of 1942, whip the Japanese quickly and be home by Christmas.

It didn't turn out to be so simple, or over so quickly.

***

1

DOGS FOR DEFENSE

When the war started, America was one of only a few countries that did not have a formal military working canine program, and no plans for dogs appeared to be in the future. Alene Erlanger, a well-respected poodle breeder, took the lead. Mrs. Erlanger had pushed for dogs to serve in World War I but was denied. Now, after the surprise attack on Pearl Harbor and the United States joining the war in the Pacific and Europe, she knew she needed to successfully organize a K-9 Section.

Alene contacted a writer at the New York Sun, Arthur Kilbon, who often wrote about dogs in his articles. Arthur wrote a column named *Popular Dogs* for the New York Sun, and after speaking with Mrs. Erlanger, wrote columns expressing the need for a K-9 Section. Articles were published in the Saturday Evening Post and other family magazines found in middle class American homes.

In January 1942, Mrs. Erlanger officially founded the Dogs for Defense. She also coerced Kilbon to be the publicity director for the new organization. Soon, celebrities joined the cause, and Americans across the country began donating their treasured family pets to help win the war.

Dog breeds were lightly restricted at the beginning. DFD was looking for dogs between one and five years old, breeds such as German Shepherds, Belgian sheep dogs, Collies, Huskies, and Doberman pinschers. As the organization began receiving dogs, they weren't exactly sure what to do with them. What were the best training techniques for dogs serving in a war? For that matter, for what tasks could dogs be trained? Erlanger called on the best trainers she knew. As a renowned Poodle breeder, she called on her own kennel trainer, Henry Stoecker, to develop a K-9 Section training program. Ironically, Henry grew up in Germany but immigrated to America in the 1920's. Henry followed in his father's footsteps as a dog trainer, and while in Germany trained dogs for both military and police work. Stoecker began working with the first dogs to arrive. Those he found unsuitable were sent home to their families.

In February, Mrs. Erlanger opened her kennel, Pillicoc Kennels in Elberon, New Jersey, to military police to begin sentry training. Stoecker had developed an early training syllabus that would introduce the military men to the dogs. The dogs were a mixed bag, including German Shepherds, black poodles, Dalmatians, and a Huskie.

In March 1942, the Quartermaster Corps of the United States Army officially took over the K-9 Section. The QMC not only trained dogs for the U.S. Army, but also the U.S. Navy, Marines, and the Coast Guard. As the training program matured, the K-9 units (both men and dog) went through 8-12 weeks of basic obedience training. Now that the Army oversaw the program, they created six War Dog Training Centers, in Virginia, Nebraska, California, Mississippi, North Carolina, and Montana. It was about this time that the Quartermasters decided to officially designate the unit the K-9 Corps.

This is the program that brought Penny and Jackson together in ways they would never forget.

***

Christmas 1941, Greensburg, Tennessee

Both Gilmore boys returned to their respective schools to finish the last few days of the winter semester. Eugene needed to see his counselor to discuss leaving school to enlist in the U.S.

Army, and Jackson was withdrawing no matter what the future held. Neither boy discussed leaving school to enlist; they knew their parents would strongly protest them dropping their education. Eugene Sr (Gene) had never attended college. When he left the Navy in 1918, he returned to Tennessee and his parents' farm. He met Faye at the county fair in the spring of 1919. Faye was three years younger than Gene, only 17, slim, long, thick dark hair that curled when it rained. (Her boys must have inherited their mother's hair because Gene was nearly bald at the age of 41.) Gene and Faye were married after a short romance, and Eugene was born in early 1920. Gene ran the farm for his parents, and he and Faye lived in the upstairs bedroom where he grew up. Gene was an only child; his mother had severe complications during her pregnancy and never became pregnant again.

In 1924, Gene's mother passed, and a year later his father died from a lonely heart, or so it appeared. Gene took over the farm for good and ran a prosperous business, raising cattle, corn, hay, soybeans, and a large garden for themselves. He never resented not attending college, but he swore to Faye that their children would obtain an education.

Eugene's counselor was also opposed to him withdrawing. He advised Eugene to wait and finish his studies, graduate, then enlist as an officer. *He's right*, Eugene thought, *I should just finish school in May and then enlist.* But he knew Jackson planned to enlist as soon as he returned home in a few days. He decided to sign up with Jackson so they could hold a united front to their parents.

Jackson didn't have as tough a decision. When he met with his counselor to discuss leaving school and enlisting, he was told he was making a good decision. Go enlist, fight for our country, then return home and finish your education.

On a cold day a few days before Christmas Day, the Gilmore brothers drove to the recruiting center in the middle of town. Greensburg was a small southern town, with a gas station, a drug store, post office, one grocery store, and a small whistle-stop train station. The recruiting office was adjacent to the post office, with a small front office full of posters and photos to capture the imagination of prospective enlistees. Eugene had already signed up a year earlier as part of the Selective Training and Service Act of 1940, which mandated that all men between the ages of 21 and 45 to register for the draft. If you were selected for the peacetime draft lottery you then were required to serve one year in the U.S. military.

Jackson and Eugene thought they should arrive early and beat the long line, but arriving at 7:30am, there was already a line out of the recruiting office stretching 30 feet. It took an hour to finally make it into the building, and as the brothers began to warm up from the cold wind outside, they looked at the recruiters. Navy, Army, Army Air Force, even the Marines and the Coast Guard were there. Both brothers wanted to fight, and both planned to join the Army. As they waited, a civilian in a tweed suit asked "Who wants to join the Navy? Who wants to join the Army Air Force? Who wants to join the Tank Corps?"

"I'm joining the Army; I'm fighting the Japs and the Huns face to face" Eugene whispered to his brother. Jackson nodded; he would follow his brother's path, maybe end up in the same unit. The line at the Army desk wasn't too long, and several men in uniform were helping prospective soldiers enlist. Eugene was first up and told the recruiter he was ready to enlist. After a few questions and answers, the recruiter told him to go to the other side of the room and talk to the officer recruiter.

"I'm here to fight, not be an officer!" Eugene said, a little forcibly. "Officers fight right alongside enlisted in this Army, son," the recruiter said with a smile. "Now go on across the room. Next!"

Jackson watched his brother as he grumbled under his breath but went to the recruiter. "Well? What's it going to be, son?"

He turned back to the recruiter, a little shaken by what just occurred. His brother would be an officer and they would be wrenched apart forever. Now, full of anxiety and not sure what to do, he hesitated again.

"Son? I need an answer, what's it going to be? Tank Corps? Infantry, Artillery?"

Jackson nervously looked at the soldier. He finally blurted out

"Infantry for me sir!" With that, Jackson was sent to another room for a physical, more questions, forms to complete, then finally was told he was enlisted in the Army and would be told when to report. Go home for now.

Eugene had a bit longer ordeal. After discussing his education (he was still a semester away from graduation) with the man, it was decided he was eligible for Officer Candidate School and would be assigned to the Army Corps of Engineers, pending officer selection board approval. "I told you I want to fight, not build bridges!" the discussion quickly turned into an argument, but he stood his ground. After going back and forth for several minutes, the recruiter appeared to back off a little and consider his request.

"Well, Gilmore, I have to say I admire your desire to fight. I'll tell you what, I'll leave your designation blank, and once the selection board assigns you to OCS you can fight it out with the higher ups there on where you land. Fair enough?"

"Fair enough, thank you sir!" Eugene was relieved as he went to the next step of enlistment. About two hours later he was told the same instructions as Jackson: Go home and wait for orders.

The boys were excited on the drive home but were also caught up in what they would tell their parents. They stopped at the drug store for coffee and cinnamon rolls and time to think. Jackson led off. "What are we going to tell them? No matter what they're going to be mad."

"That's the point, no matter what they are going to be mad, so we just have to tell them we enlisted and sit back for the barrage."

"I can't take Momma crying, and you know she's gonna cry."

"I know, but we need to stick together, okay?"

Jackson sipped his coffee and took a bite of a cinnamon roll. "Okay, I'm with you, but you do all the talking."

"Deal. Hurry up and finish that roll. Let's go home."

The boys were certainly right about their parents being upset. Gene shouted at them, their mother only cried, which was worse than the chewing out from their father.

"Get in the truck, Jackson! I may not be able to stop your brother but I can by God stop you!" Gene grabbed Jackson by the arm and took him to the truck. Eugene went to stop them, but one look from his father and he held up. They drove to the recruiter in silence, Jackson fuming. *I'm nearly 20 years old, I can make up my own damn mind!* He thought but knew better than to share that thought.

Gene towed his son into the recruiting office and forced Jackson to point out who recruited him. "I'm here to get my son out of the Army. He never should have enlisted and did not have my or his mother's permission. I want him released from this enlistment now!"

The recruiter took it all in stride, and calmly asked Jackson his name, ignoring Gene. Once he had Jackson's file, he skimmed it quickly. "It says here that you are almost twenty years old. Is that correct?" Jackson nodded quickly. The recruiter nodded in agreement and finally acknowledged Gene.

"Sir, it appears that your son here is old enough to make his own decisions. It's what we call in the service being a 'grown ass man' and doing what our country calls us to do. So, your son is enlisted in the Infantry and will receive orders in the near future to report for Basic Training."

Gene stood fuming, not knowing how to respond. Finally, he turned and walked away without a word. Jackson looked at the recruiter, who just nodded at him. The drive home was also in silence, and when Gene went inside, Jackson stayed on the back porch with Beau. He could hear as his mother began crying again, but not as hard as before.

Supper that night was difficult. Faye cooked a good dinner for them, but they could tell her heart wasn't in it, with burnt rolls and over-cooked fried chicken. Still, the boys ate hungrily, if nothing else so they would not be able to speak, not with a mouth full of chicken. Finally, Gene put his fork and knife down, and cleared his throat. "Boys, I apologize. You both are right in enlisting. I enlisted in the Navy when I was 17, and my Momma was fit to be tied, but they didn't try to stop me. So, you boys go fight, but be careful, try to take care of each other, and come back home in one piece. Now pass me the pie."

And that was the end of the argument.

1942
Camp Shelby, Mississippi

Dear Momma,
Well, I've made it through 6 weeks of basic training, or boot camp as we call it. I'm doing really good. I finished first in my platoon in the two-mile run, and second in pushups. It's not too hot here yet but it's only March. I'd hate to be here in the summer! I don't think Greensburg gets as hot as this place will.

Anyway, I'm assigned to some huge division but only for training. As soon as we all complete boot camp most of us will go to other training and to a new unit. My drill sergeant asked for volunteers today for joining the K-9 Corps. It's a new unit that pairs you up with a dog and you train and go to war. I heard that the Army is taking in pets to train for combat. Momma, please don't volunteer Beau. He's a fine dog but he doesn't need to be mixed up in this mess. I'll get my own dog and when the war is over, I'll either keep him or give him back to his owner.

I heard from Eugene too. He's doing good in Officer Candidate School, but we all knew he'd be just fine. I figure if this war last more than a few years he'll be running whatever part of the Army he winds up in! I miss Eugene, and Daddy, and especially you Momma. Give Beau a big hug for me and a piece of your fried chicken.

Love always,
Your son, Jackson

Jackson *was* performing good. He was thriving in the Army environment. The physical training was enough to make him push himself, and he was in the top of his company in classroom training. In early 1942, the Army Ground Forces was established and assumed responsibility for training 'replacements.' All men in a Replacement Training Center were trained the same, conducted in two types of instruction. The first type required personal supervision and close contact with recruits. This included physical training, company marches and bivouacs (a "bivouac" was not as fancy as the French word appeared. It meant camping out in the cold without a tent or cover), uniform and bunk inspections, and close order drill.

The other type consisted of classroom instruction, mainly technical in nature, including weapons training, map reading (which many recruits barely passed and many failed), hand grenades, booby traps, and mortar and machine-gun field firing. This training was performed by a cadre of soldiers and officers from the battalion or regimental commands.

With about 3 weeks of training left, the word was passed that the division was looking for volunteers for the K-9 Corps. An older sergeant stood in front of the group of young men, still boys in some ways, and told the story of Dogs for Defense and the Quartermaster Corps taking over K-9 Corps training. "The Army has decided it will enlist dogs to help us defend our country. We need sentry dogs, attack dogs, messengers, dogs to help medics, and finally, combat dogs."

Combat dogs? That really got Jackson's attention. He quickly raised his arm and was given an inquiry form to complete. He thought of Beau back home and was thankful that his mother didn't volunteer his old friend. The questions focused on traits and qualifications:

- Do you like dogs?
- Do you have a pet or hunting dog?
- Are you friendly towards dogs?
- What is your AGCT score? (Army General Classification Test which measured the ability to learn)
- Do you consider yourself to be patient with animals?
- Rate your physical endurance on a level from 1 – 10 (with 10 being the best)
- Do you think you are dependable in terms of taking care of a dog 24 hours a day?

After he turned in his form, he continued with training, running, pushups, obstacle course (his times were in the top five in the company), and classroom instruction, when after a few days he was called to Division HQ. He was directed to a small classroom where a Quartermaster Sergeant was waiting to interview him. A captain in the QMC (Quartermaster Corps) sat in the back of the room with a pen and pad but did not ask any questions. The Sergeant went over all of Jackson's answers but asked for more details. He was especially interested in Beau and their hunting. Jackson sheepishly explained that while Beau was a great hunting dog, he quit hunting a couple of years ago, and just took Beau into the woods and fields near their home to just enjoy the quiet and beauty of the forested land and spend time with his best friend. The captain made some notes after this response, which caused Jackson some anxiety. *Uh oh, I may have just screwed up. He must think I'm lazy to just take my dog out and not go hunting!*

The interview complete, he was told to return to training. It was only a few days later when he was notified of his selection for K-9 Training School. While he had a couple of weeks left of boot camp, his personal training was accelerated so he could depart in a week. A special K-9 training course was being offered at Pillicoc Kennels in Elberon, New Jersey, until the Quartermasters established the War Dog Reception and Training Centers. (The first War Dog Reception and Training Center was not established until August 1942, at Front Royal, Virginia.)

With no chance for leave, Jackson was provided orders and a train ticket to New Jersey. The trip took three days, but it was a welcome break from training, and Jackson caught up on a lot of missed sleep. He wrote home to his mom so she would know where he would be for the next few months and let her know he was excited to be working with dogs. *I hope Momma is relieved to know I'll probably be safer with a dog going into combat.*

Why the rush? He was told when he received orders that the Army wanted to get combat dogs ready as soon as possible to accompany troops heading to the Far East and Africa. Becoming a K-9 Corps Trainer could be his ticket to getting into the fight faster than ever.

***

March 1942
Officer Candidate School, Fort Benning, Georgia

It was already hot at Fort Benning. Eugene arrived in late March in civilian clothes, a true citizen soldier. He was a little concerned to see officer candidates already in uniform, some with sharpshooter ribbons. He had assumed that all the officer candidates would be civilians, all starting as raw recruits. It appeared there were some enlisted men with different backgrounds and experiences to be members of his OCS class. *I'm gonna have to work real hard to keep up with those guys*, he thought with a little concern. There were over two hundred men in his class, now called a battalion, broke out into four companies of about 50 men each.

Coincidentally, Army Ground Forces also took over the training of officer candidates in April 1942, about the same time as it took responsibility for enlisted Basic Training. Fort Benning was a large, sprawling post, with nearly 200,000 acres for buildings, billeting, tents, and of course room for training. Fort Benning was home to Infantry OCS, where thousands of men attempted to complete the course and become Infantry Officers. OCS was a 17-week course and designed to push each officer candidate physically, mentally, and perhaps, even emotionally. Brigadier General Omar Bradley designed the course to instill discipline and a code of honor in the men. The men were to go through rigorous physical training and class instruction designed to provide technical and tactical experience and knowledge needed by a combat platoon leader. Leadership, while difficult to teach, was trained into the men using various techniques, such as working problems, instructing fellow candidates, and field drills.

Major General Omar Bradley was also the commander of the first airborne division in U.S. Army history when the 82nd Infantry Division was redesignated the 82nd Airborne Division, headquartered at Camp Claiborne, Louisiana. Bradley was then relieved by Major General Matthew Ridgeway.

Nearly all officer candidates completed basic training prior to attending OCS. Eugene was cleared to forego basic and attend OCS because of two things: He scored extremely high on the AGCT, and the Army had already decided he would join the Corps of Engineers after completing OCS. They just hadn't told Eugene yet. The Engineering Corps began construction of two training sites which were known as Engineer Replacement Training Centers (ERTC), located at Fort Leonard Wood, Missouri, and Ft. Belvoir, Virginia. However, the centers would not be ready to take in enlisted and officer candidates until late spring of 1942. Eugene was already 7 weeks into OCS, so the Army figured he could receive his commission and then attend a five-week refresher course designed for Reserve and National Guard soldiers who had some prior engineering training.

With only a few weeks remaining in OCS and clear that Eugene would graduate and earn a commission, he was called to the Battalion Commander's office. Major Rafferty invited him to have a seat and offered coffee, which Eugene politely declined. He knew something was up, but not sure what was going on. "Mr. Gilmore, I have some good news for you. Upon receiving your commission, you will be assigned to the Engineering Corps of the Army, and will receive refresher training at Fort Leonard Wood, Missouri. Congratulations! The Engineering Corps is an elite cadre of professionals with the highest technical skills of any officer group. You should be proud."

Eugene sat silent, not knowing what to say. Major Rafferty waited a polite moment before asking him if his orders were satisfactory. "No sir, they are not. Can I be honest with you sir? When I signed up, I made a pact with my younger brother that we would both fight in this war and volunteer for combat action. Now you tell me I'm going to the Engineering Corps? Sir, I'd like to refuse the orders so I can see combat."

The major rose from his chair and sat on the front of his desk. He lit a cigarette and took a long drag, exhaling slowly. "You know Mr. Gilmore, I need to quit smoking. It's a bad habit and not doing me any favors. But it's something that I'm used too now, and a drag here and there really helps my nerves."

He stubbed out the cigarette and continued. "You have been

given a chance of a lifetime, placed in your lap. Are you sure you want to turn it down?" Eugene was certain and said so.

"Well, I did a little digging and called a friend in the Engineering Corps. They have two classifications, combat units and service units. Combat units are assigned to units that fight the enemy. The service units serve more traditional functions and remain in the rear. So you see, you can be an engineer *and* fight. Does that change your mind?"

Gilmore had to think about this. Rafferty told him to think about it over the weekend and see him Monday morning after breakfast. He agreed, stood to attention, saluted, then returned to his training. He had a lot to think about. That evening after mess, he returned to his quarters, shared with 7 other candidates (the "quarters" was a hut made of fiberboard and tarpaper and sand floors, called "tarpaper shacks" by the men). *What can I do? The Army is gonna put me wherever they want, no matter what I want. I'm stuck and will never see action!* He laid on his bunk and for a while before getting up. His platoon was scheduled for night compass training beginning at 2100 hours. He had already proven he was proficient with compass and map reading, but the drill instructors (mostly staff sergeants) continued to drive it down their throats. The drill instructors were all combat hardened or at least seasoned, and knew the importance of disciplined night operations, maneuvering quietly but quickly through the sprawling fields surrounding the fort. Tonight, Eugene and three others were placed in the back of a 'Deuce and a half' truck (GMC CCKW 'Jimmy,' 2 1/2-ton cargo truck easily recognized by its proliferation in the war). His partners were candidates from the same company, though he didn't know them well.

First was Lewis Nixon, a smart guy from the northeast who graduated from Yale. Tall, trim, and dark-haired the same as Eugene, they had an amicable friendship but too busy to become friends. Next was Richard "Dick" Winters, a Pennsylvanian with book smarts and even better at compass work and map reading than Eugene. Last was Daniel "Smokey" Hill, a good-looking kid from Missouri, and nicknamed Smokey because he smoked any free opportunity he could find away from the drill sergeants. The men were covered in a tarp and driven around for 30 minutes, with no idea where they were. The truck finally stopped and dumped them out. Smokey was designated as leader and was given a photo of the area with a grid overlay. They were instructed to make it to a station marked on the map. Smokey took charge, sending men in three directions for ten or fifteen minutes to find a road, building, pond, anything they could find and compare on the map. Gilmore went west, Lewis north, and Winters south, leaving Smokey to go east. When they met up, the men had been successful. Nixon found a stream-fed pond off the side of a gravel road, and Winters found a tar-gravel road which led to a bridge. With this information, Smokey drew out his compass and identified the features. They headed to the bridge, where Smokey shot an azimuth through the woods. After about an hour they finally ran into a gravel road, which led them to the reporting station. They were the first group in and waited in the truck.

Eugene sat silently while the other men laughed and joked about the other guys probably lost in the woods. Finally, Smokey asked him "what's eating you, pop? You ain't said a word since we got here." Eugene quietly told them what had happened in Major Rafferty's office.

"You see, I'm never gonna fight. I'll end up blowing bridges or building hospitals somewhere," he said, disheartened by his fate. Smokey piped up, "Just hold on a pea pickin' minute. I asked about this same thing when I signed up. A Captain told me to just go with whatever the Army told me to do, wait for your shot. Pretty soon, something would come along that was more important than what the Army had selected for you, and you could volunteer to get killed a lot faster than the Army intended."

They all chuckled at Smokey's "wisdom." But, as foolish as that sounded, it had merit. Eugene asked the men what they were going to do. Winters and Nixon both answered with a loud "Paratroopers!" with passion. *That sounds like a good plan! I need to check on Jackson and see what he's doing now. Maybe we can end up in the Airborne together.*

"Why paratroopers?" Winters spoke first. "Look around, Eugene. Who are the best soldiers and officers around? Who looks the most fit? The Airborne is the unit for me. If I'm going into combat I want to go with the best soldiers in the Army. I think that's paratroopers."

Eugene let that stew for a minute, then turned to Nixon. "What about you?" Nixon just grinned, and said "I'm going where Dick goes, he needs somebody to explain the world outside of Pennsylvania to him." They laughed at Nixon but soon quieted down.

"What are you going to do, Smokey?" Winters asked. Smokey took a long drag of his cigarette (he was already on his third since they climbed in the truck), and said quietly, "I've already been assigned to the 16th Infantry Regiment, assigned to the 1st Infantry Division. The 1st just left Fort Benning a few weeks ago. I figure they'll be fighting Japs or Krauts real soon, so I need to hustle up and join them. From there I'm gonna try to join the Rangers. That sounds like a lot of fun and plenty of chances to kill Japs or Germans."

"Yeah, both those sound like a fun way to die real quick too," Eugene said with a laugh. But both ideas had merit, he thought. *Do I really want to fight, or am I just full of malarky? Both of these units need good men, good leaders, to lead enlisted men into battle, fight beside them.*

Eugene closed his eyes to rest, the other men soon quieted, and soon snores filled the truck bed. The next thing Eugene heard was "Everybody out! You're home!" He didn't even wake when the truck moved out, a sign of how tired all the men really were. The last thing he remembered was thinking that he needed to write home...

***

2

TRAIN, TRAIN, TRAIN!

1942
Pillicoc Kennels, Elberon, New Jersey

    When Jackson arrived in New Jersey, no one met him at the train station. It was late afternoon in early May 1942, the weather mild and clear, but you could tell it was getting ready to be hot. Jackson looked at the address on his orders again. "REPORT TO PILLICOC KENNELS, ELBERON, NEW JERSEY, ON OR BEFORE 10 MAY 1942."

    Well, he was a little late and had no idea where to go. He decided to ask the ticket agent where to go for the night. "Where are you heading, Private? We try to help you soldiers heading off to fight...oh Pillicoc Kennels? Why it's only a few miles out of town. Hang on, ole Henry is a friend of mine, let me ring him and get you a ride."

    Thirty minutes later Jackson was sitting in an old beat-up truck while a soldier about his age drove. "Are you a dog trainer too?" Jackson asked. "No," the soldier answered, "I'm here as part of the Quartermaster Corps to help you all train the dogs. Basically I help with logistics, getting you and your dog from point A to point B, and make sure you have the food and materials to train your dog. The men who help you train your dog are civilians. Maybe I'll volunteer for K-9 Corps myself, you know, after I see how you fellas do."

Jackson was excited to be at the kennels and could hear several dogs barking in the training area. A man approached him from the building next to the kennels, wearing a cowboy hat, flannel shirt, blue jeans and boots. He looked like he had been working since sunup, and he had. The man had a big smile while holding his hand out to shake hands. "Hello Mr. Gilmore, I'm Henry Stoecker, I'm the head trainer around here. We just finished up for the day, getting the dogs settled in after dinner. C'mon, I'll take you to your room so you can get settled before dinner."

His room turned out to be a large bunk room not far from the kennels, where seven other GIs were already settled on bunks. He took the last available bunk (next to the front door, of course). The other men were cleaning up around the bunk room but stopped when Henry let go a loud whistle. "Listen up men! We have here the last man of our team. This is Private Jackson Gilmore, joining us from Camp Shelby, Mississippi. Make him welcome, introduce yourself, then let's get ready for dinner."

The other guys introduced themselves one by one, which Jackson quickly forgot. *I'll get with them later and get their names.* Right now, he was hungry, having only had a hard biscuit for breakfast and no lunch on the train. He was in his service uniform while the others wore utilities. They all strolled to the main building of the kennel facility, where they went into the kitchen door and into a large dining room set to feed over a dozen people. Paintings of huge, curly-haired poodles adorned the walls, and photos of poodles with trophies and ribbons were placed on tables and nightstands around the room. As Jackson studied the paintings and photos, a middle-aged woman with short, brunette hair, a roundish face, and carefully applied makeup entered the dining room. Mrs. Erlanger had opened not only her kennels to the Army, but also her kitchen. "Please gentleman, take your seats. Dinner will be served shortly." Henry helped her to her seat at the head of the table, then took the adjoining chair. The soldiers all sat quickly but shyly. It's doubtful any of the young men had ever sat at any kind of formal dinner, but Mrs. Erlanger set them at ease.

"Don't worry about rules or formalities. Tonight is a special dinner, now that we have all of you together. We have eight beautiful dogs here waiting to become your partner for the duration of the war. Tomorrow you will meet your new partners and begin training. For now, let's enjoy a nice dinner, because tomorrow night you'll be too tired to eat."

That surprised the men, they figured they were in good shape after completing basic training. Henry would explain it tomorrow. Right now, dinner was delivered. Starting with a green salad, followed by a clam chowder, and then the main meal, roasted chicken with onions, potatoes, and carrots. It was simple but tasted wonderful. The men ate quietly, only speaking when asked a question by Mrs. Erlanger or Henry. When dessert was served, Jackson was stuffed, but he took a saucer of ice cream and hot apple pie. It was delicious.

When Mrs. Erlanger stood, Henry popped up quickly, and the men quickly followed. "Please finish your coffee, gentleman. I'll give you time to talk and then Henry will show you out. Good night." The men returned to their chairs, and Henry took over. "Men, you are the first K-9 Trainers in the Army. Some of you were selected from the Quartermaster Corps, but a few of you were plucked from boot camp. Our government is concerned about German attacks on our factories on the eastern coast. Several U-boats have been discovered in the last few months, some even delivering spies to our land! So our first job is to train you and your partner as sentries to keep our country safe. We begin tomorrow."

Whoa…. what? Sentry duty? I signed up to train a combat dog! "Mr. Stoecker, umm, are we all going to train Sentry dogs? Because I thought I was training for combat." Jackson looked at Henry and the other men, some of whom appeared just as disappointed as he was. Stoecker took a gulp of hot coffee before speaking. "I know what you were told prior to coming here, men, but the Army has been given orders to train sentry dogs, so that is what we will do. Tomorrow, Sergeant Wilson will arrive and take charge of the unit, but I'll still train you how to train your dog. So let's get a good night sleep and I'll see you bright and early at the kennels at 0600. Goodnight."

With that, Henry stood and walked out of the dining room and out of the house to his quarters. The men just looked at each other, stunned. They quietly stood and returned to their bunk room. Several men lit cigarettes as they digested the news. "Dammit, I knew this was too good to be true. The Army screwed me again."

Private Jonathan "Johnnie" Moore, from Philadelphia, Pennsylvania, was the first to speak up and complain. Johnnie was a small kid, only 5 foot 6 or 7, maybe 130 pounds, but he was built like a bantam weight boxer. He had a square jaw, white-blond hair, and dark, piercing eyes. Jackson figured he was best to keep on his good side. In actuality, Johnnie was a good kid that never went looking for trouble, avoided it when possible, but if trouble came looking for him he was more than capable of handling himself. He had signed up just as Jackson had, thinking the K-9 Corps was his ticket to seeing combat now.

The other men were split between Sentry duty and combat. The four QMC soldiers had known they were assigned to train sentry dogs. The Quartermasters had been in the Army since 1940, were career men, not civilian soldiers, and volunteered when the QMC took over the Dogs for Defense program. Two of the other men were out of boot camp, same as Jackson and Johnnie, though they didn't appear as worked up over it as the two young men were.

He caught Johnnie's attention, nodded to the door, and walked outside. It was dark with no moonlight, though a light on the corner of the bunkhouse provided plenty of light. "What's up Gilmore?" Johnnie asked not unkindly. "You got the scoop on this place or how to transfer to a real fighting outfit?" He took a last drag on his cigarette before grinding it out, then field stripped it.

"I do have an idea. A smart guy gave me some good advice. My brother said if you don't like your assignment, do a good job anyway, and then volunteer for the job you want when the time is right. I say we go through the training, then when they're ready to train for combat, we jump on it. By that time the Army will have plenty of sentry dogs trained and will need combat dogs. That's my plan."

Johnnie lit another cigarette and took a long pull from it. "I suppose you're right, but I don't have to like it. Okay Gilmore, I like the way you're thinking. I guess I can make it through with a good pooch to keep me company. But I'm gonna sneak in some combat training if I can. You wait and watch."

"Have you seen the dogs yet?" Jackson asked. He could hear some of them whining or barking but didn't want to go see them and stir them up. Tomorrow would be fine. Johnnie told him that Henry took them by the kennels where the dogs were being handled by Stoecker's trainers but didn't really get to see them. "I saw a couple of German Shepherds, a Doberman, a big Huskie, and some dog I couldn't tell the breed. But they all looked in good health and strong. I guess we'll find out tomorrow who we get partnered with."

With that, Johnnie took a last drag and again field stripped his cigarette and went back inside. It was after 2000 hours and Jackson was ready to get settled in and get some sleep. It would be a big day tomorrow.

***

Eugene arrived at Engineering Corps Refresher Training in June 1942. Fort Leonard Wood, Missouri was a sprawling piece of land about a two-hour drive northeast of Springfield, located in the Missouri Ozarks. Fort Leonard Wood was created in late 1940 and became fully operational in June 1941. While building of the fort was underway, non-divisional units, from companies to battalions, trained on the post. With nearly 100 square miles of land, there was plenty of space to grow and train. In March 1942, the initial elements of the first Engineer Replacement Training Center arrived, and Eugene began refresher training.

By June, construction crews had built 1,600 buildings, including bunk houses for the thousands of soldiers that would train there. Eugene was assigned to a class that would start in mid-June. He was ready, and he had a plan. The refresher course, while new to him, was not difficult and he scored in the top 5 percentile of his class. Six weeks in length, officers were provided high-level instructions in theory and practice of Army engineering. As soon as the course was completed, the newly branded engineers would be sent to new units or to the Engineering Replacement Training Center to become instructors. Both selections were not in Eugene's plans.

Two weeks before completing the course, Eugene applied for the Airborne. He was immediately called to the office of the school's commanding officer. "Lieutenant, I have a request for you to transfer to Paratrooper training. Now what's this all about?"

Still at attention, he didn't know how to start. "Well, sir, when I first enlisted, my brother and I, my younger brother, Jackson, well we both decided we wanted to fight in the war. I wrote to him and let him know I planned to become a paratrooper. He went through boot camp about the same time I went through OCS. I don't know where he is right now but we both still want to be paratroopers."

Gilmore took a deep breath and tried to continue. "At ease, Lieutenant. Take a seat. So, your younger brother, Jackson? Jackson completed boot camp and is now angling to get into Airborne? And you want to join him, is that it?"

"Yes sir. We told each other we would do our best to serve together, if not in the same unit then in the same outfit. But sir, it goes deeper than that. I want to fight. Nothing against the Engineering Corps, sir, but when I joined up, the Army hijacked me during OCS and assigned me to the Engineering Corps."

Major Lee sat quietly for a moment, reviewing Eugene's personnel record. "Yes, I see that right here. They looked at your university records, mighty impressive if I say so myself, and they put you where they thought you would serve the Army best." The Major rose from behind his desk, so Eugene quickly stood at attention.

The Major approached Eugene, looking him straight in the eyes, no smile, no expression, no emotion. "I'll tell you what I'll do. Let me think about this tonight and I'll give you my decision tomorrow. Fair enough?"

"Fair enough sir!" The Major reached out and shook his hand, a firm, strong handshake that Eugene returned in kind. He saluted, about-faced and departed the office. *I may have a chance to fight and see Jackson after all*, he thought hopefully. He figured he had a 50-50 chance of the Major approving his request. Even though the airborne received preferential treatment when it came to recruits, he wasn't so sure about officers. The Engineering Corps was an elite unit and usually received the best officers and enlisted as possible. *The Major will have to reconcile allowing me to depart for the Airborne against letting an engineer go.* Since both the engineers and paratroopers are high-priority units and volunteering for them cannot be denied, Eugene knew that the Major had a tough decision to make. As it turned out, he didn't give the Major enough credit.

***

Pillicoc Kennels, Elberon, New Jersey

The morning air was warm already. The trainers were taking care of the dogs first thing, before the soldiers would meet their partner. Breakfast was simple but filling, and the men ate in a hurry, anxious to meet the dogs.

At the kennels, they could hear the dogs barking, not angrily but excited as well. The dogs knew today was special, some by the way Stoecker talked to them, and also because of the scent of new humans. Henry had the men line up according to rank, so Jackson, being the last to graduate boot camp, was also last in line to receive a partner. The first man walked forward and was introduced to a large huskie, probably 70 pounds, with silver and black markings. The soldier took the lead from the trainer and they both went to the training area. Next, a large Doberman was introduced to his partner, and off they went. So it continued, with a German Shepherd, a large black poodle, and a dalmatian, finally a couple of beautiful collies were assigned to soldiers. That left Jackson.

Stoecker stood for a moment next to the last kennel. A dog was in the cage but had not come out of his kennel. Jackson tried to make out the breed but couldn't see in the dark shelter. "Jackson, I'm glad you are last. This dog is special. He isn't a purebred like the others, but the little I've worked with him, I can tell he is an amazing animal. Let's go meet Rufus."

Rufus? What a name for a war dog! Well, here goes nothing. Stoecker opened the cage door and the trainer retrieved Rufus from the kennel. Jackson almost laughed. He saw a large Shepherd mix with…something he couldn't determine. *A cur maybe, or a coon dog?* "This is Rufus," Henry explained. "He comes from Tennessee, same as you. His mother is a full-blooded bluetick hound, his father a full-blooded German Shepherd. Rufus is unique in a few ways that you'll discover. Go ahead and meet Rufus."

Jackson stepped forward, and Rufus came toward him slowly, a little unsure. Rufus had been through a lot in the last few weeks; his world had been turned upside down, ripped from his family, his *master*. He didn't understand why, but he was being taken care of, fed, watered, walked when he needed to go. But he missed Penny so bad he thought of running away, return home. He could still smell her scent and knew he could find her. Instead, he stayed with the man who had brought him here. Henry had picked him up at the train station, was gentle with him and talked to him softly, not like those mean men on the train. Henry brought him to the kennel, gave him time to explore all the strange smells around the camp. He could smell and hear other dogs but wasn't able to see any of them. Some were scared, he could tell, but he decided he would be brave and get through this. He thought back to his last day with Penny, and it made him miss her more.

***

1942, Tennessee

Dogs For Defense advertisements were all over the papers and radio. Penny could not miss any of them if she tried. At 12 years old, she spent her time after school reading about the war, listening to radio reports, and training Rufus. She was scared for her brother, James Jr. Jimmie had graduated high school in May 1941 and had been working on the farm with his father. He planned to make a little money and then go to the local junior college and study to be a lineman for the electric company. Linemen made good money and worked outside, something he loved. When the war started, he enlisted immediately, and like thousands of others, was told to go home and await orders.

Jimmie's orders arrived in January 1942: attend basic training at Fort Benning, then join an infantry unit. Penny was more distraught than her parents, but that was her perception. Her parents kept their fear and anxiety from Penny as much as possible, but they both worried for their son. When she first saw an advertisement for Dogs for Defense, she was scared someone would take Rufus from her. But as she learned and read about the program, she saw that it was a way for her to help her brother. It took her a couple of weeks to convince herself to sign Rufus up.

"Momma, I've been thinking, I believe Rufus would be a good war dog. He can smell a rabbit a mile away, can see a squirrel in the next county, and even though daddy said he ain't much of a huntin' dog, I know he can do the job. He knows how to sit, lay, stop, stay, and fetch. Plus he's about the strongest dog I've ever seen. I want Rufus to help our soldiers, help them be safe and come home."

That was a lot for a 12-year-old girl to say. Her parents thought about it and asked her repeatedly if this was what she wanted. Jim made sure she understood what she was offering. "Once Rufus is gone, there's no turning back. The Army will take him, train him, and you may never see him again. Are you sure about this?" She wasn't completely sure, but said she was.

The Army sent two privates to pick up Rufus. Penny hugged him hard, trying not to cry. Rufus knew something was wrong and rubbed his head against her face. He didn't know why she was upset, until she gave the leash to the soldiers, who loaded him into a kennel in the back of a truck. Why are they taking him away from Penny? He's supposed to keep her safe! Penny removed his collar and took his leash, then she gave him to these strange men, crying. The truck tailgate was closed and Rufus was driven away. He watched Penny cry, hugging her mom as he left the farm.

The train ride wasn't too bad. He was fed, watered, and every now and then the train stopped and let him and a few other dogs out to go. The men weren't mean, mostly, just indifferent. One man was short-tempered with the dogs and tended to push them along faster when they were let out, but mostly just ignored the dogs. He didn't understand or know what was happening. The trip took two days, then he was offloaded and placed in another truck. This time the men talked to the dogs gently, soothing their nerves and anxiety. The boss man looked them over, soothed each dog, talked quietly to them while checking them for injury. At last they arrived at the kennel, where they were led to a large complex where kennels were arranged in a row, so that the dogs could not see each other. Henry spent a few moments with each dog, gave them small treats while he petted them and earned their trust. The dogs could sense that Henry was the leader and took to his kindness and strength.

Now Rufus was introduced to a new man, a young man, and he sensed this was his new master. Jackson talked to him quietly, petted him, rubbed his fur backwards and forwards, scratching his fur in a way Rufus enjoyed.

"So why does he look kind of...different?" Henry laughed loudly at that, giving Rufus a small start. "I don't know, except when he was born his genes got mixed up. But I think he may have inherited the best traits of his mother and father. We'll know when you start training him."

Training began immediately. The dogs had been at the kennel for two weeks, working with Henry's instructors, each highly regarded in the world of pedigree dogs. Henry had a veterinarian check the dogs, and once accepted, the vet tattooed an ID number in their left ear. So that the dogs would not bond to one of the instructors, the men would rotate between dogs. They tested the intelligence of each dog, their willingness to please the trainers, and ability to perform physical training. Each dog passed with exceptional scores.

It was basic training all over again. Jackson and the other K-9 trainers were in training as much as their partners. The men learned how to train their partner to walk on a leash, heel, sit, stay down, cover, crawl, jump, and retrieve. The K-9 trainers went to training themselves, some during the day while the instructors took care of the dogs, and other days after the dogs were fed, groomed, and put to bed. Staff Sergeant Wilson had arrived and took charge of the unit. He was an older man, at least thirty years old ('old' to the younger men), but very affable and approachable. Wilson was a career man from the Quartermaster Corps, assigned to oversee the men and dogs for the Army. He brought with him three privates to help. It was evident to the K-9 trainers that the Army was taking the use of dogs seriously and provided the resources to be successful.

Rufus turned out to be a great dog. He took to Jackson a little hesitantly, but after a few days they were best friends. Rufus already knew the basic commands, he just had to learn to do them the Army way. The same went with Jackson; on his first day with Rufus, he was instructed how to walk Rufus on a leash, form up in a line with each dog on the left side, and how to give commands. Each training period lasted about half an hour, then the dogs were allowed to rest or play. The trainers would continue training in the classroom.

At least twice a day, the trainers were given a 30-minute period to relax and play with their dog. Jackson discovered Rufus loved to chase a tennis ball. He learned that Rufus would chase and return the ball to Jackson all day if allowed. Rufus would wait frantically for Jackson to throw the ball and would speed off to catch it on a bounce. He would march back, almost prancing, stop at Jackson and drop the ball at his feet. Then he would stare at Jackson, not moving, until Jackson would reach down and grab the ball. Then the process started over again.

As training progressed, Jackson and Rufus grew closer. Jackson was the only man allowed to touch Rufus, to feed, groom, and exercise him. This instilled a genuine relationship between them and all the dogs and trainers. These were the best weeks of Jackson's life, as far as he was concerned. Even though he was working 10 and 12 hour days, he took to it with enthusiasm. After the first four weeks had passed, it was evident that Jackson and Rufus were a great partnership. Rufus was intelligent, playful, but always under control and followed commands perfectly. Jackson took him on long runs around the compounds, him in utilities and Rufus with a canvas vest. As part of training, Rufus was allowed off leash to run with Jackson, but always in the Heel position. At the command 'HEEL', Rufus would walk or run by Jackson's left side, his shoulder even with Jackson's left knee, though Rufus was given more latitude when running.

The fifth week brought new training: the obstacles course. Already trained to jump, Rufus was trained to climb a small log wall at the command UP. Soon he was climbing 6-foot walls, crawling through tunnels, up and down ramps, through barrels lined in irregular rows. Rufus excelled in all the training, as did most of his dog buddies. Now it was time to get them accustomed to gunfire and explosions. Again, Rufus performed well, remembering his days with Penny's father. Jackson began by giving Rufus the STAY command, walked about 50 yards from Rufus, and fired a 38-caliber revolver. Rufus was unfazed, even as Jackson walked closer. When Jackson finally stood next to Rufus, he gave the HEEL command and walked forward, firing the revolver at a target. Rufus stayed exactly where he was supposed to be, on Jackson's left side.

***

With only two weeks to go before graduation, Jackson knew he had to do something. At the end of the day, after feeding and grooming Rufus and attending his last class, he sought out Henry Stoecker. He found him working with one of Mrs. Erlanger's black poodles, one of her prize winners. "Give me a minute, I'm almost done with Francis." Henry led Francis from the training room (inside rather than outside like the K-9 dogs) to the main house. Once the dog was delivered, he waved for Jackson to catch up to him and walked to his office.

"What can I do for you, Private Gilmore? Should I bring in

Sergeant Wilson?" Henry nearly always called the young men by their first name, only by rank when he thought it involved the Army. "No sir, Mr. Henry, I'd like to talk to you and get your thoughts." Calling him 'Mr. Henry' was about as far as Jackson would go to calling Henry by his first name, something his southern upbringing had been trained into him.

"Sir, me and Rufus are doing swell. He's an awfully good dog, smart as a whip, not scared of anything. I really think he will be wasted as a sentry dog. He deserves to show what he can do in combat. I was hoping you could make a call or something and maybe get me assigned to a combat unit."

A slow smile crossed Henry's face. He reached into a pile of paperwork and brought out a mail folder. He handed it to Jackson.

"Take a look at this. I just received it this afternoon. I was going to find you after dinner, but now is as good a time as any."

Jackson looked at the large, yellow folder, marked from COMMANDER, AIRBORNE COMMAND. He retrieved the letter inside, signed by Brigadier General William C. Lee. "What's this about? Orders to an infantry division?" Jackson sure hoped this is what it seemed. "No," said Henry, now with a huge grin on his face. "Go ahead and read it."

***

Brigadier General William "Bill" Lee was famous for the formation of airborne units in the Army. As a Colonel in 1940, he was a strong proponent of airborne warfare, and fought aggressively for it against higher-ranking generals. In 1940 he organized the initial test platoon of paratroopers. The training was so successful that the War Department created the Provisional Parachute Group in early 1941, which later in March 1942 was transformed into the U.S. Airborne Command, led by Lee. It was here that Lee started thinking of deploying combat dogs with airborne platoons. In the late 1930's, Lee had toured Europe and observed German airborne forces performing an exercise attack on another unit. The Germans had several German Shepherds parachuting alone, not tethered to a soldier. He chewed on this for several years, until he was finally in a position to make it happen.

In mid-June 1942, Lee sent the Quartermaster Corps a letter requesting K-9 Unit volunteers for paratrooper training. He requested only four K-9 units, which he would split between subordinate commands. Lee saw that two airborne divisions would be formed, one of which he would command. He put the call out for volunteers hoping to get units trained and integrated into an airborne unit and ready to go fight.

Jackson read the message again, hardly believing his luck. Then he was concerned. *Only four units? What if they've already been filled?* He looked sharply at Mr. Stoecker, who was still seated at his desk, smoking a pipe. "How do I volunteer? I'm ready to go now!"

"Hold on son. When I read this, I thought about you right off. I made a call to the QMC headquarters, who had sent this down to me. I've already received two billets, based on the level of training we've already performed. I need two volunteers."

"No sir, you only need one volunteer, because me and Rufus are going." Henry chuckled, rose from his desk and led Jackson toward the mess hall. "I figured as much, Private Gilmore. Let's go get Sergeant Wilson and see who's going with you."

***

3

CURRAHEE

> *"Toccoa was the heat of the Georgia summer and fifty torturous minutes three days a week, pounding six miles up and down a mountain. Toccoa was murderous twenty mile forced marches done at 130 per minute. Toccoa was where men and officers learned how to take and give orders. But above all Toccoa was the crucible which forged the spirit of this regiment, and where men discovered they could go much further and do much much more than they ever imagined."*
> - *506th PIR Scrapbook*

1942
Camp Toccoa, Georgia

Though Currahee Mountain rose over 800 feet above the local land, Eugene had trouble finding it. The Norfolk Southern Rail was heavily wooded alongside the right-of-way except for a few fields that randomly abutted the highway. He was excited to be arriving at Camp Toombs, where he intended to be the best paratrooper in the regiment. Major Lee had approved his request to volunteer for paratroopers, he now had orders to join the 506th Parachute Infantry Regiment (PIR) at Camp Toombs, Georgia.

Eugene had a 10-day furlough prior to arriving in Georgia,

which he spent at home in Greensburg. The town seemed even smaller after all the travelling he had completed, and the people looked tired and ragged. Except for his Momma, that is. Faye looked as beautiful as ever, and he enjoyed his time home. Most of the young men from his high school were gone, somewhere in a military unit. A few young ladies asked about him when he returned, and he took one named Julie to a movie in Murfreesboro. He was too focused on the upcoming training to think about anything else. He ran three miles twice a day for his week at home to stay in good shape.

His mom and dad drove him to the train station in Greensburg (actually just a whistle stop). He gave his mom a hug and kiss and shook hands with his dad. "Work hard son but take care of yourself. And write your Momma more." He promised he would let them know what his new address was as soon as possible, boarded the train and settled in for a 12-hour train ride.

A few Army buses were waiting to take the soldiers to Camp Toombs, about a 10–15-minute ride. It was here he finally set eyes on Currahee. It was impressive, rising quickly to a height of 1,735 feet, and he knew he'd be running that mountain. *Why else would they build a camp next to the dang thing?* The bus pulled through the gate and took the men to get checked in. Officers and enlisted men were split up to go to their respective areas. It was obvious to Eugene that some of the enlisted soldiers had only just been taught how to wear their uniforms. He found the 506th Headquarters, finally found someone to tell him where to go, and was told to wait for the commanding officer. He and three other officers waited for over an hour before Colonel Robert Sink hurried into the office and closed his door.

Another ten minutes and Sink's clerk showed them into the colonel's office, neatly decorated with photos from past assignments in the Philippines, Arizona, and good ole Fort Benning. The young officers stood at attention and saluted. The colonel looked them over quickly then gave the order "At ease, men."

The orderly returned with their officer records (each officer hand carried his records from their last command). The

Regimental administrative officer arrived as well; Sink waved him in. "You men are almost the last to arrive. We'll get you assigned billets and you can get squared away. For most of you, this is your first assignment after your commissioning. You better prepare yourself for the toughest training you'll ever see. The parachute infantry is a brand new concept in the U.S. Army, and it's my job to turn you men into the best paratrooper officers in the Army. The 506th is nearly formed up, and you will be assigned to a company. 1st Battalion is already formed, so you men will be assigned to the 2nd and 3rd Battalions. I expect each of you men to do your best and lead by example. Any questions? No? Dismissed."

The regimental S-1 stepped to Colonel Sink's side and called out to Eugene. "Lieutenant Gilmore, could you wait a moment in the outer office?" The captain turned back to Sink with what appeared to be orders. *Uh oh, this doesn't look good. Am I being sent back to the engineering corps?* He only waited a few minutes when he was called back into the regimental commander's office. Before he could snap to attention, Sink waved him to sit. "Son, I have new orders for you." Eugene knew it, he was getting yanked around again. Colonel Sink saw Eugene's disappointment. "It's not that bad, Lieutenant. You are assigned to the 101st, but in the 326th Airborne Engineer Battalion. Now, this means you will complete parachute infantry training here, get your jump wings, then be re-assigned to Camp Claiborne. You understand?"

Eugene understood and was deeply disappointed. Sink saw that same look so ordered Eugene to speak up. "Sir, I've done everything I can to get into this war and fight, but the Army keeps throwing up walls. I just want to fight, not build bridges. Is there anything you can do?"

Sink looked hard at Gilmore before replying. "Son, what gives you the idea that the men in the 326th won't fight? Every man in the 326th will jump along with the paratroop infantry. You are fortunate, Gilmore. Only a few engineering battalion officers were selected to complete the 506th training. Most men from the 326th or other service units would attend a four-week training course at Fort Benning. You, Lieutenant, are one lucky SOB. So quit bitching about your problems and go learn how to fight!"

Eugene stood so fast he swore his boots left the floor. He saluted, gave a loud "Yes Sir!" and retreated as fast as possible. Once out of sight, the S-1 looked at Colonel Sink with a grin. "You really do enjoy scaring the young officers, don't you?" Sink's grin grew wide. "I don't *not* enjoy it, Toby, but someone's got to light a fire under these kids. And by God I'm ready to do it."

Eugene grabbed his gear and found another lieutenant to direct him to officer quarters. He laughed. "Quarters? Good luck finding a tent not mired in red clay." Still, he directed him where to go. Tents were set up for W Company, construction was going on everywhere. Tarpaper shacks were being finished as quickly as possible, as the battalions were filling up. Assigned to the Regimental Headquarters Company, training would start in a few days. He lucked out; Headquarters Company had a couple of barracks for the junior officers to bunk in.

Something else of importance happened during this time. Colonel Sink had been wary of the name of the camp, "Toombs." He wanted it changed so the men would not feel superstitious (Toombs – Tombs) about the name. Sink worked the request through the Adjutant General's office and the name was officially changed to Camp Toccoa, after the nearby town.

***

Jackson didn't have as hard a path to the 506th as his brother. Sergeant Wilson quickly approved the change, and after asking the other men if any wanted to volunteer, only Johnnie stepped forward. After Henry went over the dog and trainer records, he determined both men and dogs were fit for parachute infantry training. "I think you boys will do just fine. Take care of Rufus and Gunner and they'll take care of you. And don't worry about jump school. I'm working on a few ideas and will see the both of you before you start jump training."

While Jackson was traveling to Georgia, Johnnie was going to Camp Claiborne, Louisiana, to join the 82nd Infantry Division, soon to be the 82nd Airborne. The men and dogs traveled together to Chattanooga, Tennessee, where Rufus and Jackson departed. They said their goodbyes and said they'd meet up again soon. Then Johnnie and Gunner were gone.

The pair transferred to a Norfolk Southern train to make their way to Camp Toccoa, riding in a storage car with the kennel. He allowed Rufus out of the kennel for most of the trip, shutting him in at night so they stayed in a routine. With frequent stops, the trip took nearly three days. Jackson would bounce a tennis ball off the side of the car for Rufus to chase, which he did, nonstop. By the time they arrived at the Toccoa train station both man and dog were a disheveled mess and Jackson's arm was sore. Jackson cleaned up as much as possible, shaved, and changed into his service uniform. He groomed Rufus, fed him (he didn't know when they would have a chance to eat again so took the opportunity before entering Toccoa).

After checking in and receiving orders on where to bunk ("find a cot in a tent that ain't got a bag on it"), both man and dog were instructed to report to Colonel Sink's office. He cleaned the muck from his paws and put a quick spit shine on his boots (which was a waste of time since the entire camp was covered in mud, wet red clay or sand and dirt). But they walked side by side, receiving stares and smiles as they marched. A few soldiers snickered at the sight of Rufus, but they ignored them. *Just wait, fellas, just wait until you see what Rufus can do. Then we'll see who's laughing at who.*

Rufus sat at perfect attention on the left side of his master, looking at him for a signal or order, but did nothing else. The training was obviously a success, and Jackson was both proud and relieved. Soon the orderly/clerk called his name and led them into Sink's office. Jackson didn't know it, but his brother had been here only a few days prior to him. In the office were Sink, the admin officer (S-1), and two battalion commanders; Major Strayer, 2nd Battalion, and Regimental Headquarters Company, Major Hinton. (Hinton was dual-hatted as Regimental HQ Company Commander and as the 506th S-3 Operations Officer). Both soldiers (one man, one dog) came to attention, and Jackson saluted. After Sink returned the salute, he told them to stand at ease. Jackson gave the SIT command and hand signal to STAY. Sink watched this with amusement.

"Private, you are here because I requested you for my regiment. The parachute infantry is a brand new concept in the Army, and I will by God lead them to victory. Now, the 506th is also a new concept. We are taking men, civilians, and turning them into soldiers and paratroopers. You will go through the same basic training as paratroopers, including your dog. You will train with your dog, moving through several companies during training so the men will become accustomed to you. But you will be assigned to Headquarters Company and designated as supernumeraries to companies during training. You'll also work with the riggers to develop a vest for your dog to jump with you. Understood?"

Jackson stood silent, with a confused look. "Do you have a problem, Private?" Sink was a little agitated by Jackson's lack of response. Finally Jackson spoke up. "Sir, do you mean that I'm to go through basic training again? I completed basic months ago before assignment to the K-9 Corps." That probably was not the response Sink looked for." He stared coldly at Gilmore; his eyes grew dark. He turned and lit a cigarette, took a drag, as if acting in a stage play that called for a dramatic pause. "Son, do you *want* to be a paratrooper? Because all my paratroopers will be trained here, together, as one unit; the 506th Parachute Infantry Regiment. If you aren't willing to complete the training, then you need to get you and your dog off my camp. Is that clear?"

He realized the mistake he had made. "No sir, I mean, yes sir, clear as a bell. Rufus and I will go through training with the other men, and you will be proud to have us in your Regiment. SIR!" That was a better response and Sink calmed down. "Now, you are a private, correct? I'm promoting you to Private First Class as a show of respect for your training and handling of your dog." Jackson was pleased but now he had another issue: K-9 Corps dogs were awarded one rank higher than their trainer, as a reminder to the trainer and others that the war dogs must always be treated with respect. "Sir, um, I was instructed by my former

First Sergeant that my dog would always outrank me. Rufus is a Private First Class now."

Sink actually showed surprise. "Are you telling me that your dog outranks you? Holy Sweet Jesus, I've never heard of such a thing." The Colonel inhaled a large puff from his cigarette, then exhaled slowly, a yellow-brown cloud of smoke climbing to the ceiling. "Okay, I think I got it. You are now a PFC and Rufus is a Corporal. Orderly! Orderly! Why do I have to call you twice?"

"I've been here all the time Colonel," the orderly answered from behind Sink.

"Well, be quicker next time. I need PFC stripes for Gilmore and—"

The orderly held out two PFC stripes for Jackson and two corporal stripes for Rufus. Sink just looked at them. *Damn smartass*, he thought, not unkindly but more amused by the orderly than upset. He handed the stripes to Jackson.

"Thank you, now get back to work. Gilmore, go with Major Hinton, he'll get you squared away. Dismissed." Jackson saluted and stepped out of the office with Rufus to wait for Hinton.

Major Hinton grinned at Sink, who now sat behind his desk. Strayer was grinning too. "Major Hinton, Major Strayer, this K-9 unit will succeed. I had to throw in about every damned chip I had to get a K-9 unit assigned to the 506th. When I discovered General Lee was getting some war dogs I couldn't let him get away with that. So now we have a unit, let's get them trained. I want the company commanders in 2nd and 3rd Battalions to understand that they will not be singled out and treated any differently than the other men. They will complete training as a team, understand?"

Strayer and Hinton understood completely. They would call the company commanders together and brief them on Sink's orders. Hinton would come up with a plan of training for them and would oversee their progress. To do that he would assign a lieutenant and a staff sergeant to help. Strayer took the initiative to call his company commanders and executive officers together in the morning. Hinton, as HQ Company CO, attended with the other six company commanders.

"Colonel Sink has requested and received a K-9 training unit for the 506th. The unit is made up of PFC Gilmore and Corporal Rufus." The men laughed at that, then quieted as they saw Strayer was serious. "You will ensure that the K-9 unit is treated fairly, no hazing whatsoever, understood? If I hear of any mistreatment of the trainer or the dog, outside of normal basic training, it will not end well. Since the trainer has already attended basic training, Major Hinton is giving him a few days to get his dog settled in at HQ before assigning him to companies. You'll be provided a training schedule of when the K-9 unit will be assigned to you. Clear? Dismissed"

***

Major Hinton told Jackson to grab his gear and go to the Regimental HQ Company headquarters to receive his billeting. No 'W' Company for Gilmore and Rufus. W Company was a holding center for soldiers coming in, and sadly, soldiers going out. The place was a complete mess; tents built over red clay, and rain had turned it into mud pits. Cots sank into the mud so deep that anyone in a cot was laying in mud. He was very happy to be moving.

Jackson had two bags: his and one for Rufus. The dog was equipped with:
- food and water bowls
- Two blankets (waterproof)
- Three leashes (3, 5, and 10 feet)
- Boric acid (eye cleansing)
- Two boxes of swabs (ear cleaning)
- Flea powder
- Four towels and 4 hand towels
- Trimming and grooming Kit
- Four 16-ounce cans of water
- Five days of food (canned meats, cereals, canned vegetables and eggs)

With this load, Rufus' bag was heavier than Jacksons, who only had uniforms, boots, and skivvies. (It was later told in folklore that Rufus ate better than the paratroopers he served with in combat.)

Rufus' kennel had been delivered to Regimental HQ but was moved to HQ Company. Major Hinton had his S-1 Personnel clerk take care of them. The kennel was placed nearby one of hundreds of the tarpaper shacks where Jackson was quartered. Immediately upon review of the kennel, Jackson knew he needed help. He found his platoon leader, 2nd Lieutenant Douglas, and requested help. Douglas had been briefed by his company commander; he was to treat the unit as he would any paratroop candidate, but also to help Jackson with his dog. "Sir, in New Jersey, the kennel was fine. But here it will sink into the mud and become unusable. Could I please request a kennel for hot, wet climate? It needs to be off the ground at least a foot, with a lean-to roof –"

Lieutenant Douglas cut him off with a raised hand. "Just give me a drawing of what you need, as detailed as possible, and we'll get the construction crews to build it. There's enough of them around here you can't swing a cat by its tail without hitting someone carrying a hammer. Get it to me now and we may have it tomorrow."

"Sir? Is there anything in the regs about my dog staying in the bunk house with me? He's real good sir and won't make a fuss." Douglas thought about that for a moment. "I'll get back to you. Now get me that drawing. Dismissed." A returned salute and the lieutenant was gone.

He put Rufus on the 10' foot leash and chained him to the kennel, then he began getting the kennel set up. Next, he drew the kennel with detailed length and width, the type of roof, ventilation, everything Rufus needed. After watering, he took Rufus for a walk/run around the camp, finding where everything was located, seeing troops in PT gear running at quick time or double time. The place was lousy with soldiers. Jackson estimated there were 5,000 or 6,000 soldiers here already. He saw soldiers returning from a path that appeared to lead to the mountain top. As they approached, he began a slow trot with Rufus in HEEL, and started up the trail. It was rugged, loose rocks, washed out trenches, but they continued. He gave Rufus some additional leash to allow them both to avoid rocks, tree trunks, even a few large boulders. It was a long run up, but they made it. He had to stop and rest at the top, but Rufus was ready to go. *I better get in better shape real fast,* he thought. The run down was easier, and they made good time. Getting back to the barracks, he checked Rufus out for any injuries, but he was fine. After a shower and changing to fresh utilities he delivered the drawing to Lieutenant Douglas. "Here you go sir. I tried to be as accurate as possible." The drawing was very accurate and detailed. It seemed maybe Jackson had learned a little from his engineer brother.

"Don't run off so soon, Private. We start training tomorrow. You'll start in my platoon, but Major Hinton said you needed a few days to get settled in." Jackson had been instructed by Major Hinton to take a few days until he was sure Rufus was ready. But he also felt as if this was a test, to see if he was going to take the easy road. "We're good to go Lieutenant. But I'd like Rufus to stay in the barracks tonight just to keep him calm and get some rest. If that's okay, sir."

Douglas looked at both of them, dog at rest beside Gilmore's left leg, watching his every movement. *Why not? Heck, if they make it through training and into war they'll be sharing a foxhole!* "Okay Private, take him with you tonight, and until you hear different, he can stay with you wherever you go. But some platoon leaders and company commanders may not be as easy as me." The lieutenant looked at the drawing. "Nice work, kid," and left.

***

The men lined up as best they knew. The non-commissioned officers acting as drill sergeants began whipping the men into shape. With so many men training, classroom time was scheduled to the second. Physical training, or PT, was scheduled in intervals to give the men time to rest between exercise. A two-mile run in the morning, calisthenics, followed by mess and classroom work. After lunch more instruction, and then a run up Currahee. Jackson and Rufus attended classroom instructions unless it was training he had mastered in basic. He spent this extra time tending to Rufus and training for war. Jackson didn't run into Eugene until the 2nd day of training.

Rufus was running a small version of an obstacle course when Eugene happened by. He noticed the dog first, and thought it looked a little odd, but appeared to excel at running the course. Once finished, Jackson took Rufus over to his bowl and filled it with water from his canteen. That's when he noticed his brother. "Eugene! You made it!" He nearly sprinted the 20 feet to the gravel sidewalk to grab his brother but pulled up when he recognized the gold bars of a 2nd Lieutenant and struck a smart salute. "Eugene! I mean, uh, sir! When did you get here? What unit are you assigned?"

Eugene grabbed his younger brother without returning the salute. "Good to see you brother! I got here a few days ago, assigned to Regimental HQ Company. I see you made it through K-9 school, who's your buddy?" Rufus watched the interaction and could sense these two were close, friends, family. He stood still as PFC Jackson Gilmore, or Jackson, or Gilmore, his *master*, talked excitedly with the other man. Rufus could also derive a scent from the man closely resembling Jackson's. "What? I'm in the Regimental HQ Company too! Well, assigned to it, but I'll be rotating through the 2nd and 3rd battalion companies to work with the other guys. Oh yeah! Lieutenant, meet Rufus, Corporal Rufus I mean." He told his brother about the rank structure in the K-9 Corps (he would explain this at least a hundred other times over the next weeks).

They wouldn't see much of each other for the next 13 weeks.

***

PT was tough on all the men, which is the reason for most of the dropouts to occur. Some men were not prepared for the rigorous training, others couldn't take the pressure and quit.

(These 'quitters' did not go home; they were re-assigned to complete training in some other Army unit.) Jackson and Rufus were assigned to 1st Platoon, H Company, 3rd Battalion, on his third day of training. After mess he loaded his bag with a few things he would need for 5 days, the same for Rufus, including his blankets. When he walked in to the barracks with Rufus, the men turned and went silent. The squad leader, a corporal, got to him first.

"Private, what do you think you're doing bringing a dog in here? Get him out."

"Corporal, I'm PFC Jackson Gilmore, assigned from Regimental HQ to this platoon. This is Rufus, he's my K-9 partner and a corporal, same as you. Where do we bunk?" Corporal Ben Stockstill remembered something about a dog joining them, but had not taken any stock in it, he had enough to worry about. "Hmmm, I do recall the Lieutenant telling us something about a K-9 Corps dog joining us, and we're to make sure you both are treated fairly." He held out his hand and they shook. "What about Corporal Rufus? Can he shake?" Jackson turned to look directly at Rufus, who was already staring back at him. He pointed to Ben and Said "Rufus, FRIEND."

Rufus' floppy ears lifted, he turned to Corporal Stockstill and held out his right paw. Ben laughed and shook the paw. He tried to pet him but Rufus turned away. "It's OKAY. Sorry about that, he knows that no one touches him but me unless I tell him it's okay. It's OKAY boy, GOOD FRIEND." With that command, Rufus began wagging his tail and approached Ben, rubbed against his legs while Ben patted him. Rufus won Ben over. "Well, I guess he can stay, but I better not step in dog crap in the morning!" That brought laughter from the barracks, and the men came to meet them. Jackson pointed to all the men and gave the GOOD FRIENDS command. Rufus understood, he circulated among the men, receiving 'good boys' from everyone and belly rubs from a few.

A large soldier, about 6 foot 2 inches and 220 pounds came over to see them. He looked like he could tear the place apart by himself, powerful shoulders and arms were evident through his uniform. "Hi Jackson, I'm Greg Maher, can I pet Rufus?" Of course he could. Maher dropped to a knee and scratched Rufus behind both ears. "I sure miss my dog. He's a huskie, I named him Honcho. I bet he'd make a good war dog too but he's too old." He continued to rub Rufus, clearly thinking of Honcho. After a minute he stood up. "Let me know if you need help with anything, or anyone gives you trouble. Ole Rufus is a fine soldier."

That was how most of the men acted from then on. Some were indifferent, and a very few cautious, perhaps never owning a dog and unsure how to react. A few made remarks on how strange Rufus appeared, but nothing to complain about. It looked like Colonel Sink's orders were taken seriously. Thanks to Corporal Stockstill and Private Maher, word got around the company that Rufus and Jackson were a good team and okay.

The next morning in 1st Platoon, H company, the men fell out for run and calisthenics. Jackson took Rufus on a short leash to ensure he stayed in formation. They sang cadence songs on long marches and runs, which helped keep morale up. Once, at the end of a song, the platoon sergeant ended with "1,2,3,4, 1-2-3-4!" and Rufus barked twice. His bark came out as a blue tick hound, like "Barooooo! Barooooo!" That got the men laughing until the platoon sergeant shut them up. But after that, the men began teaching songs to Rufus and prodded him to interact at certain points. Jackson was cautious but allowed it. The men really seemed to perk up around Rufus, and Rufus, in turn, showed his gratitude to the men. He never left Jackson without permission. But soon Rufus was given run of the barracks once they returned each night.

Mess was difficult. Rufus needed a specific diet, and he couldn't get it from the mess. He reached back to Lieutenant Douglas, his actual platoon leader, for help. "Sir, Rufus needs meat, horse meat if available, he needs vegetables and real eggs. Who can I talk too?" Douglas took it for action. That afternoon, after running Currahee, the men returned to camp and dinner mess. Douglas had finished his training for the day and waited for Jackson. He had a box with him and turned over to Gilmore. "Gilmore, this is from the Quartermasters on post. They said for you to come see them every day or anytime Rufus needed anything." The box held raw hamburger meat, raw horse meat, vegetables in a broth, some rice and two uncooked eggs.

As always, he fed Rufus first before eating himself. This sometimes would make him late for chow and maybe even missing dinner. The first time this happened the guys went back to the mess and begged for a couple of sandwiches. After that they fixed him a plate if it looked like he wouldn't make it. This happened in whatever unit he was assigned. The men took to them, accepted them into their platoons once they saw that Rufus and Jackson were working just as hard as they were. They moved to I Company, 3rd Battalion next, and he was quickly accepted, almost as quickly as Rufus.

One other note; Rufus never spent a night in his kennel until he was assigned to Easy Company, 2nd Battalion.

***

Eugene had a little more flexibility than his brother, so he was able to keep up with Jackson and watch him between classes or after PT. He was proud of his brother, how well he handled the pressure on himself but also on Rufus. He had heard rumors that while the enlisted men allowed Jackson and Rufus to 'blend right in,' some officers thought the K-9 unit was of no use. What good is a dog in battle, much less try to jump from a plane? He withheld comments but it infuriated him. *He's working so hard, Rufus too, he deserves respect of enlisted and officers!* Then he realized that his brother would have to overcome narrow-mindedness on his own. He made a vow to see Jackson as much as possible to encourage him. Unfortunately, training intensified, and he was only able to talk to his brother a few times more before transferring to Fort Benning.

Eugene enjoyed the physical training, building his strength and endurance. By week 10 he could run Currahee in 45 minutes. *Not bad for a bookworm engineer!* He held a leadership position in HQ Company, serving as an assistant platoon leader, but had minimal supervisory duties. But even more, he found to his surprise that he enjoyed the leadership courses and field problems, which took squad and platoon-level units and worked attack or defense exercises and enabled the men to use their new skills and physical strength (now honed to a sharp edge) to gain experience and confidence in their abilities. But he was not impressed with the officer corps. He saw officers skipping out of class training, night marches, even night field problems. He felt the enlisted men, like Jackson (and Rufus) deserved the officer's best effort. *How are we going to lead these men if we don't earn their respect?* This attitude would prove to make Eugene one of the best junior officers in the engineering battalion in the coming battles.

***

The attitude in Easy Company was much different than the other companies in which Jackson had trained. He and Rufus reported to 3rd Platoon, Easy Company, 2nd Battalion, 506th Parachute Infantry Regiment on a Sunday afternoon, eight weeks into training. They made a good team and seemed to be accepted everywhere they served. Easy Company Commander, Captain Herbert Sobel, called him to his office. The K-9 unit reported, saluted, and stood at attention. "At ease. Private Jackson, while serving in my command, you will be assigned to 3rd Platoon. You will comply with all regulations and complete all physical training as a team. You will not receive any help from other soldiers, understand? I've had your dog's kennel moved to your barracks so you can bed your dog down each evening. Clear?"

Jackson was intimidated, to say the least. Rufus sat quietly, sensing the change in Jackson's demeanor, and he didn't like it. But Jackson held firm, and when dismissed, took Rufus for a walk. It had been a tough eight weeks, but they had persevered. Jackson had gained physical and mental endurance, and so had Rufus. The K-9 unit was able to run Currahee in company formation, never falling out of formation. Today was going to be a new test. "You, Corporal, and your dog, will learn the importance of discipline and will complete your training or you will be sent back to Regiment. Clear?"

"Clear Sir!"

"Dismissed."

He was disappointed that Rufus would be relegated to his kennel. Rufus had been welcomed into other platoons and companies as a soldier. It almost seemed that Captain Sobel did not want his men to mix with Rufus. *Why? Rufus has performed above and beyond all expectations! I'll have to bull my way through this week and move on.*

A few days later Easy Company ran Currahee in the late afternoon. As in other companies he was assigned, he formed up in the rear so Rufus would have room to run with room to avoid rocks and debris. Sobel wouldn't allow it. "Gilmore! Get up here in front of 3rd Platoon. You will lead them in PT!" Unsure what to do, he tightened Rufus' leash so he was in Heel position, close to his left knee. The pace was quick but they held it. About halfway up the mountain, Rufus was unable to avoid loose rocks and stepped on a sharp shard of rock. He yelped and nearly stopped running, but Jackson pulled on his leash to make him continue. But it was obvious Rufus was hurt, so Jackson pulled him out of formation to check his paw. There was a small gash in his right front paw, it was bleeding but not bad. Sobel pounced on him. "Get back in formation Gilmore or you will be punished. And your little dog too!" (Sobel didn't realize he had just quoted a line from 'The Wizard of Oz' but the men did, and snickered quietly, so not to draw Sobel's ire.)

Captain Sobel made another harsh order. "No one will help the dog except for his owner! They train together, they fail together. Clear?" As Sobel ran on to the top of mountain, Rufus limped but did not give up. He sensed that the angry man was an enemy, even though he wore the same uniform as his master. He didn't understand, but knew he needed to continue up the hill. Sobel was waiting for them at the top. "Twenty-three minutes, Jackson! You and your little dog need to do better or you'll never make it as a paratrooper!"

The trip down was easier, but Rufus' limp worsened. Jackson was on the verge of stopping and taking whatever punishment Captain Sobel dished out, when a large soldier pulled alongside him. "Give him to me," the soldier said. Jackson was surprised by the command but answered quickly. "I can't, Captain Sobel said no one can help us."

"I don't give a shit, give him to me. I'll get him down the mountain then you can take him to medical. Now give him to me."

Jackson gave in, stopped, and gave Rufus the OKAY command. The soldier, PFC Denver "Bull" Randleman picked up all 70 pounds of Rufus easily, slung him over his shoulders and took off. With Sobel at the top of the mountain, he couldn't see Bull helping Rufus. They charged down the last part of the mountain, reformed into platoon formations and finally switching to quick time march to cool down. Randleman unloaded Rufus and hissed at Jackson, "Get back in formation before Sobel sees us. Now!" Rufus had bled on Bull's t-shirt, so he scooped up a handful of red Georgia clay and rubbed it on his shirt. Sobel was none the wiser.

That evening, the medics looked at Rufus and decided he didn't need stiches. They cleaned the wound, applied disinfectant, and wrapped it tightly with a bandage to apply pressure. Rufus was brave, appeared to shake it off and was ready to go. Jackson led him carefully back to 3rd Platoon barracks. True to his word, Rufus' kennel was waiting. It was the new kennel, built to Jackson's drawing. He outfitted the kennel with blankets, fed Rufus dinner, though he missed chow. After dinner he took him for a walk, Rufus relieved himself (Jackson picked up the residue like any good dog owner should) and led him back to his kennel. "I'm sorry, boy, you'll have to stay out here tonight. I'll check on you before I go to bed."

Rufus didn't understand why he was again in his kennel instead of with his master, but he followed his order without argument, and limped into his kennel. Jackson decided to stay outside with him to make sure his partner was okay. Of course, after the long day, he fell asleep leaned against the kennel. "Jackson! Jackson! Wake up! But be quiet." It was Bull. He helped Jackson to his feet, then asked "What are you doing out here? It's after midnight!"

Jackson was still drowsy but answered, "I fell asleep looking after Rufus. Captain Sobel said he can't stay in the barracks so I stayed out here with him." Bull's face drew up in a strange expression, one Jackson never wanted to see again. "Get Rufus and bring him inside. I'll take care of any fallout. Now git."

The morning came early, the men fell out for morning run and calisthenics, but Captain Sobel was not around. Lieutenant Winters, 2nd Platoon leader and de facto Executive Officer of Easy Company, led the men in the run and PT before releasing them for mess and class instruction. Winters stopped Jackson to ask about Rufus. "How's your dog, Private? Does he need to go on sick leave for a day or two?

"I don't think so sir, he seems to be okay. But I'd like to have him checked again later today before we go through any more PT. If that's okay, sir." It was fine with Winters.

But after class instruction, Easy Company was sent on a forced 10-mile march, but this time a new addition had been added. Instead of stopping at the barracks, the men, dressed in battle gear, including weapons, were led to a new obstacle. Barbed wire had been stretched across a muddy field with trenches, covering about 50 yards. The barb wire was stretched about two feet above the muck, and pig guts and entrails had been slung across it and spread in the mud. To make it more realistic, instructors fired .30-caliber machine-guns over the men to increase the realism of combat. When it was Jackson and Rufus' turn, he gave the CRAWL command and off they went. When they reached the muck and pig entrails, Rufus broke training protocol and pulled down a length of pig guts for a treat. "Rufus! Spit it out! NOW!" Shamefaced, Rufus let the guts fall from his mouth and pushed on. When the course was completed, the men crawled to the side to be out of gun fire before exiting the pits. Rufus kept crawling as Jackson hadn't given the command to stop. "You just keep crawling for a while. Eating pig guts on the obstacle course? What got into you?" The men close enough to hear this exchange broke out in guffaws. Jackson was embarrassed but the men didn't think anything about it, except it was funny!

That night, after getting Rufus checked out (he was fine), washed him down, groom him, and fed, Jackson led him into the barracks.

"There's the pig killer!"

"Hey Rufus, you should have held out for hot dogs!"

"Hey Jackson, why didn't your dog offer you a bite?"

"Hey, he probably thought it was a German Sausage!"

Good natured ribbing was the Army way and Jackson took it with a smile. A few guys came over to check on Rufus and talk to Jackson. He was still in awe of how Rufus improved morale, especially after a day like today. Many men in Easy Company suffered from low morale, so Jackson took Rufus through all the barracks to help. It worked, the men responded to Rufus and many actually smiled. When he returned, Bull came over to talk. "How's Rufus? Any injuries?"

"He's fine, his paw is healing up fine. But I just don't understand why Captain Sobel is so hard on Rufus. I'm fine with taking whatever he throws at me, but not Rufus!"

Bull chewed on that for a minute. "You know what? I think Sobel did it on purpose. By going after Rufus, he made sure we'd try to protect him, and accept y'all into the company. You remember what Colonel Sink passed down to the companies, no hazing. So instead of us turning our backs on you, and snub Rufus, we took him in as part of the company. I'm not saying I agree with his methods, but it seems like it's working. Ole Rufus is gonna be a great paratrooper."

Randleman was right. Through Sobel's harsh and unfair treatment of Rufus, the men circled around Rufus (and Jackson) to protect them. The men may not have really understood Sobel's treatment of Rufus, but his actions more than likely had the desired effect.

***

4

JUMP WINGS

"'LONG WALKIN', LOUD TALKIN', NON JUMPIN' SONSOBITCHES 506'ES'. That's what they called you during your initial training in Benning but you backed up all your talk with plenty of action and hung up one of the finest records in the history of the Parachute School in reply and the critics had plenty of words to eat. First Battalion ran the instructors ragged the first week, so the Second and Third didn't have to bother with 'A' stage at all 'B' stage with the mock up towers, harnesses and tumbling apparatus was old stuff and the instructors showed a marked reluctance to run you, when you goofed off, the way they did the PTR students. Plenty of pushups were a fine substitute however, and served to keep you in line as much as could be expected. 'C' stage and Christmas Eve on the towers. Everybody sweating out the slightest sprain that would keep him from jumping with the rest of the guys, and the hard ball that formed in your stomach every time you were marched down to the field only to turn back because the weather wouldn't permit jumping. And finally-THE day!! The odd feeling being airborne was to the guys who had never flown before, the galloping butterflies that were having drunken family reunions inside of you, the first feel of the prop blast as you hurtled earthward, the opening shock that left you limp in your harness and the heady sense of overwhelming power that ran thru you as you gazed at the ground below. And that final jump when you knew you had it made. It was great to be young and alive ... and a Paratrooper."
- 506th PIR Scrapbook

Eugene and Jackson took different roads to earn jump wings. Lieutenant Gilmore was placed on a train in late November 1942, departed for Fort Benning, Georgia, with the rest of HQ Company. The trip took most of a day, but the men used the time to rest and sleep. Jackson, still assigned to Easy Company, 2nd Battalion, took part in a field march from Camp Toccoa to Atlanta.

Prior to leaving Toccoa, the men spent hours jumping from platforms of various heights to learn how to jump from a plane, control a parachute by pulling on the risers, and correct body position for landing. They jumped from eight-foot platforms, then twenty, and finally from a platform nearly 30 feet in height. Jackson practiced all with Rufus attached to his chest by a harness he had designed. Working with the Para riggers and jumpmasters, he was able to come up with a design that ensured Rufus' safety but allowed him to jump and control the parachute. The weight of Rufus, nearly 70 pounds, wasn't difficult to manage; Jackson didn't know how to jump any other way. From the day they started practice, Rufus was attached to Jackson. Rufus, for his part, thought it was a game and relished the drills. After each practice jump, Jackson would land and roll on his back, the preferred method he quickly learned, release Rufus and stand up. Rufus would jump with excitement and start to take off for the platform for another jump until his training kicked in, and he fell into place by his master.

In early December, 2nd Battalion was ordered to depart Camp Toccoa in the early morning for Atlanta. The march was about 118 miles in cold, harsh weather. Jackson and Rufus were allowed to march free of formation from the companies and platoons. Jackson used a longer leash to give Rufus freedom and not worry about remaining in the Heel position. He carried his gear as well as most of Rufus' equipment. Rufus carried about 20 pounds of gear in a halter the Quartermasters had measured and sewn together made of waterproof canvas. It was a tough march for the entire battalion. About an hour outside of Toccoa a cold winter rain began falling, but soon turned to snow. The men completed forty-four miles the first day, then were allowed to rest.

Tents went up but the men were soaked through to their skin. Fires were difficult to maintain, but they did as best they could. A few men came to see how Rufus was doing. This was the furthest Rufus had marched in training. Jackson had checked his paws earlier in the day, after they had stopped for lunch. Besides a little abrasion he was fine, but it was something that concerned Jackson.

One man who stopped to see Rufus said "Did you see the pooch Dewitt picked up? He saw a little yella dog following us just out of camp, and when it started limping, he picked it up. I thought maybe you could have a look at him." He asked him to bring him over and he'd look at him. The poor dog was a stray, hungry and hurt. Its paws were worn, and his hind leg looked like it was strained. Jackson cleaned his paws with warm salt water he had mixed for Rufus and soaked his paws for a few minutes. Next, he covered his paws in gauze, then cotton, and finally bandaged. "Tell Dewitt to keep him off his paws tonight, he may be better tomorrow. But I'll check on him in the morning."

Rufus received the same treatment. He soaked his paws in a warm saltwater solution, then carefully cleaned between his claws. Next, he fed Rufus from his food stores; a tin of horse meat and a tin of mixed vegetables, followed by a hard-boiled egg and dried milk mixed in his water bowl. With all this done, they laid down in Jackson's tent while he groomed Rufus. His fur was a mess from the march and the wet snow. Jackson dried him as best he could, then brushed his coat until it was clean. As they were getting bedded, a private from 2nd Battalion HQ found him. He was told to report to the battalion commander.

Major Strayer waited in his tent. "At ease, soldiers. I just wanted to see how you were holding up after the first day. Any worries?"

"No sir, we're fine, ready to get some sleep and start again in the morning." Strayer looked hard at Rufus, as if trying to stare the dog down. But Rufus kept his eyes on his master, waiting for the next command. "Well," Strayer finally said, relenting, "If you say he's fine then I guess he's fine. But if there are any problems I expect to find out about it, so use your chain of command.

Clear?"
"Clear, sir!"

***

The next two days were the same as the first. Wake up and march through rain and sleet. Unlike the first day, the men marched until nearly ten o'clock that night. Rufus held up fine but Gilmore could tell he was sore. With not much time, he put up his tent, built a fire with whatever he could find along the wooded road, and checked Rufus. Again, his paws were red and raw but not so bad he could not go any longer. Rufus had been through forced marches before, as far as twenty miles, and his strength helped him carry his pack with no problem. Still, Jackson was concerned. An Easy Company sergeant stopped to check on them, making sure they were okay.

The third morning was tougher than the first two. Men throughout the battalion had sores and blisters on their feet. Some men had removed their boots to allow them to dry out but found that their feet had swollen in the night, their boots were frozen, and they could barely get their feet into the boots. Rufus awoke slowly, only when Jackson called him out of the tent. "Time to go, boy!" Rufus opened his eyes, crusted over during the night. His nose, usually wet and cool, was warm and dry. He was sick. Jackson quickly got his kit, cleaned his eyes, and made sure there were no irritants. He gave Rufus plenty of water, not sure what to do next. He remembered the order from Major Strayer, but also knew if he reported this, they would be pulled from the march. Gilmore was torn between caring for his partner and meeting the rigorous march conditions. But he knew if he dropped out, the men would remember, and though they may not hold it against him, they would all look at him and Rufus differently, maybe not quite paratrooper material. Rufus stood and stretched, then wagged his tail repeatedly. *I'm ready to go!* He seemed to say. "Okay, boy, we'll give it our best shot today."

The march started in early morning, cold and wet as normal. Rufus seemed fine so Jackson let him off leash for a while to relax. He ran ahead of the Easy Company platoons, then circled back along the left flank of the formation. Rufus didn't understand why he and all the men were marching so far, but he could sense their tiredness, their heads hung down and no one was calling songs. He put his tail in the air and marched around the men and gave them a loud bark to wake them up!

As he passed each platoon, he gave a loud "BARROOO!" which got the men laughing. *They really do react to him*, Jackson thought. *Maybe this is something that should be reported up the chain. If dogs help with morale, maybe we should have more!*

As he returned to his master, Jackson stopped and checked on him again. The red congested look was gone, and his nose was wet again. It looked like he will be alright, at least for now. After lunch, the men could feel a change, as they felt proud of what they were accomplishing. *"We're out-marching the Japs!"* was making the rounds through the men and everyone could sense they were making history. Finally, that afternoon the battalion marched into the outskirts of Atlanta and made camp at Oglethorpe University. Dinner was prepared for them; they were able to clean up and finally rest.

The next day 2nd Battalion marched into Atlanta to thousands of cheering Americans, and after a civic reception, they marched to the railroad depot and boarded a train bound for Fort Benning, Georgia. Jump School.

***

Eugene received his jump wings after his fifth jump, a night jump. His first jump had taken a lot of nerve to go out the airplane door, but he didn't hesitate one bit. He guided his parachute to the open field below and landed a little harder than he expected. Still, he rolled on his back, stood up, gathered his parachute and trotted to the retrieval area. On his second jump, he was the first man out of the airplane, and felt no hesitation or fear; he actually enjoyed it! The last jump, in pitch black of night, changed his mind about this being fun. Yet, through the darkness, he could see the red light turn on, stood up with the rest of the men, hooked up, checked equipment, and was ready to go.

"Go! Go! Go!" screamed the jump instructor, and each man stepped to the door and jumped into blackness. Eugene took his turn and slipped his legs into the air stream and was whisked away. His chute opened as expected, and he checked it to make sure it was fully expanded. He tried to discern the ground below but saw nothing. He felt like he had been in the darkness for hours, but finally caught sight of shadows below him. *I'm going too fast!* he thought, pulling on his risers to slow his descent. Luckily, he had time to brace for the impact and hit the ground hard, but not as hard as he imagined. He had made it.

***

Camp Toccoa was in the rear-view mirror for the 2nd Battalion, 506th PIR as they boarded a train for a half-day trip to Benning. 1st Battalion completed jump training and wore their jump wings with pride. 3rd Battalion marched 136 miles from Atlanta to Fort Benning to show 2nd Battalion that they were just as proud and strong, though no one in 2nd Battalion ever thought different. Now 2nd Battalion was prepared to win their wings.

Fort Benning, as far as the 506th was concerned, was about one thing: jump school. The training was divided into four, one-week courses. A was physical training, B would train men to pack parachutes, train them in harnesses suspended from the ground and jumping from thirty-four-foot towers. Phase C would see the men training to jump from a 250-foot tower, control the canopy with your risers, and land without breaking parts of their body. D was five jumps from a C-47, four jumps in daylight and one in the darkness of night. Complete the five required jumps and you earned your jump wings.

Jackson arrived with all his gear, plus Rufus, at Fort Benning, along with the rest of 2nd Battalion. He was tired, sore, and a little overwhelmed. Rufus appeared to withstand anything thrown his way. He loved the train ride, where they rode in a storage car (again) by themselves. While Jackson slept, Rufus stuck his head out a window, loving the feel of the wind on his nose and ears, smelling thousands of wonderful new scents of cattle, goats, horses and even a few strange feline animals he found familiar but couldn't quite name. When it was time to disembark, Gilmore struggled with their gear, just as he had during the forced march. Luckily, a couple of men came over to help and took most of Rufus' load so the dog could walk with only a small pack of equipment. Jackson smiled at the help, *I think the guys are more worried about Rufus than me, but that's just fine with me!*

After the forced march to Atlanta, the men were still feeling the effects of the long road when they started physical training. Many men had sore feet, shin splits, you name it, but they all kept at it. They were surprised that the physical training was easy compared to what they had gone through at Camp Toccoa. The men ended up running circles around the highly skilled non-commissioned officers who served as instructors. That ended the first phase of jump school. Jackson had his first run-in with the instructors on the second day of Phase A. He and Rufus were training with Easy Company, as Major Strayer had left it up to Jackson what company he trained with, so long as they made the rounds between companies. Rufus and Jackson gravitated to Easy Company more and more as they both enjoyed the comradery of the men and felt accepted. After completing PT on the second day, it was evident the men of the 506th were in excellent condition, and the decision was made to move on to Phase B. But two sergeants called Jackson to stay behind.

"Son, what are you doing here with a dog? We cain't allow no dog to jump, we ain't even got a rig for him!" Before he could answer, the other sergeant jumped in. "Plus the Army don't allow you to take pets to war with you. Now get this mutt out of here and join your unit."

Jackson was speechless. He had been told that the instructors were aware of them attending jump school and didn't expect any problems. As the instructors continued to badger them, Gilmore caught the eye of newly promoted Corporal Randleman, who approached the instructors. "Sirs, this here is Corporal Rufus and PFC Gilmore. They are assigned to Easy Company for the duration of jump training, by order of Major Strayer. Do I need to run and get him?" The sergeants looked blankly at each other, but quickly shifted tactics.

"No, Corporal that won't be necessary. But I don't believe he and his dog will meet weight standards. That's a lot of extra weight." Bull didn't like that; it sounded more of an excuse than actual policy. "Jackson, what do you and Rufus weigh?" Jackson gave him the numbers. "So Gilmore weighs 150 pounds dressed out, Rufus is 70 pounds, so 220 pounds together. I weigh 220 pounds myself. So if they can't make the limit then how am I gonna jump?" The sergeants just looked at each other, but finally relented. Jackson felt this wasn't the last of any problems he would have at Benning.

***

Jackson had to make a call on the Quartermaster Corps that afternoon. Rufus needed supplies and he needed help with his harness. The riggers at Camp Toccoa had done a good job, but he was concerned the instructors may be right. After picking up a few days of rations for Rufus (which had increased two-fold since they departed New Jersey and started the tough physical training at Camp Toccoa) Jackson and Rufus visited the Packing Building. This was where parachutes were packed, repaired, cleaned and dried after a jump. The riggers worked here. Jackson saw long tables about 3 feet wide spread through the main room. Several chutes in disarray on the tables, as men were busy packing them. He stopped a private and asked directions to the maintenance room, and shortly walked into a smaller room filled with T-5 assemblies of chute bags, canopies, and suspension lines, connected to four cotton web risers by metal rings, or connector links. Four NCOs were in the maintenance room, or "Rigger's Shack" as it was nicknamed, each working on sets of chutes. A tall, slim sergeant saw Jackson and Rufus waiting quietly just inside the door.

"What can I help you with, private? Oh! Excuse me, I mean Corporal!" He had just noticed Rufus' rank sewn on his harness and grinned from ear to ear. "Say, you must be that K-9 unit we heard was coming with the 506th! Good to meet ya! I'm Sergeant Clyde Sellers, I run this shop." Clyde had blonde, nearly white hair, wore glasses, was trim but muscular. He wore jump wings and appeared confident without any cockiness you saw in most paratroopers. Still, Jackson was cautious and didn't want to be given the bum's rush.

"Hi Sergeant, I'm PFC Jackson Gilmore, and this is Corporal Rufus. You are correct, we are the K-9 unit assigned to the 506th. And…well, we started jump training yesterday, and I started thinking about the rig Rufus has used. I think I need something sturdier, you know, to take our weight and keep Rufus tied to me until we land. You think you can help?"

Clyde looked at the harness attached to Rufus. It appeared adequate for short tower jumps but he wasn't sure if it would take the force of jumping from a plane in flight. Clyde went to take the harness, but Rufus growled and bared his fangs. "Whoa, Corporal! I just want to look at this rig." Jackson placed his hand on Rufus' nape and said "It's OKAY. FRIEND. GOOD FRIEND." With that, Rufus wagged his tail and sniffed Clyde's hand, then licked it.

Clyde was amused rather than angry. "Well don't that beat all! Can I take his harness off now?" With Jackson's help they removed the harness for Clyde to inspect. "Not a bad design, just a little short on strength." That comment pleased Jackson tremendously. He continued to study the harness while asking Jackson about their training, where Rufus had come from, small talk. Finally, he looked at Jackson. "I think I know what you need soldier. Come see me in a couple of days and I'll have something for you."

***

The next day started with calisthenics, breakfast, classroom work, training on a suspended harness, and a demonstration of the 34-foot tower. Phase B had begun. Jackson used the original harness for Rufus for this training. All he had done so far was jump with Rufus from a 30-foot tower at Camp Toccoa. Watching the suspended harness, he saw that Rufus would be in the way if he was strapped to his chest. He would need to be strapped closer to his waist. *I need to see Sergeant Sellers today and make sure he understands.*

After the day was over, the team returned to the Rigger's Shack and found Sergeant Sellers in the back, working on a large, heavyset sewing machine. "Howdy Corporal Rufus! Come see what I'm building for you!" Clyde pulled his work out of the sewing machine and held it up for them to see. It was a jump harness for Rufus, but this one appeared much sturdier than his original. Clyde had started from scratch, using thick water-proof canvas, with thick canvas doubled over that lined the edges. Attached to the harness body were four broad canvas straps ending in metal rings. It looked durable and strong.

"These straps will tie directly to your T-5 harness. Wrap Rufus in his harness, then you'll need to drop to your knees, attach the harness like so," Sellers said as he showed Gilmore how to hook up the new gear. "Okay, I think I got it."

Clyde gave him a T-5 jump harness to try. Jackson slipped it on, wrapped Rufus up tight in his new rig, then followed Clyde's instructions. After connecting the straps to his harness, Rufus could nearly walk on the floor while strapped in. Sellers had anticipated the need to lower the K-9 harness to give Jackson freedom to control the risers and to release the T-5 harness once alit.

"If you duck-walk, Rufus will be able to carry himself. But the easiest way, I think, is to get into the plane with Rufus on leash, hook him up when it's time to jump, then waddle on up to the door. Before you know it you both will be swinging free on your way to the ground." Sellers had done a great job, Jackson thought. *Now I just need to hold up my end of the bargain and jump!*

***

"Gentlemen, your first jump will be in sticks of 12 men to an aircraft. This first jump will be from 1200 feet AGL (Above Ground Level). Just remember what you were taught, follow instructions, and before you know it, you'll be on the ground. Any refusal to jump, either in the aircraft or at the door, and you can be certain that YOU WILL BE OUT OF THE AIRBORNE. Understood?" "Yes sir!" The men knew this was the last item they had to complete to receive jump wings. Jackson was excited, with a little fear mixed in. But it was a fear of failure, not measuring up to his brothers, that caused him the most anxiety. *We've worked so long and hard for this chance, don't blow it now!* Jackson even thought that if he failed, he could persuade the K-9 Corps to take Rufus back through training with another trainer assigned. But what if Rufus failed? Jackson had mulled these things over for days. He finally decided, that if for any reason, Rufus did not complete the jumps, then he would take Rufus and be reassigned somewhere else, doing whatever the K-9 Corps decided. He needn't have worried.

The men climbed into a dark green C-47 and settled in. Gilmore had Rufus leashed but dressed in his jump harness. Once sitting down, he secured Rufus to his harness, sinched it tight, then let Rufus settle on the floor. The dog appeared alert but calm and ready to follow directions from his master.

Rufus had felt exhilaration the first time he had been dropped from the 250-foot-tall tower. The wind across his ears and nose only caused him more excitement. He loved it! Once safe on ground, he couldn't wait to go up again. He tugged at his harness, trying to get loose. Jackson quickly unhooked him and then watched as Rufus made a beeline for the tower. "Rufus. Heel! HEEL!" That got his attention, and he remembered his training—stay with master. He hurried back, sat down by Jackson's left knee and awaited instruction. "You crazy mutt, you're gonna get us kicked out of this unit! Now pay attention!" They went on to complete two other tower jumps, one in the pitch black of night. Rufus never flinched.

But this jump was the first from a real aircraft. Two Pratt & Whitney R-1830 air-cooled radial engines filled the air with turbulence as a barrage of engine noises and fumes crept into the aircraft causing the men to get nauseous. But as soon as they took to the air, the fumes disappeared, the aircraft smoothed out and the men could hear the jumpmaster. "Stand up!" the jumpmaster called loudly. "Hook up! Equipment Check!" Each man checked their gear and harness, and also the gear of the man in front of him. Then they called off their status. "Twelve Okay! Eleven Okay! Ten Okay!" And so on to the first man in the stick. Jackson and Rufus were the last in line. The jumpmaster had been concerned that Gilmore could hold up the rest of the stick trying to get Rufus to the door. As each man reached the door, the jumpmaster screamed to be heard over the roar of the wind and engines. "Go! Go! Go!"

No one hesitated, each man followed his training. Gilmore waddled close behind the man in front of him, being careful to keep his left foot in front, his right always behind, so that when he reached the door, he would pivot on his right foot into the door. In only a few seconds he was in front of the doorway, he pivoted on his right foot exactly as trained, his left foot forward, and placed both hands on the outside of the doorway. The jumpmaster tapped his leg and screamed "Go!" Jackson threw his left leg out of the plane, but before he could push off into the slipstream, Rufus jumped, pulling him out of the airplane.

The airplane tail swiftly passed on his right, the ground on his left, as the static line pulled his upper body toward the doorway, until the canopy cracked open with a violent shock. The ground quickly moved to his front as he swung in the open air, but soon settled down beneath his feet. He opened the risers and looked up to check his canopy; all good, no blown panels. He reached down and felt for Rufus.

Rufus didn't understand why they jumped from the loud machine, but he felt much better in the air than in the stinky enclosed place. The smell of sweat and fear had been overwhelming; he could smell distinctly separate scents from each man. Even his master was giving off a scent of fear, though not as bad as most of the other men. Now, as he swung in the air, he felt elated, this was a game for him to play! He could clearly see the ground approaching and readied to land.

It seemed only a few seconds had passed since he left the airplane when the ground was suddenly close. Jackson bent his knees slightly to be able to take the shock of landing, but he pulled strongly on the risers and landed with only a small jolt to his body. Rufus landed on all four paws but fell over as Jackson rolled onto his back. He quickly hit the release to allow Rufus to get up, then began pulling in his canopy. Their first jump was done!

The next three jumps went good for the duo. They jumped from 1,000 feet, followed by two more from 800, and finally a night jump at 1,000 feet. But on the last day jump, things went amiss for two troopers. Jackson was the first out of the airplane this time. He had proven they could move as well as any other trooper in jump gear, while Rufus walked between his legs as he shuffled toward the door. This time, he followed the instructions from the jumpmaster, pivoted toward the door, and when given the "Go!" command stuck his left leg into the slipstream, Rufus jumping at the same time and out they went.

He should have been the first man on the ground, but as he watched the horizon, he looked over his shoulder and saw a man go streaming past. The canopy had not opened cleanly, with a line crossing over the top, entangling his chute so that it did not open properly. The trooper tried to clear the line but ran out of time and hit the ground hard. As Jackson watched, he saw no movement, just the canopy billowed behind him.

Once safely on the ground (another good landing), he released Rufus, gathered his canopy and called Rufus to heel as he headed to the injured man. An ambulance arrived and medics were attending to him. He was conscious but was bleeding from his mouth and nose. He watched as the medics loaded the man into the ambulance and sped off. Jackson never saw the man again. Later, in another stick, a trooper never had a chance. Once he departed the aircraft, his parachute was pulled from the pack, but never opened. His chute streamed behind him, wrapped by several chords. He tried to open his reserve but jumping from 800 feet left no time and the man struck the ground, bounced three feet into the air, then landed again, no movement. These were the first two losses for the 506th. There would be plenty more later in the war.

The last jump came on December 26th, 1942. The fourth day

jump was completed on Christmas Eve, and the men were given Christmas Day off. That evening dinner was the best meal the men had in months. Real turkey, dressing, mashed potatoes, yams, and several vegetables. Many of the men wrapped turkey into kerchiefs to take back to the bunk rooms. Jackson had already fed Rufus but needed to check him over and give his coat a good brush. When he arrived at the bunk room, Rufus was waiting outside. They entered the building and found most of the men drinking beer (someone had made a beer run to the post exchange, or PX) and sharing turkey. "Jackson, can Rufus have some turkey and dressing? He deserves it as much as we do!"

Gilmore had closely guarded Rufus' caloric intake, mainly to ensure he received enough protein and energy foods. *Well, maybe just a little turkey wouldn't hurt.* "Sure!" he replied, "But I need to feed it to him. Just something we were trained to do. Sorry." Several guys came over to share with Rufus: Bull Randleman, DeWitt Lowery, Don Malarkey and Skip Muck, even Sergeant Carwood Lipton. Rufus began licking his lips at the scent of the goodies. Jackson hand-fed Rufus and he devoured it all. "You sure you been feeding him? He acts like he ain't eaten in a month!", one of the men called out laughingly. So, against his better judgement, Gilmore fed him more, and more, until Rufus had put a couple of plates of turkey and dressing away.

He took Rufus for a good walk, keeping him on the 10-foot leash to give him freedom. After about 15 minutes Rufus found a spot and let it go. And go. And go. *Uh oh, I hope he doesn't get sick. If we miss the last jump because of a sour stomach I'm gonna be real upset, and probably be chewed out by every officer up to Col. Sink!* But Rufus finished his business, wagging his tail and ready to go. Jackson buried the pile where it was and returned to the barracks. It was cozy if not warm, as a small potbelly stove in the center of the room gave out as much warmth as it could. After a little while everyone settled in for the night, expecting to finish the last jump the next evening and receive jump wings. Jackson got into his cot, settled in, then motioned for Rufus. Rufus jumped on the cot, curled up on his blanket, his back and haunches pressed against Jackson's side. Tomorrow was a big day.

***

The day after Christmas, the men were ready for their last jump. It was pitch black, no lights marking the landing zone, nothing. Jackson and Rufus boarded the C-47 without difficulty, Rufus happily jumping up through the doorway while Jackson was helped up by a couple of men. They were again in the middle of the 12-man stick. Once airborne the pilot flew past the drop zone, passed over the Chattahoochee River and on into Alabama before turning back to the drop zone. The red light came on, easily visible in the darkness. The jumpmaster called the orders: "Stand up! Hook Up!"

As Jackson checked on their equipment, Rufus gave a belch, then a muffled 'pffffffffft.' It only took a few seconds for the odor to spread through the close quarters of the airplane. "Jesus Christ!!! Who did that!" The jumpmaster was livid. "Which one of you yellow bellied quitters crapped their pants? You gonna live, boy?" The men laughed even though they were nervous. Jackson raised his hand. "Sir, it was me. Or well, my dog sir. Sorry about that."

That got a bigger laugh, but the jumpmaster quickly gained control. "Equipment Check! Sound off!" As Jackson checked their gear, the man in front of him sat down, his head in his hands. *Uh oh, he ain't jumping,* Jackson thought sadly. Jackson reached up and removed the parachute hook from the static line, making it easier for the men behind him, for now they wouldn't have to unhook and hook up again. The light turned green, and the jumpmaster sent the men out as quickly as he could. "Go! Go! Go!" Jackson and Rufus stepped to door, but the man before them was gone, so Jackson just jumped, without pivoting into the door frame.

The wind caught him with great force and swung them both side to side. Jackson held Rufus to ensure he was firmly attached, then grabbed his risers as the canopy blossomed above him. He could barely make out the earth below him, the horizon was as dark as the sky and gave no hint of where he was. Suddenly, Rufus let out a loud "BAROOOO!" When Jackson looked down he saw they were only twenty feet or so from the ground, but quickly assumed a good landing position and alit not too hard onto a hard patch of ground. They were okay! But as he released Rufus and gathered his chute, he heard a crash from a copse of trees off to the west. "Rufus, HEEL. Let's go!"

They ran for about 100 yards before they reached the small trees, surrounded by brush. There was no sound until a jeep and ambulance swiftly arrived. With the headlights shining, Jackson saw a dreadful sight. A trooper had fallen straight through the trees onto the hard, packed ground. His chute had partially opened, and when he opened his reserve chute it became tangled in his primary chute. He never had a chance. This put a dimmer on the men's celebration, but only for a moment. They were becoming hardened, not only physically and mentally, but also emotionally. Death would soon be all around them, each man knew, and struggled in his on way to cope with that thought. Soon, the party livened up and beer was flowing freely.

The pinning ceremony was the next day, the men in Class A uniforms (except for Rufus, who wore his normal vest). That afternoon another party kicked off in one of the large Day Rooms, all Easy Company was there, including the officers, even though they had received their jump wings weeks prior. Suddenly, the room was called to attention with a loud "Room TENSHUT!" Colonel Sink arrived followed by Major Strayer and Major Horton.

"At ease men. You deserve this party, each one of you has worked damned hard to receive your wings, and you succeeded. Now we have a lot of training in front of us, and you will show the rest of the Army what the best company in the 506th is made of!" Cheers drowned out the next few words. "Now, I was informed of an oversight earlier today, and I apologize. Private Gilmore, Corporal Rufus, front and center!"

Jackson was surprised, but quickly led Rufus to the front and snapped to attention. "Private First Class Gilmore and Corporal Rufus reporting as ordered, sir!" Sink had a smile on his face and his eyes twinkled with happiness. "At ease, paratroopers. Men, Private Gilmore received his wings at the pinning ceremony today, but we overlooked another trooper. Corporal Rufus completed his jumps and should have received his jump wings. But some fool in Regimental HQ only listed the men that qualified. So, Corporal Rufus, stand at attention."

Jackson gave the Attention command and Rufus shot up on all four legs, looking straight ahead. "Private, you do the honors" Sink said as he handed the jump wings to Jackson. Jackson trembled a little as he received the wings, but swiftly knelt by Rufus. Quietly he said, "Here you go, boy, you really deserve these as much as any of us." Once pinned the men shouted their approval, and the party continued. "Buck" Taylor hollered across the room, "Hey Gilmore, you ought to change that dog's name to something that fits, since he floated a 'biscuit' in the airplane!"

Later, Major Horton tracked Jackson down to discuss a topic that would change their fate forever. "Private, I know you were instructed to move about the companies, but now that we're moving to platoon and squad level field training, I think we need to find a permanent home for you." Jackson was ecstatic. *Finally! We are getting assigned to a unit!* "That sounds good to me sir. Where do you think I'll go?" Horton thought for a moment before answering. "Tell you what. Colonel Sink is giving all of you a ten-day furlough. Go home, relax, and when you get back come see me. But be thinking about where you feel you can do your best work. And think about some things you and Rufus can do in the field to help the men."

***

Eugene found Jackson and they both took off for home. They caught a train to Atlanta, transferred to a train bound for Chattanooga, and finally arriving in Greensburg. They had to request for the train to stop and let them off. Rufus and Jackson rode in the baggage car most of the way, but once in Chattanooga, they changed to a local train system and the conductor told him to bring his War Dog to the front. Only two cars carried passengers, and plenty of seats were available. A few kids were traveling with parents and took a shine to Rufus.

"Is he really in the Army?" "He jumped out of an airplane with you?" "Does Rufus know any tricks?" So instead of catching some sleep, Jackson and Rufus played with kids for an hour before the parents came and dragged them away. Rufus loved every minute of it. The last time he was around children was when he left Penny nearly one year ago but seemed an eternity to him. After the kids left, Rufus curled up on the seat next to Jackson, placed his head in his lap, and fell asleep.

No one was there to pick them up at the depot, and since it was New Year's Eve, only a few townsfolk were around. But once they walked into the drug store and sat at the soda fountain for hot coffee and a sandwich, folks recognized them and welcomed them home. Eugene called home and their dad arrived in a few minutes. It was a warm reunion; Rufus shook hands with Gene and jumped into the truck bed. Faye was crying with joy; her boys were home! Rufus impatiently waited for Jackson to call him out of the truck, finally letting loose with a loud "BAROOO!" to get Jackson's attention.

"Rufus, Heel! Momma, this is Rufus, my partner. We do everything together. Rufus, BEST FRIEND." With that Rufus tail set to wagging as fast as Jackson had ever seen it. The dog approached Faye timidly, sat down next to her. When Faye knelt, Rufus gave her a huge lick of his tongue. "Well, if I didn't know better I'd say y'all two have met before!" He didn't realize how close he was to the truth.

Rufus smelled Jackson's mother from the truck. The scents brought back so many memories of his home with Penny. She smelled like Penny's mother, Marilyn-- soap, but traces of bread, sweet smelling cookies, chicken. He realized that this must be Jackson's mother and wanted to be close to her like he had been with Marilyn. Rufus was torn between being happy to be there with Jackson, but sad because of memories of his home with Penny. Even though he loved Jackson with all his heart, and loved the work and excitement, he missed Penny so, so much. But as he entered the home he felt better. He could smell another dog too!

Beau was in the back mud room and barked until he was

finally allowed in to meet visitors. He ran to Jackson and jumped into his arms, causing Rufus to nearly attack Beau to protect his master. But he saw how Jackson was greeting his old friend and knew he was safe. Jackson spent a few moments greeting Beau while Rufus watched on with mixed feelings. Finally Beau made eye contact with Rufus and went to meet this new dog in the house. Tails were up, wagging tentative, both dogs tense but not aggressive. Jackson commanded Rufus to Heel position to make sure the dogs didn't fight. But Beau and Rufus continued to smell each other until satisfied, neither dog tried to assert dominance over the other, and soon were best friends. Rufus had not played with another dog since New Jersey and enjoyed the freedom.

It was both good and strange to be home for both boys, as their mother continued to call them. They answered hundreds of questions about what they had been doing, even though both men wrote home often. But when they went to town, folks welcomed them but seemed unaware they were training to go to war. Only the young men, not yet called to duty, were very interested in what they had been through for the last 10 months. They especially had lots of questions about the Airborne, how tough was training, jumping from airplanes, which Jackson told them instead of 'jumping from a plane in flight' they were 'jumping from a plane in fright!'

Neither brother had seriously dated a girl while home, but friends set them up with blind dates, usually a sister of a friend or younger sister of one of the boy's girlfriends. It was nice to go to a movie, hang out late, but something nagged them both. Eugene figured it out on the way home one evening. "Jackson, some of those boys haven't shaved in a couple of days. Did you see how sloppy they all look? Only the girls looked like they took time to wash their face! Boy have we changed! It's hard to believe that I probably looked like that a year ago!" He was right, they had changed. Both men were disciplined, mentally and physically tough, and walked with a confident, nearly cocky swagger.

When it came time to return to Fort Benning, their mom cried again as she hugged them, but sent them with a box of food to eat on the train. The ride back took longer, but they arrived in time to make it on post before the furlough expired. A new type of training was awaiting them.

***

5

TRAINING FOR WAR

"That stop and go train ride...The pretty Red Cross girls with the ever welcome coffee and donuts....Waving at all the girls enroute...The engineer was a beer hound and side tracked every time he saw a bar....Finally, Sturgis...And 'Rat Race Ridge'...Digging in and pitching tents...Having to carry that rifle to chow all the time...Situation tactical ya know...Waking up in the middle of the night to find a snake sharing your blankets...Starting to wish the whole damn maneuver was over...Getting the hot poop about the first jump...Attached to the Red Army they said...And down to Sturgis Airfield."
- 506th PIR scrapbook

January, 1943

    Eugene made his way to North Carolina, finally joining his unit. Sporting shiny new jump wings, he joined the 326th Airborne Engineering Battalion at Fort Bragg, where the 326th had relocated in September 1942. The men in the 326th were nearly all wearing jump wings, though they had gone through the four-week jump school at Fort Benning instead of the 17-week (13 weeks of Basic training plus four weeks of jump school) Paratrooper training he had just completed. He felt like he was a little better than his peers, and rightly so. The physical training he had gone through made him tougher, both physically and mentally, and the rest of his training would be nowhere as difficult. Still, he needed to fit in and become an engineer now. The 326th was formed and ready to train. The commanding officer was Lieutenant Colonel John Pappas, a native of Washington, who led the battalion in division exercises and maneuvers. Eugene thought the exercises were becoming more detailed as the training proved that engineers could build bridges and fight. The 326th moved around the southern states throughout 1943, practicing in simulated attacks against the enemy (be it Japan or Germany), until September. It was time to load up on a train bound for New York Harbor and set sail for England. He hadn't seen Jackson since January, when both were home on furlough, though he had followed the 506th as much as possible. He had known Jackson was assigned to Camp Mackall, North Carolina, in early 1943, but was not provided an opportunity to travel the 40 miles west to see him. But he knew they would see each other before going to battle.

***

Rufus and Jackson arrived at Major Horton's office two days after returning from furlough. As the 2nd Battalion XO, Horton carried out many of the administrative duties for the battalion CO, Major Strayer. After a short wait, the K-9 unit was escorted into Horton's office, where Jackson stood at attention and saluted, Rufus stood still at Heel position. "Welcome back Gilmore, at ease. Take a seat." Major Horton came around from behind his desk and sat in a chair across from Jackson, as Rufus sat next to him.

"I hope you had a good break and were able to get home. Tennessee, right?" Jackson said he did get home with his brother and Rufus, and it was fine. "Now, the regiment is getting ready to cross over the Chattahoochee River and camp in Alabama for a while. I'd like to get you situated into a company that you feel fits your unit. Have you any thoughts?"

"Well sir, me and Rufus, well, we've trained with a lot of the guys, and they were all swell, nobody mistreated us at all. But if I could have my choice, sir, I'd like to stay in Easy Company." Horton gave a small smile which he quickly covered. "Why Easy, Private Gilmore? I think all the companies are well trained, and you said it yourself that all the men were good guys."

Jackson thought for a moment. "Well sir, it's just that I think Easy Company took to me and Rufus real quick, and they appreciate Rufus as much as I do. I think Easy will be a good fit for us. And I think Easy is the best company in the Army, sir, and Rufus deserves the best!"

Horton nodded his head slowly, taking all Gilmore said into account. "Alright Private, you and Corporal Rufus are assigned to Easy. Now what about the other thing I asked you to think about?" He meant the other tasks that he and Rufus could do to help in the field. "I did do some thinking sir, and I came up with a few ideas."

Jackson had thought of a few ways they could become more useful. He explained his ideas to Major Horton. Rufus could be trained as a combat attack dog, a scout dog, going on reconnaissance patrols, messenger dog, and finally, help the medics with finding wounded soldiers. "That's quite a list Private. Can you train Rufus to perform those missions?" He couldn't, but he knew who could.

"No sir, I can't, but I know who can. Either we go to New Jersey for a month, or the Army sends Mr. Henry Stoecker here." He told the Major all about Henry, what he had done in such a very short period of time, getting the K-9 Unit formed and trained.

"I think I'll try to get Mr. Stoecker here for a month, I'd like to meet him. Okay, Private, that's all for now. I'll let you know when your next orders are ready. For now, report to...Orderly!" The door opened quickly as the orderly stepped into the room. He handed Major Horton a folder containing Easy Company's current manning. "Yes, report to 3rd Platoon, Lieutenant Moore. He'll get you squared away. Any questions?"

Jackson stood quickly, as did Rufus without waiting for the command. "No sir! Thank you sir!" He saluted, and quickly departed. *I can't believe it! For once things worked out for me and Rufus!* Lieutenant Moore was a good officer, fair and looked after his soldiers. He reported as ordered and was assigned to 3rd Squad. Jackson was elated. After so long in training, nearly a year, he finally had a home!

Horton had a big grin on his face as he walked to Sink's office. He pulled out a five dollar bill and laid on Sink's desk. Sink looked up from the training plan he was reviewing, saw the bill and saw Horton's huge smile. "So, what'd he choose?" Sink obviously knew what was happening with his K-9 unit, now he wanted to know where he landed. "He chose Easy Company, sir, just like you said. How'd you know?"

Sink and Horton had a bet. Horton thought Gilmore would select H or I Company in 3rd Battalion, Sink thought he would pick Easy Company. "I've been watching that boy with his dog. He takes care of that animal like it was his son. I've heard that he missed evening mess several times because he was taking care of Rufus. And Major Bounds over at the Quartermasters HQ told me he never misses an opportunity to outfit his partner and make sure he has the best chow he can get. So I knew he would want Rufus to be with the best company. And right now, that's Easy."

Sink took the fiver and slipped it into his pocket. "You thought he would pick H or I Company, right?" Horton nodded with a smile. "I sure did sir. I saw how the men of 3rd Battalion took to him and Rufus, I just assumed he'd go where the men took to his dog so well."

It was Sink's turn to nod and grin. "His decision shows you what the boy is made of. He knows being in Easy Company is tough, Captain Sobel hasn't let up on those men for one hour. But he figured Easy was where he belonged. And don't forget about Corporal Randleman carrying Rufus down Currahee when he was hurt. He's lucky Captain Sobel didn't see that."

Not much got past Colonel Sink.

Jackson and Rufus reported to 3rd Platoon just in time to go to chow. Though Rufus did not eat, he went with Jackson to the mess hall. No officers were present, but somehow Captain Sobel was aware of the K-9 in the mess. That afternoon Jackson and Rufus were called to Captain Sobel's office, where they both were called to attention and not put at ease. "Private, you took your dog into the mess facility today? That is strictly against regulations. You will no longer take your dog into the mess hall, do you understand?"

Jackson was nervous but had to speak up. "Sir, I understand. Permission to speak, sir?" Sobel glared at him but allowed it. "Sir, I was instructed that my K-9 partner and I go everywhere together, do everything together, train together so that we fight together. Rufus is as much a paratrooper as I am, sir. So, well sir, if he is not allowed into the mess hall, well sir, I request permission to eat outside with Rufus. Sir."

That infuriated the CO. "Request denied, Private. From now on, you will tie the dog up at the barracks and retrieve him after each meal. Is that clear?" Jackson knew he was on thin water, so he quickly saluted with a "Yes Sir!" and so low that only Jackson could hear, he heard a low growl escape Rufus' throat. *Dammit Rufus! Just shut up and we'll be out of here in a second!* "Permission to leave, Sir."

"Get out." Jackson saluted again, did not wait on a return salute and quickly departed. Once back at his barracks he sat on his bunk with Rufus on his pad next to him. Shifty Powers approached him. "Hey Jackson, what's wrong? I declare, you look like you lost your best buddy?" Powers was from southwest Virginia, a self-described mountain man, and usually soft-spoken. But concern for his squad member was great. Jackson told of his encounter with Sobel. "I bet I know who told Captain Sobel, it wasn't one of us, had to be one of the senior NCOs who don't have nothing better to do."

Shifty reached over and petted Rufus gently on his head. Since all Easy Company were GOOD FRIENDS, Rufus was able to enjoy the attention. Powers thought for moment, still rubbing Rufus, then said "Tell you what. Let me do a little checking for you and I'll see what I can find out." With that he stood up and turned to go to his bunk. "Hey Shifty," Jackson called, "Don't go and get yourself in trouble on account of me and Rufus. We'll be just fine, okay?" Shifty nodded his head and went on.

The next day the 506th loaded up and marched 10 miles across the Chattahoochee River to the Alabama side of Fort Benning. It was a great improvement in living conditions for the men of the 506th. The barracks were spacious and warm, the chow good, and there was a PX and a movie theatre. Jackson got Rufus squared away, left him tied to a post at the back of his bunk house and went to chow with 3rd Platoon. When he arrived, without Rufus, his platoon sergeant, Staff Sergeant Kudla, stopped him. "Where's your partner, Private Gilmore? I thought you two were inseparable?"

"Well Sergeant, I was ordered to leave Rufus at the barracks while eating chow, he's not allowed in the mess hall." His platoon sergeant glared at him. "Well, I say he can come inside with you. Go get him. I'll take care of this. Now git." He got.

This meeting was not happenstance, it was on purpose. Shifty had mentioned this to Kudla the prior evening. Kudla went around his chain of command because he knew where the order originated. He went to the 2nd Battalion First Sergeant. The next day, Kudla waited for Jackson and sent him back to retrieve Rufus. As Jackson and Rufus entered the mess hall, First Sergeant Evans stood and approached him. "Private, I thought you were ordered to leave your dog outside the mess hall. Is that not correct?"

Gilmore was about to answer that he was instructed to bring Rufus with him, when Sergeant Kudla stepped in. "Excuse me First Sergeant, this is my fault. I haven't had the chance to brief Private Gilmore on his mess procedures. Gilmore, come with me." Kudla left Evans standing there turning red, but quickly followed the pair behind Sergeant Kudla. He took them to the rear of the mess hall, where a table had a placard on it which read K-9 UNIT AREA. First Sergeant Evans sputtered "Who ordered this? I know for a fact that Captain Sobel ordered this man to NOT bring his dog in here!"

Kudla gave a slight smile but quickly lost it. "Sorry First Sergeant, this came down from Regimental HQ. You know, squad integrity must be maintained, and all that." With that,

Evans stormed off, probably to find Captain Sobel. Jackson was relieved when Evans left, but quickly sat down and put his head between his hands. "It's gonna be okay, paratrooper, hang in there." But as Kudla turned to go, Gilmore stopped him. "What have I done? Now Captain Sobel is gonna be on the lookout for me, I'll never do anything right, and probably get busted to E-1!"

Some other men came to the table to sit down for chow, Shifty Powers with them. They were all in on it. "Don't worry Jackson, we got your back," Shifty said gently. "Whatever happens from here on, you are one of us, and we stick together." That helped Jackson, so he left Rufus at the table and went through the chow line. When he returned, Rufus was watching him intently, waiting for his next order. "At ease, boy, let me eat." He tore off a small piece of toast covered in creamed chipped beef, or what the men called 'shit on a shingle' and gave it to Rufus. Jackson routinely gave him snacks during the day, but table food was rare. Rufus licked his lips and stared at Jackson, as if saying 'more, please?' Gilmore gave him one other small bite and told him "That's all." Rufus lowered his ears and laid down next to Jackson's feet. *I'm in the Company less than a week and I'm already causing trouble*, he thought, not without humor. *Oh well, I asked for this!*

***

Training was fast and furious. The men continued training in squad and platoon-size exercises, but then training intensified, becoming more complex and involving multiple companies, the men jumped with M-1s and packs. Rufus was packed with about 25 pounds of gear during jumps, and once on the ground helped troops move quickly by taking on stores of ammunition. Jackson saw that he needed to design a new vest with metal rings to attach ammo boxes.

Moving to Camp McCall, North Carolina in March 1943, Easy Company and the rest of the 506th were part of three-day combat problems in the woods, focusing on quickly forming up in the assembly area, moving silently but quickly to combat positions.

By the end of May, the regiment had moved to a camp in Kentucky, Camp Breckenridge, near Sturgis, Kentucky, where they bivouacked for weeks at a time. Here, the 506th officially joined the 101st Airborne Division on June 10, and the men sewed the 'Screaming Eagles' insignia on their left shoulder. Large scale maneuvers ranged over hundreds of miles. They made three more jumps, as the Blue Army opposing the Red Army. Night marches occurred regularly. Jackson and Rufus were an integral part of the exercises, working as sentries and with patrol teams. Jackson gave Rufus freedom during these problems, allowing him to catch scents of other soldiers, listening in the quiet of night. On one patrol, Rufus caught the scent of something and quietly followed it, weaving back and forth across the trail as he was taught. Suddenly, Rufus froze, stuck his nose in the air, then softly growled; he had the enemy, and pointed where he was.

Jackson told the patrol leader where the enemy was located, "Just aways down that gorge. If we go along the top we can ambush them." The patrol leader, Corporal Owens, agreed, and quietly led the patrol to the gorge, then swiftly attacked. The enemy soldiers were asleep and were quickly captured and taken back to HQ. At the end of the maneuver a few days after the patrol, recently promoted Lieutenant Colonel Strayer addressed the men. He congratulated the men of 2nd Battalion for a job well done and called out Jackson and Rufus for the excellent patrol work. 2nd Battalion had performed so well, that in July they received a commendation from the 101st Airborne Division commanding officer, Major General William Lee.

After a ten-day furlough, the 506th and the entire 101st Airborne Division rode trains to Fort Bragg, North Carolina. The men took hot showers, the food was much better, and were reoutfitted with new gear and uniforms. It was obvious to the men they were preparing to deploy. But east to Europe, or west to the Pacific? Rumors of fighting in the Mediterranean was also a hot topic.

***

Dear Jimmie,
I just got your letter, gosh! I had to look at the globe to see where in Italy you are. I am so glad you are doing so good and are safe. I miss you very much, it is hard working on the farm without you. Daddy works hard but he can't work so hard anymore. But I do whatever he tells me to do and maybe it takes longer than you to do it, but I finish it. Momma says I'm getting bigger and stronger every day and that soon I'll be as strong as you. I giggle because I won't ever be that strong! School starts next month and I will be in the eighth grade! Boys pick on me about my red hair but Momma says it's because they are too shy to tell me they think I'm pretty. I'm not so sure.
I am sending you a picture of me and Rufus before he left to join the Army. I haven't heard anything about Rufus, so if you see him give him a big hug for me. I added some candy too, but don't give it all away to your Army friends. Well I need to go feed the animals. I will write you again soon. I love you and miss you.
Your sister, Penny.

***

July 1943
Sturgis, Kentucky

True to his word, Major Horton got Henry Stoecker to travel to Kentucky for a few weeks. By now, there were several DRTCs (Dog Reception and Training Centers), located in Virginia, Nebraska, California, Mississippi, Pennsylvania, and other states. Henry had played a major role in getting the DRTCs operational and following the same training guidelines. When Major Horton contacted him, he quickly accepted the request and took civilian orders to travel to Sturgis. Henry persuaded Major Horton to procure a C-47 so he could bring a K-9 unit with him to help train Rufus.

They landed at Sturgis Municipal Airport, only a few miles from where the 506th was assigned, at Camp Breckinridge, Kentucky. Sturgis Airport had been constructed in 1941 to train

Army pilots, and was bustling with training airplanes, hopeful pilots, and instructor pilots. A truck was waiting for them, and they quickly offloaded gear from the C-47 and traveled to the 506th. Major Horton was waiting for them.

"Good to meet you, Mister Stoecker. I'm Major Oliver Horton but call me Ollie."

"Please call me Henry, sir. This is Sergeant Andrew Whatley, and his partner, Corporal Digger." Digger was a large German Shepherd, larger than Rufus by at least 10 pounds, but he had true Shepherd ears, standing straight up and aware of all around him. Stoecker brought the pair to aid in training, as Digger had just completed nearly the exact instruction that Gilmore had requested. Jackson and Rufus soon arrived outside of Regimental HQ and were happy to see Henry. Even Rufus was happy to see Henry and Digger, but never broke his training, staying in Heel position.

"I thought the dog always outranked his trainer?" Horton asked, remembering Sink's conversation with Gilmore. Henry chuckled. "Normally you are correct, but Sergeant Whatley is my lead trainer and brought Digger with him. He's not his partner but Digger loves the man."

Stoecker didn't waste a minute. He was given a small office, Whatley was shown where he could bunk in the NCO quarters, and that afternoon training began. Jackson was excused from all field maneuvers so they could train for the next month. They had only a few weeks, as the regiment was rumored to be ready to return to Fort Bragg, and then prepare for deployment. They started with refresher training for Sentry. This took the rest of the afternoon, with Rufus quickly remembering his earlier training, he and Digger went through the drills flawlessly. Stoecker called it a day to give the men and dogs a chance to get settled. Whatley went with Jackson to take care of the K-9s. By the time they were done it was time for chow, and both men and dogs went to the mess hall and ate at the K-9 Corps table. (Staff Sergeant Kudla took the table sign with him to whatever camp or fort they went.) The chow was very good, pork chops, green beans, peas, cornbread, and ice cream for dessert. Whatley was impressed.

"You sure got a great deal going here, Gilmore. Nice bunk room, good chow every night, not much PT. I thought you paratrooper types had it rough."

Jackson didn't much care for that comment but kept quiet. After a moment, he thought differently. "Hey Sergeant Whatley, I'm taking Rufus on an early run tomorrow, just to keep him in shape, you know? How about you and Digger join me? We have a good running trail here that we can take before breakfast. Sound good to you?"

"Sure, we'll meet you at your bunkhouse at zero six hundred, if that's good." It was good with Jackson, and he grew a big smile while eating his ice cream. He even snuck Rufus a spoonful.

The next morning, Digger and Whatley were there bright and early. Whatley wore PT shorts and sneakers, but Jackson was in utilities, jump boots, and musette bag. "What's up with the uniform, Gilmore? I thought we were going for a run?" Jackson just smiled. He had a five-foot leash for Rufus but would let him free once on the trail. "This is my running gear, Sergeant. We train like we fight around here. Let's get loosened up and I'll show you the trail."

Once at the trailhead they started with an easy trot, letting the dogs get into a rhythm. He slowed and released Rufus. Whatley did the same and both dogs quickly took the lead, but not straying off the trail. Jackson kicked it in, about a seven minute mile pace. The trail was a big circle, six miles in length. Whatley couldn't keep up the pace and soon lagged 100 yards behind. Digger kept up with Rufus with ease. At the half way point Jackson stopped, called the dogs and waited for Whatley. Whatley arrived, red-faced and out of breath. "Thanks for waiting for me. How much further?"

Jackson grinned and told him three miles. Whatley could only grin back, he knew he'd been had. "Okay Gilmore, you little shit, you proved your point. I'll set the pace the rest of the way. Let's go." Whatley set a good pace but slower than Jackson's by a minute per mile. Whatley caught his breath and they talked while running. "I see that you and Rufus are in great shape. I guess the paratrooper training was tough?"

Gilmore smiled and thought back to Camp Toccoa. "Sergeant, it was the toughest thing I've ever been through in my life. We had 13 weeks of hard training, we were beat down both physically and mentally. Then we had a 118-mile march to Atlanta. When we arrived at jump school, instead of being tough it was a relief! But we made it, and now we know we're ready to go to war and make a difference. And we go together. Our NCOs are the best in the world, and the officers, well, most of them, are darn good. They went through the same hard training as the enlisted, and that makes them okay in my book." They stopped about a mile from the end of the trail and walked the rest of the way. "I need to start running more, I'm beat," Sergeant Whatley admitted. "But I work 12-hour days as it is, six days a week. Taking care of these dogs is important to me, so I'm usually the first man up and the last guy to turn out the lights. At least I have my own room with a bathroom, and the food is great. Ole Mrs. Erlanger sets a damn fine table."

"Why are you still in New Jersey and not at a DRTC?" Jackson asked. Whatley whistled for Digger, and both dogs came back to the Heel position without orders. "I spent a few months setting one up in Missouri, then on to Nebraska, but the men training the dogs weren't following the same procedures. I told Henry and he talked to the Quartermaster Corps about the problem. The Army started sending K-9 trainers to New Jersey, where we trained the trainers. We get a group of about 12 soldiers in every couple of months and train them the right way. I came into the K-9 Corps a little after you left New Jersey. I was a corporal in the QM Corps, went through K-9 training, and found out I took to it real good. When I came back to work for Henry I got promoted, and it's been great so far. The only thing that bothers me is that I'll probably spend the rest of the war in New Jersey, unless I volunteer to go with a Quartermaster unit to a fighting unit."

A few days later, while training under the instruction of Henry, Jackson saw Easy Company go off in formation, wearing service uniforms without the jacket. *They must be going to classroom instruction,* he thought. The men deserved a break, after spending weeks at a time in the field around Sturgis, sleeping in pup tents, eaten up by deer flies and mosquitos all night, and eating K-rations. A few guys saw Rufus and made a few catcalls at him. Rufus looked at Jackson, gave a small whine, and looked back at the men. Jackson leaned down to him and said "Okay." With that, Rufus took off for his friends. He marched next to them, lifting his legs like he was marching too, circling the platoons one at a time, giving his famous "BAROOOO!!!" bark. The men laughed as usual and told Jackson to take care of 'our' dog. Henry watched it all without saying a word, only smiling broadly.

A loud whistle from Jackson called Rufus to return, which he did immediately. Henry was impressed. "You know what Jackson, you just showed me another valuable thing the K-9 Corps offers. From the look of your friends I'd say Rufus lifted their morale quite a bit when they saw him. I think I'll write a paper to the Quartermaster Corps and suggest they provide training for units to have a dog go with men to war. They don't have to be trained like Rufus but enough that they will make it through combat and give the men companionship in the battlefield."

While this was a remarkable idea, the Army never adopted it. However, single soldiers, marines, and airmen throughout the battlefields of the world adopted strays and took them wherever they went. So, in the end, Henry was right.

A few more weeks of training and Henry said Rufus was ready. The 506th had already taken trains to Fort Bragg, which by now was obviously a staging area, preparing units for overseas service. Henry and Sergeant Whatley said their goodbyes, shaking hands and rubbing Rufus. "Thank you sir, I really believe this will help me and Rufus support Easy Company, maybe even the battalion. I can't thank you enough for coming here to help, both of y'all."

Jackson packed up his gear the next morning, boarded a train, but this time he rode in a passenger car with Rufus in a seat beside him. No one said a word, as Rufus wore his jacket with corporal stripes and jump wings. Jackson thought that Rufus looks more like a paratrooper than a paratrooper does. He was ready to join his buddies again and get ready to ship out. But when he arrived at Fort Bragg, Major Horton had instructed Sergeant Kudla to send him immediately to his office.

Major Horton was in his office, along with the Easy Company XO, First Lieutenant Dick Winters. Horton offered Jackson a seat and sat down in a chair next to him. He gave Rufus a good rub before talking. "Private Gilmore, Colonel Sink has a mission for you. Next week, the 506th will deploy on trains to ship overseas. But he wants you to return to Fort Benning for four weeks. You will help the jumpmasters train other K-9 units to jump and help them get outfitted correctly. Do you think you can do that?"

Jackson was concerned and it showed. "Yes sir, I can do that. But sir, how will I catch up to Easy Company if y'all deploy without us? How will I find you? I don't want to stay behind, sir!"

Horton looked at Winters, who nodded. "We have that figured out, Private. When you're finished training K-9 units to jump, you'll be sent to an Army air base, and you and Rufus will board an Army Air Force airplane to join us. I can't say where we'll be, but we'll send for you as soon as we get there. Sound good?"

Lieutenant Winters had helped him, he calmed down. "Yes sir, that sounds just fine. But I need some help." After Horton told him to continue, Jackson made a request. "Sir, I need to outfit Rufus with new gear. The Quartermasters can help. And I need to get the men and dogs outfitted to jump, like I was. I'll need the Quartermasters to understand and support me. Could you take care of that?"

Horton nodded his head and smiled at Winters. *This kid is on the ball, he'd have made a good paratrooper without his dog,* Horton mused. "Well then, it's settled. Join your squad, we'll get your orders ready for Fort Benning. And Corporal Gilmore, you'll need these too." He handed Jackson a pair of corporal stripes and two sergeant stripes for Rufus. "Now take care of Sergeant Rufus, Corporal. We'll see you overseas."

***

August 1943
Fort Benning, Georgia

    It was awfully hot in Georgia in late August, and even though Jackson was from the south, it was still tough on him and Rufus. Especially day jumps. The planes were hot, stuffy, smelled of sweat and vomit. Gilmore had settled in quickly at Fort Benning, given quarters with the other jumpmasters (even though he wasn't a trained jumpmaster), he had a bunk, chow hall was close, and they had an attached latrine, so no more walking to take a shower. Without any fuss, the jumpmasters allowed Rufus to stay in the barracks. Jackson thought he could sense that the men thought he was doing something important, something that might help soldiers in combat. They were right.
    The first K-9 unit to show up was his old friend, Johnnie Moore. Private Moore had already earned his jump wings, about the same time as Jackson. After handshakes and introductions, Moore explained. "Dammit Gilmore, after me and Gunner got our jump wings, we were good to go. But a couple of months ago, he just up and died." Johnnie stopped for a moment, lit a cigarette with a shake in his hands. "Gunner was a good dog. A great dog. The docs think he had an enlarged heart and it just quit working. I buried him in Kentucky."
    Jackson was truly saddened and told his friend so. "So who is your new partner?" Johnnie brightened up from his dark thoughts of losing Gunner. "This here is Toby. He's been a great dog too. After Gunner died, I was given a choice, either stay in the 82nd as a paratrooper, or go back and get another dog and go through jump school again. I decided to try again with a new dog. Sergeant Wilson sent a dog to the DRTC in Saint Louis, turned out it was Toby. Toby was fully trained as a replacement, so we just had to take time and bond. Oh, Sergeant Wilson sends his regards and says keep up the good work."
    Toby was a two-year old bull mastiff, brown and white, thick chest and legs, and nearly 90 pounds. He was muscled and stood taller than Rufus, but Jackson thought Rufus could outrun Toby in the field. "Good thing you are scrawny, they don't make a

parachute big enough to carry that dog with a regular soldier!" Johnnie laughed. "You know, you're right, I do need to see about getting a better harness for him."

That's part of why Jackson was here. During the first week of jump school, while the men were going through physical training, he would work with the Quartermasters to get new, stronger harnesses sewn. Later that afternoon he visited the Quartermasters and asked for Sergeant Sellers. "He's gone, joined up with the 101st a couple of months ago." Jackson was startled, he had a friendship with Sergeant Sellers and had depended on him. Now he was gone. "Do you know what unit he joined?"

"Yeah, the 502nd, can't remember which unit, but you ought to be able to find him when you get to wherever you're going." That soothed his anxiety, and he found the man that replaced Clyde. Sergeant Walker was aware of the K-9 Corps arriving and had already been working on harnesses. They looked fine, very strong, good straps and ties, nearly exactly like the harness Sergeant Sellers had built for Rufus. Jackson thought he probably should get a new harness; he'd been hauling it around for nine months, through mud, rain, even snow. It was certainly to fall prey to dry rot.

The next week the K-9 units went through tower jumps. Jackson showed the men and dogs the best method to strap their dogs to their bodies, and how to walk. There were eight total units and would make up one stick. None of the dogs appeared scared of jumping, so they moved to the actual jumps. The jumpmasters took over, but Jackson rode along with the stick.

The first jump occurred early in the morning, before the sun baked the earth, and the planes became unbearably hot. A stick of 12 paratroopers went first, all replacements for the 101st and 82nd Airborne Divisions preparing to deploy soon. Once the first stick cleared, the pilot took the airplane in a wide circle and returned to the drop zone. The jumpmaster put them through the paces, standup, hookup, equipment checks, and sound off. Each trainer shuffled to the door, eyes wide (except for Johnnie). But each jumped without hesitation. When he caught up to the men and dogs, they were excited and animated. "Let's go again! That was a doozy!" "I jumped out, the plane disappeared, then I was jolted harder that I could believe. Next thing I knew I was hittin' the ground!"

Three more successful jumps and the teams would be ready for the night jump. The last day jump was from 800 feet AGL. The K-9 units were alone this time, no other stick with them. It was an afternoon jump, but fortunately the heat had subsided and the plane was bearable. Jackson had Rufus with him, harnessed and ready to jump. He told Moore why he had Rufus. "I swear Rufus was upset because he knew I was getting in an airplane. He ignored me for two days, until I told him we would jump. He really loves this stuff." Johnnie nodded, he felt the same way about Toby, and Gunner.

Jackson and Rufus were the last out. When it was their turn, the jumpmaster hollered "Go! Go!" and tapped him on his leg, Jackson jumped. He felt the same quick jolt as always, felt his chute deploy, but looked up to make sure no panels collapsed. It was only a few seconds before he was on the ground, unhitched Rufus, who took off running to the west.

"RUFUS! HEEL!" But Rufus never slowed down. Jackson rounded up his chute and took off for his wayward dog. He found him a few hundred yards away, where other men and an ambulance were. Panting from a full sprint, he grabbed Rufus by his harness and began correcting him, but then stopped. Gilmore saw what had set Rufus off. He saw Toby lying motionless in the scraggly bushes off to his right. Then he saw the twisted parachute, and then Johnnie. Both were dead. "His chute never opened, it was tangled from the second he left the plane," said a jump trainer on the ground. "He didn't have time to deploy his reserve. Wouldn't have mattered, he was already dead, too low to discard his primary and deploy his reserve."

Stunned, Jackson could only stare at his friend as the ambulance medics loaded both bodies into the back and drove off. There was no time for sorrow. "Let's go, back to the assembly area. You too, Gilmore."

At his barracks Jackson sat alone on his bunk, Rufus laying at his feet. Rufus was affected too. Rufus had never imagined that this much fun was dangerous. He had enjoyed playing with Toby, a good boy just like him. He didn't understand what happened, only that his friend was gone. In that small way, he was luckier than his master, who knew exactly how dangerous this work could be. Suddenly, Jackson jumped to his feet. He rounded Rufus up and went to visit the other K-9 teams. They were alone in one of the smaller tarpaper shacks spread throughout the larger barracks used by platoons or squads. When Jackson entered the bunkroom he saw each man with his dog, all seven K-9 units together but alone. He needed to speak up. "Listen up fellas, come with me and let's go for a walk." The men slowly responded to Jackson, each man leading his dog outside and joined Jackson. Again, Rufus could sense the sadness, grief, even fear coming from the men. From the dogs he sensed anxiety, probably due to the men's uneasiness. He softly keened, only loud enough for Jackson to sense more than hear. Jackson realized that the dogs were suffering as much as the men.

"Fellas, what happened to Johnnie and Toby was awful. I don't know how well you knew Johnnie, but me and him were in the first group to complete K-9 training under Henry Stoecker." That surprised the men; Stoecker had become a legend among the K-9 Corps. Not only Henry but also Mrs. Erlanger and her furious work to get dogs into the Army to serve our country, and maybe save a few soldiers' lives along the way. "You know Henry Stoecker, sir? I mean Corporal?" one young Private asked.

"Yes I do. Mr. Stoecker is one of the finest men I've ever met. He took me under his wing when I arrived at Mrs. Erlanger's training facility and is the biggest reason me and Rufus are Paratroopers. And I'll tell you this: Henry would be grief stricken, just like you, on the loss of Johnnie and Toby. But I know what he'd say. He'd say 'Boys, this is tough, but you have a job to do, and you owe it to your partner to be strong, to lead him, to give him comfort."

The men took that in quietly. Jackson continued. "Let's go for a walk, maybe run a little bit. What do ya say?" Not waiting for an answer, he turned Rufus toward the running trail and began a slow run pace, slower than double-time and easy to keep up. The other trainers watched Jackson quietly, then each team turned and caught up with them. Once together, Jackson released Rufus from his leash; the other men followed his lead. The dogs ran ahead but not far, only as far as they had been trained to go without orders. Still, the dogs ran together, tails high in the air, ears up (except for Rufus' goofy ears), running from side to side of the trail, taking in the scents of the trail, men's sweat, and even a few varmints that had crossed during the night. Jackson increased his speed, catching the dogs, who then sprinted forward to expand the gap. He tricked the dogs, though; when they ran forward to continue the six-mile course, he turned onto the three-mile course route with the men behind him. Rufus saw it first, gave a loud 'CHUFF' and turned back at a sprint, the other dogs following. Now the men saw what Jackson had done and turned on the speed. Jackson was now nearly sprinting, the men behind him, but Rufus quickly caught and passed them, followed by the other dogs.

After the dogs passed by, Jackson slowed to a walk. He called to Rufus to heel, and the other dogs returned to their masters as well. They all walked together, the dogs panting, the men breathing hard, but all were in better spirits. As they walked back to camp, Jackson took the opportunity to talk to the men again. "Guys, we are among an elite few in the Army. We are K-9 Corps trainers, with our partners, who can depart a perfectly good airplane deep into enemy territory with our dog. But no matter what job you are assigned, you owe it to your partner to do the best job you can. If you feel beat, your dog will sense it. If you feel dread, so will your dog. It is up to YOU to lead your partner into combat, to take care of him, to lead them, and to keep them safe. Tomorrow, we have the last jump, a night jump. After you complete that, you will earn your jump wings, and so will your dogs." He pointed to the wings sewn onto Rufus' harness (his regular harness, not his jump harness). "We will always be a team, dependent on each other. But don't forget that we're here to help win a war, help our fellow paratroopers, our fellow soldiers. So remember our fallen brothers but do whatever you can to make their death worth it and make every action you carry out from here on to be worthy of the men that have fallen and will fall in battle."

Wow, did I just say all that? Where'd that come from? I'm acting like a platoon sergeant, not a lowly corporal. Jackson was quiet, but the men, all Privates or PFCs, listened as if Jackson was a senior instructor. And in a way, he was. He'd been through the toughest training the Army offered, survived Camp Toccoa, 20-mile night marches, forced march to Atlanta, and field exercises lasting weeks. He was hardened, and though only a corporal, he was becoming a leader.

The next day was the last jump scheduled for the K-9 Corps. One of the young men, Caleb Ratliff, found Jackson to talk. "Hey Jackson, are you and Rufus jumping with us tonight?" That startled him for a moment. *Perform a night jump? We've done this a few times already! Why would I jump again at night?* Then, he saw the concern in Ratliff's eyes. Caleb was a kid, really, only 18 years old. He had volunteered as soon as he turned 18, completed boot camp, K-9 training, and volunteered for Airborne Infantry. While he hadn't gone through what Jackson had at Camp Toccoa, he had completed some tough training. He suddenly realized that these men needed a leader. They were here, alone, no unit, no platoon sergeant, not even a squad leader. Jackson was it.

"Heck yeah, Ratliff! Me and Rufus wouldn't miss a chance to jump from an airplane in 'fright', especially at night!" Caleb laughed at the old paratrooper joke. It also gave him a little boost knowing that Gilmore would be jumping with them on their last jump.

Night jumps were indeed frightening. There were few markings on the ground observable from 1,200 feet AGL, few lights were spread across the countryside. Inside the C-47, all eight men were ready. Jackson had Rufus at the front of the airplane, next to the pilots. He walked through the plane, helping the men get their equipment ready. He double-checked their dog harness, ensured it was cinched tightly and tied correctly. After that he shuffled to the front, attached Rufus and harness, and waited. Soon, the red light appeared, the jumpmaster went through the jump protocol again, everyone was ready. Then, Jackson smelled it. Rufus farted, a bad one. With the door open in the rear, the smell quickly travelled to the back. As it passed each man, they gave aloud groan and cursed. It hit the jumpmaster. "Jesus! Again? Who crapped their pants? You that scared? You don't have to jump boy, just sit down and it'll all be over, and you can go on back to the Army!"

Jackson raised his hand. "It was my dog, Sergeant. He gets a little excited on night jumps, he loves it!" Guffaws filled the airplane before the jumpmaster shut them up. "Knock it off! Now get your head back on straight if you want to survive!" The light suddenly turned green, and the jumpmaster screamed "Go! Go!" Each man and dog departed the aircraft without a second thought. They went so fast that Jackson was behind as he shuffled with Rufus up to the door. Rufus whined in excitement. Jackson didn't have time to square up at the door, he just jumped.

"One thousand, two thousand, three thou---" and the canopy opened with a sharp crack and forcibly threw them backwards. The oscillations slowed and he was able to find the horizon, even in the darkness he could discern the difference in the ground and dark sky. He looked for any other paratroopers but saw none. Rufus chuffed, which meant 'Get ready boss! The earth is near!' Jackson looked down and could see trees and shrubs scattered over the field. He readied himself, bent his knees, pulled strongly on the risers, just as his feet hit the hard ground. He rolled onto his back, Rufus rolling on top. They were down. He unhooked Rufus, unhooked the chute, gathered it up, found his bearings and they both trotted to the muster area. He was the last to arrive, flashlights and jeep lights lit the area. He counted the men and dogs; one, two, three...seven! All made it! Private Ratliff saw Jackson and walked over excitedly. "We did it! Piece of cake! Let's go celebrate!"

Gilmore tended to agree with Ratliff, and as the men climbed into the back of the truck, they were all energized and euphoric, knowing they were paratroopers now. The men had bought beer from the PX earlier in the day, had it iced down and waiting in the barracks. After tending to the dogs, they all returned to the barracks. But once inside, they saw Johnnie's empty bunk and the celebration quieted. Jackson grabbed a beer from the bucket, took a long swig to quench his dry throat. "Guys, I know you are still thinking about Johnnie, but I tell you, he wouldn't want you to waste one tear. He was doing exactly what he wanted to do and loved every second doing it. So grab a beer, let's have a drink to Johnnie!"

After a few moments, the men loosened up and returned to their good cheer. Jackson checked on the dogs, outside in kennels in a small fenced in area. They were all good boys, strong, brave, and ready to serve. He said his goodbyes to the men and returned to his barracks with Rufus. It was late, but he needed to feed Rufus; all the dogs had a small meal in the morning to get them through the night jump. He fixed Rufus a bowl of horse meat, rice and two raw eggs. He was tired too; it had been a long day. He took off his boots and uniform and climbed into his bunk. He was asleep before Rufus finished supper. Rufus eased up onto the bunk and curled up at his master's feet. Rufus thought he should wake his master up to go pee, but then decided he could hold it, and immediately went to sleep as well.

***

September 1943

The flight to England was scheduled to take a few days. At Godfrey Army Airfield, near Bangor, Maine, Gilmore and Rufus, along with another K-9 unit, boarded an almost new B-17 Flying Fortress. Godfrey AAF was a key location, where airplanes, as part of the Lend-Lease Act, were ferried to Newfoundland, then on to England. The B-17 they boarded was part of a squadron heading to England as part of the Eighth Army Air Force. The squadron would fly to Newfoundland, rest and refuel, then continue to Scotland, and finally, England.

The airplane was crewed by only the pilot, copilot, navigator, radioman and engineer. No gunners were aboard, leaving room for the K-9 units. It was cold. And although they were issued heavy, insulated flight suits, boots and gloves, it was still cold. The pilot flew at 10,000 feet AGL to help, but the cold crept in.

Private George MacGrath and his dog, a huskie named Trigger, sat on thick mats brought aboard for the long trip. Of the seven K-9 units Jackson trained, only he and MacGrath were traveling to England. He supposed the other guys were going to the Pacific, or even Italy.

The flight to Newfoundland was without problems, but once at Gander Lake, the winds shifted, and the squadron had to wait for tail winds to make it to Scotland. After a few days of waiting for fair winds, they finally received good news. Winds had shifted and the 12-hour flight to Scotland was on. At Scotland, they again took a day of rest before departing for Thorpe Abbotts, a new Army air force base in South Norfolk near the North Sea. The trip had taken seven days, but he was finally in England.

***

6

TRAINING IN ENGLAND

"Training became intensified. Both day and night assemblies were practiced over and over again. The difficult art of assembling large numbers of scattered troops can be learned only by actually assembling and assembling again. Small and large unit "Attack, Reorganization, and Defense problems" were constantly on the agenda. Many of them were of two and three day duration. All were designed, not only to give a man working knowledge of the mechanics of combat, but to teach him about the ground: how to use it to his advantage, how it fits a plan of battle, and above all how to live on it for days at a time without impairment of physical efficiency. These things are important. They make the difference between life and death. They must be instinctive. And so the regiment walked through England for a year before D-Day, attacked towns, hills, and woods, and dug countless foxholes, and slept on the ground many nights. The regiment went on fire problems in which they attacked with artillery, mortars, and machine guns, crashing into the objectives ahead. And finally, when spring came in 44 the regiment knew it was ready, and furthermore, it knew it was good."
- *506th PIR Scrapbook*

December 1943
Basildon Park, Southern England

First Lieutenant Eugene Gilmore was tired. The 326th had just completed a week-long field exercise where they practiced demolishing communication facilities, built bridges across small rivers, then defended them from Germans. They worked day and night, slept in foxholes, and ate C-Rations. But tired as he was, he felt that the training was good and preparing them for the invasion of Europe. He was 3rd Platoon Leader in C Company, a parachute company. Companies A and B were glider companies. The glider companies were comprised of two glider platoons and one parachute platoon. C Company consisted of two parachute platoons and one glider platoon.

The 326th Headquarters were in the Basildon Park Manor, built in 1783 for Sir Francis Sykes. With 91 rooms, the officers had their own rooms and each company had offices. Basildon Park, located less than one mile west of the River Thames, between Upper and Lower Basildon, provided hundreds of acres for combat training. Nearby towns and boroughs, such as Reading, provided the men with pubs to drink beer and relax.

Eugene took a hot shower, dressed in his service uniform, but packed two sets of utilities. He was headed to Littlecote, 30 miles to the west and where the 506th Parachute Infantry Regiment was located. He requisitioned a jeep and made the 30-mile trip in an hour. He had volunteered to meet with the 506th Operations Officer (S-3), battalion and company officers, along with senior NCOs. He was directed to discuss the 326th status and capabilities and determine special requirements the paratroopers may need for the liberation of France. Meetings lasted a few hours each day for four days, where Eugene took part in operation planning, intelligence and logistics briefings. Each day after meetings, he would return to S-3 offices and prepare for the next day. But he had requested and received a three-day furlough to allow him to find his brother.

He took the effort to find Easy Company officers and NCOs and introduce himself. Lieutenant Meehan, who had recently replaced Captain Sobel as CO, was surprised to meet Eugene, and Winters was just as surprised and happy to see his old OCS buddy again. After the second day of briefings, Winters invited Eugene to come with him to Aldbourne for the night. He already had a room in the manor secured for him.

During the 20-minute drive to Aldbourne, Winters caught Eugene up on Jackson and Rufus. He told him about the mess hall table, leading a group of K-9 units in jump school, and how they captured a Blue Army unit because of Rufus. Gilmore was proud of his little brother and was ready to see him. "So how do you think He'll do in combat?" Eugene asked, a little hesitantly. He was concerned for Jackson going into combat, he wished he could be in the same unit to watch over him. Winters soothed his fears.

"Your brother is gonna be just fine. He's become one of our best paratroopers, even without Rufus. Major Horton told me he has leadership skills and could use him as a platoon sergeant if he wasn't a K-9 trainer. Which, by-the-way, is why Jackson is a Corporal instead of a Tec-5. Horton said, and I agree, that Jackson should get some additional NCO leadership training. I watched him work Rufus on patrols, they make a good team. But we'll all find out about ourselves when we jump into France." Eugene nodded silently. He thought about the jump also. Where would the 326th go? He hoped it would be near the 506th.

They arrived at Aldbourne, Lieutenant Winters got Gilmore squared away in the old manor, then they went to find Jackson. Easy Company had just completed some squad level training, marksmanship, and map-reading, and were back in their barracks. Aldbourne was a huge change for 2nd Battalion. The men bunked in a horse stable, Nissen huts or tarpaper shacks, similar to barracks at Fort Benning and Toccoa. But similarities ended there. Aldbourne was an isolated, small village, consisting of cottages with thatched roofs, cobblestone roads, and an eleventh century Norman church. Up to now, the men had always been on isolated, military-only posts. Now they were in the middle of a quaint English village. The men learned to behave in town and leave the heavy drinking for weekend passes to London.

Jackson was tending to Rufus, combing his fur, cleaning paws, eyes, and ears, when Eugene found him. They were in one of the stables occupied by Easy Company. He snuck into the stable and bellowed "Hello Corporal Gilmore!" Jackson jumped up at attention, not knowing who it was. When he saw his brother, he broke into a huge grin and rushed to him. He pulled up a step from Eugene, saluted but didn't wait for a return, and hugged his brother with all his might.

"Eugene! I mean, Lieutenant Gilmore! Boy it's good to see you! I heard your battalion wasn't too far away, I was gonna try to come see you. But up until a few weeks ago weekend passes were hard to get."

They quickly caught up, Eugene reintroduced himself to Rufus (Rufus didn't forget him, he knew he was family). Eugene wanted to take him into town to eat dinner and have a beer, but Jackson had to get it squared away with his squad leader, Sergeant Shifty Powers. Next, he needed to finish getting Rufus settled in and fed. Finally, he asked Corporal Floyd Talbert to watch over Rufus for a few hours. Rufus bunked in the stable with the rest of 3rd Platoon, and off duty he roamed the stables, greeting the men for rubs and play. But Jackson had always remained with him, never departing even for a moment without him.

Gilmore told Rufus he would be back, and to stay. With that, Eugene, Jackson, Shifty and PFC Walter "Smokey" Gordon (from Jackson, Mississippi, not far from where Eugene attended college) piled into the jeep and took a short drive to The Crown Inn, where the men went directly to the basement. Here, enlisted men of the 506th were able to get away for a few hours and put the war out of their minds. The officers of the 506th made the Blue Boar their place, but both enlisted and officers kept the cocky paratrooper bit to a minimum.

Each had a beer served and ordered dinner, but then Floyd Talbert found them. "Jackson, we got a problem. Rufus is going nuts! Once you left, he was okay, for a minute. Then he started running around the stable looking for you. Then he started barking that crazy bark of his. We brought him with us, he's up on the street with Popeye."

Jackson jumped to his feet and raced up the stairs. On the street, Rufus sat in the back of a jeep, he ears high in the air, which is difficult to do with floppy ears. When he saw Jackson, he jumped from the jeep, ripping the leash from Popeye's hand, and quickly took the Heel position next to Jackson's left knee. Gilmore picked up the leash and knelt next to his dog.

"What's wrong, boy? It's okay, I'll be home in a little bit. Go on with Floyd, okay?" Rufus refused to budge. He didn't even look at Jackson, just stared straight ahead. Jackson wasn't sure what to do. Then he realized, they had not been separated since the time he went with the K-9 units to Fort Benning, and he rode with them on their first jump, alone.

"Okay, boy, I understand. Let's go home." Jackson turned to his brother. "I need to go back to the barracks, Rufus needs me. Y'all go ahead and eat, I'll be okay. See you when you get back."

The elder Gilmore had another idea. "Hold up Jackson, let's take him downstairs and see if they care. He's a paratrooper, right? I see his rank and jump wings, so bring him down to the cellar."

He was right, the owners of The Crown Inn, and the small pub in the basement, only concern was that Rufus was clean and well behaved. Rufus sat next to Jackson and was a perfect gentleman. He never begged for food while the men ate and told stories. Most paratroopers already knew Rufus so it wasn't a big deal. Colonel Sink was right, getting Rufus out in front of all the men in 2nd and 3rd Battalion made them aware of the K-9 team and knew they were Toccoa-trained. Still, Jackson was concerned about Rufus' actions.

The next day Gilmore rode to Littlecote with Winters and Nixon, and the Easy Company XO, First Lieutenant Patrick Sweeney, who had come over from Able Company, 1st Battalion. The evening before, the enlisted men had told Eugene about Winters' court-martial and the 'Revolt of the Sergeants.' He was stunned by the story. *How could a company commander try to court-martial his own XO for being late for a latrine inspection?* He soon learned the background of Captain Sobel and Easy Company, how the men pulled together to protect each other. Jackson had never said a word about mistreatment to Eugene.

The visit with Eugene was good, even though it was short. Both men had work to do and it was time to get back to it. A week after Eugene departed, Easy Company made a night jump, followed by a three-day field problem. Part of the training involved the loss of officers and NCOs as casualties, and other junior men were placed in roles of responsibility. Jackson got caught up in one of these, with Shifty and Talbert listed as casualties, he was made squad leader. Even though he was still considered a supernumerary to the platoon, he took his responsibilities of leadership seriously. He got the rifle squad moving into a fixed position that was defendable, found the new platoon sergeant, and was instructed to put together a patrol. Jackson selected four men to go with him from 3rd Platoon, PFCs Smith and Walters, and Private Jones. He led the patrol into the forest, walking quietly, letting Rufus listen and smell. Rufus stuck his nose high in the air for several seconds, then gave a soft, high-pitched whine; he had the scent.

Rufus worked the trail, moving ahead quickly. Too quickly. Rufus suddenly pulled up, his head down and tail up. He started searching back and forth, going further out, until he came back to Jackson and sat. "What is it boy? What do you smell?" It was as if Rufus was confused and didn't know what to do. "C'mon boy, let's go," Jackson urged, but Rufus wouldn't budge. He tried to get him to heel on the leash but Rufus still wouldn't budge. *He'd never done this before. Why is he acting like this?* Gilmore decided to send two men back the way they had come. "Go slow, be quiet, listen for anything, and don't get caught. Report back here in 10 minutes." He had a hunch. Rufus wouldn't move, which meant there was danger all around.

The two-man team made it back. They were excited. "Holy moley! We found a squad trying to sneak up on us! How'd you know they was there?" Private Smith asked, somewhat amazed. It was Rufus; he knew they were in trouble, so tried to get Jackson to remain in place. Jackson made a quick decision. "Look for cover, there's got to be foxholes here, by God we've dug enough over the last six months." They found a couple of fallen logs and hunkered down behind them and waited.

The other squad snuck in as quiet as possible. Rufus heard them first, releasing a low growl. Jackson heard them next; it was just a small sound, of wet ground being stepped on, but it was enough. If they had been moving or talking, they would not have heard it. In the darkness, Jackson saw eight men's silhouettes walking about 15 feet from them. When the middle man passed, Jackson stood and screamed "HALT!" Smith, Jones and Walters also rose with rifles at the ready. The other patrol knew they were caught. They were from the 82nd Airborne Division, working night problems too. 3rd Platoon, Easy Company, got the jump on them. Jackson knew Rufus saved them, but he doubted it would be so easy in combat.

***

March 1944
Aldbourne, Southern England

In late March, 2nd and 3rd Battalions made a combined jump, the largest jump by the 506th to date. It was purely for show, as Prime Minister Churchill, General Eisenhower, Lieutenant General Omar Bradley and Brigadier General Maxwell Taylor attended the show. Taylor had just assumed command of the 101st from General Bill Lee, who suffered a heart attack in February. The jump was perfect. Three-plane V formations of C-47s streamed overhead at 800 feet, and the paratroopers hit the ground without incident. Over 1,000 men of 2nd and 3rd Battalion, 506th Regiment, 101 Airborne Division, rained down upon the field at RAF Wellford.

Jackson and Rufus were in one of three planes carrying 3rd Platoon. He sat beside a new replacement, Private Arvil "Freddie" Spiers. Freddie had been sent to Easy Company from the 501st PIR, which had joined the 101st in January. Though a replacement, Freddie was a Toccoa man, and proud of it. The 501st had been activated in November 1942 at Camp Toccoa, shortly before the 506th departed for Atlanta and Fort Benning.

The 501st arrived in England in January 1944, and Colonel Sink immediately requested replacements for men that had fallen out for whatever reason.

They followed protocol for the jump, shuffled to the door, and when given the green light, they departed the airplane into open air. The sky was full of parachutes and airplanes. Jackson was in the middle of the stick, along with Freddie, and they jumped among hundreds of other paratroopers. It was difficult to see the horizon there were so many parachutes. But he landed safely, quickly gathered their chute and gear and ran to the assembly area. Jackson and Rufus ran as fast as they could and outraced most of the other paratroopers. Freddie was only a little behind them, running nearly as fast as Jackson. It didn't hurt that they were in one of the first C-47's to drop men. Still, his and Rufus' speed caught the eye of Churchill, who watched the display with admiration and awe. Churchill mentioned the fast dog and man to Eisenhower, who just smiled proudly.

After the regiment was formed, Churchill accompanied Ike on an inspection. They both stopped and spoke to many men, including PFC Malarky from 2nd Platoon, and PFC Freddie Spiers, 3rd Platoon, Easy Company. General Eisenhower asked one of his favorite questions; "Where are you from?"

"South Mississippi, sir," Private First Class Spiers answered without nervousness.

"Hmm, good fishing and hunting in that part of the country. What did you do before the war?"

"I was helping my dad with his plumbing business, and served in the Mississippi National Guard, sir."

"How did you end up in the paratroopers?" Ike asked, genuinely interested.

"I volunteered to join the paratroopers, sir, so my unit had no choice but to let me go. I joined up and went through training with the 501st PIR, and when we got to England I was transferred here."

Ike was surprised. "Well, you certainly arrived at the right time. Prime Minister Churchill may have a question or two," and stepped away, leaving Churchill standing near Freddie.

"How do you like England, son?" Freddie wasn't sure how to answer, so he gave an honest reply. "Frankly sir, I haven't had time to look around at the sights. I just got here a month ago and I've been so busy I'm still a little dizzy. But what I've seen so far is just swell, sir." Churchill smiled at the remark and said, "Well, lad, perhaps we can make your stay hospitable but short, and get you boys back home as swiftly as possible." Jackson and Rufus were at the rear of 3rd Platoon, on the far left and witnessed the entire conversation. Churchill caught sight of Rufus but didn't leave Eisenhower's side.

After the inspection, the men were told to fall out and circled around Ike, who gave them a stirring speech and promised to do everything in his power to win this war and bring a speedy end to it. Next, Churchill spoke to men about their courage, strength, and defeating the Third Reich. "Soon you will have the opportunity of testifying to your belief in all those great phrases embodied in the American Constitution. I thank God you are here, and from the bottom of my heart I wish you all good fortune and success."

After the men were released, Jackson led Rufus away, but was stopped by a tall British soldier. "Excuse me Corporal, but the Prime Minister would like to talk to you." *Me? Why?* Jackson wasn't sure what to do, but he followed the Brit to a small gathering of high-ranking officers, reporters and photographers.

"Mister Prime Minister, allow me to introduce Corporal Jackson Gilmore and Sergeant Rufus." Churchill, smoking his traditional cigar, raised eyebrows as Jackson came to attention and saluted. Rufus had automatically come to attention when he sensed Jackson doing so. Churchill returned the salute and shook hands with Gilmore but looking at Rufus with amusement. "Tell me, Corporal, how does your dog outrank you?" It was a question Jackson had answered a thousand times but did so eagerly for the PM.

"I am very impressed with the speed of you and your dog, Corporal. Were you and your dog selected for Paratroopers because of it?" Gilmore smiled at the remark, he knew he was fast and had gotten faster from all the running they had done at

Toccoa. He explained the tough training both he and Rufus had gone through, along with the rest of the 506th, which impressed Churchill. "May I pet Rufus?" Churchill asked, genuinely wishing to get closer to the dog. Gilmore quickly told Rufus it was OKAY and GOOD FRIEND, and Rufus immediately stepped close to Churchill, wagging his tail, and offered his right paw to shake. Churchill was impressed and quickly took the offered paw. He knelt slowly (Churchill was nearing his 70th birthday) and gave Rufus a good rubbing. He had one more question. "Son, Rufus is a good, strong lad, but may I ask about his ears? He doesn't appear to be a full-blooded German Shepherd, does he?"

Gilmore laughed at the questions, and explained his heritage, even getting Rufus to bark his patented "BAROOOO!" which set the people around them off in laughter. After the quick meeting, Gilmore led Rufus away, but was stopped again, this time by a photographer and reporter. They had witnessed Churchill's infatuation with Rufus and wanted more information for an article. Jackson told them who he was, his home, and how he and Rufus had become Paratroopers. Finally done, he departed for the trucks.

Jackson found Spiers and they began walking to the trucks to take them to Aldbourne. Before he could go far, he felt another hand on his shoulder. When he turned, he was surprised as anytime in his life. "Sergeant Sellers! Boy it's great to see you!"

They shook hands and caught up. Sellers had originally shipped out with the 502nd PIR, but had recently been assigned as First Sergeant, Able Company, 506th. "That's really good to hear, First Sergeant. I was hoping to run into you here in case Rufus needs help with gear." Sellers was happy to help. He was at Aldbourne with the rest of 1st Battalion, but he had visited the men in the rigger section quartered at Chilton Foliat working at the new packing sheds. He could get Jackson, and any other K-9 units, whatever they needed. "Just tell your squad leader that we talked so your platoon sergeant knows what's going on. I don't want any complaints coming back to me about going around the chain of command!"

Rufus was happy to see Clyde as well. Sellers knelt so he and

Rufus were eye to eye. As he petted Rufus' thick fur, he talked to him. "I'll take care of ole Rufus, we'll get him all the supplies he needs." Sometimes it takes knowing the right folks to get things done, and that was certainly true in the Army.

***

Gilmore and Spiers became good friends, and both were crack shots with the M-1 rifle. They practiced together and kept score, though Freddie won nearly every time. Even Shifty said Freddie was a good shot, maybe better than him, but Freddie didn't think so. Spiers became Jackson's de facto backup to Rufus, and Rufus was okay with that. They practiced splitting up a few times, with Jackson going away during training, and Freddie taking Rufus through his paces, and Rufus performed just fine. But each time they returned to find Jackson waiting, Rufus would bolt from Freddie and run to his true master. Besides from these times, Jackson and Rufus (and most times Freddie) were inseparable.

Spiers was the same age as Jackson, now 23. Both volunteered as soon as they could. Freddie was working with his dad as a plumber in South Mississippi but worked plenty of construction jobs in New Orleans. He graduated high school but knew he would work for his dad, William "Bill" Spiers, as he had been helping him since he was big enough to carry a pipe wrench. Once word got out of his skills, Freddie was kept busy with plumbing repairs in the bunk rooms and latrines, even helping in the mess halls and battalion headquarters. A few times he helped some of the locals who had graciously opened their homes to officers.

When they had time off, Jackson and Rufus would accompany Freddie to The Crown Inn, where beer flowed forever, and Rufus barked at whomever played the piano. It was never a problem bringing Rufus to the bar, the men loved him and took turns rough housing with him. But each paratrooper couldn't help thinking of what awaited them in a few weeks. They were ready, they knew they were the best in the Army, and were ready to take it to the Germans. But each man knew the dangers that faced them and knew the training they had completed prepared them to be tough and fierce. But at The Crown, the men were able to take time away and forget the war for a few hours.

There were dances and parties to attend as well, even sporting events between different regiments. Freddie and Jackson attended a dance held in Aldbourne for the men and took Rufus with them. Besides the local ladies, there were numerous Women's Royal Naval Service (WRENS) and WAAF (Women's Auxiliary Air Force) there to dance with the men. Jackson and Freddie were shy but looked forward to dancing with the women. Rufus was nearly overwhelmed by the event, the aromas of perfume from the ladies was almost too much for his senses. Jackson took Rufus along to get a bottle of coke and met a group of young ladies from town. They had seen Rufus and Jackson before but never introduced. One girl was the first to see Rufus and knelt beside him. Rufus, always wary, knew the rule, no touching. But before Jackson could tell him it's OKAY, the girl was petting Rufus and rubbing his ears with both hands. Rufus looked up at Jackson with happy eyes. Jackson just looked at his dog, shaking his head. He surmised, correctly, that Rufus understood he was around friends and everyone was OKAY.

"He is beautiful! What's his name?" the young girl asked. Freddie answered quickly. "Rufus. And I'm Freddie. What's your name?" Jackson grinned as Freddie stepped in quickly. Her name was Kate, she was only 17 and lived in Aldbourne. The other girls quickly surrounded Rufus and Freddie and began peppering him with questions. Freddie, soon over his head, looked to Jackson. "To tell the truth, ladies, Rufus belongs to Jackson. They're a K-9 unit and together are gonna bite Hitler right in his britches!" The girls laughed royally at the joke, and Jackson told them all about Rufus, where he was from, why he had floppy ears, and even got Rufus to bark his Tennessee bluetick hound roar, and that brought another huge laugh.

By this time, several Easy Company men wandered over to the crowd. The men knew they had two choices, join in or go find some other ladies to dance. They figured, correctly, that the best chance was to let Rufus be their front man. After a few men took ladies to dance, Jackson walked the dance hall and introduced Rufus to more ladies. Each time he stopped, the girls would surround him and Rufus, then men would appear and introduce themselves while petting Rufus, telling stories of Rufus' exploits then off to the dance floor with a lucky young lady. Until the men would depart for the invasion of France, Easy Company men would track down Jackson and ask if they could take Rufus to a dance or party with them. Jackson wouldn't let them, instead he would take Rufus for 15 or 30 minutes and let the young men use him to meet girls. Easy peasy.

***

7

NORMANDY

What was it like? Well, you went out into the flak and tracer filled night sky, and the chances were good that it was water below you instead of land, and you hoped the water wasn't too deep. Or perhaps you landed in St. Marie-du-Mont or St. Mere-Eglise. It's not nice, landing in an enemy city in the middle of the night. You fought through and around the little towns trying to locate the rest of the unit, and when you found it you fought through Pouppeville, Vierville, Angoville au Plain, St. Come-duMont, and Carentan; and you piled up the enemy dead until you gave up trying to 'figure ratios because an attacking force was supposed to lose more than the defenders, the Book said, yet there were the grey dead stacked like cord wood and only an occasional body dressed in tan. You learned the taste of an 88 shell exploding ten feet away, and you discovered the Burp gun. You discovered too the sweet wine of standing in a town you had fought for and won; and above all you found out you were a better man than the enemy.
- *506th PIR Scrapbook*

    The 506th moved to Upottery in late May. RAF Upottery was built in 1944 near East Devon and the small village of Upottery. The 439th Troop Carrier Group was assigned here, with four squadrons consisting of over 80 C-47 Skytrains. In late May the 101st made several jumps from Upottery, preparing for the big jump.

In early June, Easy Company was called together in a large pyramid-shaped tent. They were finally informed of their DZs (Drop Zones). Easy Company would drop near Ste. Marie-du-Mont with the order to destroying the German garrison in the town, and seizing the south exit of causeway number 2, leading the landing troops from Utah Beach into Normandy. Lieutenant Meehan instructed 3rd Platoon of their special task of destroying a communications line leading inland. That excited Jackson, they had a mission! For a few days Gilmore studied the sand tables, aerial photos and large maps hung on the walls, memorizing the DZ and surrounding area, roads, and train tracks. He was ready. Unfortunately, Colonel Sink had other ideas.

***

June 5, 1944
Upottery, England

The 326th Airborne Engineer Battalion were on the move to several airfields. Instead of jumping as a battalion, units had been assigned to the 101st and 82nd Airborne Divisions. Eugene, assigned to Charlie Company, would jump with the 506th from Upottery. The older Gilmore was elated; he may have a chance to see Jackson before they departed England. The truck ride took over two hours, but they had departed Basildon Park in plenty of time to get to Upottery, take a break and rest before departing for the airplanes. Eugene told his CO he was going to look for his brother but would be back in a few hours. He asked a few MPs where he could find the 506th, and finally found Easy Company.

Rufus was sleeping, he had a busy day on June 4th. Getting ready for the jump had excited him, but then, they didn't go get in the airplane, and he didn't know why. He remained keyed up, so much so that Jackson took him for a long run around the hedgerows that imprisoned them for security. Later, Jackson went over his equipment, checking the fit on Rufus and ensured everything was in good shape. They both were too keyed up to sleep, so Jackson led him to the large facility tent set up for them and watched a movie. *Mr. Lucky*, starring Cary Grant and Laraine Day was a movie about a gambler and con man who falls for a wealthy socialite. Most of the men had seen it a few times, including Jackson, but they didn't have anything else to do.

On June 5, Jackson was resting with a few others, waiting for word to depart the marshalling area for the airplanes. After asking a few Easy Company men, Eugene found Freddie, who took him to Jackson. After handshakes and hugs, they told each other their plans, where they would be dropping (*planned* to drop, to be precise), and would try to keep track of each other. A few moments later, a 506th HQ sergeant called for Corporal Gilmore. "Take your dog and report to Colonel Sink, on the double!"

He said goodbye to his brother and followed the sergeant to the HQ area. Sink had a large tent separated by canvas walls. He was finally let in to Sink's office, where he saluted the Regimental CO, and saw Major Horton, Lieutenant Colonel Strayer, and First Lieutenant Meehan, his CO. *Oh boy, what did we do now?*

"At ease paratrooper, and you too Sergeant Rufus." Sink was still amused by Rufus outranking Gilmore. "Well, son, I know you don't know why you are here, so I'll tell you. You are being assigned to my stick when we jump. Sergeant Miller will take care of you and get you settled in. Now go get your gear and report back to Sergeant Miller."

He was stunned. *Jump with HQ? But I have a mission!* When he didn't move or respond, Sink asked "Corporal, did you hear me? Now git! Dismissed!"

Jackson stood still. He finally was able to talk. "Sir, permission to speak sir."

"Hmmph. Granted."

Jackson wasn't sure what he was going to say, but it came out in a hurry. "Sir, we're assigned to 3rd Platoon, Easy Company, 2nd Battalion. We're part of a mission to destroy communications leading to Normandy. I, I mean *We* need to go with my men, sir. We've trained together for so long, and we belong with them! Sir."

Sink took a drag on his cigarette, exhaled, and looked at Gilmore sternly but not without compassion. "Son, I understand how you feel, and I appreciate it very much, Hell, I admire you for your loyalty to your platoon and company. But other things outside of my ability to control have intervened."

Sink took another drag and exhaled. He told Jackson to sit down, and he sat beside him. Sink was also a GOOD FRIEND of Rufus, so he reached and petted and scratched his ears. "I'll never get over how funny his ears look on a German Shepherd. You've done a damn fine job, son, a damn fine job. I've had reports of your ability and how you and Rufus have performed in the field. Both of you are great assets under my command, and I plan to use you to your fullest abilities. But it will be later. Right now, I need you to accept this order with faith that I know what I'm doing. Can you do that?"

Jackson didn't understand, but he was a good soldier; no, a good paratrooper. He stood quickly, saluted Sink with a "Sir, yes sir!" They left the tent and went to retrieve their gear. He was still shaken, but he had orders, and it was obvious someone much higher was pulling strings.

When he returned to Easy Company, the men were beginning to get there gear together before dinner and heading to the departure area. He told his platoon sergeant and squad leader what happened. Shifty Powers was barely able to hide his anger. "This here ain't right, I tell you, it just ain't right! We need you and you deserve the chance to drop with your platoon. Let me talk to Lieutenant Meehan and see if he can stop it."

Jackson appreciated the thought, but knew it was no good. "The CO knows, he was in Sink's office. I think the order came from General Taylor. What set him off about me and Rufus...well I guess I'll never know."

The men circled around the team, giving him pats on the shoulder or back, and rubbing Rufus. They told him they'd find him at the DZ near Ste. Marie-du-Mont. Freddie helped him carry their equipment to the HQ marshalling area, about a quarter mile away. "Hey Gilmore, don't sweat the jump. We'll find you and Rufus and y'all will rejoin the platoon." They shook hands and Freddie returned to Easy Company.

Dinner was a grand meal, with fried chicken, buttered bread (real butter!), fruit cocktail and ice cream. Gilmore was careful not to feed Rufus from the table, remembering the night farts in the previous night jumps. After dinner, Jackson took a walk, let Rufus do his business, then returned to the marshalling area. Everyone else was resting or sleeping, so he decided to bunk down for a nap as well.

At 2030 hours, the HQ First Sergeant came through and woke them up. Time to go! Jackson grabbed their gear and fell into formation with the rest of the men in his stick. There was still light to see fairly well, as sunset wasn't until after 2200 hours (10:00p.m.). He had both his and Rufus' gear but would receive his other gear at the hangar. Men marched in formation, separated by airplane number. They marched the mile to their hangar, where they found men waiting to help them gear up.

Jackson had tried to prepare Rufus for the jump, fed him horse meat early in the day so that he had time to digest it and then do his business. He hoped it would help Rufus from having gas in the airplane. D-Day was no place to pass gas in an airplane full of men preparing to jump into enemy territory. Rufus would jump with his gear, about 25 pounds worth, Jackson carried less but had his M-1 rifle, ammo, a few grenades, two knives, and a revolver. While lighter than the other paratroopers, their combined weight was close to the limit of the parachute. He decided not to wear his reserve chute; they would jump at less than 1,000 feet, and if the primary parachute failed, he didn't think he would have time to remove it and deploy the reserve.

They threw their gear into waiting trucks, hopped in and rode to the airfield. Rufus put his front paws on the side rail to look out at the thousands of paratroopers marching to airplanes. They passed Easy Company, walking to C-47's numbered 66-73. The men saw Rufus' head poking over the side and called to him.

"Hey Rufus! You be safe!"

"Don't eat any German sausages you find when you land!"

"See you in France Rufus!"

Rufus let out a loud "BAROOOOOO!!!!" to the men of Easy Company, who laughed loudly and heartily. Just as it had happened in numerous other times, the men were lifted by the presence of their friend, Sergeant Rufus. Jackson waved at the men, and they hollered at him too. He saw Freddie near the front, waved and hollered, "Freddie! See you in Normandy, pal!" Freddie grinned and waved his arms. "Be safe and take care of Rufus for me!"

Jackson sat down for the remainder of the short ride. It hurt him to not be going to war with his friends, the men he trusted, and who trusted him, and Rufus too. He hoped he could get this fixed and find Easy Company once in Normandy. As the truck stopped near their airplane, a dull green C-47 Dakota, or affectionately known as the 'Skytrain'. He shook off his dejection and got Rufus to his designated spot. Both their jump gear were in two bags, and he placed their other gear alongside them. Men began strapping on jump gear, packing leg bags, and checking rifles, hand guns, and knives. Rufus was suited up and carried some of his own gear, while Jackson took the rest. Fortunately, Jackson didn't have to carry to war all the things the other paratroopers did. He limited the amount of ammunition he carried, reduced his food rations to two days, and carried most of Rufus' food instead. He figured he could bum a K-Ration from another paratrooper, but it would be difficult to find Rufus the food he needed.

He didn't know many of the men he was jumping with, a few men that had transferred from a company or battalion HQ platoon was all he knew. But the men knew he was a good soldier and that Sink has personally required the K-9 unit to jump with him. They didn't ask why, nor cared, as long as he was a paratrooper that was fine with them. The men were ready, all were sitting down in two rows, waiting for word to board. Finally, Colonel Sink arrived, fully geared up and ready to go, with four officers from his staff and the regimental First Sergeant. He said a few words of encouragement to his men, then shook their hands as they boarded. Rufus was the first to board of the 2nd stick of eight men, so he and Rufus would be near the cockpit wall. Sink stopped him and shook his hand. "Corporal Gilmore, I will see you on the ground. Now let's go kill some Germans."

***

About a half mile away, Eugene was preparing himself to parachute into enemy territory. Along with his stick of 16 enlisted combat engineers, they were to destroy bridges north of Carentan and defend a lock on the Douve River. As the 3rd Platoon Leader, it was his responsibility to get the men assembled as quickly as possible, get to the gliders which would deliver men and equipment, and report to his CO for orders. He was the jumpmaster for his aircraft, flying in Serial #12, behind his brother with Colonel Sink in Serial #11.

Eugene had worked hard and had been promoted to First Lieutenant a few months ago. He was requested to fill in as the S-3 for the company in mid-May but begged off to remain as 3rd Platoon Leader. "Libby, I don't want to leave my men so close to the invasion. We know what we need to do and are trained and ready. Can Battalion HQ send someone to help?"

Charlie Company CO, Captain Francis 'Libby' Liberatori, was a good officer and a strong leader. From Springfield, Massachusetts, Libby was an architect before joining the Army. He thought for a moment. Gilmore was basically turning down a promotion to stay with his men, men he had been with for 18 months. Libby wouldn't be in this situation if his S-3 hadn't broken an ankle on the last training jump. But, while he needed a new Operations Officer, it made sense to leave his platoons intact.

"Okay Eugene, I'll try to find a replacement, maybe from Able or Baker Companies. But after we get to France and settle in, I'm going to look at you again. Deal?" Gilmore saluted and said "Deal!"

As they boarded their airplane, he helped each man up the steps. Each man carried his weapons and gear, but they weren't overloaded as the other paratroopers. Most of the 326th Airborne Engineer Battalion equipment would be delivered by gliders. Once all the engineer paratroopers were aboard, Eugene climbed in and sat just in front of the door. The men were quiet, no singing, no jokes, just a cigarette lit here and there, checked equipment (again), or just relaxed against the wall. The pilot passed word to the crew chief, and Eugene helped him mount the door to the aircraft hatch. The plane taxied to the runway, the pilot ran the engines up to full speed, and released the brakes. Eugene saw the airfield slowly begin to move past them, then faster, until they lifted into the air. Thousands of planes filled the sky, and after circling the airfield, they arrived in their position with two other C-47s to form a 'V', which in turn formed with two other 'Vs' for a total of nine airplanes. About twenty minutes into the flight, the crew chief removed the door, and Eugene moved to the rear side of the hatch to look.

What he saw astounded him. To the east were thousands of ships, as far as he could see. The invasion fleet of 6,000 ships steamed toward Normandy. The seaborne invasion would begin about five hours after the paratroopers landed in their drop zones. He looked out at the airplanes nearest him, then saw hundreds of C-47s, all in V of V formations, filling the sky. The sky was clear, but once over the coast they ran into a thick cloud bank. No longer able to see the single blue light on each C-47, the pilots veered off, away from their flight patch, gained altitude and moved off to the left or right.

After they broke out of the cloud bank, the formation was lost. Only the lead plane in each of the V formations had been able to maintain his course. Now, separated from their lead plane, the other pilots were on their own. They had no way to find the drop zone, being totally dependent on the lead pilots with airborne transceivers to lead them to the Pathfinders' Eureka signals. (The Pathfinders were a group of Paratroopers who led the invasion by jumping prior to the 82nd and 101st paratroopers arriving and setting up beacons in the drop zones for the lead pilots to follow.)

Now lost and disoriented, and most likely frightened, anti-aircraft rounds with red, blue, and green tracers exploded everywhere, above, below, behind, in front, and sometimes direct hits. Against orders, some pilots began flying erratically, weaving to avoid the ack-ack. Eugene's pilot increased speed to 150 miles per hour, much faster than the planned 90 to 100 mile per hour.

The pilot also dropped to 400 feet altitude, instead of the normal 600 feet. Now, not even knowing his position, only that he was over Normandy, the pilot instructed the co-pilot to hit the green light. Eugene had the men ready, and when the light changed to green, he hollered "Let's go!!!!" and out he went.

***

Colonel Sink was in Chalk #1, Serial #11, one of the first formations to fly over Normandy. Lieutenant Colonel Charles Young, Army Air Force, and group commander of the 439th Troop Carrier Group, piloted the lead C-47 of Serial #11. Young hit the cloud bank covering western Cotentin, climbed through the darkness using instruments and radar, but he could not find the Pathfinder's signal or Aldis lamp. Instead, Lieutenant Colonel Young recognized the landmarks around DZ C, and dropped Sink and his men on the northeast side of Zone C at 0114.

Jackson and Rufus were sitting near the cockpit when Chalk #1 went airborne. The plane was in very good shape and didn't smell so much of oil, fuel, and sweat. But once the men settled in, Rufus could smell the sweat and fear released by the men. He could sense which men were nearly overcome with fear, and others he sensed were more anxious than scared. After reaching altitude and getting into formation, Sink called for Gilmore and Rufus to move aft.

"Corporal Gilmore, I want you and Rufus to jump behind me, we'll meet up and stay together. Clear?"

Jackson nodded and sat down in a seat cleared by a 506th HQ officer. Colonel Sink had requested the door remain in place so the men could smoke. He lit a cigarette and took a deep pull on it, releasing the smoke into the air. Rufus sat quietly at Jackson's feet, taking everything in with intense concentration. He sensed this jump was different than the others, the men he didn't know were tense and scared, though his master was less tense than many of the others.

Even though Jackson had taken precautions with his diet, Rufus was getting an upset stomach. It may have been the early supper, which was rich with horse meat, eggs, and grains, but Rufus couldn't help it. He gave a loud burp, then a subdued 'pfffffff' left him. It only took a few seconds before the awful smell filled the airplane. Sink turned to Gilmore with a surprised and disgusted look. "Damn son, is that your dog? What did you feed him, a dead skunk?" That brought a roar of laughter from the men, and the tension, heavy in the air, lessened. All Jackson could do was to offer an embarrassed apology. Sink told the jumpmaster to remove the door, "Because we need some damn relief in here!"

Sink wasn't mad, just a little ruffled by the smell. He looked at the men in his stick. Nearly all the men had been with the 506th at its inception at Camp Toccoa. He felt a fierce but sentimental pride in all of them, he could only describe it like the love you feel for family. Each man had been through extremely tough training, but having completed it, he felt, rightly, that they were one of the finest units in the Army. Nearly all the men in his regiment had come from humble beginnings, especially the young enlisted. Some came from poor families, poor farmers, factory workers, or even on their own to fend for themselves. The $100 they received in monthly pay was more than most had ever seen. Many soldiers sent most of their pay home to family. Yes, he had a right to be proud of his men, and he knew they would do their job superbly.

The red light appeared, and the jumpmaster had the men stand up and prepare to jump. Jackson checked Rufus' harness once more, then checked all equipment. He was ready. Standing behind Colonel Sink, who was already at the door with his head out the hatch. The light turned green, and the jumpmaster yelled "Go! Go! Go!" With his head in the wind blast, he didn't hear the jumpmaster. As the jumpmaster moved to tap Colonel Sink on his leg, Rufus stuck his nose in Sink's butt. Sink jumped. Literally.

Jackson followed a second later. The air turbulence hit him, followed by the shock of his parachute opening and sending him in large oscillations. Tracers were everywhere he looked, some concentrating on airplanes, other, smaller machine-guns aimed at falling paratroopers.

He looked below and saw that he was about 300 feet above a

flooded field, so he slipped to his left to land on the other side of a hedgerow. When he was 30 feet from earth, Rufus let out a loud "BARROOO!" to make sure he knew they were close. He landed with a thump, rolled on his back, released Rufus, and began getting his parachute and harness off. Rufus paced around him, searching the area for movement and smell. As he stood, he looked for Colonel Sink, but he was nowhere to be seen. Even though he had jumped only seconds behind him, the speed that they were flying had spread them apart by hundreds of feet in different directions. He told Rufus to heel and removed his jump harness and threw it aside.

Jackson wasn't sure if he was in DZ C or not. He knew he was walking east because of the hundreds of aircraft flying overhead. He didn't know where Colonel Sink landed so he decided to continue to move east, where he would find the drop zone or the causeways 1 and 2, which were the primary objectives to secure. Suddenly, Rufus looked up and barked. Coming down almost on top of them was a paratrooper. He hit a few feet in front of them, hit with a hard thump, rolled, and stood up. It was Corporal Maher from H Company, 3rd Battalion. Maher was supposed to jump into DZ D, about three or four miles to the south, but both men had only a vague idea where they were. Other men began falling near them, and they soon had a group of over a dozen paratroopers, a mixture of 2nd and 3rd Battalions and two men from the 82nd Airborne Division. The 82nd guys were well out of their drop zone, far to the east, but again they had only a vague idea where they were. Still, the men formed up and began moving east.

Rufus led the way, in scout position. His senses were on edge; he sensed the danger around them and knew his job was important. He listened for sounds of men and machines but heard nothing in front of them. Suddenly, he stopped, his nose high in the air. What is this strange new smell? A cigarette…but not one he recognized. It was coming from somewhere in front, not far away. He set his legs and pointed directly ahead, releasing a low growl.

Jackson raised his left hand and the men stopped and crouched. He slowly moved up to Rufus. "What is it, boy? You see something?" Rufus didn't look at his master, but moved a step forward, then froze again, letting out another low growl. Gilmore looked closely but saw no enemy movement. But he *had* to trust Rufus. He told Rufus to stay and returned to the men in a crouch. He turned to Maher. "There's something ahead that set Rufus off. I think there's a German unit hiding ahead. We need to get off this road and take 'em out."

Maher looked wide-eyed at Jackson. They had only been on the Cotentin Peninsula for an hour and were now in their first contact with Germans. "What do you want to do? Split up and try to sneak up on 'em?"

Jackson agreed with Maher. "Take half the men and go to the north. I'll take the rest and go south. When we get close, we'll open up on them, then you move in and flank them. Let's move out."

Jackson signed for Rufus to join up, and they set out through the south hedgerow and into a field which was partly flooded. With Rufus in the lead, the men quickly but quietly moved east toward the German unit. He didn't know how many they were facing, but he knew they had to kill them, or more paratroopers would get wounded or killed coming down this road. Another hedgerow, running south to north, joined the hedgerow along the road. Rufus suddenly crouched on his belly, his head down, and crawled forward about twenty feet. He stopped, his fur up along his back. Jackson saw his muscles tense, and without warning, Rufus jumped through the hedgerow in front of them. Barking and growling, Rufus attacked. Jackson rose and ran forward, but did not fire his rifle, fearing he would hit Rufus. He heard Germans screaming and several pistol firings and burst through the hedgerow to find four Germans manning a machine-gun emplacement. Raising his Garand M-1, he shot one German in the shoulder, turned on another, but didn't fire. Rufus had one man pinned down in the mud, his neck clinched in his jaws. The German soldier looked at Jackson with fear in his eyes, but too scared to move or speak. The Germans surrendered, and it was over almost before it began.

Maher and his team came through the hedgerow and joined

him. "You take them out on your own? I only heard one shot so we never let loose."

"No, Rufus got them all by himself." As they searched the German prisoners, Rufus remained at alert, growling but no longer in attack mode. The prisoners kept their eyes on Rufus, not on the paratroopers. Now they had a problem; what to do with the prisoners? They had been told (not in any written order, just verbal) to take no prisoners. But Jackson couldn't kill them in cold blood. "We have to take them with us," he told Maher. "I know we were told no prisoners, but I can't kill them, it just don't feel right."

Maher looked hard at Gilmore, his eyes cold and black. "I'll take care of them; you take Rufus and get us back on the road." Jackson wasn't sure what Greg meant by 'take care of them' but he got the men together and on the road heading east in short time. He turned to look back and saw Maher getting the prisoners marching forward, their hands atop their heads, except the wounded Kraut who held his wounded arm in the other. Rufus took lead again and they moved east at a fast but safe pace. The prisoners moved slower, with one wounded in the shoulder and one limping. As the paratroopers moved ahead, Maher got further behind, almost out of sight in the twilight.

Jackson was following Rufus when he heard the sharp crack of an M-1 Garand, followed quickly by several more. The men hit the ground and began searching for enemy gunfire, their M-1s aimed and ready. Rufus stood on all fours, looking back down the road, fearless. Within half a minute, Maher came walking up the road, alone. They stood, Rufus wagging his tail in an easy manner, looking at his friend. "You alright Maher?" Jackson asked, concerned that something happened, maybe the prisoners attacked him.

"What happened, where're the prisoners? They try to escape?" Maher kept walking through the men until he reached Jackson. "I told you I'd take care of them, so I took care of them. Let's go." Jackson looked at Maher, he kept walking. But he could see that Maher still had the cold black eyes and stone face. *Just let it go, he'll tell me about it later,* Jackson thought.

After walking another mile, they joined another group from several units, among them 1st, 2nd, and 3rd Battalions, and a few from the 502nd PIR. Several officers, including a couple of Lieutenant Colonels were in the group, so Jackson's de facto squad leading was over. However, he and Rufus were ordered to scout ahead for enemy positions. Luckily, no more Germans were discovered, and soon they marched into the township of Le Grand Chemin, not far from the small town of Culoville, where Colonel Sink would eventually set up the 506th regimental command post.

Rufus led the way to the command post, giving a loud 'BARRROOOO!!!' to let the others know he was there. Several Easy Company men heard the loud bark and found Jackson and the other group. Freddie was the first man to greet him, limping from a twisted ankle but giving Jackson a hug around his shoulders. Rufus raised up and put his front paws on Freddie's chest and big lick across his face. "Yeah, I missed you too, Rufus. Boy, I'm sure glad to see you. I thought I was gonna have to fight the Germans on my own!" Spiers led them to Easy Company's post, but there were few men collected. The sun was just beginning to rise in the east, and each man knew that the seaborne invasion would be starting soon. Colonel Sink had sent men out to secure the two southern causeways, only a few miles to the east past Ste. Marie Du Mont.

There was no sign of Easy Company leadership. No officers had shown up and the highest-ranking enlisted man was a sergeant from the HQ platoon. As the sky brightened, more men arrived, including Lieutenant Buck Compton. Buck was the assistant platoon leader of 2nd Platoon, easy going and friendly, and liked by the men. Compton had joined Easy Company in December 1943, and while not considered a 'Toccoa' man, he soon earned the respect of the men and was accepted by them.

By early morning, over a dozen Easy Company men had gathered, including Lieutenant Winters. Sergeant Lipton also arrived along with Sergeant Guarnere and PFCs Malarky, 'Popeye' Wynn and 'Smokey' Gordon. Each told stories of their jump, who had made it, and who hadn't. No one had heard or seen anyone from Lieutenant Meehan's stick, which included most of the senior leadership of Easy Company and HQs Platoon.

Jackson found a quiet place off the side of the town center to check Rufus. He removed his vest, checked for any places that may have rubbed him raw, but found none. His paws were healthy but dirty. Jackson poured some water in a bowl and put down a tin of dry horse meat. Rufus was hungry and ate everything Jackson gave him. He laid down beside Jackson and fell asleep. Soon, though, Freddie found them. "Easy Company's going on a patrol, Lieutenant Winters wants everyone up front."

Captain Hester (Battalion S-3) had ordered Lieutenant Winters to take Easy Company and take care of a German artillery battery firing down Causeway #2 onto Utah Beach. Winters gathered up what Easy Company men had made it to the assembly area and laid out his plan. When Jackson volunteered, Winters looked away and moved on. After the assault team was selected, and Jackson was left out (both he and Freddie had been passed over, Freddie because he was limping), he went to see Lieutenant Winters.

"Sir, me and Rufus would like to help. I can shoot real good, sir, and Rufus can carry ammo and find Germans waiting to kill us."

Winters looked at Jackson with concern, "Sorry Jackson, but I already have my team. You need to stay here with 2nd Battalion and help round up Easy Company stragglers. Clear?"

Jackson didn't like it, but he would follow orders. With a sigh, he answered "Clear, sir." Winters went on with his work, getting rid of anything but weapons and ammunition. Soon, the team took off to Brecourt Manor, where a battery of four 105mm artillery guns continued to fire shells at the seaborne units coming ashore. He found Freddie and sat beside him, disappointed that he was not selected to go. Jackson was getting a feeling that there was an effort to keep him out of action.

"I don't know, Freddie, it's like everyone from Winters on up is trying to keep me out of danger. I think I need to speak to Lieutenant Colonel Strayer." Freddie nodded his head. "Good idea, but don't get your hopes up. If they don't want you getting shot at, take it that they see you as a high priority asset!"

Freddie continued. "Hey, I haven't had time to congratulate you and Rufus yet!" Jackson was confused. "For what? Stumbling our way into this place?"

Freddie grinned. "No, you goofball, for what you and Rufus did on the way here. Some 3rd Battalion guy told everybody who would listen about Rufus attacking a German machine-gun nest that was hiding in the hedgerows. It's no telling how many paratroops they would have killed if y'all hadn't took them out. You two should get a medal or something!"

Jackson was humbled by the praise, but it didn't mean anything to him. He wanted to help his buddies, they still had missions to complete. He stood and Rufus quickly followed into heel position. "I'll be back in a little bit." They took off across the courtyard to the 2nd Battalion temporary headquarters. Strayer was talking with Lieutenant Nixon and Captain Hester, reviewing a map of the local area, the causeways, and Utah Beach.

"Lieutenant Colonel Strayer, could I please speak with you, sir?" Strayer looked up, clearly irritated by the interruption. But when he saw it was Gilmore and Rufus, his face relaxed, he picked up his helmet and spoke to the other men. "Give me five minutes. And find us a path to Causeway #2." Strayer nodded his head for Jackson to follow him outside.

"Speak up, Corporal, what's on your mind?" Jackson knew what he needed to say. "Sir, I want to volunteer to help Lieutenant Winters, or go with another team to the Causeway. Me and Rufus can help, sir, I know we can."

"I know you can help, Corporal, but right now I have orders to follow, so you are staying here." That surprised Jackson. *Orders? Concerning me and Rufus?* "Sir, if I may ask, what orders?"

Strayer looked like he was going to berate him, then his face relaxed again. "Look, Gilmore, you and Rufus are doing good work. I heard about what you two did on the way here, and I'll personally make sure you get a medal. But Colonel Sink gave me specific orders to keep you and Rufus safe. Got it?"

Jackson didn't let it go. "Sir, I understand what you told me, but could you tell me *exactly* what your orders were?"

"Colonel Sink received an order to ensure you two made it safely into Normandy, and he passed it down the chain of command. And that's the end of it." He turned to go back to his headquarters, but Jackson continued. "Sir! We *ARE* safely in Normandy now! So Colonel Sink completed his orders, right sir? I think your orders are complete too sir, and me and Rufus can help. Sir."

Strayer pulled up short, turned to look at the pair. Rufus was staring back at Strayer with intense dark eyes, his ears up (as much as he could raise his floppy ears). Strayer thought a moment, then said "Hmmm. You have a point. Okay, you and Rufus are free to join your company. But for God's sake don't do anything stupid! I'll have a hard enough time explaining to Colonel Sink why I let you go without you or Rufus getting hurt. Go on." With that Strayer departed, leaving Jackson stunned. When he finally was able to digest his win, he hurried to Freddie.

"Strayer said we could go help! Now I just need to figure out what we can do, right now." Freddie thought a minute, then barked "Hey! I got an idear. (He said it just like that, 'idear'). "Let's get some ammo boxes together and fill them with whatever we can find. M-1 clips, mortars, grenades, magazines for Tommy guns, and volunteer to take it to Easy Company. What do you think?"

Jackson thought that was a swell idea, so they quickly scrounged ammo. After an hour, they had three ammo boxes filled and ready to go. He strapped two boxes to Rufus' harness and made sure he didn't put his dog in a bind. He guessed Rufus was carrying about 60 pounds of gear. Heading to headquarters, they ran into Captain Hester carrying ammo. "Captain Hester, we rounded up three boxes of ammo, can we go with you? Rufus is loaded up and ready to go." Hester didn't hesitate. "Let's go. Give me a handle on that box." Jackson and Hester took off at a trot, with Rufus in the lead.

It was simple to find Easy Company. The big guns were firing shells every 10 seconds, the noise was deafening even a few hundred yards away. Hester led the way, Jackson careful to order

Rufus to remain at Heel position. He didn't want him running off again and getting into trouble. They caught up to Lieutenant Winters at the 2nd gun; the first already destroyed. Hester was first into the trench and then to the gun emplacement. Jackson led Rufus quickly behind.

Guarnere saw Rufus first. "Hey Rufus! Where you been, boy? What'd you bring me?" Rufus rubbed on Guarnere and gave him a quick lick, then returned to Jackson. Gilmore untied the ammo boxes and gave them to the men. Winters watched the resupply as he took TNT and a grenade from Captain Hester. "Good job Gilmore," Winters said with a smile. "Now get out of here before you get Rufus hurt."

Jackson smiled, turned to his friends. "Yes sir! We can make another ammo run as soon as we get back." They took off, swiftly departing the firefight but watching for Germans. Rufus led the way back to the town with no problem. After a quick rest and drink of water for them both, they started rounding up more ammo. It took another hour, but they gathered up two boxes to take to the firefight. Then Jackson noticed something; quiet. No artillery rounds had been fired for a few minutes. They could hear machine-gun fire, both American and German. Heavy machine-gun fire erupted, definitely American .50-caliber and .30-caliber machines guns filled the air. Then, nothing. No gunfire of any type, not even M-1s. It wasn't long before Easy Company returned to the battalion command post.

Easy Company had destroyed the artillery guns, killed over a dozen Germans, and captured twelve. But, Easy, along with Lieutenant Speirs from Dog Company and his platoon, lost four men and six wounded. The destruction of the 105's meant the men at Utah Beach had a safe route up Causeway #2. The fight had taken nearly three hours. Now, early afternoon on June 6th, the 4th Infantry Division were making their way off the beachhead, along Causeways 1 and 2 and into Normandy. Jackson learned that after Lieutenant Winters had led the fight to take the 105s, he later directed U.S. tanks arriving from Utah Beach to destroy the remaining machine-gun placements.

The members of the 506th departed for Culoville, where they

would spend the night. Easy Company was now up to over 80 paratroopers, but no one had heard from Lieutenant Meehan or anyone in his stick. It wasn't long before word came down that Meehan's plane had been hit by flak and went down with all aboard. No survivors. Winters was now the Easy Company CO.

Jackson settled down with Freddie and a couple of other men under a large rectangular tent set up just outside of Culoville. Jackson unpacked their gear, laid down a waterproof blanket, and cleaned Rufus. His paws were a mess, full of dried mud. His coat was dirty but brushed out easily. Finally, he cleaned his eyes with a mild Boric acid and checked his ears. All done, he opened his last can of water and poured it into Rufus' dish, opened canned meat and vegetables and set out for him to eat. Rufus ate heartily; it had been a 'Day of Days' for everyone, two or four legged.

Gilmore was finally able to take stock in himself. He bummed a K-ration from Freddie, took a long drink from his canteen, and ate silently. *We made it through the first day, and ole Rufus performed just about as well as anyone could have believed.* He hoped his officers knew how good Rufus had performed. A thought suddenly struck him; he never put Rufus on leash, not once the entire day. But Rufus had stayed with him, following voice commands. He thought he should keep it that way until something forced his hand. His last thought as he fell into a deep sleep was of his brother, and he prayed that he was alive and safe.

***

Sink set up the 506th command post in Culoville, with his battalion CPs close by. Lieutenant Colonel Strayer found Sink in his temporary CP. 2nd Battalion, while not engaging fully in securing the causeways, had assembled quicker and with more men than 1st and 3rd Battalions. Sink was happy to see him. They caught up on the day and the next objectives. Sink's problem was that, even though he had plenty of men, he had no radios or communications for most of the day. With that problem remedied, he was ready to lead the 506th into combat as a regiment.

Strayer explained the events at Brecourt Manor and several other engagements, and about Rufus nearly single-handedly taking out a German machine-gun nest. Sink listened attentively, then let out a loud guffaw. "Let me tell you what that damn dog did to me." Sink told him how he moved Gilmore and Rufus to the rear next to him. "I had my head out the door when the light turned green, didn't hear the crew chief tell me to jump, but the next thing I knew I had that damn dog's nose up the crack of my ass, and by God I jumped!"

They laughed loudly for a moment, enjoying a respite from the day's fighting. "Colonel, what *were* your orders for the K-9 unit?" Strayer asked with a questioning look. "And who gave them?"

Sink smiled again. He explained that he received a call from General Maxwell Taylor, the 101st Airborne Division Commander. "Taylor told me he had received a call from Ike himself and told me that Ike had received a personal request from Churchill. He said Churchill asked that if there was any way to make sure 'that splendid dog would make it safely to France to please see to it.' That's why he jumped with me. But I never saw them after I jumped, until tonight. Churchill took a shine to Rufus, you think?"

Jackson didn't hear this until weeks later, but when he did it all made sense to him. He felt he should apologize to Colonel Sink, but finally decided to let it go.

***

First Lieutenant Gilmore hit hard, with a loud thump! He felt a flash of pain run from his lower back down both legs. He rolled over onto his back and didn't move. No Germans were shooting at him, so he slowly sat up and released his parachute, removed his harness, and stood in a crouch. He was alone, not another member of his platoon anywhere near him. His platoon was supposed to have dropped in DZ D, but he knew he wasn't in the drop zone. He thought he was north and west of DZ D (he was correct), so started off to the east. More men were falling nearby, and he quickly formed a squad of eight men from various units; H and I Companies, 3rd Battalion, and a few men from the demolition platoon of Regimental HQ Company. The men from the demolition platoon had the same mission as Eugene – destroy or hold the bridges at Le Port.

As the only officer in his tiny unit, Gilmore quietly took command and continued eastward toward the assembly area. They picked up a few more troopers, until they ran into a large group heading south, led by Colonel Howard Johnson, commander of the 501st PIR. After looking through the assembly, he did not recognize any of his men, nor anyone from the 326th. He found Colonel Johnson, reported in as a combat engineer, and was ordered to stay close; he would be needed later.

Remarkably, Colonel Johnson and his stick landed in the middle of DZ D. Planes carrying his 1st and 2nd Battalions had dropped well short of the drop zone, but when the jump signal flashed, an equipment bundle was wedged in the door. It took a moment to clear the bundle, which caused them to fly another mile or so before dropping.

Johnson led his men south to the La Barquette lock, situated on the Douve River and less than two miles north of Carentan. The men had traveled through swamp land, crossed streams as deep as their waists, and crawled through hedgerow after hedgerow. Now they were only 300 yards from the lock. Mortar fire was sporadic and overshot the men. Captain Shettle, 3rd Battalion S-3, 506th had about 30 men with him, and requested permission to attack the bridges at Le Port, their original assignment. Johnson approved but told Shettle to take Lieutenant Gilmore with him; he would need a combat engineer. Gilmore took the men from the demolition platoon with him.

Johnson sent fifty men to secure the lock. The unit raced to the lock, facing only sporadic rifle fire. Several men quickly crossed the lock and secured both sides, and hurriedly dug foxholes in the soft, wet clay. Minutes later the Germans finally reacted and fired mortars and machine-guns at the invaders, but with no or little damage. The lock belonged to the Americans, though more troops were needed to keep the lock *and* destroy the bridges two miles to the east.

Gilmore joined the 3rd Battalion men to destroy the bridges. They moved out a little after 0400, traveling quietly along the Douve. The lead man was crouching, held up his arm to stop. Everyone took a knee and listened. No sound was coming from down the road toward the wood bridges, only sporadic gunfire from the north. The lead man, a corporal from A Company, 1st Battalion, 501st, stood and began walking again, then he wasn't walking. Machine-gun fire covered the road, the corporal was hit several times across his chest and gut. The entire group scrambled off the road and into the ditch. They quickly returned rifle fire, covering each other as they slowly progressed. A mortar team set up and hurled mortars as quickly as they could load them. Several were direct hits and the German machine-guns were silenced.

A medic was already on the corporal, but there was nothing he could do. They moved the dead body off the road, took one dog tag, and continued onto the bridges. The small group reached the first bridge at 0430. One of the demolition sections, led by Sergeant Jake McNiece, was already there and had wired the bridges for demolition.

McNiece, a native Oklahoman and half Choctaw, had landed alone well away from DZ D. He quickly gathered some men, including a few from his demolition section, and headed south to the Douve River. Along the way, he ran into Colonel Johnson (but well before Gilmore arrived) and was ordered to take up a defensive position. After arguing with Johnson about his orders to take the bridges, he finally agreed to follow orders, and he and his men set out.

However, McNiece had no plans to follow Johnson's order, and instructed his men to follow him to the bridges. They arrived at Le Port at 0300 hours and immediately wired the two wooden bridges for demolition. Shettle sent a squad across the smaller bridge to the west to occupy the east bank. The men dug in as best they could.

Shettle had decided to wait until he received reinforcements to take the second bridge. When another group of 20 men joined him, he decided he had the forces to take the other bridge as well. A First Lieutenant from H Company led the assault to the east bank but crossed under the bridge to take the far bank. Shettle and a small team followed them across the river and the bridgehead was secure, at least temporarily.

Shettle was concerned. Though he felt they had killed several Germans and wounded others, his men were running low on ammunition. With no reinforcements nearby, he withdrew his team to the west bank to hold there. Colonel Johnson, holding the lock, could not send any troops. The men hunkered down for the rest of the day and into the night.

In the early evening, help walked into Shettle's group. About 40 men from 1st Battalion, 501st joined the "Battalion" providing the reinforcements he needed. But they were still short on ammo and held a precarious defensive position.

Eugene was in a foxhole when the Germans made a push toward the west bridge. He saw two Germans running toward the bridgehead on the left and two others on the right. He fired and one fell and did not move. He switched to the next German, aimed, fired, and that one dropped alongside his fellow soldier, not moving. Paratroopers opened up on the other Germans, but they had retreated out of sight. That was the only attempt to retake the bridge. Later that evening, Captain Shettle found Eugene in his foxhole. He was needed by Colonel Johnson.

Three other troopers accompanied him on the mile trek to the La Barquette lock. The bridgehead was now over 200 yards deep from the lock in all directions. They soon saw that Colonel Johnson's group had grown to nearly 300 men. Johnson was sending 100 men to support Lieutenant Colonel Ballard, commander of 2nd Battalion, 501st PIR, who had 250 men but were under fire and could not join Johnson's force. Instead, Ballard moved west toward St. Come-du-Mont, which beyond the town were two bridges over the Douve that was his mission to destroy. But German forces at Les Droueries were too strong to move through, so orders changed to an attack on Les Droueries.

Eugene didn't know any of this; he only knew he was ordered to support Lieutenant Colonel Ballard with demolition actions. Ballard had demolition and soldiers, but he wanted at least one officer to direct the combat engineers. Eugene joined the group, all tired, hungry and dirty, and they began the march to Les Droueries. It was after 2300 hours, they had all been fighting or marching for over 20 hours. Hopefully they would be able to rest when they arrived. As he trudged on, he thought about his brother and prayed that he was alive and safe.

***

8

MARCH, FIGHT, MARCH, FIGHT

Never before had the Krauts run into anybody who fought with the savagery and deadliness of the Trooper. They had grown used to grinding over all opposition as though it didn't exist. Being torn apart and killed so efficiently was unique in their experience. They didn't like it in the least. When they were walked to the beach and put in the PW cages and they saw Troopers from behind the wires they would mutter "Butchers with Big Pockets". They were definitely scared.
- *506th PIR Scrapbook*

Rufus was tired, wet, dirty, and hungry, as always. Jackson had little time to scrounge up food for him, mainly scraps from any meal they received from Battalion, and those were scarce. He needed to find meat, today.

It was D-Day plus 10, June 16, 1944. The 2nd Battalion had marched to Vierville, then onto Angoville-au-Plain, only a few hundred yards south of their location. After Colonel Sink's regiment cleared Ste. Come-du-Mont on June 8, he set up his CP at Angoville-au-Plain. Easy Company remained at Sink's CP for three days in defensive positions around the regimental HQ. Jackson took time to let Rufus rest and scrounge for food. He had carried three days of rations for Rufus on D-Day, but now was out of canned goods. Men from Easy Company, and men from 1st and 3rd Battalions had donated cans of meat and vegetables to Rufus after he ran out on June 9. He was humbled by the many selfless acts and pledged he would take Rufus to the other battalions to thank the men.

On June 10, he needed to find meat. Shifty Powers, his squad leader, said he would check with Battalion Supply. A couple of hours later he got his answer. The Battalion S-4 (Supply Officer) had sent word back that they had no supplies for a dog and to see the Quartermaster Corps.

Shifty Powers didn't let it go. "Go over to Regimental HQ, somebody there will help you." Back to Angoville-au-Plain he and Rufus went. After asking for the Regimental S-4, he was shown into a tent where several sergeants and PFCs were busily going over orders attached to clipboards. He stood and watched quietly, not drawing attention. Finally, a sergeant saw him and asked what he needed. "Sergeant, my dog needs meat. I only brought three days of food for him, and I stretched it out as far as I could. But he's been so busy I had to feed him twice yesterday."

The Sergeant wanted to help, but he didn't have much. "Let me look, we might have a few cans of tuna or stew. About all we have are K-rations." A few moments later he came back with a couple of K-rations and some individual tins. "Take these, they're Supper kits. And I found some loose tins of meat and stew. This ought to get you through a couple of days."

He took the food with a big "Thanks, Sergeant!" and returned to Vierville. He found Freddie, just back from patrol. Jackson and Rufus were going on night patrol, so he needed to get some sleep. "Be careful out there, there's a lot of sniper fire and mortars will rain down with no warning. We ran into a patrol, and engaged them, and found out it was a trap. They knew exactly where we would hunker down and zeroed in on our position with mortars. Owen and Willie got hit but will be okay. Just be careful."

The patrol would go out at 2200 hours. A force of eight men, plus Rufus, would patrol to the south and east of HQ, trying to find German patrols and engage them. Again, Rufus was lead scout. Jackson gave him the command to commence 'Patrol,' and Rufus quickly led off into the night. He remained within 20 feet of Jackson, but again off leash. Rufus was in hunt mode, his nose to the ground, going back and forth across a road and through hedgerows. As they moved south, they could hear rifle and machine-gun fire coming from the area near Carentan, their next objective. Rufus stopped, listened, put his nose in the air for a few moments, then continued. He allowed Rufus to go a little further out, but when he lost sight of him, he called him back.

With no contact to the south, they moved east. Rufus followed his same routine, his nose to the ground, trying to find a scent different from his friends. After another hour of patrol, they were ready to return to HQ, but suddenly Rufus locked up, his tail pointed while he gave a low growl. Gilmore held up his left arm to halt the patrol, who all knelt and looked nervously around for Germans.

"What do you smell Rufus? A German? German cigarettes?" Rufus looked straight ahead without flinching. He stood like that for several minutes, as if he couldn't move or he would lose contact. Jackson eased back to the patrol leader, Shifty Powers. "He's got something that is setting him off, Shifty, but I don't know what it is. If it's Germans, they must not be close, or they would have opened up on us."

Shifty took that info and called it in. "We have possible contact; I need a mortar team here fast." He gave his coordinates, then had the men get off the road and in the hedgerows. Jackson told Rufus to Heel, and Rufus reluctantly followed his command. It took fifteen minutes for the mortar team to find them. Powers had the mortar team set up behind a hedgerow. He gave them the azimuth of where Rufus had pointed, then called Jackson over.

"How far do you think Rufus can smell Germans? Fifty yards or so?" Gilmore smiled. "Try about half a mile, maybe further." He looked at Rufus, who was still focused on the direction of the scent he picked up. He turned to Shifty. "Give me a minute, I'll see if I can get you a better answer."

He led Rufus back to the road, where he immediately got low, into attack posture. Jackson led him further into the field, staying low. Rufus stopped, dropped to Cover position, and growled again. Jackson knew Rufus felt the Germans were close, so they returned to the patrol. "He thinks they're close, he can smell them and probably hear them, which means they may can hear us and are waiting for us to walk into their kill zone. I think you can probably start at about 50 yards down that way and walk them out further with each round." Shifty agreed. PFC Don Malarky, lead of the mortar squad, gave his men orders to set the mortar fire. He signaled Shifty that they were ready. Shifty nodded his head, giving a silent order to open fire.

The mortar fire was fast and deadly accurate. Malarky had them firing a round every two or three seconds, firing two rounds at the same target, then changing the distance but always the same direction. They heard a short scream from a distance away, maybe 100 yards, but it was silenced quickly. After firing 40 rounds at the Germans, Shifty had them cease fire. After the last rounds exploded, they waited for the night to go quiet again. Just a moment later, they could hear a moan and a cry for help, at least it sounded like that, but no one understood German. Jackson wanted to take Rufus ahead and stalk the injured patrol. Shifty wisely said no. "Our patrol is about over, and we don't know what's out there, how many or nuthin' bout them. I'll report the contact and a team can go out in the morning. Now let's go."

***

The 506th had no break after D-Day. After taking the guns at Brecourt Manor, they marched a bit over a mile from Ste. Marie-du-Mont to Culoville, where they settled for the night. On June 7, they marched nearly two miles to Vierville, cleared the village, then fought off German counterattacks the rest of the day. The next day they marched to Angoville-au-Plain, only a mile or so to the south, where they stayed for three days in reserve and defense of regimental HQ. It was here that Easy Company men not seen since June 5th began streaming into the village, and soon Easy Company had over 100 men. Paratroopers from other regiments joined the 1st and 2nd Battalions to bring them up to nearly full strength. The company then moved to Ste. Come-du-Mont and spent the night.

But the march and fight continued on June 11, when General

Maxwell Taylor ordered a three-pronged attack on Carentan, and the 506th would perform a forced night march around Carentan to the southwest. The battalion marched through marshlands, small creeks and thick hedgerows, until they finally crossed the Douve River. On the morning of June 12, Easy Company was in position to attack Carentan. At 0600, the order was given to attack. Jackson and Rufus were ordered to remain at 506th HQs, which they reluctantly followed.

2nd Battalion attacked the Germans holding Carentan along a road leading into town, ending in a Y junction. They faced tough machine-gun fire, but eventually defeated the Germans and took Carentan. Meanwhile, Jackson and Rufus were in a pickle.

Colonel Sink had followed the same route as his 1st and 2nd Battalions to Carentan. But while his battalions had stopped at Hill 30, about half a mile southwest of Carentan along Rte. de Periers, Sink was lost and mistakenly moved his CP south of Hill 30, well forward of his battalions. Not realizing his location, he ordered the attack to commence at dawn. When the fight began, German fire came from all directions. They were surrounded but Sink quickly ordered 1st Battalion to attack east to get the regiment out of trouble. He told his men to dig in.

Jackson took Rufus out along the hedgerows to protect the CP. There were men dug in along the perimeter, waiting for the Germans to attack. As they moved to the west of the CP, Jackson saw a stand of trees just past a hedgerow and decided to clear it. When they were about 40 yards from the trees, two Germans stepped out and began firing. Jackson dropped and returned fire. Then he stopped, Rufus was in his firing line. Then he wasn't so he raised his rifle, but then Rufus was again in his line. The Germans originally fired at him, but quickly saw the real threat and aimed at Rufus.

Jackson was stunned. Before he could order Rufus to return, the dog jumped and hit the lead German in the chest and knocked him down. Rufus bit into the man's neck, who elicited a loud scream and began screaming, "Aussteigen! Aussteigen!" The other German, only 10 feet away, aimed at Rufus, but didn't fire as he didn't want to shoot his sergeant. Jackson stood, aimed, and shot him through his throat. He ran to Rufus, gave the command to Heel, and pointed his M-1 at the German sergeant. "Aufstehen," Jackson ordered the German. The prisoner stood, clinging to his neck, not paying much attention to Jackson; Rufus had his undivided attention, growling lowly and baring his teeth.

He marched the prisoner back to the CP but was met by several paratroopers running his way. "What happened? You get lost?" He didn't get lost, he explained. "I was just checking out the perimeter, and two Germans took a shot at me."

"Where's the other one?" Jackson didn't smile, he just pointed to the trees. "Over there, but he won't be joining us."

At the CP, Jackson turned the prisoner over to the regimental intelligence officer, or S-2. Sink saw the exchange but said nothing, he'd speak to that man and his damn dog later, after they were safe. He didn't like Gilmore taking chances with Rufus' safety.

1st Battalion arrived in force about 30 minutes later, but the Germans had moved in close, and fighting among the hedgerows was fierce. Mortar fire was intense, but A Company overran the Germans, created a wide gap in their encirclement, and Sink gave the order to move out. This time, Jackson was happy to stay close to Colonel Sink. Machine-gun fire was whizzing by their heads as they ran in a crouch across one hedgerow after another. They dove into a ditch, and Rufus happened to land atop of Sink.

Instead of getting mad, Sink laughed. "Gilmore, you better get control of this damn fleabag dog before I court martial him for striking a superior officer!" Sink threw his arm over Rufus and hugged him close. "Rufus, you're my kind of paratrooper. Let's go!" With that, Sink jumped up and took off to the north, along with the other HQ men and 1st Battalion paratroopers. It took about an hour to get to safety, but artillery fire cut off the Germans and they made it to Hill 30 safely.

After the regiment HQ was secure and contact was made with the other forces, Gilmore was called back to the Regimental CP. "Go see Colonel Sink in the farmhouse over there," was all he was told. When they reported, Sink was tied up with getting the battle in good order. But he took the time to call Jackson and

Rufus over. "I received a request from the 501st to check on you. Seems your brother is helping Colonel Johnson take Carentan from the northeast. I told Colonel Johnson that you and Rufus were fine, and he said the same for your brother. We should meet them later today."

Jackson thanked the Colonel and departed. He was so relieved to hear that Eugene was alive and they would meet up later.

2nd Battalion had moved into Carentan against heavy machine-gun and artillery fire. They pushed on until they met up with 1st Battalion, 401st Glider Infantry, which had attacked from the northeast. The Germans had been pushed out of Carentan, the town cleared of the enemy, now orders came down from division for the 506th to attack west to the town of Baupte, over five miles west of their position. Both 1st and 2nd Battalions began the long march west, along the road and railroad to the north to attack the withdrawing Germans.

Jackson and Rufus were scouts for the battalion. They pressed on but received no machine-gun or mortar fire for an hour. By early afternoon, though, heavy machine-gun fire hit them from far down the railroad. They retreated to the railroad embankment, then made their way back to Easy Company. Machine-gun fire continued, but 2nd Battalion repulsed the German counterattack. Lieutenant Colonel Strayer quickly ordered his battalion to pursue the Germans. They caught up to them near the small village of Douville. The Germans were dug in and the fire was intense. It was later discovered that 2nd Battalion was up against the German 6th Parachute Regiment along with elements of the 17th SS-Panzer Grenadier Division. Fighting went on all day and into the night. Finally, both sides halted fire for the night and hunkered down for the battle that awaited them in the morning.

On Lieutenant Winters' order, Jackson fell back to 2nd Battalion HQ, a small stone house about 500 yards to the rear. He dug a foxhole for him and Rufus, deep enough to allow them to sit up and not be seen. He wasn't ordered to go on night patrol, so he took care of Rufus. Cleaned him up, combed his fur, checked his teeth, cleaned his eyes, and paid careful attention to his paws. They had been walking and running over tough terrain for several days, but Rufus appeared to weather it well. Jackson soaked his paws in salt water for a few minutes, then dried them with the cleanest towel he had. Finally, he settled Rufus on his blanket and prepared dinner.

Several men had donated a tin of meat or stew for Rufus. He filled the bowl with water from his own canteen as he ran out of tins of water days ago. While Rufus ate, he scrounged for something to eat himself. He had a candy bar and a tin of stew; that would have to be good enough. It was about 2200 when he was finally able to sleep. Rufus woke when he climbed into the foxhole, but then laid next to Jackson and fell quickly asleep.

Just as he was falling asleep, someone whispered his name from the edge of his foxhole. Jackson opened his eyes and sat up. Rufus quickly raised in alert at the interloper, growling lowly. "Easy, Rufus, easy," the stranger quietly said. It was First Sergeant Sellers, from Able Company. Rufus immediately lowered his floppy ears and wagged his tail, then jumped out of the foxhole to greet his friend.

As he rubbed on Rufus, Sellers explained what he was doing. "I've been trying to catch up with you for a few days, but we're moving so fast I never could find you. How have y'all been fairing? Had much action?" Jackson smiled and told the story of Rufus' exploits. "I'm real short on food for him, but the guys have all donated whatever they could. My buddy Freddie, you met him at Wellford, remember? Anyway, Freddie caught up with me on our way to Carentan and gave Rufus his only K-ration. I tried to give it back but he refused and left. I did get a message to the Quartermaster Corps through Regiment S-4, but nothings shown up yet."

Clyde smiled, that's why he was there. "I'm on it, kid. Just hang on for another day and I'll have Rufus fixed up. Now take this for tomorrow." Sellers held out a K-ration, but it had been opened. Inside, Jackson found it full of canned meats and vegetables, but a chocolate bar, cigarettes, and other items were removed to make room for more tins. "This should get you through tomorrow. I'll catch up with you later tomorrow night. Get some rest, we're attacking in the morning." Jackson stood and shook Clyde's hands. "Thanks First Sergeant, this is awful good of you, and I appreciate it. And Rufus will too!" Clyde gave Rufus a last scratch between his ears, nodded to Jackson and departed.

Sporadic firing continued throughout the night, but Jackson (and Rufus) were so tired they slept through it. He woke at 0500, stiff, cold, hungry, dirty and tired, the same as all the other fellows. After taking Rufus for a walk to do his business, he set out the last of his water for Rufus. *I'll bum some from the guys later,* he thought with a smile. He knew his buddies would share, especially if he told them he gave his last bit of water to Rufus.

They walked carefully to the main line of defense and saw men moving into attack formations. He found Lieutenant Welsh, Easy Company XO, and asked where he was needed. "Take this to Private Spiers and assist him." 'This" was a M1919 Browning .30 caliber machine-gun and two ammo boxes, received from 2nd Battalion, 502nd PIR. Welsh was hurrying along the line. "And tell Gordon to move down to the left." Jackson turned to leave but Welsh called him. "And Jackson, keep your head down and don't do anything to get Rufus in danger. Clear?" It was clear.

At 0600, the 506th began the attack, but so did the Germans. Both the Americans and Germans attacked with everything they had, artillery, machine-gun, rifle fire, and mortars. 2nd Battalion had formed a skirmish line from north to south, with Easy Company anchored to the railroad embankment, with Dog and Fox Companies on their left flank. The two attacking forces became confused as they passed one another, columns of German armor heading toward Carentan. The German attack was fierce, most of the German infantry had light machine-guns and German artillery was raining down. The German force attempted to overrun the right flank, almost exactly where Jackson was helping Freddie with his machine-gun. Jackson ordered Rufus to DROP and STAY. This made Rufus remain at the base of the machine-gun nest where Gilmore and Gordon were firing and reloading as fast as possible.

As the fire intensified, Easy Company took casualties. The right flank was in danger of falling to overwhelming German forces, but Colonel Sink had requested support, and 2nd Battalion, 502nd PIR joined the 506th and firmed up the right flank. Still, the 506th had to give ground, and fell back to the battalion reserve line due to the superior firepower from the Germans. Easy Company was deployed along a road that crossed the battalion area. Fox Company faced a fierce tank and infantry attack and fell back to join Easy Company at the 2nd Battalion command post, which now was on the front lines. D Company was on F Company's left flank, with 1st Battalion further down on their left. 1st Battalion was under a heavy attack, but 3rd Battalion was called up from reserve to support 1st Battalion.

Now under heavy tank and artillery fire, Fox Company broke and fell back, leaving Easy's left flank exposed. Dog Company's right flank was dangerously exposed as well, and fell back, though not too far so that they could still cover Easy Company's left flank. The Germans tried another flanking maneuver on the north side of the railroad track, but Lieutenant Winters ordered mortars to concentrate in that area, causing the Germans to fall back. A German tank came rushing through a hedgerow on Easy's left flank, the machine-gunner tearing into Easy positions. Gordon returned fire but the gunner was protected by a steel plate and continued chewing up Easy. Spiers also let loose with a barrage of machine-gun fire but had no effect on the tank.

Lieutenant Welsh and PFC John McGrath rushed out from their cover to attack the tank with a bazooka. As McGrath aimed, Welsh loaded a bazooka round, but when the round hit the tank, it just bounced off the heavy shielding. Welsh reloaded and ordered McGrath to wait until the tank showed its vulnerable underbelly. This time the bazooka round entered the belly of the tank and stopped the tank cold. The tank had gotten one last shot off, which screamed over Welsh and McGrath's head, and hit just past Spiers and Gilmore's foxhole. The blast blew both of them out of the foxhole, but Rufus was safe below. Things quieted for a moment, and Rufus slowly raised his head over the ledge. Spiers and Gilmore were nearly unconscious from the concussion. Rufus jumped up, bit into Jackson's collar and dragged him into the foxhole, where he tumbled down. Next Rufus did the same for Freddie, who was just beginning to gain his bearings. Rufus dumped him into the foxhole just as heavy machine-gun fire blazed over his furry head.

After a brief moment, Spiers came around and was able to man his machine-gun, firing at the German line. The rest of the company was firing as fast as they could, mortars flew through across the field into the enemy's hedgerow. Jackson, stunned but okay, fed the belt into the gun. Meanwhile, Lieutenant Colonel Strayer got Fox Company back in line and ordered Dog Company to shore up Easy's left flank.

Fighting continued all day, with any respite doubtful. But at 1030 hours Combat Command A, 2nd Armored Division, charged in with Sherman tanks and infantrymen. The 2nd Armored Division routed the German forces and pushed them all the way past Baupte, the 506th's original objective. Finally, the paratroopers could rest, and fell back to Carentan into division reserve. Jackson took time to look Freddie over. He had a jagged hole in his thigh from shrapnel, a deep cut on his forehead, and more shrapnel in his shoulder. "Let's get you to the aid station. Can you walk?"

Freddie could walk but with a heavy limp, so he put his arm around Jackson's shoulders and leaned heavily on him as they made their way to the aid station. He told Freddie he'd check on him later and departed to rejoin Easy Company. As he neared Easy Company, he saw soldiers from another unit, not paratroopers, entering the area. He heard "Rufus? Is that you Rufus?" Jackson turned and saw a soldier from the 29th Infantry Division staring at him. The soldier walked over to him, staring at Rufus. His tail wagging swiftly, Rufus let out a low keen, dancing on his front paws. But he didn't break the Heel position. "How do you know Rufus?" Jackson asked.

"My sister donated Rufus to the Dogs for Defense program. I never thought I'd see him again." The soldier was Penny's brother, Jimmie, who had enlisted at about the same time as Eugene and Jackson. He was a light machine-gunner in the 116th Infantry Regiment and had come ashore at Omaha Beach, which later became known as the most difficult and deadly of the five landing beaches in Normandy. He was tall, trim, and had short, blondish-red hair. Jackson told Rufus "ITS OKAY," and Rufus rushed to Jimmie, jumping on his chest and nearly knocking him down.

They only had a few minutes to talk as the 29th was moving toward Baupte. But Jackson got Penny's address and told her brother he would write her and tell her all about Rufus. They said goodbye, and another chance meeting that affected Jackson's life had happened again.

That night, the 506th was relieved by the 502nd and moved to division reserve in Carentan. After a hot meal served by the Service Company, he took Rufus to look for Able Company and First Sergeant Sellers. He found Able Company easily but couldn't find Sellers. He found the company command post, full of very tired enlisted and officers. He saw a staff sergeant that seemed alert and got his attention. "Hi Staff Sergeant, I'm looking for First Sergeant Sellers, do you know where he is?"

The sergeant looked gently at Jackson and Rufus. He spoke softly so not to wake any soldiers (He could have yelled and not woke the men, dead-tired from two days of hard fighting). "What business do you have with the first sergeant?" he asked, but not unkindly. Jackson explained his connection to Sellers. "He told me he'd find me tonight and help get food for Rufus, my dog. I thought I'd find him and save him a trip."

The staff sergeant slowly stood, motioned for them to follow him outside. He lit a cigarette before speaking. "Kid, First Sergeant Sellers got hit bad. We were reinforcing the left flank when we were hit by artillery and tank rounds. Clyde took a hit in his left arm; he nearly lost it. Hell, it was hanging on by a tendon and a prayer. I was nearby in a foxhole; he was running around to men giving them orders and directing fire when he got hit. He went down without a word. I rushed to him, hit him with morphine and called for the medics. We got him to the aid station, but they immediately moved him to the regiment hospital in town. I don't know how he's doing."

Jackson was stunned of the news. He didn't know Clyde well at all but knew he was a good man and a good soldier. Before

Jackson could leave, the sergeant stopped him. "Hang on a minute, I think he left something for you." He stepped out of the room and returned quickly with a shoebox-sized container. "Yeah, he definitely left this for you and Rufus."

Inside the container was at least four pounds of fileted horse meat. The meat was salted so it would keep. *Good ole First Sergeant Sellers!* Jackson thought, but then lost his smile when thinking of his friend. After thanking the sergeant, Jackson led Rufus into Carentan, looking for the hospital. He found it easily and asked about his friend. The doctor had to take the arm, but it looked like he would make it. He would be sent back to England as quickly as possible for more surgeries, and then he would be on his way home. "Please tell him I came by to see him, okay? It means a lot to me. I'll write a letter and bring it in the morning if that's okay."

It was okay, the Corporal said, but he wasn't sure when the patients would be shipping out. "Could be the morning, could be tonight, depends on how stable he is. But come by, someone will be able to help you."

Jackson returned to the company area, found Shifty and sat down on the floor in an undestroyed house. It was after midnight now, and Jackson still had to get Rufus squared away. He went through his routine of cleaning Rufus and making sure he was fine. They finally laid down to sleep at 0100 hours. It had been a long, hard day, but they survived. And Rufus' legacy grew even more when Freddie told the story of being dragged into his foxhole by that 'big ole furball'.

***

Eugene had been in a few firefights as well. After helping with demolition of bridges at Le Port, he had tried to get through to 2nd Battalion, 501st at Les Droueries. But heavy fighting and Germans were between Lieutenant Colonel Ballard's troops and Colonel Johnson at La Barquette. They returned and reported that they were unable to contact Ballard. Colonel Johnson, 501st PIR, told Gilmore to return to Le Port and took the remaining men in his command and marched north. Johnson thought that with additional strength he could destroy the bridges over the Douve River.

Eugene returned to Le Port and crawled into his foxhole. He was dead tired, wet, grimy, and hungry. Even so, he fell asleep easily. He remained at Le Port with Shettle and McNiece for five days, defending the bridges from sporadic German attacks. They had very little food and water, but the men shared what they had. A German sniper harassed them for a few days, killing five men, until finally PFC Jack Agnew spied him in a two-story building and filled the window with bullets.

Seaborne forces from Utah Beach, originally planned to meet them at the bridges on D-Day +1, had still not appeared by D-Day +3. Colonel Sink had no contact with 3rd Battalion and assumed the demolition team had failed to secure the bridge. Late afternoon on the 3rd day, four P-51 Mustangs bombed the bridges, then bombed the paratroopers, not realizing they were Americans. The mission completed for them, the group began moving north on June 11 to join Colonel Johnson and the 501st PIR. They were then relieved by the 327th Glider Infantry Regiment.

On June 11, Colonel Johnson told the men of the 506th they could join their unit, several miles west of Carentan. As Eugene got ready to depart, Colonel Johnson pulled him aside. "I sure could use your engineering skills, Lieutenant. But I understand if you want to join your unit."

Gilmore paused, not sure what he should do. "Sir, I sure would like to get back to the 506th. My brother is in Easy Company, 2nd Battalion, and I'd like to make sure he's okay."

Johnson understood but offered a deal. "Gilmore, if you stay with me, I'll get word to Sink to personally ask about your brother. We'll meet up with the 506th south of Carentan at Hill 30, but my men need help building a treadway bridge. Can you help?" Johnson looked cold and hard at Gilmore, then his demeanor eased, and he put his hand on Eugene's shoulder.

"I know you've been through a lot, but I need you, you're the only combat engineering officer I'm aware of, and those enlisted need some help. I'll get word of your brother as soon as possible. Now let's go." That was not a request, but a 'soft' order. Eugene knew he needed to help so he turned south with Johnson.

Eugene made a few changes to strengthen the treadway bridge, but the enlisted men, some of them his, it turned out, had done a bang-up job. The bridge was sound and ready to allow the 501st, 327th and the 401st Glider Infantry to take the attack into Carentan. That night, artillery fire was incredible and set Carentan ablaze. The following morning, the 506th met up with Johnson's group and Carentan was taken.

Eugene was able to get away the next day after Carentan was secured. He found Jackson and Rufus near Easy Company CP; a deserted stone house partially destroyed. Jackson and Rufus had a large foxhole covered in hay along the bottom to keep warm and dry. "Eugene! I heard you were looking for me!" Jackson was excited and relieved to see his brother. They stayed near the command post as there were still lone German snipers hiding south of Carentan.

They went to get chow, near the regimental HQ temporary command post. The line wasn't too long and soon they had hot chow, stew with vegetables, potatoes, and cubes of beef. Eugene looked like he hadn't slept in a week, which was close to truth. As they sat and ate, Sink left his command post but spotted Rufus. He remembered he had a message.

"Corporal Gilmore, I want you to know that I appreciate all you did these couple of weeks, and I'm mighty pleased you and Rufus survived. But I don't need a dead hero dog. Understand?"

Jackson rose to attention while Sink advised him. Rufus rose to Heel position on his own, with no order. "So, from now on, you tread more carefully, you hear? And if there's anything you need, you let me know, okay son?" Sink looked at Rufus, reached down and scratched his ears. "What about Rufus? You need anything for him?"

He surely did! "Yes sir I do. Rufus needs supplies, I'm out of food and cleaning supplies for him, and his blanket and harness have nearly rotted. I guess, sir, well I just need to get help from the Quartermasters."

Sink nodded, he understood. "Okay. Well, you go see your platoon leader, tell him to take you to battalion S-4, with orders from me to take your order and get it filled, today. Clear?" Jackson grinned from ear to ear. "Yes sir, thank you sir!"

Sink nodded his head and turned to go, but spied Eugene. He reached out and shook his hand. "Lieutenant, I hear you did some good work on destroying a few bridges and fixing a few more. Damn fine job, son. Who are you with now?" Sink knew that Gilmore was assigned to 3rd Battalion for the jump, but after the first day on the Cotentin Peninsula plans went out the window.

"Hey sir, good to see you. I guess I'm still with Colonel Johnson, but I've been working with the demolition platoon from HQ Company. We haven't stopped until today, sir."

Sink was a little taken aback. "You've been fighting with McNiece? Let me give you some advice. Stay away from him and the rest of the 'Filthy Thirteen,' you hear? McNiece is a damn good soldier, but he doesn't care a thing for officers. He'd as soon break your jaw as he would shake your hand. So be careful."

Eugene was surprised by Sink's words. *Filthy Thirteen? What is he talking about?* "We got along just fine sir. I told him to call me Gilmore, we covered each other a few times and I helped his team rig the bridges. I shot a German bearing down on him, and after that he was just fine with me."

Sink finished his cigarette, field stripped it before commenting. "Well, even so, I want you to rejoin the 326th, now. Go to my CP, find Captain Matheson and tell him I said to get you to your unit." With that, Sink turned and departed. Eugene stayed with his little brother a few minutes more to talk and visit, then slowly departed to get going to his unit. Shifty joined them, then Don Malarkey, Wild Bill Guarnere, George Luz, and Skip Muck. They all wanted to greet Rufus.

Word had spread of Rufus's actions since D-Day. Though the paratroopers had acted with valor and pride, they were surprised to hear of how fearless Rufus had acted. Rufus ate it up. The last eight days had been very tough on him. He didn't understand what was happening, only that there were men trying to hurt his friends, and he would not allow that to happen. The men understood it too and vowed they would protect their four-legged brother with their life if called for.

***

The next day the battalion S-2, Lieutenant Nixon, ordered a patrol. Winters asked men to volunteer, but none stepped forward. Before Winters could make an order, Jackson and Rufus stepped forward. "We'll go on patrol, sir," Jackson stated firmly. Before the Lieutenant could 'volunteer' anyone, several men stepped up. Guarnere, Shifty, Lesniewski and Blithe would also go on the patrol, with Guarnere lead.

There was a cluster of small cottages and farm buildings interlocked with surrounding hedgerows. Nixon thought a German command post was located in and around the buildings. Guarnere asked Jackson to take point. "You know what to do. Stay along the hedgerow, let Rufus get a scent of Krauts and we'll cover you." Two hundred yards away from the farm, Jackson eased Rufus into a hedgerow. "Look close, boy, look close." Rufus put his nose to the earth, then high in the air. He sniffed the air for a long moment, then sat down. That meant he smelled Germans but wasn't sure how far or in what direction.

Jackson, in point with Rufus, left the cover of the hedgerow and moved to a downed tree about 30 yards towards the farm. Again, Rufus sniffed the earth, then the air. This time he left his nose in the air much longer. He moved his nose left and right several times, until he finally stopped, and pointed to a two-story cottage about 150 yards away. Jackson signaled to Guarnere: 'German 150 yards south, move up under cover.'

Suddenly Rufus jerked his head in the air. He didn't smell anything, he *heard* something. Rufus had his ears as elevated as they would go, listening with all his might. He had heard a sound, a metal-on-metal sound, one that he knew. It was the sound of a machine-gun being full-loaded and releasing the bolt. Rufus crouched into attack position, which saved his life. A bullet zinged by Rufus' head, through the tip of his right ear. Sniper! The crack of the sniper rifle was followed by machine-gun bullets spraying all around them. Guarnere opened fire on the farm house, along with the rest of the patrol. Jackson pulled Rufus back to the hedgerow, not caring about enemy fire. Guarnere watched the German machine-gunner track the pair, as the bullets got closer and closer. Wild Bill took aim and opened up on the gunner with his Thompson and laced the 2nd story window with round after round. The machine-gun stopped, only M-1 Garands were firing. Lieutenant Welsh ordered a cease-fire, and the men regrouped. No one was wounded. Well, not quite true. Jackson was tending to Rufus' ear, a bloody mess as the bullet had gone through the tip of his ear but shredded it along the way.

Lieutenant Winters joined them as they checked on Rufus. Winters sent for a medic to treat their point man, which was how many of the men now thought of the large, black-brown dog. Even as he sat there calmly, Doc Roe, Easy Company medic from Louisiana, poured a sulfa treatment on his ear, then covered it in a bandage. "Let's get him to the Aid Station now."

Two men carried Rufus on a stretcher, although Jackson said he could walk. The bleeding had slowed, thanks to the sulfa. Rufus kept his eyes on Jackson, walking beside the stretcher. His ear hurt, but not too bad. Rufus didn't know what hit him, but he heard it as it zinged through his ear. The trip to the battalion aid station only took a few minutes, and they hurried inside the large tent.

A few of the men went with Jackson into the aid station. The doctor at the BAS had no issues treating a dog and allowed the men to remain near their platoon buddy. He looked at the ear, a nurse had cleaned it thoroughly, and he thought he could save most of it. "I think I can cut off the tip just below the bullet hole, and he'll be fine. He may look funny but he'll survive."

When all the men broke out in huge guffaws, the doctor looked up in surprise. "What's so funny? I said he'll make it!" Jackson laughed again. "Doc, we're laughing because Rufus is already the funniest looking dog in the U.S. Army! This might help his looks a little bit!"

Rufus healed up quickly, and the men of the 506th were finally called off the line. On June 28, the 83rd Infantry Division arrived from Omaha Beach to relieve the 101st. The men were pulled back to a field camp near Utah Beach. For the first time in 23 days, the men had hot showers, clean uniforms, and new socks and skivvies. On July 11, Easy Company marched aboard a large LST, or Landing Ship, Tank, for the short sail to England. The following night, the men arrived in Southampton, and by the next day, July 13, they arrived home, in Aldbourne.

***

9

ALDBOURNE AND HOLLAND

The folks of Aldbourne welcomed 'their' soldiers home with open arms. They had read of the exploits of the paratroopers and were proud of 'their boys.' The papers had reported nearly daily on the exploits of the American paratroopers. But once the men received new uniforms and back pay, most of them departed for London.

The paratroopers were busy after returning to Aldbourne. After returning from London or other places, the men began training. They were first refitted with new uniforms and weapons, and men were promoted. Winters had been promoted to Captain and officially named the Easy Company CO in early July. He recommended First Sergeant James Diel for a battlefield commission to Second Lieutenant. Don Malarkey, Skip Muck, Mike Ranney and Paul Rogers were promoted to sergeant. Also promoted were 2nd Lieutenants Welsh and Compton to First Lieutenant. Bill Guarnere and Leo Boyle became staff sergeants. But Captain Winters didn't know what to do with Gilmore and Rufus. He talked to Lieutenant Colonel Strayer and Major Horton, and finally saw Colonel Sink.

"What are your intentions, Dick?" Sink was behind his desk at Littlecote, a warm fire making the large office cozy. He removed a cigarette from a pack, lit it, took a deep breath, and looked squarely at Winters.

Winters was not intimidated by Sink. He'd been around the

man long enough to know he was a good soldier, fair with the men except for a few cases, and had promoted Winters twice. "Sir, I've discussed this with my NCO's and officers. I'd like to promote Corporal Gilmore to sergeant. He's done an incredible job, the men like him and Rufus, and he's needed in 3rd Platoon."

Sink was dismissive. "Fine, fine, promote him to T/4, and don't forget his dog gets promoted too. Anything else?" He looked at a stack of papers needing his review, picked up the top report and began reading. Winters wasn't done. "Sir, I'd like to promote Gilmore to sergeant and make him a rifle squad leader in 3rd Platoon. I think he's earned the right to lead a squad, but I know he has other…uh, responsibilities, with Rufus."

"Promote him to sergeant, as a squad leader? What about his dog? You just going to ship him back to the states?" Winters had a plan, and he explained it. Keep Rufus as his partner. Allow Gilmore to perform any functions required, such as night patrol or silent scout. "I know Gilmore can handle the work, and Rufus will help keep the men in line."

The Colonel sat back in his chair, took a long draw on his cigarette, and licked his lips before he spoke. "Captain Winters, I think that is an excellent idea. Get it done and make Rufus a staff sergeant. Anything else?" There was. "I'm putting Gilmore and Rufus in for a Silver Star, and also a Purple Heart for both of them."

Sink guffawed loudly. "Son, you can put in all the awards you want, and I'll approve and send up to Division HQ. But the Army decided a few months ago to not allow dogs to receive awards. So write them up and I'll approve. But tell me this. Which action are your writing them up for? Taking out that machine-gun nest on D-Day? Or helping you at Brecourt?"

"Well, sir, I was actually thinking of the machine-gun nest for Gilmore and Rufus, and then Rufus' actions at Carentan, when he pulled Spiers and Gilmore to safety after they were hit by a tank round,"

"Hmmph. Alright then, see the 506th S-1 for help. Good job."

The promotion was a surprise to Jackson. He'd led squads in training and did good work. He studied the field manual while other soldiers spent their nights in pubs. What he needed was soldiers that believed in him and trusted his abilities. He asked and received a promotion for Spiers to Corporal, who would act as Jackson's assistant squad leader. He felt comfortable with Freddie and Rufus by his side. But he also had five replacements that had no experience and needed to be trained.

Jackson stayed in Aldbourne with Rufus. His ear was healed but Jackson just wanted to rest and write letters home, especially to his mother and Penny. And there were men in the hospital that he needed to visit. Jackson found Freddie, Lipton, and Popeye Wynn at the Army hospital in Marlborough. Freddie and Smokey had been wounded on the line outside of Carentan, at "The Battle of Bloody Gulch." Lipton had been wounded by an artillery round while taking Carentan, Popeye had been shot in his buttocks while taking the 105's at Brecourt Manor. They were happy to see Jackson and Rufus and commented about his ear.

"He looks better, maybe let him take a bullet in his other ear."

"At least he can raise one of his ears now!" Jackson laughed along with the fellas as Rufus made his rounds to see the men.

Gilmore returned to the nurse's station. He asked for First Sergeant Sellers but was told he wasn't taking visitors. "Could you tell him that Sergeant Jackson Gilmore is here to see him? Please?"

The orderly shook his head. "The first sergeant said he didn't want any visitors. Period." Jackson made another try. "Would you please tell him that Staff Sergeant Rufus is here to see him? Just tell him that, please?" The orderly let out a sigh, followed by a grunt, but walked down the hall into a small ward. He was gone for only a minute when he returned. "Hmmm. He said for both of you to come on back. Is that dog clean?" Gilmore smiled. "He's cleaner than you or me both, I promise."

The ward was small, with only eight beds along the walls. There were overhead lights but only one light near the door was on. Each bed had a table lamp, but few were on. Sergeant Sellers was in the last bed on the right, in a dark corner with his lamp off. Jackson approached slowly, Rufus walking as slowly and light as possible. Clyde was awake, but his skin was pale, he appeared weak and pallid, and looked like he had lost 30 pounds. His left arm was wrapped in gauze just above where the elbow would have been. Jackson gulped when he saw the wounded man. Sellers was an 'old man' of 30 years, which is old for a paratrooper. In reality he was only seven years older than Jackson, but that seven years was spent in the Army in numerous positions of leadership. Clyde had been selected as First Sergeant for many reasons, mostly because of his natural leadership and management ability. Now he was going home.

Jackson spoke quietly. "Hey First Sergeant, we sure have missed you. Did you get my letter?" He had written a letter to Sellers just as he said he would and hustled it back to the field hospital in Carentan the morning that Sellers shipped out for England. It had been a month, but Jackson had not received a reply. Now he knew why. Clyde was not well, physically, mentally or spiritually. One look at him and you knew he was on the verge of giving up, on everything.

"I wanted to thank you for the food for Rufus. Without your help, well, I'm not sure what would have happened. Rufus made it, though, and boy did he!" Now Jackson got excited as he told Clyde of Rufus' exploits. Clyde didn't respond at first, until Rufus left Jackson and placed his head on the right side of the bed. He placed his nose on Clyde's good arm, nudging him for some attention. Clyde looked down at a furry face, and after a moment began rubbing him along his head, neck and back. He didn't say anything, just quietly petted Rufus while Jackson told his tale. Rufus wagged his tail, licked Clyde's hand, then jumped and placed his front paws on the bed.

Clyde was surprised but visually brightened up with a big grin and laugh. Rufus began licking Clyde's face and neck, until Clyde finally had to tell him to stop. But his demeanor had changed drastically, and he thanked Jackson. "It sure is good to see you too, Rufus." Then his face turned dark again. He lowered his eyes. "I haven't let anyone in to talk, until you and Rufus. I don't want to see anyone, see their sorrow, their sympathy, their *pity*. I just want to get out of here and go home." He looked away from Jackson, but in doing so looked directly at Rufus. He resumed petting him again.

"I can't explain how I feel, you know? I feel…I feel…like I've let my men down. I was supposed to make sure they were safe and doing things the smart way and not going off to be heroes. Now look at me. I'm useless to the Army, and I don't know what else I'll ever do."

That was hard to listen too, Jackson wasn't ready for this kind of conversation. But he had to help his friend. "First Sergeant, that's about the biggest load of malarkey I've ever heard. You took a shot from the Germans and survived. Now get healed, go back home. Go through rehabilitation, then see what the Army offers. They may make a drill instructor out of you, or training soldiers and paratroopers. Heck, I bet I could even swing a gig with the K-9 Corps if you want to try. I may be just another K-9 trainer, but I have friends that can make stuff happen. What do you think?"

Clyde *did* perk up at the mention of K-9 Corps. More than anything, he needed to be useful again. "You know what, Gilmore, you may just have a good idea. Okay, suppose I go through rehab, get checked out. Then the Army releases me. What then? Army pay and disability will only go so far."

Jackson explained. He would write a letter to his old friend and trainer, Henry Stoecker, from the Pillicoc Kennels in New Jersey. Henry would find a spot for Clyde; he knew he could. As they talked, Clyde seemed to ease up and talk about his family, his wife and two small girls. He last saw them in August 1943, right before he shipped out with the 101st. Jackson stayed a little longer but could tell Clyde tired easily, so he said goodbye. "But I'll be back as often as I can, you just keep getting better." Sellers smiled and said he would, then asked "Hey, be sure to bring Rufus too, okay?"

As Jackson quietly left the bedside, he was stopped by one of the other patients. "Hey Sergeant, would you mind coming over here for a minute? You and your dog?" It came from a private, on the opposite side of Clyde but down a few beds. Jackson looked and saw that he was missing both legs. His head swirled for a moment, then he fought it off. "Sure Private, what's your name?"

His name was Joseph Dolan, from the 505th PIR. He landed at Zone A on D-Day, formed up with a group of about 50 paratroopers and officers, and attacked a German garrison near Sainte-Marie-du-Mont. The garrison had artillery support and killed and wounded numerous men until paratroopers overran the position. Joe was from Kentucky, age 21, enlisted in 1943 and joined the Paratroopers in early 1944.

As he and Jackson talked, Rufus eased up to Joe's bed, finally placed both paws on the bed to be close to Joe. Dolan smiled as he rubbed on the thick fur along his back and neck. "I miss my dog a lot. He's just a mutt, but he sure is a good dog. When I get back I can't wait to take him hunting agai….."

Joe lowered his head, closed his eyes, and quietly sobbed. Rufus, sensing the pain, keened softly and leaned in to lick Joe's face. Joe put an arm around Rufus and just held him, until his tears went away. Jackson wasn't sure what to say, but he could not *not* say anything. "You know what Joe? I bet you go hunting plenty of times when you get home. You may not walk or run like you used to, but the Army will help you. Give me your address and when I get home I'll invite you to come hunting on our land. Deal?"

Joe was better but asked Jackson to come back and visit. As they turned to go out again, several men asked to see Rufus. Jackson took his time and spent equal amounts with each man. Rufus didn't have to be told that these men were 'Good Friends.' He sensed their pain and suffering and knew it was his job to ease it. He did so by giving love to the soldiers.

When they finally left the room, Jackson stopped and leaned against the wall. He started shaking, his head in his hands. Rufus nudged his nose against Jackson's leg, getting his attention. Jackson was still shaken but began to calm himself. He knew he needed to do something.

He returned to the orderly station and asked to speak to someone in charge of the recovery ward. He was left waiting in the hall outside the nurse station when a doctor, a full bird colonel, introduced himself. "I'm Doctor Harrison, I was told you needed to speak to someone in charge?"

Harrison was a small man, wore glasses and was balding. But he looked every bit a competent surgeon. Jackson wasn't sure what he wanted to say but he tried. "Hello sir, I'm Sergeant Gilmore, and this is Sergeant Rufus. We're a K-9 unit assigned to 2nd Battalion, 506th PIR. We came to visit some of the fellows and see them off. But something happened…well, it's like this. When the wounded men saw Rufus, they brightened up and wanted to see him, rub his fur, just be with him, you know? Pretty soon they'd be smiling or even laughing."

Doctor Harrison saw where Gilmore was going but prodded him on. "Go ahead, son, it's okay." Jackson struggled to continue. "Well sir, a thought occurred to me, that if we brought a few dogs through here, it might cheer the men up a little bit. Just make sure the dogs are good natured, the smaller the better. Why, bring a small dog in here to put in a soldier's lap and I bet he'd forget his pain for a few minutes." He realized he was telling a colonel how to run his hospital.

"Uhhh, sorry sir, that was just a thought I had. Thank you for your time, sir." The colonel was impressed. "Hold on, Sergeant. You say you saw the men smile, and laugh? Just because they got to pet your dog?" It was simple, really. Rufus was so friendly and funny, you couldn't help but feel better around him.

Harrison thanked him for his help, then added, "Let me know when you come back. I have a few men I'd like to introduce you too. Some men are having a very hard time with injuries, and maybe your dog could help them." Jackson quickly agreed, and over the next few weeks made several trips to the hospital. The Colonel, impressed with Jackson, wrote a letter of commendation to Colonel Sink for Jackson and Rufus' actions.

***

On August 10, 1944, the 101st Airborne Division, spread throughout southern England, formed up in Hungerford to conduct a general review for General Eisenhower. The 506th departed Aldbourne at 0530 hours and rode the eight miles in worn out trucks. Soon, other units arrived, including units from the 439th Troop Carrier Group, the same group that flew the

506th to the Cotentin Peninsula on D-Day.

Rufus rode along with Jackson in the back of a Dodge 2 1/2 ton truck. It was a short ride, but as always, it was crowded and dirty. No one talked, a few smoked, a few chewed tobacco or dipped snuff, but most just rode with arms crossed and eyes closed.

The review was not scheduled until 1000 hours, the men would form up at 0800, until then they had time to find breakfast. The regiment had sent an advanced party to set up mess tents and CPs for the battalions and companies. The men wore Class A uniforms, with medals and ribbons adorned on both chests. Rufus wore his vest with jump wings and staff sergeant rank. They tagged along with other 3rd Platoon men to the mess tent. Jackson sat with Rufus in the back, alone. He gave Rufus water in a bowl and a piece of toast to carry him over until supper. This was when he missed his buddy, Freddie. Freddie always had the scoop on what was happening, where to go, when to hide, and when to get in line for the goodies. He hoped Freddie would return soon and made a note to go visit him again.

They began forming up for review at 0800. The 101st was made up of 13,000 troops, formed up by units, beginning with regiments:

- 327th and 401st Glider Infantry Regiments
- 501st, 502nd, and 506th Parachute Infantry Regiments
- 377th Parachute Field Artillery Battalion
- 321st and 907th Glider Field Artillery Battalion
- 101st Airborne Signal Company
- 326th Airborne Engineer Battalion (Eugene's unit)
- 326th Airborne Medical Company
- 426th Airborne Quartermaster Company

It took over an hour for the units to form up for the parade in review. At 0955, General Eisenhower arrived with his entourage. After introductions, handshakes and courtesies, the review started. It took 10 minutes before the 506th passed in review. Jackson had Rufus on a short leash as they marched. He was located on the back left corner so Rufus could march on his left.

Rufus was perfect, no barks or unnecessary movements; he marched straight ahead with his eyes intently on Jackson.

With the review completed, the units stacked up in front of the review stand. A captain took the microphone. "The following personnel are to fall out and form up in front of the reviewing stand. First Lieutenant Walter G. Amerman, 506th, Sergeant Jackson J. Gilmore, 506th, Captain William P. Lee, 501st..."

The list was not long, only a dozen or so men. They were instructed to form up in one row. General Eisenhower was led by his staff to a position in front of the men. The first man called was a staff sergeant from the 501st. He was presented the Distinguished Service Cross by Ike himself. Only two men from the 506th were out front, Gilmore and Ammerman. Jackson was at the far left, at the end. Finally, his name was called, he marched smartly, turned in front of Ike and saluted the Supreme Commander of Allied Forces in Europe. Ike returned the salute. A major on Ike's staff read the award:

"..For conspicuous gallantry in action on the 6th of June, 1944 at Normandy, France. Corporal Gilmore formed a small group of paratroopers from multiple units and led the attack on an enemy machine-gun nest. He quickly gave orders to his unit, then single-handedly attacked the enemy, knocking out the machine gun nest while taking no injuries to his unit while taking four enemy prisoners, thereby allowing many paratroopers to advance safely. His courage and devotion to duty reflect the highest credit upon himself and the United States Army."

Jackson was astonished. He didn't deserve this! Rufus did the work! He would say something. As Ike approached with the medal, Rufus remained attention. "Thank you for your service, son," Ike said with obvious sincerity. "Where are you and your dog from?"

"We're both from Tennessee, Sir. Sergeant Rufus was donated to the Dogs for Defense program and I was lucky enough to be paired up with him." Ike took a step back after pinning the medal on Gilmore's jacket and gave a good look at Rufus. "He looks like he's seen some action too, how'd he do?" Ike seemed genuinely interested, so Jackson told the truth.

"Sir, Rufus deserves this medal, not me. He led the attack on the machine gun nest, he attacked two Germans outside of Carentan that were trying to overrun the Regimental CP, and he saved my life the next day by dragging my unconscious body into my foxhole before another tank round killed me. He deserves this more than I ever will. Sir."

Ike was taken aback by Jackson's confession. He didn't know what to say, so he looked at Rufus. "Can I pet Rufus?" Ike was a little wary of military dogs. Last year, in Italy, he met Chips, a German Shepherd-Collie mix with some Huskie mixed in too. Ike was talking to Chip's handler, Private John Rowell, when he bent down to pet Chips, forgetting that K-9s were trained to bite anyone but his handler. Chips didn't make an exception for Ike and nipped him on the hand.

Jackson had decided on his own that Rufus would be more relaxed around soldiers, and trained him to let others touch him, IF Gilmore allowed it. The FRIEND, GOOD FRIEND, and BEST FRIEND orders were Jackson's way of allowing the men around him to enjoy Rufus. Now, he bent to Rufus, pointed at Ike, and gave the BEST FRIEND command. As Ike went to bend down, Rufus jumped on Ike, putting his front paws on his shoulders and gave Ike a huge, wet lick on his face. Ike tumbled back on his haunch, his hat flying off, Jackson pulled Rufus back, while several of Ike's staff and personal guards hurried to help the general to his feet. All Jackson could think of was how much trouble he was in. One Sergeant, a guard, glared at Gilmore as he helped lift his General to his feet. "Sir, I'll detain this man and his dog until you decide what to do with him," the Sergeant said with a chill in his voice.

Instead, when Ike stood and someone handed him his hat, he was laughing. He waved off the statement by his Sergeant. "No need for that, it was quite unintentional." He reached down and let Rufus smell his hand, then petted him on his head and neck, and rubbed his ears. Rufus took it all, enjoying the attention. Ike laughed again. "I don't seem to have much luck with K-9s. But Rufus looks like a good boy and a good paratrooper. He really jumped with you into Normandy?"

Relieved, Jackson took a breath. "He did sir. He loves to jump. We have over 20 jumps together. It's the only way we know how to jump, together, I mean." Ike suddenly remembered something. "Is Rufus the dog that Prime Minister Churchill took a shine to and called me about before you jumped into France?"

"He sure is sir! And you can see, we made it just fine. We're paratroopers, sir, we take care of each other." Ike was impressed and made a note to call Churchill and let him know Rufus was fine.

After the awards, the men were dismissed to join their units, and Ike gave a short speech where he expressed his tremendous appreciation for what the division did in Normandy, and that the 101st would soon return to fight the enemy.

Eisenhower's guard hunted down Gilmore. "Hold up kid, I need to talk to you." Jackson stopped and turned to the Sergeant. "Sergeant, I'm real sorry about Rufus jumping on General Eisenhower, but it was an accident. Rufus was already on his way to the General when he bent down. It was an accident, and the General said as much."

Sergeant Lonnie Oakes looked straight at Rufus. Oakes was older, in his mid-thirties, tall and slim but with chiseled features and appeared very fit. He grew up in Attalla County, Mississippi, and enlisted in 1942 when he was 34 years old. Being older than all his fellow soldiers, he was given leadership positions throughout basic training, was a crackerjack sharpshooter with the M-1, but wise men decided to send him to Europe in 1943 to join Eisenhower's staff as a personal guard.

He spoke to Jackson in a kind voice. "Sorry Gilmore, I'm here to apologize to you. Ike brushed it off and enjoyed meeting Rufus. I just want to apologize to being a little heavy-handed back there. No hard feelings?" Jackson smiled and stuck out his hand. Oakes grabbed his hand and shook it with a powerful grip. "Shucks, Sergeant, you didn't have to come out and look for me. No hard feelings! Now meet Rufus. Rufus, GOOD FRIEND."

Rufus looked at Sergeant Oakes, wagged his tail, and brushed up to the Sergeant. Lonnie broke into a huge smile and knelt down to pet him. "He sure is a good looking boy, a little odd looking, but still a good looking dog." Jackson gave him the story about Rufus' lineage and his heroics. "Well, he's sure done his part to defeat the Nazis. Ike said y'all are going back into action soon. Keep your heads down, both of y'all." He shook hands with Jackson and Rufus and hustled back to Eisenhower's staff.

Gilmore thought about what Ike had said. *He said we'd be back in the fight soon, but where?* Just over a month later, Ike was true to his words.

***

September 3, 1944
Aldbourne, England

    Dear Jackson,
    I was so happy to receive your letter! Jimmie wrote and told me all about meeting you and Rufus in France! I am so relieved to hear you are both doing well and are safe. Please send me a photograph of you and Rufus if you can. I am enclosing some hard candies and cookies mother and I made for you and Rufus (but we know you will share them with your friends).
    I cried when you told me about taking Rufus to the hospital. Rufus is such a good boy, no wonder all the soldiers want to pet him and give him a hug. I am so proud of both of you, and I'm going to call the newspaper and tell them all about what you are doing.
    Mother reads every newspaper article she can about the war. Now that she knows about you and Rufus, she said she will save all articles about the paratroopers for you when you return. We are so worried about all of you brave boys in France. We pray for all of you every night and every Sunday at church. We now have three Gold Stars in our windows, for Jimmie, you, and Rufus!
    Please take care of yourself and Rufus. I hope I will get to meet you when this war is over. I included my freshman school picture, my red hair is a mess!
    With constant prayers, I am forever grateful, and your friend,
    Penny

***

The next few weeks saw Easy Company get outfitted in new uniforms, field gear, and rifles. They spent hours at the rifle range to zero them in. They spent several days and nights working field problems to provide experience for the replacements. Jackson spent most of his time with the new fellows, teaching them tricks he had been taught that were not in the paratrooper basic field manual FM 31-30. Freddie rejoined Easy Company in mid-August and fell right in as assistant squad leader.

One night in early September, Jackson led his squad on a night field exercise. They were taken to a field and 'dropped' from the back of a truck, what they called a 'tailgate drop.' Their task was to clear any 'enemies' from a few abandoned barns, donated to the paratroopers for training. Jackson split the men into two sections, with him and Spiers leading them. They approached from the north, behind hedgerows, and split to make a pincer movement.

A new kid, a replacement, would not remain quiet. He was complaining about everything. "Why are we out here in the middle of the night? It's wet, cold, and I'm hungry!"

The other men tried to get him to be quiet. "Shut up Smith, you moron! Be quiet!" Jackson heard the grumblings and sent Rufus to the rear. He gave the sign for SILENCE (covered his ears), and said "get 'em in line, boy." Rufus quickly but quietly went down the line of soldiers, looking each in their eyes, until he reached Smith. Private Smith was still mumbling and trying to get to something in his musette bag, making too much noise. Rufus looked him in the eyes and growled lowly. Smith looked up at Rufus, then slapped him across the head, hitting his damaged ear. Rufus didn't make a sound but pulled away and growled again.

Two men grabbed Smith and took him down, hard. Smith screamed and fought, until Gilmore joined them and held Smith down. "Shut up you fool! Billy, get the section together, we're falling back." He sent a runner to Freddie's section so they could both fall back together. Gilmore formed them up and they marched back to camp.

He released the men when they returned to Aldbourne, except

for Private Smith. Spiers joined him as they took Smith to the First Sergeant's tent. Lipton was already at work, reviewing the training schedule Captain Winters and Sergeant Boyle had planned for the day. "First Sergeant Lipton, we have a problem and need help."

Gilmore told Lipton of the events from the night. Lipton was angrier than any time Gilmore had seen before. "You put the lives of your fellow soldiers at risk because you can't follow simple orders? And you struck a superior officer? I don't see how you ever made it through paratrooper training!"

The problem was quickly becoming a big problem for the 101st. Replacements did not have the training required to join the paratroopers. They had gone through boot camp, then a four-week paratrooper course at Fort Benning. Even soldiers who have been fighting, veterans of D-Day, only completed a two-week jump school at Chilton Foliat. While difficult, it was nothing like the training the men had gone through at Camp Toccoa, not the many field exercises they had performed in the states and England. The Army provided them with replacements barely out of boot camp, it was the 101st's job to turn them into paratroopers.

Lipton wanted to court martial Smith, but Gilmore had another idea. "Let me and Freddie take him out on a three-day field exercise, just the three of us. We'll leave Friday and return Sunday. If he isn't better then you can do what you want with him." Lipton thought about it, then said "If that's how you want to spend your weekend, then okay. But you might consider taking all your replacements."

***

September 8, 1944

Jackson got his replacements in a loose formation and Freddie led them out. They marched for five miles, took a break, then continued. He marched them the rest of the day until they arrived at the abandoned barns where Smith had caused a scene. "What the hell? We could have ridden in a truck like we did last time!" That was from Smith.

Gilmore remained calm. He ordered the men to make camp. Some had brought K-rations, but Smith hadn't. Spiers lost it. "You mean you were told to prep for a field exercise and didn't bring any food? You can starve as far as I care, you dumass!"

It was late afternoon, and the temperature was getting cooler. Gilmore set up his tent, set out Rufus' gear and began grooming him. Never short on sarcasm, Smith looked at Gilmore and said "I don't see why you have a stupid dog with you. And you treat him better than you do us. Maybe I ought to say something to First Sergeant Lipton about that?" Gilmore continued grooming Rufus, cleaned his paws, nose, face, and ears. He set out his water and food bowls and prepared a meal of horse meat, vegetable stew and rice. After he was done, he turned his attention to Smith.

"Y'all come on over here, I have a few things to say." The men stood in front of Jackson. All of them young, none more than 19 years old. There was Johnny Morgan from Baltimore, Ralph Mize from Oregon, George Parker from Pennsylvania, Frank Hall from South Carolina, and Smith from Missouri.

He sat and had the men do the same. "Look guys, we're all in this together. I know y'all are new guys, replacements, and the old guys don't take to you very well, but they will. It's my job to train you how to fight at a squad level, how to walk a night patrol or be a silent scout. Besides our last exercise, have any of you been on a night patrol?"

They hadn't. Jackson explained the basics of night patrol, emphasizing the need for silence, while looking straight at Smith. "Well, I think we understand the need for silence now. We all depend on each other to stay alive, and when we go back into battle, I need to know that each of you have my back, and the back of every paratrooper, just like I have yours. And the same goes for Rufus."

Smith took issue to that. "I ain't risking my life for your mutt! And he tried to bite me last time we were out. Yeah, he did!" Smith looked angrily at Rufus, who sat patiently by Jackson. "Look," Gilmore pleaded, "Rufus has been through K-9 Corps training, 13 weeks of basic at Camp Toccoa, a 115-mile march through ice and rain, and jump school at Benning. He's been with the 506th since we formed up. He is a staff sergeant in the U.S. Army, and you will by God treat him with RESPECT!"

Gilmore let out a deep breath. He had allowed his temper to rise and needed to calm down. But he had the men's attention. "Rufus saved my life on D-Day by capturing a machine Gun nest all by himself. At Carentan he saved me and Freddie's life by pulling our unconscious bodies into a foxhole after we took a tank round that nearly killed us. All the men in Easy Company accept Rufus as a paratrooper and treat him with respect. If any of you have a problem with that, then we need to settle it right now." Gilmore stood up. He didn't realize it, but he had a look of authority, toughness, and his face said, "I'll whip every one of your replacement asses if I have too!"

Smith didn't respond, but the other men did. Each of them agreed to everything Gilmore had said, they were ready to learn and become useful to the squad, and Easy.

After dismissing the men, he told Freddie he was going hunting. "I should be back before nightfall, but if not make sure the men set a perimeter and take turns at standing watch." He headed west with Rufus to a small stand of trees leading to a valley. Jackson had calmed down but was still frustrated. He had his work cut out for him. Right now, he wanted to find game, a rabbit, squirrel, even a deer. He took Rufus and sat near the edge of a clearing and waited quietly. It wasn't long before a large grey rabbit appeared along the edge of the clearing, not far from Them. Rufus zeroed in on the rabbit immediately, his ears perked up and his body tense. Jackson was ready to shoot the rabbit, but decided Rufus needed some fun. Quietly, he said "you want to get him, boy? Okay, get 'em!"

Rufus bolted from his position so fast that the rabbit had little time to react. The rabbit darted back and forth, ran through brush, but Rufus was unstoppable. After only a two-minute chase, he came back with the rabbit in his mouth. Still alive, Rufus wouldn't let him go. Jackson took the rabbit for his jaws and quickly put the creature out of his misery. He took out his knife and cleaned the rabbit on the spot.

It was dark when he finished field cleaning the rabbit, so they quickly returned to camp. As he approached, he saw a fire and men surrounding it. Not trying to maintain silence, he walked on toward the camp. Suddenly someone yelled "Halt! Identify yourself! Don't come any closer!" He stopped but had a big grin on his face. "It's Gilmore and Rufus, request permission to join camp."

Freddie took the rabbit and cooked it on a spit over the fire. When it was ready, Jackson cut a piece off and gave to Rufus. He then gave each of the men a slice, and then had one himself. Smith thanked him for the food as he had none. He appeared to have lost some of his cockiness too. "So, Sergeant Gilmore, we didn't hear a gunshot, how'd you catch a rabbit? You trap him?" Jackson grinned. "Nope, ole Rufus caught him. He's faster than any jack rabbit I've ever seen and can turn on a penny. That rabbit never had a chance. So tomorrow, keep your eyes peeled for any game, we'll keep it for dinner."

After supper, the men kept the fire going, and settled around it, some smoking. Freddie pulled out a pack of chewing tobacco and put a bit in his cheek. They told stories of training, getting to England, what they did before the war.

Freddie had a story to tell. "Let me tell you a story about learning respect. I was about four or five years old, spending some of my summer with my Papaw, helping him weed the garden. It was hot, and I decided I'd had enough, dropped my rake and went looking for a water hose. I found the hose, connected it to the pump and stated filling up a big tin bucket. I was gonna go for a swim in that bucket. Papaw saw me and hollered 'Put that water hose down, boy, and get back to work.'

"I was hot, so I hollered back, 'I don't have to listen to you, you old bastard!' I had heard my older brother call him that, just not to his face, so I figured I could call him that too. I kept pumping, the bucket was filling up, and then I caught a glimpse of my Papaw, he was almost on me, his eyes were red! I dropped that water hose, slipped under his arms and took off down the dirt road. I crossed the gravel road out front, found the railroad tracks and took off. I don't know how far I ran, but I think I ran for about ten minutes. I stayed in the woods for a couple of hours, then decided I'd better go home.

"When I got near my grandparent's farm, I peeked around and saw my Mamaw at the end of the driveway, waiting for me. I told her I wasn't coming inside cause Papaw was mad and was gonna kill me. She said 'Come in boy, Papaw is just worried about you. He won't hurt you.' She hugged me and took me home.

"So, I went inside and saw Papaw, jumped in his lap and cried on him, told him I was sorry and I loved him. He looked at me with a solemn face, and said, "Son, don't ever say that to your Daddy, he'll kill you.' So, I never did."

The men chuckled at the story. He spit tobacco juice into the fire, making a hiss leave the fire. "I learned to respect my grandparents and my parents. They never had to teach me about respect again. I guess I learned to respect the guys over me as well. We all have a job to do, we may as well do it together, and do it good." He spit into the fire again. It was late, so the men settled in for the night. It had been a good day.

After three days in the field, Jackson marched them back to camp on Sunday afternoon. They were all tired, Gilmore had worked them through field exercises all day and night. But he thought he saw a change in the men. They opened up to him and Freddie more and seemed to have more pride in themselves. It wasn't that the replacements were raw, they just needed some personal training and to be accepted. They now felt like they had each other's back, and soon the older men would help them blend into the company.

Smith turned himself around. He never complained again about a long march or being hungry or cold. He had been a loner, but now realized he depended on the men around him, just as they would depend on him. And Rufus? He made up to Rufus by bringing him a big slab of venison he got from a trooper in 2nd Platoon.

A few days later the men were at dinner in Easy Company's mess. Rufus and Jackson were at a table along with Freddie, Popeye Wynn, and a few of his new guys. The weekend exercise had helped tremendously. Gilmore's squad was in good shape, the veterans helped the new guys as much as possible and it showed. While his rifle squad was fully operational and ready for combat, the veterans weren't as anxious to return to combat as the replacements were to show the old guys what they could do. It wasn't based on a fear of fighting Germans, they were more than ready to kill more Germans and end the war. Now they knew what to expect because they had lived through it, had seen their brothers get injured or die, and that weighed heavily on most of the old guys. Each 'seasoned' veteran had looked back at his actions, and more often than not, realized they had made some foolish decisions, such as when Sergeant Lipton climbed a tree to shoot Germans at Brecourt Manor. Lipton left himself vulnerable to German machine-gun and rifle fire, something he vowed to never do again. They would still fight hard, but no longer make foolish decisions.

After supper was over, the men stayed for beers and games of pool or darts. Suddenly, First Sergeant Lipton called them to order. All leave cancelled, they were moving out again, getting back into the fight. Some didn't believe it; there had been over a dozen airborne operations planned since the men returned to Aldbourne, but each had been cancelled because the Allied forces, mainly General George Patton's Third Army, kept overrunning the drop zones. This time there would be no scrub.

***

For the jump into Holland, the paratroopers were taken to Membury on September 14. They received a briefing the next day, Operation MARKET-GARDEN would be a larger airborne operation than D-Day. The 101st would land north of Eindhoven, liberate the city then move on north through Son and a few small towns to secure the road for the British Guards Armored Division to pass through to the north. This meant the 101st had to hold and control the road running north-south from Eindhoven to Veghel to Uden. Eventually the British XXX Corps would drive through Arnhem and over the Rhine.

The drop would be in daylight, shortly after noon on September 17. The mission of the 506th (and Easy Company) was to capture the bridge over the Wilhelmina Canal near Son. Jackson had his squad ready, a mixture of veterans and replacements. Some of the PFCs in his squad had been with him at Toccoa. Johnny Young, Raymond Fields, and Joe Hill were good friends since joining Easy Company in August 1942. Gilmore didn't know them very well but good enough that they knew they could rely on him and Rufus in a fight.

***

D-Day September 17, 1944
Holland

The sky was extremely clear and a beautiful blue over Holland, shortly after noon on September 17, 1944. Many of the Dutch families in or near Son were in the street following church. Suddenly, the sky turned dark, not from clouds, but from over 1,500 C-47s and nearly 500 gliders that approached from the southwest. Soon the airplanes began disgorging men and equipment, adding to the apparent darkness. At 1315 hours the 506th landed exactly where planned, Drop Zone C, just northwest of Son. This day drop was very different from Normandy, where paratroopers landed alone and didn't see men from their company or battalion for hours, even days. In Holland, the aircraft pilots held steady on course. All the "V of V" airplanes remained in formation. Green lights activated and the men dropped in unison, landed in a soft, open field, and immediately ran to the Assembly Area, north of Son. 1st, 2nd, and 3rd Battalions quickly formed up, passed out gear and equipment, and were combat ready in under an hour.

Jackson and Rufus were second out of their plane. A new assistant platoon leader joined them and acted as jumpmaster. Second Lieutenant William 'Bill' Batson joined Easy Company in mid-August. Batson always wore a three-day shadow on his face, but with light red hair, it barely showed. Only 22 years old, he had volunteered after graduating from Auburn University. He had tried to join the Army Air Force as a pilot, but he was partially color blind and was turned away. Bill decided to join the paratroopers. How did he join paratroopers being color blind? He cheated! After graduating from OCS, he went through Fort Benning and jump school, received his jump wings, and was thrown on a boat full of replacements for numerous Army units. Arriving in August, he went through the 506th HQ and was assigned to Easy.

Being an officer offered no quarters by the veterans; you were a replacement until you proved yourself. Batson understood, his father was a Navy Senior Chief with 25 years of service. His dad was serving in Norfolk now, assigned to the 5th Naval District HQ. From day one, Batson was on fire, getting dirty with the troops, digging foxholes with the enlisted, going on night field problems and leading the platoon like he was born to it. The replacements took to him immediately, and the officers saw he had mettle and spirit. However, Captain Winters throttled him back a notch; he didn't need heroes, he needed good leaders.

Rufus was trembling with excitement. He knew what to expect now; *flying through the air, landing, then finding bad people to protect my friends from!* No farts this time either, Gilmore was pleased to see. When the light turned green, the Lieutenant was out the hatch without a word, with Gilmore and Rufus a second behind. His parachute opened with a mighty pull on his harness, but they sailed easily to the ground and landed lightly. He released Rufus, who made circles around Jackson until he got rid of his parachute and harness and took off for the assembly area. Rufus was running ahead, dodging paratroopers and equipment coming down in front of him.

It is worth mentioning the different parachute harness used in Market Garden. The parachute was the same, a T-5 used in Normandy. This was the same harness used by the British, with all the ends of the harness located in the center of the chest, and fastened to a large, circular buckle. Once on the ground, a paratrooper would turn the buckle to the left, strike the buckle with his fist, and the entire harness fell away. Oddly, this type of harness had been invented in the U.S. but only used by the British until now.

They made it to the assembly area within a few minutes and units began forming up. After gearing up, the 2nd and 3rd Battalions moved out through the northern part of Son, heading directly through the city to get to the bridges. 1st Battalion was ordered to form up units of 15-to-25 men, place them under an officer, and take off due south to secure the main bridge over the Wilhelmina Canal, and possibly a few smaller bridges.

With Spiers' help, Gilmore quickly got his squad in order, and Easy Company reached the outskirts of Son. Dog Company, followed by Easy, Battalion HQ, and Fox Company, and finally 3rd Battalion, walked into the small town without taking fire. The roads were empty except for a lead platoon from Dog Company. As they moved into town, a sharp crack of artillery fire boomed over them, quickly followed by an explosion in the middle of the road. The lead platoon men went down, some wounded, some dead, others able to get to the side of the road and around the first row of buildings. Another round hit but no injuries occurred. A trooper from 2nd Battalion HQ Company fired a bazooka round at the 88mm gun and destroyed it. The Germans attempted to run but were all shot dead. Jackson took his men along the left side of the road and began clearing buildings. Before they moved further into town, they saw German soldiers scattering out of windows and doors before they could fire on them. As Jackson told his men to clear a house, a machine-gun from the other side of the canal began firing and hit a few Easy men. With Rufus at his side, Jackson hurried to the injured man and quickly dragged him into a building. He saw two holes through the soldier's steel helmet and saw that the bullet had caused a deep graze along his temple. The soldier, George Gipson, was unconscious and bleeding badly. He treated the wound with sulfa and placed a bandage over the wound and gave him a dose of morphine. Easy Company medic Eugene Roe showed up and took over. Jackson whistled at Rufus and they rejoined the fight.

Easy Company had destroyed the machine-gun across the

canal and 2nd Battalion moved on through Son, nearing the bridge. When they got within 50 yards, some men from 1st Battalion arrived from the west and moved toward the bridge. Suddenly (that word appears many times during battles) there was a huge explosion in front of them. The bridge exploded in a thousand pieces, throwing debris everywhere, some even as far as 100 yards. Colonel Sink was 70 yards from the bridge and was hit by debris. The men hit the ground as pieces of lumber, metal and concrete rained down among them. Fortunately, only a few injuries were counted, none needing aid, and they continued to the destroyed bridge.

Even though the bridge was destroyed, the central support column was still standing, undamaged. Some men from 1st Battalion dove into the canal, crossed to the south bank and retrieved a couple of row boats. Jackson was standing near Sink when his brother arrived. First Lieutenant Gilmore, now the C Company S-3, arrived with 3rd Platoon, C Company, 326th Airborne Engineer Battalion. 3rd Platoon had jumped with the 506th and caught up to Colonel Sink after retrieving gear from gliders.

While Jackson was happy to see his brother, he couldn't interrupt. Captain Liberatori joined them a moment after Eugene arrived. 'Libby', the CO of C Company, had promoted Eugene to Company S-3 as soon as they returned to England. Lieutenant Gilmore quickly assessed the damage and thought they could get a footbridge constructed to span the canal. While Jackson couldn't interrupt the planning discussion, Rufus could, and did. Rufus came up behind Eugene and stuck his nose in the crack of his buttocks. Eugene jumped, and when they saw what had happened, the men burst into laughter, even Sink. "I know how you feel Lieutenant," Sink said with humor. "Sergeant Gilmore, please get Staff Sergeant Rufus under control!" The younger Gilmore turned red but quickly got Rufus and moved away. He held Rufus and leaned down to whisper. "I swear, Rufus, I'm gonna put a one-foot leash on you if you don't stay put." He didn't mean it. Come to think of it, he hadn't put Rufus on leash a single time in Normandy, and Rufus had performed exceptionally well. He'd just make sure to remind Rufus to heel.

Within 90 minutes of arrival, 1st Platoon had put together a rickety footbridge to allow the 506th to cross the canal. As the men took turns (the temporary bridge, made of rope and wood scraps, was only strong enough to hold a few men at a time), Eugene finally had time to take a break and find his brother. The K-9 unit was sitting outside a small shop on the main road, along with several of his squad and platoon members. They caught up with news, what they had been doing, news from their parents.

"I met up with the brother of the little girl who donated Rufus to the Dogs for Defense program! He's a rifleman with the 29th Division. He gave me his address so I wrote his sister and told her about Rufus. She wrote me back and sent me a picture." He pulled a photo out of his top left pocket and handed to Eugene. "She's a mighty cute kid, Jackson. How old is she?"

"She's thirteen or fourteen, I think. Yeah, I guess she's cute, in an awkward kind of way." He took the photo back and quickly put it away, now a little embarrassed by the letter.

It had taken most of the evening to get the regiment across the canal. There was no way Sink would attempt to attack Eindhoven at night, too risky, so he ordered the regiment to set up a defensive position about a mile south of the canal, near a small hamlet outside of Eindhoven. It was after midnight before Jackson was able to lay down. He had positioned his men as ordered by the platoon sergeant, made his rounds to ensure his men were where they were supposed to be, and left Freddie in charge of the watch. He found a large haystack to lay down beside. Even as late as it was, he went through his care procedures for Rufus before finally laying down. He was asleep before Rufus could get settled next to his side. A light rain started, Jackson roused himself and made a hole in the haystack, and fell asleep, Rufus curled up on his side.

***

D-Day +1 Near Eindhoven

The morning dawned clear of rain, and Jackson hurriedly took care of Rufus, even feeding him early. He didn't know when he'd get another chance to feed him, so he gave Rufus some canned meat and chicken and rice. He found the platoon sergeant, received orders to form up, called his squad together and joined 3rd Platoon. Jackson had just a moment to say goodbye to his brother. The Engineers, along with a platoon from Able Company remained behind at the footbridge. He joined his men just as they began the march.

The men had little to no sleep, all were wet from the rain (except those lucky enough to spend the night under roof) and ate British rations as they marched to Eindhoven. Rufus again marched around the men, prancing and picking his front paws up high, keeping pace with Easy Company. A few men called Rufus over and gave him a quick rub, almost as if for good luck. 3rd Battalion led the march to Eindhoven, followed by 2nd Battalion, with 1st Battalion in reserve. The 1st had taken a beating the day before, fighting their way south through the Zonsche Forest, then fighting machine-guns and 88mm artillery once they reached the canal.

They were only 600 yards along the road when they received machine-gun and rifle fire. Gilmore considered putting Rufus on a short leash, just to ensure he didn't run off and attack a machine-gun nest all by himself. In the end, he decided to trust Rufus' instincts. He took his men down the road, maintaining as much cover as possible. His squad soon came under direct fire, and they returned fire without being ordered. The attack stopped, and the 506th continued. Again, small arms fire opened up on them, but was quickly silenced by 3rd Battalion. For the next few miles, they were continuously attacked by small groups, but 2nd and 3rd Battalions drove them back into the city or left them dead where they fell.

But once they reached the outskirts of Eindhoven, German 88s and mortars began falling around them. 3rd Battalion was stopped and received punishing fire. Colonel Sink stopped 2nd

Battalion and sent them to the left. Lieutenant Colonel Strayer ordered Easy Company to lead the battalion down another road to out flank the Germans attacking 3rd Battalion. Captain Winters directed 3rd Platoon to put scouts out and take off down the road. Jackson immediately moved to the front of Easy. He found the platoon leader, Lieutenant Brewer. "Sir, let me take the lead. Rufus will find us a way through." Brewer thought about it for a moment, then agreed. "You have lead, Gilmore. Take your squad and put scouts out fast."

Captain Nixon arrived with a member of the Dutch Resistance, who would show them where the 88s were located. Lieutenant Batson arrived with a piece of cake and slice of apple pie in his hands and took a group of men following the scouts to destroy the 88mm guns firing on the 506th. Batson ate the cake and pie as he moved into attack position.

Jackson led his scouts, made up of all replacements—Morgan, Mize, Parker, Hall, and of course, Smith. Corporal Spiers joined them to support the mission. The seven of them moved quickly, spreading out, making it more difficult to hit. Rufus led the way, moving faster than the men could but had the instinct and training to find safe cover and wait for the men to move and catch up, but never bunching up. A group of soldiers made an enticing target for 88s, machine-guns and mortars.

Smith, who had given Rufus so much trouble in Aldbourne, now rushed to the front and knelt next to Jackson and Rufus. "What do you think, Sergeant? Any machine-guns in front of us?" Jackson was sure there were machine-guns ahead, and most certainly snipers. He was hesitant to send anyone, especially Rufus further without supporting fire. "I don't know, Smitty, but we'll move forward fast until we make contact."

Gilmore looked at Rufus; the dog was tingling with excitement. *Good God, he really enjoys this!* Gilmore was amazed at Rufus' ability to attack, to sense the enemy, and to instinctively know what he needed to do. He made his decision. He would send Rufus forward about 50 yards to the corner of the block. Once secured they would have a clear view of the 88s attacking the 3rd Battalion. He called Rufus. "Listen, boy. Go forward. Go fast. Stop on my whistle. Go!"

Staff Sergeant Rufus didn't hesitate. He literally tore out of their safe position, running along the road, crossing behind street lamps onto the sidewalk, running a random pattern no sniper could guess. Just as Jackson went to whistle for Rufus to stop, a shot rang out from a sniper. The round hit in front of Rufus, ricocheted off the road and hit him in his chest. He didn't go down but continued to a covered position. Rufus looked back at Jackson, one ear up and one flopped over, eyes intent, as if to say, 'What're you waiting on, c'mon!'

The sniper had let onto his position, a tall church steeple where he could see the entire area and enemy movement. But he made a mistake by firing on Rufus. Gilmore called back for a rifle grenade. As the scouts fired on the steeple, without effect, Freddie dashed forward and dove behind the steps providing cover to Rufus. He had his M-1 Garand Rifle and attached the M7 grenade launcher to the barrel. Spiers sighted his target using the M15 auxiliary sight mounted on the left side of his M-1. His range locked in, Freddie fired. The special round loaded in the rifle launched the grenade on its path, a high arc above the church, then hit exactly where the sniper was located, ending the threat.

The rest of the scouts moved forward, maintaining intervals until safely behind cover. They heard the 88s firing, but a few mortar explosions later and the artillery fire stopped. Batson had attacked the artillery position with mortar and rifle fire, killing the Germans manning the position and destroying the guns. Jackson ran forward to check on Rufus. The ricochet had hit him in his vest, a thick strap ran across his chest to keep it tight. The bullet piece had gone through the vest and into his chest. Freddie called for a medic while Jackson removed the vest. The wound wasn't deep, it was more like a slash, but it bled freely. Jackson had Rufus lay down on his back, cleaned the wound with water and boric acid (He always carried a pack for Rufus) and poured sulfa powder on the wound. Doc Roe arrived and took over. He looked at what Gilmore had done, said "Nice job. He'll be fine. Keep an eye on him and see me tonight, I'll stitch him up and he'll be good as new."

The 506th regrouped, and Sink ordered the regiment to move on into Eindhoven. Only sporadic resistance met them, a few snipers and machine-gunners, but as scouts moved forward, firing rifles and grenades, the Germans departed. A few lone Germans remained in houses, sniping at the paratroopers, but they too were either killed or run off. Lieutenant Brewer moved forward of the scouts, scouting the road ahead with binoculars. He continued to move forward on his own, even though Captain Winters called him to fall back over the radio. A single shot rang out, hitting Brewer in the neck. He fell like a puppet released by a puppeteer, collapsing upon himself.

Jackson saw the home where the sniper had fired and ordered scouts to clear it. Johnny Morgan, Ralph Mize, George Parker, and Dave 'Smitty' Smith took off, moving quickly along the road, using any cover available. They flanked both sides of the home, Smitty went to the front door and kicked it in. He entered the house with Morgan right behind him. The stairs were to the left and turned to the right at its midpoint. Smitty took a quick look but couldn't see anything. "What do ya think?" asked Morgan. "Go quiet or rush him?" While Smitty thought that over, Mize and Parker joined them. Smitty made his decision. "Let's go!" he said with an urgent whisper. They raced up the stairs, but as they reached the mid-landing, a German M-24 grenade rolled down the top of the stairs. Smitty, closest to the grenade, jumped forward a few steps, grabbed the grenade and flung it up the stairs. The grenade exploded only a few feet from Smitty, in mid-air.

Morgan ducked down and wasn't hit by shrapnel. Now he rose, ran up the last few steps, stepped over Smitty, and fired two rounds into the room immediately off the landing. The sniper had tried to hide behind a large dresser, but Morgan shot him between the eyes. Mize and Parker rolled Smith over, but there was nothing to do. Half of his face was gone, along with his throat and upper chest. Morgan took his dog tags and they carried the body down the stairs and outside, where they left the dead trooper next to the house. They would mourn later.

As the 506th moved into Eindhoven, they met no further resistance. By midmorning, with Easy Company leading 2nd Battalion, they marched into the heart of the city, Rufus and Jackson in the lead, followed by his squad of riflemen-scouts. Sink ordered Lieutenant Colonel Strayer to send out teams to round up enemy lingering in the city and continue to clear the southern outskirts. Strayer, sitting high atop the city with Nixon and Hester (S-2 and S-3, respectively) in the Oude Toren steeple, ordered Easy and Dog Company to go south and hold the bridges over the Dommel River.

Rufus led the scouts south, using his sense of smell, hearing and sight to find the enemy. Luckily, only a couple of stragglers were met as they made their way to the Dommel River. The rest of Easy quickly followed, along with Dog Company. No more Germans were encountered, and Easy Company took control of four bridges over the Dommel. The road was clear for the British Guards Armoured Division to roll through Eindhoven.

Then, something amazing happened. As the men continued to clear the town, the inhabitants began coming out into the streets, thanking the soldiers for liberating them from the hated Germans. Orange banners broke out all over the city, hanging from windows above, streaming high and proud. Kids quickly surrounded Rufus and Jackson. Although Rufus was very good with children, soon there were tens of children crowding around them, and some parents as well. Jackson clipped the three-foot leash on Rufus so they would not get split up. The same was happening to other troopers, the Dutch were so grateful and welcoming, it was nearly impossible to move further.

Freddie saw what was happening and gently, but with purpose, pushed his way through the crowd to Jackson. "Need some help?" Freddie was grinning, but knew they needed to press on. He made a hole in the crowd and Jackson followed, until they broke out and had breathing room. As more paratroopers marched into the city, the citizens cheered them on, giving them treats of beer, schnapps, and baked delicacies. Finally, through the crowd, Captain Winters gathered his platoon leaders and ordered patrols sent out to the outskirts to search for enemy troops.

Gilmore's squad formed a defensive position just north of the Dommel River crossings. They built defensive cover from whatever they could find, scraps of wood, concrete blocks, anything. Nearby civilians brought down whatever they could to help, a door, a board, firewood. Soon Gilmore thought he had an effective cover and split his men into two groups, one to sleep and one to remain on watch. He ordered Rufus to lay down and rest, then got him water. Rufus drank thirstily, drinking all the water in the bowl. A little girl, probably eight or nine, came out of a house across the street, carrying a small box. She gave it to Jackson with a shy grin and ran back to her home. Inside the box was a can of beef stew, a tin of roast beef, and some small, hard biscuits. He decided to feed Rufus again. It had been a busy day, and Jackson remembered Normandy, how difficult it was to find food for his partner. He poured the roast beef into the box and Rufus ate quickly, licking the box so hard he chased it down the road. That tickled the boys and they teased Rufus. "He sure is a chow hound, that one!"

Jackson called Rufus to heel, and they walked over to the house where the young girl had entered. A knock on the door was quickly opened by a tall, middle-aged woman. Behind her was the girl who had brought Rufus gifts. "Hello ma'am, do you speak English?" She did and welcomed them into her house. "I wanted to thank your daughter for the gifts of food for Rufus, my dog. He was really hungry and the roast was very helpful."

A look of surprise, then concern raced across the woman's face. Obviously, she didn't know her daughter had gone outside to see Rufus. She decided to deal with that point later. "It is us who should thank you, for freeing us from those monsters! Wait just a moment, please, sit." Jackson sat on a small couch with Rufus at his feet. The girl shyly approached Rufus, who stared at her intently. "Come closer, he won't bite you. He only bites Germans! What is your name?"

She giggled at the joke. "My name is Zoe. Your dog is very pretty, may I pet him please?" Zoe was smitten with Rufus, who loved attention from kids. As she petted him, Rufus licked her face and neck, making her laugh and squeal with delight. Jackson reached into his leg pocket and pulled out a packet of chocolate and some hard candies. "Here Zoe, this is for you. Do you like chocolate?"

She did, but had not tasted chocolate in years, shortly after Holland was invaded in 1940. Zoe went to the kitchen and asked her mother if she could eat the chocolate, and even though it was only a few hours from dinner, she allowed it. Zoe's mother returned with a pot full of soup. "For you and your men, thank you for coming and killing the Germans."

Gilmore was humbled by her thankfulness and told her so. "Is there anything me and my men can do? Is your husband here?" She bowed her head for a moment to compose herself. Jackson realized he shouldn't have asked the question. "My husband was killed by the Gestapo. He was a member of the Nederlands verzet, the ahh...Dutch Resistance. One day the Nazis broke down our door and took him. I was notified a week later that he had died. So I have no feelings for the Germans. None! They cannot tell us what to do with our country! Kill them! Kill them all!" She broke down and began sobbing. Zoe rushed to her, and they hugged each other for a long moment. Long enough for Jackson to feel deeply uncomfortable, but also long enough for Rufus to inch his way forward, move his head in between the mother and daughter. They both dropped to their knees and hugged Rufus. Rufus licked their hands and faces, and soon both stopped crying.

"Thank you for coming. And thank you Rufus, for your kindness." Jackson nodded and left as quickly as he could without being impolite.

Back with his men, Freddie took the soup and served to the men using their tin cups. The soup was delicious, a mixture of vegetable stock, carrots, celery, pasta, and meatballs. He later learned the soup was called *Groentesoep met balletjes*. Lieutenant Batson showed up just in time to eat. "What's up Lieutenant? You just showing up for the chow or we got new orders? We staying here tonight?" Batson was what the men called a 'chow hound.' He always found the guy who just got a box from home full of cookies or treats. He never missed a meal at the mess hall either. Amazingly, Batson was as trim as any of his fellow paratroopers. The men wondered where he put it away.

"We're moving east to Tongelre," he said between bits of soup. "Finish eating and clean up. We move out in thirty minutes." Jackson interrupted. "Hold it. I need each of you to give up as many packs of cigarettes and chocolates as you can. The woman who cooked this soup and gave to us is a widow, her husband was killed by the Gestapo. I want to give her whatever we can before we move out." His squad came up with eight cartons of Camels, Pall Malls, Lucky Strikes and Chesterfields, plus a dozen chocolate bars. He called to Freddie, "Take them for me, would ya?"

Jackson couldn't face the mother and daughter again.

***

D-Day +2 September 19, 1944

Early that morning, the British Armoured Division were at the Wilhelmina Canal, ready to cross to Son. The previous day, Eugene and his platoon had worked all day to clear debris from the bridge. British engineers arrived with a Bailey Bridge, and overnight installed it across the canal. By 0700 the Guards Armoured Division were moving across the bridge and into Son.

Easy Company was the lead again. Winters received orders to move out toward Helmond, eight miles to the east. They were charged to widen the Eindhoven section of the road, nicknamed 'Hell's Highway' and clear a buffer zone on both sides.

They had just started the forced march when they learned a large German force was in the area and were recalled to defend Eindhoven. Both 2nd and 3rd Battalions returned to Eindhoven, 2nd came from the east, 3rd from the west. They formed up in the outskirts of the city, formed defensive positions and patrolled the rest of the day and night. As Jackson and Rufus were settling down for the night, The German Luftwaffe bombers carpet bombed the center of Eindhoven. The next day they were told several thousand civilians had perished.

D-Day +3 September 20, 1944

The Germans attacked Son several times but could not defeat the Allied forces. Artillery and British tanks, along with dug-in paratroopers, held their positions and forced the Germans into retreat. Later in the morning, Captains Nixon and Hester joined Captain Winters and Lieutenant Colonel Strayer for more orders.

Regimental S-2 had an intelligence report (most likely from the Dutch Resistance) that 50 German tanks were between Neunen, east of Son, and Helmond, a few more miles to the east. The Germans were moving on the 101st's flank, and Easy Company was ordered to reconnoiter and engage if practical. Easy Company would join a squadron of the British Armoured Guard, allowing several men of Easy to ride on the British tanks. Several jeeps were also available. As they were about to set out, Winters ordered Gilmore and Rufus to ride in a jeep in the rear. Reluctantly, Jackson ordered Rufus to heel and started to the rear. Rufus didn't budge. He looked at Jackson, then back to the fellows, back to Jackson, finally back to the fellows. Then, he sat and would not move.

Technically, Rufus outranked Jackson, but that was only for external concerns. Jackson was the boss. "Rufus, HEEL!" No movement. "HEEL!" Nothing. Jackson realized what was happening. Though he was the master of Rufus, his trainer, the men of Easy were his fellows too. *He belonged with them.* Jackson knew it too and stopped Captain Winters.

"Sir, I appreciate the ride, but I think me and Rufus should stay with our squad. See, he won't budge unless he's going with his buddies. If it's all the same, sir, we can do some scouting as well. Alright, sir?"

Winters was impressed. *He just turned down a safe ride in a jeep to be up front with his men, and all because of Rufus.* "Alright Jackson, join your men."

The convoy rolled through Neunen without engaging any Germans, not even scouts or patrols. Jackson was walking with

Rufus near the front of the column. The tanks made too much noise to listen for enemy, but Jackson took Rufus forward after Lieutenant Batson held up the tank squadron commander. As they moved forward, Rufus used his fine senses as best he could. He could smell the gas and oil of the British tanks, the sweat of his buddies, but other scents were faint. He crouched to the road and worked his nose as hard as he could. Finally, he had it. It was a scent of fuel, but different from the gasoline used by Allied forces. Germany had been receiving petrol from Russia, up until the Germans invaded. Since then, most oil and gas were produced in Romania at the Ploesti oil fields. Rufus couldn't tell you why, but he knew the gas had a different smell. It turned out that the Germans were fuel starved and were using low octane gasoline, whereas the Allies used high octane fuel. Doubtful that a man could tell the difference in feel or smell, Rufus could.

    He turned to look down the road, then sat. That was the sign of Germans nearby. As Jackson moved up, an 88mm artillery round was fired and hit 30 feet in front of Rufus. "Rufus! HEEL!" The dog bolted toward Gilmore, and they beat a hasty retreat into a roadside ditch. The lead British tank bolted forward to engage German tanks, and the others followed. The men advanced under cover of the ditches on each side of the road. A tank battle ensued around Easy Company, men were pinned down by machine-gun fire and mortars. A German half-track moved along their right flank, but British tank rounds smashed into it, causing it to explode in flames and flying debris, leaving Germans crawling out, on fire. It was compassion that caused paratroopers to shoot them instead of watching them suffer.

    Several German tanks fired at the Brits, setting one on fire and another blew up in a crushing explosion. Sergeant Bull Randleman hollered at the men to get up and move forward, anywhere but staying still. Jackson, in the ditch on the other side of the road, hollered for the men to move forward as well. He grabbed Rufus, leaned down and said loudly, "Rufus, RUN LEAD, GO!" Rufus looked over the road, looked for cover, then took off. Jackson ran as fast as he could, but Rufus left him behind. But that was the order, run fast, find a safe place to stop.

A hundred yards further up, Rufus stopped on the west side of a barn. Jackson caught up and banged against the barn door. Shortly, his entire squad was beside him. He ordered one section to go left and the other to go right, he and Freddie would go through the barn.

Freddie led the way, slowly opened the door just a bit. He threw a grenade in and moved back. A short second later the explosion rocked the little barn, Freddie opened the door and rushed in with his rifle ready. There were three German infantry men on the hay-covered ground, two were dead, the other unconscious. Jackson grabbed some rope and tied his arms and legs so he couldn't move. "We'll get him later, let's go!"

The fighting was fierce. Badly outnumbered by German troops, at least a couple of battalions, Easy Company took a beating. They hunkered down and returned fire, while slowly retreating to Neunen. Gilmore led his squad from the barn back to the road, using whatever cover he could find. By late afternoon, his men had safely retreated to the town of Neunen, where they joined other small groups of men returning fire. Finally, after night arrived, Winters ordered the company to break off contact, make your way west as best you can, and regroup in the outskirts of Neunen.

Jackson was dog-tired. His position as squad leader took more out of him than he realized. He was constantly talking up to the platoon sergeants and officers and relaying orders down. Always checking their welfare, always thinking about the next thing, and the next thing. Then, there was Rufus. He would spend as much time as possible cleaning him, checking for wounds or problems with his paws. Rufus never complained or whined; he was a real trooper. Once again, Rufus proved his worth in combat. He had become a valuable asset to the entire company, and that was becoming widely recognized by the men and officers.

Luckily, Captain Nixon had arrived with trucks to give them a ride back to Eindhoven. But word soon swept through the men that several troopers were left behind. A couple showed up later that night, and a couple of men went back to Neunen and found Easy Company's mess cook, Private Elmer Meth. But Sergeant

'Bull' Randleman was missing. During the firefight, he had been cut off by the burning British tanks and machine-gun fire, hid until dark, then moved into a barn for the night. A German scout entered the barn, a fight ensued, and Bull bayonetted the German, covered him in hay, and spent the rest of the night in short fits of sleep. In the morning, Bull began walking back to Eindhoven when he ran into scouts from Able and Dog Companies.

***

After two days of staying in foxholes defending Eindhoven, on September 22, the 506th was given the task of defending Uden. The village of Uden was located about 25 miles to the northeast, halfway between Eindhoven and Nijmegen. Before loading into trucks, Doc Roe stopped Jackson to check on Rufus. His stitches were clean and healthy. Jackson took time to clean around the wounded area each day. Freddie took half of the squad to a truck about a third of the way from the front of the convoy. Gilmore didn't exactly 'hide' from Captain Winters, but he made himself scarce until it was time to load up. He quickly got his men on a truck near the back of the column, loaded Rufus and his gear and climbed into the truck bed. Rufus immediately climbed onto the seat board, put his paws up on the side rail, and let out a loud "BAROOOOOO!!!" just so the fellows knew he was with them. Some laughed and hooted but it was all good.

The drive to Uden was uneventful, almost eerily quiet. No Germans attacked them or were spotted. The sky was clear and blue, the sun burning bright, and the men looked upon the countryside, taking in the beauty of Holland. Windmills, small barns and cottages lined the road, untouched by Germans or Allied forces. The ride was a little break from the war the men desperately needed.

After the convoy passed Veghel, German Panzer tanks emerged from woods and cut the road in two places, isolating part of the troops in Uden and a smaller group in Veghel. "Find some cover! Move out!" Jackson screamed to his men. They quickly jumped off the truck and into the town, taking cover behind houses or in alleys. Staff Sergeants Guarnere and Rader were the ranking NCOs with them, along with Sergeants Malarkey and Gilmore. They had about a dozen men, including six from Jackson's squad. And, of course, Staff Sergeant Rufus. A few officers began joining up as the men from the rear hurried to take cover in town.

German 88mm artillery pelted the men in Veghel, tanks surrounded the small village and added to the destruction. The men lost contact with one another in the bombing, moving to new cover, crawling into cellars, where they discovered Dutch families hunkered down, sobbing, praying, some screaming. Children were the most upset, rightfully so, not understanding the explosions and rumblings. Rufus approached the young children, laid down between them and placed his head in the lap of a small girl. She immediately began petting him and talking to him in Dutch, "You will be fine, doggie, you will be fine."

The attack went on for hours, through the rest of the day before it finally let up. Rufus remained alert, went where Jackson went, as he checked on the men and attempted to get intelligence on the battle. In Uden, Winters and Nixon watched the attack on Veghel from atop a church steeple, stunned by its ferocity. Tank rounds, artillery, Stuka bombers and mortars pounded the British and American forces for hours. Freddie, safe for now in Uden, was worried about his friends trapped in the village.

During a lull, Lieutenant Peacock, 1st Platoon Assistant Leader, arrived, and hurriedly moved the men further into town. Jackson and Rufus moved down a road toward the center of town, where several roads came together. The barrage started again, and men hunted for cover, again going into homes and entering cellars, again shared with frightened civilians.

Colonel Sink arrived in a hurry, rambling up in a jeep all alone but shouting orders before his boots hit the road. "Get out here now! All of you men! I don't care what unit you belong. Get out here NOW!" Men crawled out of cellars, sheds, and storage rooms, some having just arrived. There were British soldiers, men from the 501st, and parts of the 506th. Sink ordered a perimeter defense near the outskirts and told them to dig in. Gilmore offered his squad to Able Company and moved to the west of town. They dug foxholes as deep as possible but discovered that water seeped in to cover the bottom at little more than three feet deep.

It wasn't long after they had dug foxholes that another attack was launched against the town from the west, almost exactly where Jackson and his squad were dug in. It began with artillery fire, brutally accurate. Next, German tanks began pummeling the town. The 327th moved up and drove them back with mortars, 57mm anti-tank cannon fire, and bazookas. In the lull, Jackson checked his men. No one was hurt bad, just a few wounds from shell fragments which were fixed up quickly.

As evening came on, the German attacks let up, until darkness arrived, and attacks ceased completely. Guarnere showed up with Sergeant Malarky. "Easy Company, listen up. Grab your gear, we're digging in on the northeast of town. Let's go!" About a dozen men rose up and followed Guarnere. Jackson caught up and asked what was going on. "We got about 10 Easy men south of town heading this way. We're digging in with Colonel Strayer to the north with 3rd Battalion."

***

D-Day +6

More attacks came, starting at dawn on September 23. A heavy assault started at 1300 hours but only lasted an hour. The 501st counterattacked and found the Germans had withdrawn from their front. Sink ordered the 2nd and 3rd Battalions to clear the road from Uden to Veghel. They cleared the road out past 2,000 yards on either side and met up with the Grenadier Guards attacking toward the south. Relieved, the 506th returned to Veghel. A few firefights to the south occurred the rest of the day, but by night all fighting had ceased near Veghel.

During the day, gliders landed with reinforcements. This freed up the 321st Field Artillery Battalion to join up with the 506th and go to Uden the next day. No more attacks occurred during the night; Jackson had his men not on duty to stay together but find a place to sleep. Private Morgan found a large sturdy shed nearby, and after Jackson talked to the owners, they invited Jackson and his men to stay on the first floor while the family went to the cellar.

That evening they had a delicious hot meal, graciously cooked by the lady of the house. She even cooked Rufus a plate of hamburger and rice. The men were weary and fell asleep quickly. Jackson went through the nightly ritual of cleaning Rufus. He saw a small cut on a front paw, but it appeared to be not too bad, and no debris remained in the cut. He cleaned the cut with warm water and soap and wrapped it in a clean bandage. Rufus had not limped or complained once, so Jackson had no idea when it occurred.

Finally ready to settle down, he made one walk around the outside perimeter of the house, leaving Rufus inside. After checking on the sentries, he returned to the house, took off his boots and laid down on a rug near the fireplace. The chill soon left his body, and as Rufus snuggled against him, he fell asleep. Rufus, his senses always alert, waited a few moments, listening keenly for any intruders. Finally, satisfied his master was safe, he put his head on Jackson's leg and fell asleep.

***

10

HEALING WOUNDS

October 5, 1944

The 101st had carried out it's orders with great credit. They had cleared the 50-mile corridor that allowed the British Guards Armoured Division to move north to Nijmegen. But the mission had failed to get Allied forces across the Rhine. Still, the Allies had liberated large parts of Holland. This proved to be important later as it provided a critical buffer zone for the opening of the Port of Antwerp, where thousands of tons of fuel and supplies poured into France.

The British were hurting. They were clearing the Antwerp area and had no resources to send to the 'Island,' a long narrow area near Nijmegen between the Lower Rhine and Waal Rivers. The 506th moved north and took front-line positions near the border town of Opheusden.

Easy Company held its own against the Germans. Fighting units two or three times their size, the men continuously drove the attacking Germans back. The British provided round after round of artillery fire, which greatly helped to repulse the Germans.

On 5 October, Jackson and Rufus were on a pre-dawn patrol with Morgan, Mize, and Parker. Gilmore led the patrol to the west from Easy Company's CP, located in the village of

Randwijk. Rufus walked about 40 feet ahead of Jackson, atop a dike running east/west along the Lower Rhine River. They went as far as the Lexkesveer Ferry Crossing but had no enemy contact. They turned southwest and moved toward 3rd Battalion and the town of Opheusden. Dawn had just broken when the patrol took heavy machine-gun fire. They scrambled into a ditch on the south side of the road and returned fire.

The machine-gun fire stopped, as the Germans were probably probing the Americans, and pulled back to lose contact. Jackson got his men up and moving, continuing toward Opheusden. He recalled that his brother was somewhere to the west of Opheusden, with parts of the 326th Airborne Engineer Battalion. A couple of days earlier, Colonel Sink had requested the engineers be turned into a rifle platoon to help with the defense of the line. Eugene was probably only a few miles away.

It was tough going along the dike trench, so when Jackson saw an opportunity to get off the dike and onto a road, he took it. As the men moved south, they approached a T in the road. Jackson had Rufus continue west, and the men followed. Then, WHAM! An 88mm artillery round hit close, knocking them all to the ground. Mize fell on the road, taking shrapnel to his head and chest. Jackson turned to the rear, saw Mize down, and as he ran to pull him off the road (because they *knew* two more rounds would quickly follow), Rufus sped past him, grabbed Mize by the back of his collar, and pulled him off to the side of the road. Jackson got there in time to help get Mize completely off the road and into a ditch. As soon as that was done, two more rounds hit in the field alongside the road, where the squad was hunkered down. Obviously, the German 88mm guns had a spotter.

Gilmore quickly sized up his position, and it wasn't good. His men were in a field with no protection. He had to get them moving. "Get up! Run this way! Get up! LETS GO!"

The men got up and ran across the road and into a ditch on the east side. Another round hit in the middle of the T, where the men had been. Jackson picked up Mize, through him over his shoulder and ordered the men to fall back to the east, fast! He waited until the last man passed him, then he and Rufus followed.

WHAM! An 88mm round hit a small storage shed to his left, sending shrapnel and wood splinters everywhere. Jackson was peppered with wood splinters in his left arm and shoulder, but he took a piece of 88mm shrapnel in his left buttock. He ran another step or two before he collapsed. He rolled Mize over to make sure he was okay. Mize was breathing but needed medical care. Jackson looked for his men, but they were gone ahead, hopefully safely behind a sturdy building.

He looked back for Rufus but couldn't find him. Then he did. Rufus was only 10 feet behind him and to his right. He was lying in a small dip in the land, with his ears barely visible. He raised his head slowly, one ear up, one ear down, with an incredulous look on his face. When he saw Jackson, he gave him a look of 'what the heck was that?' and hopped up and ran. He was limping, almost dragging his left hind leg. Jackson wanted to check him out, but he had to get Mize stabilized. He gave Mize a morphine syrette, poured sulfa over his wounds and covered in a bandage. There was nothing else he could do.

Gilmore turned to Rufus. He had a deep gash across his haunch, blood was pouring out, but not as if an artery had been cut. He thought about giving a morphine shot to Rufus, but examining him, Rufus was awake, coherent, and not wild-eyed. After he spread sulfa on Rufus' wound, he noticed another injury. At least a third of his tail was gone. It wasn't bleeding bad, but Jackson treated it with sulfa anyway. It was time to go and go fast.

88mm rounds started falling all along the road as they marched east. Jackson stood, but there was terrible pain in his leg and back. He soldiered through it, grabbed Mize and slung him across his soldier, looked at Rufus and said, "Let's go fast, boy!" Rufus looked at him and barked an 'Okay boss!' He didn't go fast, he waited for Jackson.

Jackson was struggling. He made it about 50 yards, to the east side of a barn, then had to rest. He was out of breath and strength. *I just need to rest for a minute, that's all. Then I'll catch up to the fellas, and…they'll help me…*

Just as Jackson was near to losing consciousness, Morgan came running up, slid hard into the barn wall next to Gilmore.

"Jackson! Jackson! You need to stay awake. I'm gonna take care of you, just hang in there." Morgan poured sulfa on his wounds, including his buttock. Luckily, he only took a hit in one cheek. Parker and Hall joined them as well. Morgan told them to carry Mize, he would carry Gilmore. Paul Morgan was big for a paratrooper, almost as tall and husky as Bull Randleman. He threw Jackson over his shoulder and took off.

No one knew that Rufus was hurt, but it didn't matter. Rufus took off fast and easily kept up with the men. They ran for another couple of hundred yards until they were in the middle of a small village. People came out of their homes when they saw the men, curious and concerned. An old man waved them to come over, he would give them sanctuary. They stomped heavily into the house, into the kitchen, and laid Mize and Gilmore on the floor.

"Pick them up, put them on the table. Let me look at them." The old man was genuinely concerned for the men. It turned out he was an old merchant marine and studied medicine to draw more money on ships where no medical men were part of ships company, He looked at Mize first. After checking the wound, he looked into his eyes, checked his breathing. "He will be fine, as long as you get him to a doctor soon."

He looked at Jackson next. Jackson's wound had nearly stopped bleeding, but it was a serious wound, the shrapnel embedded deep. The old man poured a glass of gin, took a big drink, then poured the rest over Jackson butt. Gilmore moaned but didn't complain. "You want morphine, Jackson?" asked Morgan. He didn't. The pain was not too bad, just the loss of blood had caused him to be woozy. Then, his other wounds kicked in. His arm and shoulder, and his rib cage had been peppered by the artillery round. His arm and abdomen began to hurt, badly. But he couldn't take morphine, he had to take care of Rufus. Then, as he continued to groan and grimace, the old man got Morgan's attention, nodded his head, saying 'go ahead, he needs it.'

Morgan took his morphine syrette and carefully inserted it into Jackson's left arm. In only a moment, Jackson was feeling no pain, but he was coherent enough to take care of Rufus. "Rufus," he said softly, "My dog. His leg…hurt…take care of him first…" and then he was out of it. The old man ignored him and continued to treat the shrapnel wound. With wound clean, he took a knife and carefully dug in the wound, but soon stopped. As he dug in the wound, blood flowed out heavily. He stopped, cleaned the wound again, but didn't go into the wound again. He poured more gin in the wound, then remembering the soldiers, had them pour sulfa on it. He packed the wound with clean rags and wrapped his mid-section with lengths of torn sheet. "There, that is the best we can do for now. Let them rest. Now let me see the dog."

Rufus had remained beside the table, as close to Jackson as he was allowed. The old sailor saw this. "Here, move the other man to the sofa, put the dog on the table." Morgan waited for Parker and Hall to gently move Mize, then he picked up Rufus and laid him next to Gilmore. Rufus immediately looked over his master, and after a moment was satisfied he was fine. He gently laid his head on Jackson's left side. Jackson, completely out of it, instinctively raised his wounded arm and laid it over Rufus's neck.

The old man went into action. He shaved around the wound, cleaned it with gin, then tried to clear the wound. He couldn't. A piece of metal was embedded in the leg and he was concerned that if he removed the metal piece it could cause too much bleeding. He decided to leave it in. "Tell your doctors to be careful. If that shrapnel goes much deeper, it could cut an artery."

They remained there for most of the morning, with Gilmore and Mize sleeping restlessly. It was about noon when Parker, outside on patrol, heard a jeep coming from the east. He peered carefully around a small store and saw two jeeps approaching. He stepped out, raised his M-1 above his head. They were Easy Company men, looking for Jackson's patrol. Shifty Powers was in the lead jeep.

"We sure are glad to see you Shifty," Parker said with relief. After giving Shifty the situation, they moved to the old man's home. In just a few minutes, they had Mize, Gilmore, and Rufus loaded in the jeeps and headed back to the Easy CP. From there, they would call in medics and get the men to the aid station.

Easy Company CP was a mess. Wounded men were spread everywhere, in barns and the farmhouse. The Germans had attacked 3rd Battalion in Opheusden in the west, and 1st Platoon ran into a German patrol near Heteren, at a crossroads leading to a river ferry crossing. When Captain Winters led 1st Platoon and other units in a dawn attack, they had surprised an SS Company at the crossroads. The rifle platoon fired quickly and accurately, killing 40 or so Germans and injuring twice that.

Winters then tried to beat the retreating SS men to the river, but the Germans counter-attacked near a factory, so Winters wisely withdrew to the dike. As the men crossed the dike to safety, the Germans unleashed a ferocious artillery barrage on Easy men. Almost 20 men were wounded, but none killed. Ambulances picked up the seriously wounded and took them to the Regimental Aid Station.

Doc Roe stopped to look at Jackson's wound. Roe thought Jackson was in good shape but was concerned that the shrapnel was so large. He checked Rufus too, found him in good shape as well, but sent him with Jackson to the rear. Jackson, barely conscious asked about Mize. "He's been evacuated to Eindhoven, but he'll probably end up in England. Now quit worrying and get some rest."

The Regimental Aid Station was crowded with wounded men. Some would be evacuated to a British medical facility in Eindhoven, others would go to a British hospital in Belgium, some would go back to England. Jackson and Rufus were set down on a stretcher in the hallway. A medic stopped to check on them, checked the dressings, then gave both of them a tetanus shot. The medic drew a long needle and jabbed it into his buttock next to the shrapnel wound and warned, "This is gonna hurt."

He was right, it did hurt. Jackson let out a quick "Jeez!!!" *That hurt worse than the shrapnel hit!* thought Gilmore. Rufus took his shot like a trooper, not a peep or whine from him. As the medic left, Rufus looked at Jackson, one ear up, one down, again with an expression of 'what was that all about?'

It was decided to send them to Eindhoven. They only stayed there for a few hours before they were loaded into an ambulance and taken to a British field hospital in Belgium. Though it was a mobile field hospital, it was set up to perform difficult but life-saving surgeries. Jackson didn't see much, but he saw there were lots of wounded soldiers, British, Canadians, and Americans. Having come out of the morphine-induced semi-conscious state in the ambulance ride to Belgium, he checked on Rufus and made sure he stayed next to him on his stretcher. He really was amazed at how well Rufus took everything; the explosions, gunfire, injuries, even his fearlessness toward attacking the enemy. *How did this dog get this way? Was he born so brave? I didn't teach it to him. I guess I just got lucky when Mr. Henry assigned Rufus to me, or me to him.*

Soon two medics came and told Jackson they were taking Rufus to an operating room. As they quickly put Rufus on a stretcher and walked out of the waiting tent, Rufus jumped off and hopped back to Jackson. The medics were a little annoyed, but understood they were a K-9 unit and NEVER separated. Rufus curled up next to Jackson, who was laying on his right side to leave his injured left side unburdened. "Give me a minute and let me talk to him, okay fellas?"

Jackson looked into Rufus' eyes and petted him with his injured arm. "Buddy, I'm okay. I'll be right behind you, okay? I need you to go with these boys. It's OKAY. Go on." Rufus looked at the medics, back to Jackson for a long moment, before giving Jackson a lick on his face, jumped onto the stretcher and laid down. The medics picked him up, both of them a little amazed at what they witnessed.

A few minutes later two more medics came and took Jackson to another operating room, a large tent with several operating tables, surgeons and nurses hustling about. As the medics were prepping him for surgery, he looked around and was shocked by what he saw. Soldiers were missing arms or legs, or both. Some had terrific head injuries or injuries to their neck or throat. He closed his eyes just as a medic started a drip and another placed a breathing mask over his face, and he was soon asleep.

***

The surgeon had no problem operating on Rufus. Doctor Martin and his family have several dogs and they treated them as family. He cleaned the wound, made sure no foreign particles remained, and stitched him up. Same with his tail, or missing tail. The nurse cleaned the tail, shaved a few inches back from the wound, and the surgeon stitched that up as well. Rufus was taken to another tent to recuperate and wait for Jackson.

Jackson's surgery took longer. The surgeon, Doctor Barnes, had no problem finding the shrapnel, it was removing it that was difficult. The shrapnel had twisted when it entered his buttock, with a large section hidden under the wound. X-Rays showed the shrapnel went another few inches deep under his skin, close to the bottom of his spine. He couldn't pull the metal straight out, he would have to gently twist it while pulling it out to make sure he didn't cause nerve damage.

Doctor Barnes took his time, carefully removing the shrapnel, until it was dislodged. Blood began running out of the wound, more than normal. The surgeon knew immediately what happened, the shrapnel nicked an artery. The surgery team got to work; suction removed the pooled blood so the surgeon could find the damaged artery. He knew where to look, he suspected the gluteal artery had been damaged, but did not bleed much because the shrapnel kept the artery plugged. Now that he knew where the damage was, he clamped off the artery, stitched it up, and closed the wound.

Gilmore's other wounds were quickly cleaned, all debris removed, his wounds stitched up, and after he was awakened, was taken to the recovery tent. Rufus was sitting up, waiting for him. They brought him in and placed him on a cot. The concern on Rufus' face was almost comical. Jackson was able to talk and told him he was okay. Again, laying on his right side, he rubbed Rufus and talked soothingly to him. "I'm okay, boy, we're both okay. We'll be out of here and back with the fellas in no time. Now we need to rest, okay? Let's go to sleep."

It was late evening by then, neither had eaten all day, but they were given water. Jackson didn't feel like eating anyway. Rufus ignored his hunger; he would eat tomorrow. Tired and still woozy from surgery, Gilmore fell asleep quickly. Rufus looked around the room, judged that all the men and women hustling about were friends. He gently stepped onto Jackson's cot, curled up beside him, and with one last look around, fell asleep.

***

Jackson's injuries were sufficiently bad enough to be shipped to England. He and Rufus were carried aboard a Navy troop carrier to make the short trip to England. There they travelled to the same hospital they had visited friends, in Marlborough. Rufus healed quickly and was soon anxious for duty. He no longer limped, and his tail wagged a little faster now that it was missing about eight inches.

Jackson was slower in healing. The doctor's greatest concern was not that he would walk again, it was infection. Many, many soldiers found themselves safe in a hospital after receiving a wound, only to later fall to infection. Penicillin was given regularly to treat infection, but for some it was a long road to overcome.

Even though slow to heal, Gilmore's wounds were healing on the doctor's schedule, and he could walk for several minutes before pain set in. but he toughed it out on those walks so Rufus could get exercise. And he found that by pushing himself, he got a little stronger each day. At the end of three weeks, Jackson and Rufus were going for short runs, then walking for 30 minutes. Another couple of weeks and they were running for twenty minutes, not at a Camp Toccoa pace, but still a good pace.

They returned to the hospital one afternoon, and were told to report to the convalescent ward, a large open area where soldiers could relax, read, play table tennis, or gamble. Soon, an Army captain entered with several soldiers and civilians. He presented soldiers with the Purple Heart medal, congratulating them and have a photographer take pictures. He approached Jackson and Rufus, both now at attention, Rufus at Heel. The captain read the citation, then pinned the medal on his chest. After thanking him for his service, the captain moved on.

"Captain, sir, you forgot someone." He turned to look but was bewildered. Jackson continued. "Sir, you forgot Staff Sergeant Rufus. He pulled a soldier off a road to save him from artillery, then was hit by an 88 himself. He deserves a Purple Heart too, more than I do."

The captain was confused and didn't know what to say, so he barked out Army regs. "Sergeant, the Army does not award medals to dogs, or any other animal." He looked down at Rufus, wanting to pet him, but thought better of it. "I'm sorry for you and your dog, but that's just the way it is." He turned and moved to the next soldier. His butt still hurt, his left leg was sore too, probably over-working it and nerves were raw. He rubbed Rufus lovingly, a bit disgusted with the Army and its regulations.

A couple of soldiers approached. "Hey Sergeant, can we pet your dog?" With a nod they both knelt and praised Rufus with words and rubs along his ears and neck. "He sure is a good-looking fella, even though he looks like he's been in a dogfight. One ear chewed off, his tail cut off, he's seen some action, hasn't he?" Jackson thought they must be real homesick if they thought Rufus was a good looking dog.

Bragging on Rufus was something Jackson loved to do. Soon he was telling them about D-Day, Carentan, and Holland. Other wounded men gathered around. Jackson saw a few men from the 101st but didn't know them. But they listened just as intently. They laughed loudly when Jackson told of Rufus pushing Colonel Sink out of the C-47 and were amazed at his bravery on D-Day and beyond. They were fascinated by the fact that Rufus loved to jump out of airplanes. After an hour of sharing stories, it was getting time for dinner, and the men headed off. Then, something happened. One of the soldiers stopped and came back. He removed his Purple Heart and pinned it on Rufus' harness, next to his jump wings.

"Whoa, Private, you don't need to do that. Rufus is perfectly fine without a medal. Take it back, please." Jackson went to remove it but the private stopped him. "He deserves it. I got to France two weeks ago and I'm already injured. All I did was crawl into a foxhole already dug by a dead guy, sit and wait, and then a mortar hit me and here I am. I didn't even have time to meet my platoon sergeant. Let him keep it. Please."

Another soldier, a Ranger, approached. He slipped his medal off and pinned it on Rufus without a word. Then about ten soldiers, each of them young or younger than Jackson, did the same thing. It was touching, humbling, and awoke a spirit in Jackson he hadn't felt in a long time. He nearly cried as the men kept coming forward. The photographer that accompanied the captain happened to capture the ordeal and took photographs of Rufus being pinned.

The photographs made a splash in the States, and the public questioned the Army's policy of not awarding medals to animals. The photograph also made its way into *Stars and Stripes*, which caused more grief for Jackson.

***

November 1944

Completely healed, in his opinion, Jackson ached to get back to Easy Company. He'd been gone for six weeks but had kept up with the 101st exploits by reading *Stars and Stripes* articles and talking to other paratroopers. It was time to get back to the fight.

The hospital administration had other ideas. Regulations were written in stone; once rehabilitation was completed, soldiers would go through the replacement depot. The 'repo depot' didn't care what unit you originated from, they sent you to whatever unit needed boots, infantry, artillery, armor, it didn't matter. Jackson thought what would happen to him and Rufus. The repo depot would probably split them up, send him to some unit in an infantry division. And Rufus would probably be sent to the Quartermasters. He had to figure out a way to get back to Easy.

A vague plan began to form. The next morning, Jackson dressed in new ODs (ODs- Olive Drabs were the nickname of the Army's combat uniform, called ODs for their color), took off on a morning run with Rufus. It was cold, barely in to the 40s when they started, but warmed by mid-morning. They ran four miles in full gear, Rufus with his harness filled with food and some gear. Jackson had his musette bag strapped to his back, also full of rations. Poulton Hill Road was a narrow road, barely able to allow vehicles to pass in either direction. Many parts of the road were lined with hedgerows, reminding him of Normandy.

He slowed to a walk, Rufus by his side. At a sideroad, he stopped for a break, giving Rufus plenty of water. Instead of turning back, he continued eastward, and by 1000 hours they approached the outskirts of Ramsbury. A light drizzle turned into a light rain, which turned into a heavy rain with strong winds, so Jackson began looking for cover. He entered the Square and saw an inn with a pub and restaurant, The Bell. Jackson hoped they wouldn't mind Rufus. Rufus shook the rain from his coat before entering. *Well, at least he's shown his good manners*, Jackson thought with a smile. Several patrons turned from the bar to look at them. The locals were used to soldiers and airmen visiting from the airfield to the south. That airfield was Jackson's destination. More precisely, the Quartermasters HQ at the airfield.

The inn was warm, a big fire in the fireplace made it a cozy room. He removed his musette bag and stayed near the door until a waitress approached him. "Hello Sergeant, what kept you on the road in this awful weather? Let's get you and your friend a table by the fire so you can warm up." She took his coat and hung it near the fireplace. "How about a nice cup of hot tea to warm you up?" She returned with a serving of tea, with milk and sugar on the tray. Then she poured warm milk into a saucer and placed it on the floor for Rufus. She looked at his injured ear, the shaved leg where the shrapnel hit, and what remained of his poor tail. She left with a "Be right back," and in a minute returned with a large towel, and without asking began rubbing Rufus with the towel. "He'll be good as new in no time. But he certainly looks like he's had a tough go at it, doesn't he?" For his part, Rufus enjoyed the attention. The waitress' smell reminded him of Penny's mother.

Other patrons looked on quietly, interested but not staring, which the Brits felt would be rude. Jackson was suddenly aware of how odd he must appear. A lone soldier with a dog, no vehicle, no bags, nothing but what he had on him. "He sure has, ma'am, he has. He's saved my life a couple of times too. We just left hospital at Marlborough. I'm trying to get us a ride back to my unit."

"Hold that thought, Sergeant, I'll be back in a jiff." She took care of a few patrons, pouring tea, getting scones and biscuits for them. A few minutes later she returned with two bowls of beef stew. She placed one bowl on the table, the other on the floor for Rufus. She sat down as both eagerly dug in to the stew. "Now lad, where did you say you were trying to go?"

He swallowed a spoonful of stew before he answered. "I'm trying to get to Holland. My unit is there, and I need to get back as quickly as possible. I thought I'd find a cargo airplane and catch a ride."

She nodded. "Ramsbury has plenty of planes, lad, plenty. Eat up, and I'll check on getting you a lift." Jackson thanked her and wondered why she was so helpful. For that matter, nearly all the English civilians were helpful and appreciative of the Americans, as long as they behaved themselves. He looked around the inn, and on a small table along the wall next to the fireplace was a flyer about the inn. It turned out the Bell was 300 years old, converted from an old coaching inn to what it was now, a cozy inn where locals visited for tea and talk.

Gilmore was ready to get on his way. He put on his jacket and musette bag, hooked the harness on Rufus, then waited for the kind waitress. She returned a few minutes later with an older man. "Here Sergeant, Mister Wilson is delivering milk. He can take you to the airfield." Gilmore was humbled by the help. He thanked the waitress, gave her all the British money he had (it amounted to about five pounds) and joined Mister Wilson as he walked through the kitchen to a small alley.

"Jump in soldier, we'll be there in no time. Where are you two escapees going?" Jackson was surprised, was it that obvious he was AWOL? He decided to tell the truth. "We escaped from hospital in Marlborough. I was concerned that if we showed up at the Replacement Depot, some foolish officer would decide to send me one way and Rufus another. So, I decided to get back to my unit on my own. They're in Holland now, and I need to get back."

Mister Wilson stopped at the guard gate outside the airfield. "Good luck to you Yank, keep your head down, and tell your partner to tuck his tail between his legs, he'll keep it longer." With a loud snort and a laugh at his own joke, he put the lorry in gear and slowly drove off, with a last blow of his horn. Gilmore turned to the two military policemen at the gate, showed his ID card and asked where to find the QMs. Of course the Quartermasters were on the other side of the airfield, but after only a short walk he hitched another ride, and soon arrived at the Rigger's Shack. Memories of First Sergeant Sellers flooded over him. He reminded himself to write Clyde and Mister Henry.

The riggers were helpful, once Jackson explained what he needed, a ride to Holland. "We're dropping supplies to Nijmegen in a couple of days, would that be close enough?" It absolutely would be close enough!

***

The C-47 was cramped. A crew of four loaders, a dozen containers, each 4x4 feet, didn't leave much room for Jackson and Rufus, pushed into the tail where no containers could fit. The QMs could just squeeze by the left side of the containers and go from the tail to the cockpit. The loadmaster, also serving as the jumpmaster, moved to the rear to talk to Jackson. Staff Sergeant Jones had made a new jump harness for Rufus, based on First Sergeant Seller's design. Jones also outfitted Gilmore for the jump, even providing him with a M1911 pistol and a map of Northern Holland. "Listen up Gilmore. We are going in low first to drop supplies. Once we're done, I'll tell the pilot, he'll gain a little altitude and make another pass. They'll give the green light, just like all jumps. You'll jump at 600 feet on a heading of 300 degrees. Nijmegen is northwest of your drop zone, look for our detachment to the north of the DZ, they'll get you squared away. Got it?"

Jackson was ready. "Got it, and thanks for all your help!" They shook hands, but Jones didn't let it go. "You sure you want to do this? You could wait it out and meet up with your buddies when they come off the line, you know."

"I know. I, uh, we, need to get back to my guys. But thanks."

The load crew got busy for the mission. Since this was a cargo drop, the doors to the large rear hatch were removed prior to flight and covered with a canvas hatch cover. Looking through the cargo hatch, he was able to see the landscape, still plush farmland in November. The sky was clear, just as it was on their first jump into Holland in September. The red light over the cargo hatch lit up, Staff Sergeant Jones and another QM moved the first container to the door. The green light flashed on, and Jones pushed the first container out the hatch. The men behind him already had the next container ready to go, and out it went. It only took a moment, and all the containers were out the door. Jones called the airplane commander to let him know the cargo run was complete.

The pilot made a slow right turn and gained altitude, leveling off at 600 feet. Jackson saw the red light, stood up, duck-walked to the door with Rufus, and Sergeant Jones hooked him to the wire and checked his gear. "I packed your parachute personally, Gilmore, so don't screw up," Jones said with a grin. "Good luck, hope you kill a bunch of Krauts."

The green light blinked on brightly, and Jackson was out the door. While he did have some equipment, he was lighter than normal, and floated silently to the ground. He saw soldiers to the north, just as Jones had stated. He released Rufus, released his parachute, then rolled it up in a bundle and took off to the north at a good pace, Rufus at his side. A soldier was waving for him to come his way, but before he could wave back, Rufus took off, breaking his heel position. Still over 100 yards away, he hustled to catch Rufus and give him an earful (in his good ear, of course). Rufus was running at full speed, and when he reached the man, he attacked him, hitting him high in the chest and knocking him down. *Oh crap! What the hell is he doing?*

He hustled on, thinking he would apologize and make sure Rufus didn't hurt him. But Rufus was playing with the soldier, tugging on his sleeves and bloused trousers. He grabbed Rufus with as much strength as he could muster and yanked Rufus off the man. "HEEL! NOW!"

Angry at his dog, he first had to check on the soldier. As he reached to help him up, he was surprised to see Freddie! "What the heck! What are you doing here? I thought I'd have to search for Easy Company! Where are you located? Anyone else get hurt?"

Freddie laughed loudly. "Relax, Jackson! We're all good, Easy Company is south of Arnhem, holding the line in Driel. Let's load up and get going." They loaded their gear in the jeep and took off. Freddie filled them in. "A lot's happened since you got hit. Captain Winters got promoted to Battalion XO. Lieutenant 'Moose' Heylinger took over, but he got shot by a replacement on guard duty."

"Who's the CO now?"

"Lieutenant Norman Dike. I don't know much about him yet, but the word is he's not much of a combat leader. Some of the guys already nicknamed him 'Foxhole Norman.' But I've hardly seen the guy so can't really tell you what he's like."

"So how did you wind up picking me up in Nijmegen? I figured I'd hit the ground and beg the QMs to get me to a unit in the 101st and find my way to Easy."

Freddie smiled. "Some QM radioed his detachment in Nijmegen, they reached out to the 101st, which tracked Easy down, and Lieutenant Batson sent me down here to pick you up. Easy squeezy." Jackson smiled at the story. He was a little amazed at how some soldiers go out of their way to help him. He said as much to Freddie. Freddie shifted gears, got the jeep up to 45 miles per hour, and looked at Jackson with a smirk. "They're not helping you," he said with a grin, "they're helping Rufus." Jackson quickly realized Freddie was right.

The drive took an hour, by then Freddie had Jackson up to date. It was afternoon when they arrived at Easy Company CP. He went to check in with the CO, but he was not to be found. The other fellas were happy to see them, glad they were both okay. With Freddie in the lead, he found his squad in a barn along the line in Driel. Lieutenant Batson was asleep on a pile of hay, others asleep wherever they could find a niche. Freddie showed them to a corner to put their gear, but Jackson was light on gear and needed to be outfitted, both for him and Rufus. He needed a rifle, knife, and bowls and things for Rufus. He needed to go to the battalion supply. Freddie stood up. "I'll take you, but we need to wait until it's dark. We got lucky coming in, spotters will drop artillery on top of you. Take a nap, we'll go in a few hours."

***

2nd Battalion CP was busy. As darkness set in, vehicles began moving. Something was going on. "Looks like we're going somewhere," Freddie guessed as they stepped out of the jeep and walked into the school, temporarily the 2nd Battalion HQ. They found the Supply shed, in a garage for the school's equipment. Jackson was able to get a few things he needed but no tins of meat for Rufus. He settled on K-Rations, but figured he'd see if the mess cooks had any beef or venison. Most of all, he needed a new blanket, cloths, boric acid and canned water for Rufus. "Go see the Regimental S-4, I think they have a few things for you."

He found Freddie talking with a sergeant he knew from the HQ company, Sergeant DuCarpe. "We're headin' off the line tomorrow, going south to a place called Mourmelon, France. The whole regiment is coming off the line in the morning and loading up in trucks. We're getting gassed up now. It won't be fun, it's about 270 miles of crappy roads."

"Sergeant Gilmore, we need a minute of your time over here." First Sergeant Lipton was waving for him to come over where Captain Winters was talking with Colonel Sink. Lipton pulled him aside away from the discussion Colonel Sink was having. "I received a copy of orders for you to arrive via C-47 today around noon. Is this true?" Lipton acted like he was sore, but he was kidding.

Gilmore gulped. Rufus looked up at him with a curious look that said *Well? Is it?*' "Well First Sergeant, we did indeed catch a ride on a Skytrain, but I didn't request any orders. To be honest, we're AWOL from the hospital. They were getting ready to send me to the repo depot, so I bolted. I hope this won't cause you any problems, Lip."

Lipton grinned and slapped him lightly on the arm. "You're not in trouble, just having a little fun. But," he said as he waved the orders in the air, "You know what this order means? It means you were ordered to jump into a combat zone. Yep, all of Holland is considered a combat area. So you and Rufus now have three combat jump stars. Unbelievable."

Lipton gave Gilmore the orders. It looked like the QM Staff Sergeant really pulled a fast one. Jackson went from being court martialed (which would never happen since he rejoined his unit) to being one of the only paratroopers in the 506th to be awarded three stars. He was surprised and happy but knew the fellas would give him grief for it.

Sink was getting agitated. They had a map of Holland and France out on a table, and a couple of drivers were showing Sink the route. The original plan was to travel at night, taking a route further west. But this added several hours to the route. It was safe, going through Brussels and Antwerp, but added nearly 10 hours to the trip.

Colonel Sink wanted a different route. "Now, this is what we're gonna do. We are going to load up in the morning, head south on Hell's Highway, and not stop for nothing but gas. The boys can take a leak when we stop, hold it, or pee in a cup for Pete's sake. But I want to be in Mourmelon before dawn on the 26th. Is that clear?"

The drivers, one a Captain, the other a staff sergeant, were both savvy. The Sergeant was tall, trim, powerful looking, and he was a negro. He spoke up. "Captain Griffey, to do that, we need to shift our resupply lines. That's going to take time. If we're going to do this, we need to let them know now." Captain Griffey agreed. He looked at the map, ran his finger down Hell's highway, and made an instant decision. "Tell them to set up outside of Liege and Sedan. That'll make sure we don't run out of gas." He turned to Colonel Sink. "Well Colonel, does that suit you good enough."

Sink was happy. "I wish I could thank all you boys with the Red Ball Express. Y'all have done a wonderful job in this war, now get us to France." The famous Red Ball Express. These men pulled a thankless job but did it superbly. There will be more about the men of the Red Ball Express.

***

The Regimental S-4 Supply Depot were loading up for the move south. They would actually be the first to leave to ensure they arrived before the regiment. Jackson, along with Rufus and Freddie, found Staff Sergeant Lee packing order forms. "What do you need boys, we're packing up here, and you should be doing the same."

"Hey Staff Sergeant, I was just checking to see if you had any provisions for my K-9 partner. He needs some supplies; I can give you a list or I can go---."

"I know who you are, Gilmore. And Rufus, too. Captain Sobel ordered me to set a box of supplies aside for you. He even said if you didn't come get it, to find you as soon as possible and get it to you. Hang on." That set Jackson back a step. He really had no dealing with Captain Sobel since the last time he was denied supplies. Gilmore wondered if someone had ordered him to help Rufus. It wouldn't be the first time somebody stepped in behind the scenes.

"Here you go, just sign here." Lee brought in a flight bag that appeared full. when he opened it, he was overjoyed to see everything Rufus needed; two blankets, a new harness, bowls, water, tins of beef, boric acid, wash cloths, a brush and two leashes.

Staff Sergeant Lee then pulled a duffel bag from behind the counter. "This is for you. Your M-1, 200 rounds, mess kit, jump jacket, skivvies, socks. How are your boots? You need boots?" Jackson was ecstatic. He figured he'd be trying to get outfitted for a week. "Thank you, Sergeant! I do need a set of jump boots. All they had at the hospital was regular Army boots."

Captain Sobel walked into the front of the storage office, an elementary school office with a gymnasium in the rear. He saw Jackson and Rufus and approached. "Sergeant Gilmore, I see you made it back from England. How are you and your dog doing?"

Jackson wasn't sure, but he thought he felt true concern for him. "We're good sir, thank you. And thank you for all the supplies for Rufus. It's hard to get him what he needs in the field, sir, so thank you."

Sobel looked at Jackson with no emotion, but as his glaze slid to Rufus, his eyes softened, and he reached out to rub his ears. *Oh jeez, please Rufus, don't bite him!* Rufus didn't bite, he leaned into the rub and licked Captain Sobel's hand. Sobel smiled and rubbed on him for several moments. He kneeled down so he was low and put both hands on Rufus' face. "You're a good soldier, Sergeant Rufus. I didn't mean to be too tough on you. I just wanted to make sure you were ready to become a paratrooper. And make sure the men would take care of you too. Looks like you did just fine." Sobel rose, nodded to Jackson, and turned to return to his office. He stopped, turned back, and said, "You're a good soldier too, Sergeant Gilmore," and returned to his office and shut the door.

***

Camp Mourmelon was perfect for the men to rest up after 70 days of fighting, most of that on the front lines. Easy had jumped into Holland on September 17 with 162 officers, NCOs, and paratroopers. They left with 113 men, 114 counting Rufus. Jackson had lost a man, Smitty, and another wounded, Mize. But he and Rufus were okay and back with the fellas. They quickly settled into barracks, cleared all the German propaganda and unsuitable linens, and made themselves at home. Best of all, there were hot showers. The men hadn't had showers since they had arrived in the marshalling area in England. Well, Jackson had a shower the morning he and Rufus went AWOL, but he could use another one. And Jackson gave Rufus a good bath too.

The men got to work upgrading the barracks. Bunks were moved in, enough to allow an entire platoon to bunk together.

Men were straggling in from hospitals. Bill Guarnere, Ralph Mize, and Lieutenant Compton rejoined the company after going AWOL from hospitals, caught a ship to France, then hitchhiked to Mourmelon.

As a newly promoted Staff Sergeant, Jackson and Tech Sergeant (E-7) Rufus would bunk with the senior NCOs. This promotion was a bit more complicated than his earlier promotion. Captain Winters had called Gilmore to 2nd Battalion CP. Jackson expected to see Lieutenant Dike, but only Lieutenant Welsh, the Easy Company XO, and Lieutenant Batson, Assistant Platoon Leader 3rd Platoon were there with Winters.

"Sit down Jackson. You're all healed up, I hope? Good. I called you in to promote you. I want you to take over as assistant platoon sergeant of 3rd Platoon. Think you're up to it?"

Jackson was up to it. "Yes sir, I know we can take care of the fellas, sir." Winters noted the use of 'we', nodded but he wasn't finished. "Rufus was mentioned when I talked to Colonel Sink. He asked me to tell you that he is proud of both of you and wanted me to say he is 100 percent behind your promotion." Sounded good to Jackson, but Captain Winters still looked like he had more to say.

"Colonel Sink thinks it's time for you to move on to your new duties. We can find another partner for Rufus. He can stay in the Regiment, but he won't be assigned to you, and he won't be going into combat." Gilmore was speechless. He reached over and rubbed Rufus behind his neck. "Sir, you... you don't know what you're saying, I mean asking. I'm here because of Rufus. He saved my life; he helps me make good decisions. He helps me keep the men in line. And he saved a lot of men on patrols. I *need* him with me sir. I need him."

There was only silence in the room. Finally, Jackson spoke up. "Sir, how about this? When we need a patrol, if we need Rufus then I'll take him on patrol." Winters was about to stop him there, but he held silent. "If Rufus is needed on a patrol and I can't go, then Corporal Spiers can take him. Which brings up the question, will Freddie be promoted to squad leader?"

"He's getting promoted today as well. But let's talk Rufus. Do you really need him, or is it your responsibility to take care of him that's bothering you?" Jackson thought for a second. "Yes sir, it is. Both, I mean. I need him, he needs me. He's been my dog for over three years, since we were paired up at K-9 training. I don't believe I can do my job as good without him, sir. And truth be told sir, I'm a little hurt that you and Colonel Sink want to take him away from me. If it's a choice of being promoted or keeping Rufus, well sir, I think I'd rather stay in my squad."

Winters turned red. He didn't care to be dressed down by an NCO. "If you think this is a dressing down, think again. Ike got a call from your biggest fan, AGAIN. Just be glad that the prime minister didn't call President Roosevelt. So, Ike called General Taylor, Taylor called Sink, and here we are."

Jackson didn't understand. "Sir? I'm confused, did me and Rufus do something wrong?" All he did was heal up faster than anyone else with him at the hospital and do his best to get back to the men on the line. Winters continued. "Someone dropped a copy of *Stars and Stripes* on Churchill's desk. His concern for you and Rufus is well known by his staffers. He saw a photograph of you with Rufus at the hospital. Rufus was covered in Purple Heart medals. Churchill got a little concerned that Rufus wasn't being taken care of and out of harm's way. What do you say?"

Jackson was stunned by the course of action taken concerning him, without his knowledge. "Captain, I don't know what to say. I did nothing wrong, sir, I take better care of Rufus than I do myself. Sir, Rufus is one of the best soldiers in this company. What he does for the men is…well, when the fellas see Rufus marching with them, or dropping in to say hello, the men brighten up. It's like they forget about the war for just a moment. Maybe they're back home with their dog, I don't know. But they love Rufus and would protect him like any other paratrooper."

Winters remained silent for a moment. He realized Gilmore was right. He'd have to make this right. When he spoke, the emotion in his voice was thick. "You're right, Jackson. I'll talk to Colonel Sink. For right now, go on back to 3rd Platoon, get Spiers squared away with his squad. But do not let Rufus get in the way of your duties and responsibilities to the men of Easy. If you need help with him, ask for volunteers. Clear?"

Jackson rose, Rufus fell into attention, and Jackson saluted. "Yes sir! I promise, sir. Rufus won't be a problem. Heck, the men would chase me out of camp if I allowed their dog to be taken away. Thank you, sir!" Winters saluted and Jackson hurried out. He only told Freddie how close he came to losing Rufus.

***

Mail caught up to Easy on the last day in November. Letters from his mother and Penny were waiting since he was in the hospital. And a letter from Mr. Henry. Henry had written to First Sergeant Sellers, had met him in a rehabilitation facility in Virginia.

'I was very impressed with Sergeant Sellers. In fact, he will join me here in Elberon in the new year. He's as good a man as I've ever been around and will be a fine addition to the K-9 Corps.'

Penny wrote how relieved she was that he and Rufus were healed but concerned by the wounds.

'I saw a photograph of you and Rufus in the newspaper. You look so handsome in your uniform and medals. Why does Rufus have so many medals? Please keep him safe, and please keep yourself safe. I worry about both of you and pray for your safe return home.'

He opened his mother's letter last.

Dearest Jackson,
I was so scared when I read of your wounds, but relieved that you are fine. I don't know where you are, but I pray for you wherever you are. Please remain safe and careful.
I don't know how to tell you, so I will just say it. Eugene was killed in Holland. I'm so sorry to tell you in this way. We are heartbroken, but we know he was doing his duty. The letter from his commanding officer didn't give many details, only

that he was trying to save a wounded soldier in a field, and both died on October 6.

Please keep yourself safe, don't be a hero and do something fearless that kills you. Please come home soonest.

All my love,
Mother

Stunned by the news, he couldn't move. *My brother, killed in Holland? When? I was just there!* He hadn't seen his brother since that day at the canal bridge in Son, September 18. He was killed a day after Jackson was wounded. Eugene had been a big brother any younger brother would love. Growing up, Eugene took time to play with his little brother, taught him to play baseball and basketball. When Eugene went off with his friends, he let Jackson tag along. When they were older, Eugene helped him with school, took him with him to town on weekends, and helped him with his chores. He was the best brother a man could wish for. Now he was gone.

Jackson got up and took a walk with Rufus. With a heavy heart, he walked aimlessly around the outer exterior of the camp. He thought about his mother, how broken she was by the loss of her first born. He would write her tonight. It was cold near the woods, and soon he was ready to return to his barracks. With wisdom beyond his age, he had reconciled the loss of his brother with the sacrifices of war. He would mourn later.

***

December was a good month in Camp Mourmelon. Preparations were being made for a football game on Christmas Day between the 502nd and the 506th. The fellas were practicing three hours a day to get ready. The Army put in three tent movie theaters for the men to relax and enjoy, but since they were at the end of the supply line, the movies they showed were four or five years old, and they didn't get new movies often. Reims was off limits because the paratroopers were fighting each other in pubs and in the streets. After a huge bar brawl between units of the 101st and the 82nd, word came down from division, five-mile marches and heavy calisthenics are the order of the day, maybe that would work some of the excess energy out of them.

Freddie, Jackson, and Rufus went into Mourmelon-Le-Grand on Saturday to shop and look around. Freddie saw a French barbershop and dragged them in to get treated. They each got a hot shave and tight haircut. Rufus even had his nails clipped.

Now, clean and fresh and looking like kids just out of boot camp, they stopped at a street café and had a good lunch with tiny cups of coffee. It almost felt like the world was normal again. A new movie was playing in the movie theatre in town, so they went to see *The Impatient Years*.

They ended the day at the mess. The food was excellent, and they made up for all the lousy meals they had in Holland. Throughout the day, Rufus had remained perfect, though Jackson had him on a leash in town. While they returned to the barracks, Freddie spotted Malarkey in a game of craps and decided to join.

In his bunk, Jackson read mail he received after dinner mess. His mother had written again. She had received a few letters from Jackson, but he had just mailed a letter the day before. Still, she appeared to be better. There was a letter from First Sergeant Sellers, thanking him for the encouragement and the help with joining the K-9 Corps. *I'm going to New Jersey in a few weeks, and once done there I'll be assigned to the RTC in Virginia. That will be great for my family to come live with me, not far from our home in North Carolina.'*

And another letter from Penny. She included the photograph of Rufus with his medals, she forgot last time. And she included another photo of her at home. Jackson looked at the photo differently this time. *She's just a kid,* he thought, *but she is cute and will probably be a looker. Too bad.* Still, he folded the letter carefully and placed it in his coat breast pocket.

The following days were just as nice. The men went on marches and runs, performed calisthenics, cleaned up the camp, and filled in bomb craters from World War I. Mail was one of the best deals they had. Men started receiving Christmas packages in the first two weeks of December, a truly large morale boost.

Gilmore received a package from his mother and from Penny's family. His mother sent him an Army green scarf and six pair of heavy socks ('in case you get cold') and cookies. Penny sent cookies and her father sent a pair of hunting mittens, with a slit in the right glove to allow his index finger to find the trigger.

Gilmore shared the cookies with the other NCOs but kept most for the new replacements. The company was only up to 65 percent strength, though replacements and wounded Easy men were coming in every day. Part of his job was to train the replacements, but the veterans almost refused to do field problems. Jackson depended on Freddie and his former squad, no longer new guys after Holland, but veterans themselves. Lieutenant Batson took part and did good work, taking a dozen or so men on night maneuvers.

In mid-December, Jackson took Rufus into town to see a veterinarian. The doctor, tall and thin, spoke excellent English and welcomed Rufus in. Rufus needed a good checkup, something the Quartermaster Corps could not do, so they sent him to a civilian veterinarian. The doctor was very interested in Rufus' injury to his hind leg. "The wound has healed perfectly. See here? No red tissue around the stitch area. No signs of infection anywhere. The surgeons did a wonderful job."

The vet checked his ears, nose, mouth and teeth, then his paws. He was a little concerned for his paws, they had covered many miles of roads and rocky paths. The doctor brought Jackson a large bag of Epsom salt and clean rags. "Pour a cup of Epsom salt into a bucket of warm water. Let him soak his paws in it for 10 minutes every day for five days. They will be fine."

Relieved that Rufus was in good health, Jackson walked back to camp and prepared to soak Rufus' paws. First, he soaked the front paws, cleaned him up, made a second bucket of Epsom salt and warm water, and soaked his hind legs. Through it all, Rufus was perfect. Then a thought arose. Rufus failed to Heel a few times, including in combat. He thought he might need a little refresher training. Well, that could wait until tomorrow.

The feeling around the 101st was that the men would ride out the winter in Mourmelon, then jump into Germany in March, maybe even jump into Berlin. They relaxed, watched movies, played sports, drank lots of beer and liquor. Some made friends with the local young women and spent their time away from camp partaking in French hospitality. They caught up on sack time clear back to Camp Toccoa.

Today was a Saturday, December 16, and Jackson planned to watch a movie and go to bed early.

***

11

BASTOGNE

"We weren't particularly elated at being here...that ordeal in Holland had begun to tell in the expressions of these men reeling back you could see it was a grim thing to be done. Rumors are that Krauts are everywhere and hitting hard. Farthest from your mind is the thought of falling back, in fact it isn't there at all: And so you dig your hole carefully and deep, and wait, not for that mythical superman, but for the enemy you had beaten twice before and will again. You look first to left, then right, at your buddies also preparing. You feel confident with Bill over there. You know you can depend on him."
-506th PIR Scrapbook

December 1944
Bastogne, Belgium

He was colder than he had ever been in his life. Even when squirrel hunting in the early mornings in the winter, snow on the ground and ice in the trees, Jackson had never experienced the cold that he did in Bastogne. All the men were cold. No one had proper winter clothing, winter boots, extra socks, few had long coats. Jackson had extra socks, thanks to his mother.

Even though the men had been in garrison, they had believed the Army would provide whatever they needed. No one bought undershirts or socks or skivvies in town, they relied on Army

Logistics to provide everything, as they had been instructed.

Easy's story of the Siege of Bastogne began on December 16. Adolf Hitler boldly forced his senior generals to launch a counter-offensive in the Ardennes Forest, almost exactly as they had done in 1940 and overran the French forces. Now, in December 1944, 25 German divisions stormed through the Ardennes in a surprise attack. The 28th Infantry Division fought bravely but could not stop the Germans, who broke through and penetrated 65 miles into Allied territory. General Bradley, Commander of the 12th Army Group, began sending units to the north, while General Eisenhower sent his reserve divisions to defend the Ardennes. The reserve divisions were the 82nd and the 101st Airborne Divisions.

***

December 17, Camp Mourmelon, France

After dinner, Jackson and Rufus went to one of the movie tents to see what was showing. *Seven Sinners*, starring John Wayne and Marlene Dietrich was playing in one tent, but *The Thief of Baghdad* was playing in another theatre. He hadn't seen it yet so settled in near the back of the tent with Rufus. He saw a few men from his platoon and nodded to them, a few men came by to shake hands with Rufus or ruffle his fur. The movie started, Jackson pulled out a stick of beef jerky, pulled off a big chunk and gave to Rufus. Rufus loved jerky and would make it last hours. He would chew, and lick, lick and chew, until he finally gobbled up the gooey mess.

About halfway through the movie, the lights suddenly came on and the projector stopped. Men grumbled loudly as two corporals walked up on the stage. The Corporal had to shout to be heard. "Quiet down! Quiet down! The Germans have broken through the First Army's Eighth Corps lines in the Ardennes. All leaves are cancelled, report to your units for additional orders."

Earlier that morning, General Eisenhower had intuitively (and correctly) decided that the German attack was not a counterattack against forces in the north near Elsenborn. He immediately ordered his reserve forces to move out for Werbomont. The order reached the 101st that night at 2030 hours. By the morning of December 18, 101st and 82nd Airborne were preparing to move out. The poor weather and overcast sky denied them use of an airdrop. They would travel the 170 miles or so in trucks, driven by men of the Red Ball Express.

After D-Day and the Normandy Invasion, Allied forces were moving east at an incredible rate. The port of Antwerp was not yet in service because the Germans vandalized so much of the infrastructure, and French rail lines were nearly all destroyed by Allied bombers. The only thing left were trucks. Lots and lots of trucks. Beginning in late August 1944, the Red Ball Express was delivering tons of food, ammunition, and equipment to troops hundreds of miles from Cherbourg, France. Using over 6,000 trucks, both Dodge and GMC two-and-a-half trucks were manned by two drivers. Almost 75 percent of the drivers were negro servicemen.

During Operation Market Garden, the company in charge of transportation, the 397th Quartermaster Truck Company, was first introduced to the 101st Airborne Division. The 397th became an integral part of the Screaming Eagles, delivering supplies, ammo, and men. Most of the drivers were young negroes, nearly all below 21 years of age. They had volunteered for the Army, and after serving in other capacities, were finally assigned to the 397th. These young men performed exceptionally well and became so integrated with the 101st that paratroopers began to call its members "The Airborne Negroes."

Now, in Mourmelon, the last of 380 trucks arrived in the late afternoon. It took until 2000 hours for the last man to be loaded. What the 101st didn't realize is that the drivers had been on the road for 24 hours, making emergency stops to offload equipment and hurry to Mourmelon. The drivers rushed the 101st north, driving wildly in the dark, but with headlights on so they could make better speed at the risk of being targeted.

The trucks were in badly need of maintenance. They had been running supplies from Cherbourg to Chartres for weeks, though now that Antwerp was open the demand was quickly dropping. Still, the men of the Red Ball Express made an exceptional showing of themselves, driving the 101st to near Bastogne as quickly as possible. For the paratroopers, it was an awful trip. They were loaded into cattle trailers, 40 men stuffed into a box. There were no benches in the rear for the men to sit. They were packed into the trailers like cattle, every bump or fast turn threw the men against each other or bounced them into the air.

Jackson was just about to get Rufus in the back of a trailer with Freddie and other 3rd Platoon men, when Lieutenant Batson stopped him. "Come with me, Gilmore," and strode off without waiting. At the rear of the convoy were several jeeps, loaded with a few colonels and lieutenant colonels, a few majors, and very few captains and below. Batson stopped at the last jeep in the line. "Hop in, orders from Colonel Sink." The jeep had a winter cover over it, thankfully, but it was still cold. Batson hopped in the driver seat, Jackson and Rufus in the back, and then were joined by Lieutenant Compton. Gilmore recalled that Buck had returned to Easy Company only a couple of weeks ago, escaping an English hospital, made it across the English Channel, and hitchhiked to Mourmelon.

Batson pulled out of the convoy and drove to the front, behind only one other jeep. "What are we doing Lieutenant?" Jackson didn't understand why he wasn't with his men. "Colonel Sink passed word down to get Rufus up front, act as scout and check for Germans. There's rumors about Germans in U.S. Army uniforms behind enemy lines. So, relax and count your blessings. This is gonna be a long, rough ride."

The convoy departed a little after 2030 hours with the 501st the first regiment behind the jeeps. They moved as fast as possible, but traffic jams and miscommunications caused delays. Some jams they could have gotten through, but the convoy would have been left behind, so they waited. After numerous stop-and-goes, the convoy neared crossroads northwest of Bastogne. A couple of MPs (Military Police) waved flashlights and stopped the convoy at the first jeep. Colonel Sink joined Lieutenant Colonel Julian Ewell, Commanding the 501st PIR at the crossroads. A heated discussion took place between Sink and the MPs. There were now five or six MPs at the check point. Finally, Sink left the group and departed for his ride. He stopped at Batson's jeep. "Sergeant Gilmore, I want you and Rufus on your toes. I'm not sure what's going on, lots of confusion up front. We're to continue on to Werbomont to support the 82nd. Dammed if I know what's going on, but let's roll."

The lead jeep moved ahead slowly, with Lieutenant Batson close behind. As they approached, the MPs were on the road and close to the jeeps. Rufus stuck his head out of the canvas cover, stuck his nose in the air, and growled. Jackson didn't hear the growl because of the convoy trucks and jeeps. Batson continued on, until Rufus cut the night with a loud "BAROOOOO!!!" Batson stopped the jeep. "Jesus! What the hell was that all about!"

Buck Compton turned around in the front seat to look at Rufus, and when he did, Rufus jumped into the front seat and was out the open window in a flash. He ran back to the MPs, only about 20 feet away, and launched himself at one MP, taking him down quickly. Jackson was startled and slow to follow. But once he saw what was happening, he aimed his M-1 at the other MPs and hollered "Freeze! Drop your weapons! NOW!" Four or five other paratroopers joined Gilmore with pistols and rifles, all aimed at the MPs.

Sink rushed to the front again. When Jackson explained what happened, Sink was ecstatic. "I knew something wasn't right with those boys. We received new orders a while ago to move to Bastogne, and these Krauts tried to send us on a long ride. Let's mount up and get going." Sink ordered some men to go clear out the rest of the MPs at their CP.

The two jeeps that made it past the check point had to turn around and return to the crossroads and head southeast to Bastogne. Sink stopped Batson before he could move on. "Sergeant Gilmore, that was some good work back there. You and Rufus may have just made the difference in Bastogne surviving. Stay alert, don't take anyone's word for granted. Stop and ask questions, we'll send some more boys up to you at the next checkpoint."

The rest of the journey to Bastogne was uneventful. They arrived in the early hours on December 19, sleepy, tired, hungry, and above all, miserably cold. The drivers stopped the convoy about two miles from the edge of town. The men 'jumped' out the back of the cattle haulers and trucks, nearly all of them relieving themselves before doing anything else. They formed two columns, one on either side of the road, and marched into Bastogne. Somehow in the confusion, Freddie found them and led them to 3rd Platoon. The men were cold and tired, but otherwise okay. Their morale would be something else to consider. They continued their march into Bastogne, some without helmets, some without any ammo, mortar teams with no mortars or rounds. The men thought it was crazy to expect them to hold off the Germans with no way to fight. Still, they put one foot in front of the other and marched into Bastogne.

Lieutenant Batson grabbed Jackson and pulled him aside. "Sink wants you and Rufus up front with him, he's leading the division into Bastogne. Get going!"

Jackson nodded goodbye to Freddie, grabbed his meager gear and took off, Rufus at his side. The 506th was directly behind the 501st and 502nd in the convoy, so Jackson had to hustle to catch up to Sink. By jogging most of the way, he caught up to the front of the division just as they entered Bastogne. When he reported to Colonel Sink, it was nearly 1000 hours on the morning of December 19.

Sink wanted Rufus up front with him, as scout. "I want Rufus to scout out any German spies in Army gear. Keep him close, but if you see any soldiers that don't quite seem right, check him out." Jackson thought that was a good idea, but he had to ask Sink a question. "Sir, I appreciate your trust in Rufus, but I don't understand. I mean it wasn't so long ago that you wanted to bust us up and send Rufus to the rear. What changed? I mean, what changed your mind, sir?"

Sink took a drag on his cigarette as they continued to move through Bastogne to the north. "Well, paratrooper, it's like this. I was wrong, and Captain Winters helped me see that."

"Captain Winters, sir? What did he do?" Jackson hoped he

didn't get the battalion XO in trouble! "He reminded me of something I have instructed my officers to do. He said 'What do you do with good, dependable paratroopers that men will follow into battle? You promote them and give them the opportunity to lead.' He also reminded me to treat you both like paratroopers, and I would never hold a paratrooper back from fighting, unless he was too hurt for his own good. Now git!"

Just as Jackson was leading Rufus off to the north, Brigadier General Higgins stepped in front of Colonel Sink. Higgins, assistant division commander of the 101st, ordered Sink to send a battalion to Noville. Sink did the only thing he could. He turned to his 1st Battalion Commander, Lieutenant Colonel James LaPrade, and ordered him to Noville. General Higgins ordered maps to be provided to LaPrade, but maps were in very short supply. Luckily a few 1:100,000 and one 1:50,000 maps of the area were provided by the G-3, Colonel Kinnard.

As the 1st Battalion, 506th departed for Noville, Colonel Sink ordered the 2nd and 3rd Battalions into division reserves to the north of Bastogne. Jackson and Rufus were allowed to join 3rd Platoon, and they walked south until they ran into Freddie. As the men moved north, the residents of Bastogne gave the men cups of hot coffee, which the cold men deeply appreciated. A young girl, watching the soldiers march by, saw Rufus. She hurried out to the road, took off a beautiful green scarf and gave it to Jackson. She smiled and said, "Pour ton beau chie," or "For your beautiful dog." Jackson knew what she meant and thanked her with a chocolate bar. He wrapped the scarf around Rufus' neck, then pointed to the girl and said, "GOOD FRIEND." Rufus immediately rubbed against her, allowing her to pet him. They were moving on and he had to go, but he waved goodbye to the little girl, still smiling. Rufus turned back for a last look, then let out a loud "BAROOO!" The little girl laughed, suddenly shy, and buried herself in her mother's arms.

As they left the northern edge of Bastogne, a truck and jeep loaded with supplies approached. Lieutenant George Rice, 10th Armored Division and member of Team Desobry, set his soldiers to placing the supplies into separate piles so the men could grab what they needed as they moved by. Mortars, M-1 and machine gun rounds, grenades, and rocket launchers were quickly grabbed and stowed away by the paratroopers. Some men had retrieved ammo from the retreating, defeated soldiers heading south while marching through town. They felt a little better with ammo stuffed in their pockets.

"Easy Company, listen up!" shouted First Sergeant Lipton. We're moving into the woods on the east side of the road. 3rd Battalion is moving up to Foy, so we are moving to protect the right flank. We'll place you in an area for you to dig your foxholes. Let's move out!"

***

Easy Company went on the line just south of Foy. It was cold, the men lacked winter clothing, both winter coats and boots. Some still were without helmets. All men of Easy now had a weapon and ammo, even if it was very limited. Gilmore noticed that he was one of very few men who had gloves, and the only one with mittens. He was immediately concerned about supplies for Rufus. He only had a few tins of meat and other items to feed him. He decided they would go hunting once they were dug in.

As soon as the platoon was in place, he was instructed to get 1st and 2nd squad on the line, staggered foxholes so they wouldn't make so nice of a target and helped reinforce their covers. He sent Rufus on patrol with Freddie, just along Easy's line, not probing, just watching. After helping his men, Freddie returned just as darkness approached. "Hey, have you dug your foxhole yet?" Freddie asked. Jackson had not, he had spent the last few hours helping 3rd Platoon get settled in. Freddie saw the look on his face and laughed. 'C'mon, y'all are camping with me."

Freddie had received help from the fellas. He had a large foxhole off the line about 75 feet. It was deep, about five feet in length, and fortified with downed trees. A few stronger branches were laid across the top, where Freddie had tied down a blanket. On the floor, Freddie had piled fresh pine straw to keep them warm. Jackson was surprised and said so. They crawled into the foxhole, pulled the blanket over the top, and it was almost comfortable. Jackson took one of Rufus' waterproof blankets and laid it over the pine straw. As they settled in, darkness took over the forest.

The men had been warned not to build fires. Some did and were rewarded with machine-gun or mortar fire. Freddie had built a small area for a fire, using branches and any rocks he found. He started the small fire, released the smoke through a hole in the blanket over his left shoulder. It was too dark to see the smoke and the fire could not be seen through the blanket. They warmed up to where they were only cold, not freezing cold.

K-rations were on the menu for supper, while Rufus had a tin of horse meat, rice, and water. After eating, Jackson had Rufus remain with Freddie and went to check on 3rd Platoon. They could hear the intense firefight taking place to the north, where 1st Battalion and Team Desobry were attacking Noville only 1 1/2 miles to the north of Easy Company's position.

Lipton was checking the line when he saw Gilmore approaching. "Where's Rufus, Gilmore? I'd sure like him up here to smell out Germans!" Jackson grinned but answered seriously. "He needs a break, Lip. He's in his foxhole that Freddie and some other fellas dug for me. Uh...actually, I think they dug it for Rufus." Lipton understood, he cared about Rufus as much as anybody.

They were dug in from the Bastogne-Foy-Noville Road on the left, with 3rd Battalion on their right. They were only about 15 to 20 feet inside of the woods, looking down over a sloping field into the town of Foy. It was quiet except for the fighting going on in Noville. Jackson went to 3rd Platoon, dug in next to 2nd Platoon on the left and Dog Company on his right. Ralph Mize, who joined Easy in Mourmelon after escaping the hospital in December, was in a hole with George Parker. Both men had fought hard in Holland and were no longer replacements, they were veterans.

"Y'all keep your heads down, and keep your eyes peeled for movement. I don't think the Germans will come at us tonight but be ready." Parker looked hard at Gilmore, then said "Where's

Rufus?" This was the second time someone asked about Rufus. "He's fine, I thought he needed a rest after the ride from Mourmelon. Rufus stayed awake all night, he even caught some German spies!"

Parker and Mize hadn't heard that, so he told them the story. This went around the company quickly, even across the battalion and up through regiment, adding to Rufus' lore. Gilmore moved on, checking on Johnny Morgan and Frank Hall next. They too asked about Rufus. *Dedgummit! Do I need to go get my dog and bring him up here for the fellas to see that he's fine?* He decided to leave Rufus in the foxhole, at least for tonight.

After running through 3rd Platoon, He found 3rd Platoon Sergeant, Tech Sergeant Buck Taylor, also checking the lines. Before Buck could ask, Jackson blurted out "Rufus is fine. I left him in our foxhole to rest and get warm." Taylor guffawed. "How'd you know I was gonna ask about Rufus?" "Because everyone asked about Rufus! I swear I'll never leave him behind again!"

Jackson returned to his foxhole and found Rufus alone. It was almost warm in the foxhole, with the blanket covering the logs and a small fire reduced to hot ashes providing warmth. It had been cold on the line, nearly below zero, and the fellas in the outposts (OP) were in the open and didn't have the woods to provide cover or block the wind. Buck Taylor would handle rotating men to the OPs every two hours, Jackson would do so tomorrow night, December 20th. For now, he needed to sleep. Rufus curled up alongside of him and they were both asleep in seconds. Only Rufus woke when Freddie eased himself in and laid next to Rufus. Soon he was asleep as well, both men on each side of Rufus.

***

December 20, 1944

Rufus woke at dawn, sat up and stretched, then stuck his head out from under the blanket covering the foxhole. There was new snow on the ground, and a heavy fog hung over Easy Company. Jackson woke, probably because he felt cold from the loss of Rufus' body heat. Groaning as he got up and out of his foxhole, he listened for sounds of fighting but heard nothing. He gave Rufus water and took him toward the rear so they could both relieve themselves.

This time Jackson took Rufus to check the line. The fellas were glad to see him, and Rufus reacted by jumping into each foxhole and rubbing on the men. Even for only a moment, the men felt the warmth coming from under his thick fur and warmed their hands. After checking on the men, he told Sergeant Taylor he was taking Rufus to the rear and see if he could find any game. Taylor told him to stay alert and moved on down the line.

They moved to the rear, past Lieutenant Dike, still asleep, past 2nd Battalion CP, where he saw a small commotion. Captain Winters appeared to be going over a German prisoner with a few paratroopers holding the German with M-1s pointed at him. *I better be careful*, he thought, *if we're catching Germans this far behind our lines!*

They headed south, deeper into the Bois Jacques (Jack's Woods). It was still foggy but was beginning to burn off a little bit as the sun rose in the east. They approached a small clearing surrounded by thick shrubs. *This looks like a good place to find rabbits.* He ordered Rufus to stay close and quietly worked through the shrubs to the clearing. There, he sat quietly and waited. After a few minutes, a couple of large rabbits appeared on the edge of the clearing. Rufus tensed and keened softly. Jackson leaned into Rufus and whispered, "You ready, boy? Go get 'em!"

Rufus took off, but the snow was new and difficult to get through. The much lighter rabbits quickly disappeared into their burrows. Rufus was stumped. He dove into the brush but could not get the game out of their holes. After a few minutes, Jackson called him back. "Okay, boy, my turn." Jackson raised his M-1 but didn't aim yet. He had them both sit quietly and waited for game to appear. Soon, a fox was seen scurrying along the brush line, most likely looking for rabbits too. Fortunately, the fox moved on to easier prey, and Rufus and Jackson were alone again.

After 10 or so minutes, Jackson saw movement in the brush. He slowly raised his rifle to his shoulder and aimed into the brush. Suddenly, he saw it, a large brown rabbit left the brush. But just as suddenly, the fox returned and gave chase. *Hey! That's my rabbit! Leave him alone!* Jackson thought. He aimed, trying to track the rabbit as it dodged the fox, then took his shot. The rabbit turned a flip as it was hit in its left shoulder, then collapsed. The fox, shaken by the rifle shot, stopped in its tracks. Rufus took off for the rabbit, easily beating the bewildered fox. He brought the game to his master and laid it at his feet.

"Come on, boy, let's go get you some chow." As they walked back, Jackson tied the rabbit to his jacket. Rufus was pleased that he retrieved the rabbit but didn't understand why he couldn't catch the rabbit himself.

As they returned to their foxhole, Jackson thought about how Rufus had handled himself since they jumped into Normandy. He never put Rufus on a leash, except for rare instances, like formations or in town. On the battlefield, he left Rufus free to roam nearby and scout for the enemy. He thought about how all the men had taken to Rufus, and Rufus to them. A thought hit him suddenly. By allowing Rufus to remain off leash, and allowing him to interact with so many paratroops, he thought it enabled Rufus to grow, to sense that all the men were his friends, and he needed to protect them, all of them. It allowed Rufus (and Jackson) to overcome the training burned into them—only the trainer touches the K-9. Only the trainer feeds the K-9. Only the trainer gives orders to the K-9. He thought Rufus would in no way be near as remarkable if he had held him back on a leash.

The rest of the day was uneventful. They could hear heavy fighting to the north and to the southeast from Neffe. A few mortars and artillery rounds were scattered along the line but no hits or injuries occurred. Jackson spent the day watching the line, even taking a 2-hour turn in a foxhole in the OP with Buck Taylor and Rufus, something staff or tech sergeants did not normally do. They returned to their foxhole just before dusk. It had been a long day for them, Jackson was ready to warm up and eat. Freddie was in the foxhole tending to a small fire, over which rabbit cutlets on skewers were cooking. Rufus' head was buried in his equipment bag, then he popped up with a tennis ball in his mouth. He looked directly at Jackson, almost staring him down.

"Oh no, Rufus. I'm tired boy. It's been a long day. Let's eat and go to sleep." Rufus stepped close and dropped the ball in his lap. "No, Rufus, I'm tired. Okay?" He took the ball and put it back into the bag. Rufus immediately dug into the bag and came out with the slobbery ball. He stared at Jackson, then dropped the ball in his lap. *This is gonna go on all night, I may as well get it over with.*

He grabbed the ball, Rufus jumped up in excitement. "I'll be back in a few minutes, just need to let Rufus play a little bit." Freddie nodded and told him supper would be ready in ten minutes. It was bitterly cold, thankfully no wind was blowing to make it worse. Jackson held the ball in his right hand, Rufus was ready to launch, so he threw the ball about 40 feet, where it disappeared in the snow. Rufus ran it down, stuck his snout in the snow, rooting back and forth until he found the ball. He quickly returned, dropped the ball at Jackson's feet, and stood there staring intensely at Jackson. Gilmore gripped the ball harder and let loose. This time the ball travelled about 60 feet and again plunged into the snow. Rufus took off in a flash, tracking the ball until it disappeared into the snow, then rooted it out again.

Jackson made a dozen or so throws when he was ready to quit. Rufus wanted more. "One more, okay? One More, then we go eat. Go get it boy!" He threw the ball as hard as he could, which turned out to be about 100 feet. Still, Rufus took off, tracked the ball, and dug it up in the snow. He pranced back to Jackson, but instead of dropping it at his feet, he kept it. Jackson went to grab it, but Rufus wouldn't let go. They tussled for a bit until Jackson made a lunge for the ball but slipped and fell face first into the snow. When he got up and wiped snow from his face, he saw 3rd Platoon laughing at him. "Hey Jackson, we took a vote, and we all think Rufus is smarter than you and ought to be the assistant platoon sergeant!" "Have you ever won a wrestling match from Rufus? I doubt it!" All good fun. Yeah, right.

Inside the foxhole, Freddie had chow ready. He had secured a can of beans, so with the rabbit they had a nice meal. As they ate,

Jackson saw the rabbit skin nailed on a piece of board, stretched out taut. The flesh had been scraped from the hide. "What are doing with the rabbit fur, making a fur coat?" Jackson was kidding, but Freddie had a plan. "I'm gonna tan the fur and make gloves out of them. But I need another rabbit, two if you can get them. I might be able to make a hat too."

Freddie was a true country boy. He knew things even farm boys didn't know how to do. When you asked him how he knew about so many things, he thanked his dad. "My daddy started teaching me when I was barely able to walk. We lived in the country, and Daddy taught me to hunt, fish, and clean everything I caught or shot. I'm pretty good with a bow, too. He taught me to tan hides, mostly deer, but I learned to tan just about any animal we hunted."

They saved the little bit of meat and bones left over, maybe tomorrow they could make a soup for the rest of the boys. The men expected an attack during the night, but it never came. They found out later why no attack hit them. The 1st Battalion, 506th, had put up such a strong fight and inflicted so much destruction, the Germans moved down to another sector. But 1st Battalion was decimated and could hardly be called a unit anymore. Both 1st Battalion and Team Desobry pulled back from Noville and went into reserve at Luzery.

***

Before dawn on December 21, Jackson took Rufus along the line. The men were colder than they had ever been in their life. The temperature continued to drop, now below freezing. Even so, he took Rufus to the same clearing as yesterday, and waited. Jackson shivered terribly while sitting in the snow, wondering if the rabbits were smarter than him and stayed in their burrow. Finally, he saw a big gray rabbit leave its burrow and come to the edge of the brush. Jackson didn't give Rufus a chance to chase the game. He slowly aimed his M-1, fired once, and Rufus took off in a sprint through the thick snow. One rabbit would have to do today, and they quickly returned to the line.

Instead of eating the rabbit, Jackson asked Freddie to cook rabbit stew. Under the covered foxhole, Freddie used his steel helmet as a pot. He threw cutlets into the hot water, along with the leftovers from last night. Freddie scrounged up a few tins of meat and vegetables and added to the stew. It was ready in a couple of hours, and Jackson had the men come off the line a few at a time. Each man was given a cup of stew, making sure some rabbit was included. It wasn't much, but it was hot and delicious. Jackson saved a few cutlets and bones for Rufus and fed him early instead of waiting for supper.

Only a few moments after feeding the men, snow began falling. And fall, and fall. The temperature dropped into the lower teens, and the dry, powdery snow fell throughout the day until over a foot of snow covered the land. The men suffered terribly, with no winter boots, no woolen socks or winter clothing, it was unbearable. With wet boots and feet, trench foot set out on the men. Jackson took great care to ensure Rufus' paws were clear of snow and ice and cleaned him each time they returned from the line.

The snow finally stopped in the late afternoon. The men did their best to clean snow out of their foxholes, but their labor was mostly useless. But then something curious happened. From the left, or west, the men could hear laughter, then a pause of a minute or so, then another round of laughter. This went on for a while, but as it got closer, they saw the cause. A man ran from his foxhole to the next, told a story, everyone laughed, then moved on. The cause of the laughter? One of Easy Company's men, Corporal Gordon Carson, had been wounded and was evacuated to Bastogne. At the makeshift hospital, he was told that the regiment's medical company had been captured, and that no wounded were able to be evacuated. Carson asked, "Why can't they be evacuated?" The medic replied, "Haven't you heard? They've got us surrounded—the poor bastards!"

Jackson and Rufus took over for Sergeant Taylor that night and took two men to the outpost positions to relieve the paratroopers on duty. The cold was incomprehensible, at midnight temperatures dropped below zero. Rufus went with

Jackson each time, as the men were taken back from the OP and returned to their foxhole, Rufus would jump in with them, share his body heat and let the men rub his fur. After each trip, Jackson would return to his foxhole, curl up with Rufus between him and Freddie, and try to sleep. Even with the covered roof, it was bitterly cold. He didn't know how they could survive.

Mortar attacks occurred throughout the night and into early morning. None of the men got much sleep, perhaps a few minutes between attacks. 1st Platoon sent out a patrol, made contact, but lost one dead and one wounded, both replacements who joined Easy in Mourmelon. Now it was 3rd Platoon's time to send a patrol. Jackson and Rufus would be lead scout.

Jackson selected Freddie, Johnny Morgan, Ralph Mize, Joe Hill, and Frank Hall from his old squad, and Taylor selected five men he knew and trusted. Gilmore and Taylor went to see Lieutenant Batson at the platoon CP, really just a big foxhole with a blanket over it. But it did have a small table and chair sitting outside. "What's the story, Lieutenant?" Taylor asked. Batson grinned while he ate a chocolate bar. "Winters wants a night patrol. C Company lost a couple of guys on the outer OP. The Krauts snuck up on them and took them off. Winters wants us to go west a little bit, into C Company territory and get a prisoner. I told him I agreed and thought we might have a better chance at grabbing a Kraut." He stood up, grabbed a map from his chest pocket, and unfolded it on the table. "We'll go about 200 yards past our OPs, then head north into the woods. Once we're at the edge of the woods, I want Gilmore and Rufus on combat scout. I'll take your men and Taylor take his, two columns, stay close and be quiet. If we make contact, we'll drop back immediately. If we can get the drop on a German, I'll decide if we make a move. Any questions?"

"What if we lose contact with each other in those woods. It'll be awful dark tonight." Batson had a plan. "If you lose contact, kneel and look to the horizon. You should see a silhouette of the man in front of you. If that doesn't work, just wait, the man behind you will catch up. Follow tracks of the man in front of you as best you can. If you still don't make contact, follow your tracks back to the assembly area." Batson had a good plan, there weren't any more questions.

***

The men tried to rest before the patrol. Other men had found sheets and blankets and covered their foxholes as best they could, which provided a small bit of cover. Freddie built a small fire to make hot coffee and provide warmth. Jackson slept restlessly, until Rufus put his head on his chest and Jackson unconsciously put his hand over Rufus' neck. They both slept for a couple of hours.

Freddie woke him at 2100 hours. Jackson had bagged three hours of sleep, felt tired but ready to go. Freddie handed him a cup of coffee and a biscuit from a K-ration. He gave Rufus a biscuit too. "You get any sleep?" Jackson asked. "Yeah, I'm good, I wasn't up all night like you were." Freddie looked to be in good spirits, Jackson thought, as he handed Jackson a fruit bar and put a bowl of meat and eggs down for Rufus. *Freddie sure is a scrounger,* Jackson thought, glad his friend was so resourceful. And he appreciated his help. Since taking on assistant platoon leader duties, he didn't have time for much else, even taking care of Rufus. Without Freddie's help he didn't think he could do his job, at least not very well.

Fresh snow had fallen in the short hours Jackson was asleep. It was soft and dry and didn't make a noise when stepped on. A heavy mist covered the area, making it hard to see more than a few feet in front of you. The patrol moved out in two columns, Batson and Taylor leading, with Jackson and Rufus up front as scout. Again, Jackson left Rufus off leash, allowing him to choose his own path, stopping to listen or turn his nose up at a scent. They moved into the woods to the west, through C Company's perimeter, then turned north, toward Foy and the Germans. Jackson led Rufus effortlessly, Rufus in loose heel position but watching and listening. The trees were thick, but there was little underbrush to impede them, but also not much to provide cover.

They slowly moved toward the German line. Jackson squared

up Rufus in the right direction and gave him orders. "Go see. Low. Quiet. Come back. Go!" Rufus knew what he needed to do. Jackson had told Rufus to move slow and quiet, stay low, do not attack, come back. He took off quietly but faster than the men could have moved and remain stealthy. The night was overcast so little light reflected off the snow. A low mist also rolled in, making it more difficult to see more than a few feet. After they departed, Batson put the men into a defensive perimeter facing north.

Rufus reached the edge of the woods, listened for any sounds. He raised his nose and sniffed the air. There! He had it! Those bad-smelling things his friends put in their mouths, but the enemy's sticks stunk much worse. He crawled through the snow, with only his head and neck visible. He stopped suddenly and didn't move. He heard something. Not talking, but a sound from a man. He inched closer to the sound. He was now in the middle of the field, no cover, alone. The sound was louder. He raised his head a bit more and saw it. In front of him was a foxhole like his own, except it had no cover, and there were two sleeping Germans in this one, snoring.

He listened for a moment, almost growled, but remembered his orders and quietly returned to the woods. Under the cover of the mist, Rufus quietly walked into the middle of the patrol, startling them all. Rufus stood in front of Jackson, locked eyes, then sat. Jackson knew what that meant. Germans. "Hey Lieutenant, Rufus made contact. I don't know how many, I never tried to teach Rufus to count." The men snickered at that comment. "I'd bet he ran into a German OP, so maybe two or three Germans. What do you want to do?"

Batson thought for a moment. "What do you think? You think we can sneak out there and take a couple of prisoners? I'm tired of these Krauts picking us off and sniping our patrols. So, this is what we're gonna do." He laid out a plan that was tactically sound. Four men would go out into the open field, move in from the west instead of the south. Leave helmets and musette bags behind. Go in quiet, grab them before they make a sound, bring 'em back.

Rufus led the way, with Jackson, Spiers, Mize, and Hill close behind. Jackson moved to the east about 100 feet to allow them enough room to swing back to the west. When they reached the edge of the Bois Jacques, Rufus began to crawl. Morgan caught Gilmore's arm and whispered, "Jackson! You want us to crawl through the snow? We're already freezing!" Jackson nodded and said "That's right. Now follow me." He knelt, then got into a four-point crawl and followed behind Rufus. Freddie moved past Morgan, buried himself in the snow, and followed Gilmore. The snow was bitterly cold, the only good thing was it was dry snow and didn't soak them too badly. When he thought they had gone far enough, he stopped Rufus.

"You smell the Germans, boy?" Rufus took a minute with his nose in the air, turning north, then west, north, then west again. He crouched and began moving west. Jackson ordered the men to stay down and remain quiet. He moved forward with Rufus for what he thought was about 100 feet, then stopped. He slowly raised his head until he saw the foxhole, about 15 feet in front of him. He listened hard, and heard what Rufus had heard, snoring. He turned to his men. "Okay, straight ahead of us, about 15 feet, a large foxhole. Sounds like two or three Germans are in there. Let's move slow, when we get to the foxhole, I'll raise up and jump in and hold them. You guys come up from behind fast but be quiet! Let's go."

It was nearly midnight when Jackson moved forward, still in a crawl, until he was only a few feet from the Germans. He rose to his feet as quietly as he could, but he was so cold he was afraid his knees would pop so loud it would wake the Germans. He looked over the rim and saw two young (younger than him, at least) Germans huddled together, deep asleep. He stepped into the foxhole with his revolver pointed at the Germans. Neither soldier awoke, so he reached out and tapped them both on the top of their helmets. One soldier opened his eyes just as Morgan and Mize jumped into the hole behind Jackson. The German opened his mouth to speak or scream, but Jackson shoved the revolver in his face while placing his index finger over his mouth, making a 'shushing' sign.

The German nudged his partner, who had the same reaction.

Jackson had them stand while his men took weapons and check for knives. He made gestures for them to walk south toward the woods, and ordered Morgan, Mize, Hill and Hall to take the prisoners back immediately. "Go straight south, be quiet, but hurry." As the men took the prisoners, Jackson stayed behind with Freddie. They searched for anything that may be useful, but only found an empty German equivalent of K-rations. Suddenly, Rufus' ears (well, one) perked up, and he issued a soft growl. Jackson turned to Freddie, who heard it too. Germans! They hunkered down in the foxhole, there was nothing else to do. "Get ready. Wait for them to get all the way in the foxhole. You take the soldiers; I'll take the sergeant." Jackson had assumed that the Germans handled the outer perimeter Ops the same as they did, and he was correct. A *Feldwebel Wachtmeister*, about the same rank as a staff sergeant, led the two German soldiers to the foxhole. Jackson and Freddie were sitting down, with Rufus between them. When the men jumped down, Freddie raised his M-1 and shouted, "HANDS UP!" The German sergeant reached for his Luger, but before anyone could react, Rufus moved forward, his fur up on his back, and growled deeply, menacingly. Jackson aimed his revolver at the sergeant's head, but the German had already let go of the Luger and put up his hands with the other two.

Freddie took their weapons and quickly got them moving south. By luck, they had captured the Germans at the OP just before they rotated soldiers. They moved quickly but as silently as possible, not sure if a German patrol was approaching. They made it to the edge of the woods and disappeared. Rufus led them to the patrol group, about 50 feet inside the woods. When Batson saw what the patrol had done, he was ecstatic. "Holy crap Gilmore! If we send Rufus out every night, we'll capture the entire damn German Army!"

Batson was excited about so many prisoners, but he was still infuriated with the Germans taking soldiers. He turned to the German sergeant. "You speak English? English?" The sergeant glared at him, then said with a British accent, "I say old chap, of course I speak English. And I think it is bloody well rotten of you to use our own dogs against us." Batson ignored the sarcasm but closed on the sergeant. Batson smirked at the comment. "Well, 'Old chap,' this is what I'm going to do. I'm going to let the younger kid go back to the line. But give him this message to give to your commander. Tell him that if anymore soldiers get taken off the line at night, we're gonna leave Germans exactly where we find them, with their throat cut ear to ear. Comprende?" He doubted the German spoke Spanish but was certain he got the message. Especially when Freddie, standing behind Batson, ran a finger across his neck and made dying gestures.

The sergeant understood and spoke to the young soldier. Freddie made the gesture again, and they all felt certain he got the message. Batson had him untied and walked him to the tree line. He pointed his .45 at the kid, then gestured for him to go. The soldier turned and quickly left the woods. Batson hollered at him again, and when the German turned to look at Batson, the Lieutenant ran his gun across his neck. "Don't forget, now git!" This time the soldier ran off and quickly disappeared into the fog.

"Alright, let's go, two columns. Taylor, take care of the prisoners, keep them tied together so we don't lose any." Sergeant Taylor was already tying them up but just kept going with a smile. Lieutenant Batson was a good officer; he just got a little excited sometimes. But he was solid in combat, looked after the younger paratroopers, and that meant a lot to the men.

***

December 23, 1944

The entire division was short of clothing, and food shortages were getting severe. But on the morning of December 23, the weather finally let up, the men woke to a clear sky for the first time in nearly a week. While still miserably cold, they knew that a supply drop would be coming. They could here a few planes, most likely C-47s, circling, then they were gone. But a couple of hours later, 16 planes flew over the drop zone and disgorged critical supplies. By later afternoon, over 240 C-47s had dropped nearly 1,500 bundles.

The 101st Airborne Division Quartermaster Corps did not have enough men or trucks to pick up the bundles, so each unit sent men and trucks to help. They scooped up the supplies, sorted it and began making runs to the men on the line all around Bastogne. Easy Company found out later that the Pathfinders had jumped into Bastogne to guide the C-47s in to a safe drop. They set up beacons which allowed the C-47s to guide in on the signal and make a precision drop. It took until Christmas Eve before non-combat supplies made it to Easy. They still needed M-1 rounds, mortars, and .30mm machine gun rounds.

With clear skies, fighters of the Ninth Air Force attacked German forces surrounding Bastogne. The Germans did not use their antiaircraft guns against the attackers, probably to cover up their positions. But the fighters and bombers caused so much damage on that first day, the Germans had no choice but return intense fire at the aircraft. But that first day of bombing was wildly successful. By the end of the day, there was a ring of fire encircling the men on the line defending Bastogne. Besides German tanks and trucks ablaze, the fir forests had burst into flames. The smoke was heavy and nearly covered the small town.

Jackson, Rufus and Freddie were making rounds when he heard some news. Joe Toye had lost his boots when he had taken them off to dry his socks and rub his feet, when artillery shells exploded around him. He dove into his foxhole without his Corcorans, and they were destroyed. Though Doc Roe picked him up a pair from Bastogne, his feet were in bad shape. Jackson went to visit and see what he could do. Rufus jumped into the foxhole beside Toye and received some rubs. When Jackson saw Joe's feet, he was astonished. They looked frozen! He made a gut decision. "Joe, put your boots on and go rest in our foxhole. It's warm, Freddie has coffee, and put these on when you get warmed up."

'These' was a new pair of socks that Jackson's mother had sent him in France. Joe looked to Jackson with concern. "I ain't leaving the line, Jackson. But thanks for the socks, they are appreciated." Jackson was adamant. "Look, Joe. Just go to my foxhole for a couple of hours. It's not like I'm 100 feet off the line, you know. Go on and get your feet taken care of. Freddie will help you." Toye took a moment to decide, calculating leaving his foxhole for a few hours. He didn't want to leave his men alone, and Jackson realized that. "Look, me and Rufus will stay here until your return, okay? We need to visit them anyway, I haven't been outside 3rd Platoon as much as I should, so we'll stay here."

Toye thought about it for another moment, then slid the socks and boots on, stood up, and thanked him. "Freddie will take care of you Joe, get warm and take care of those feet." As Freddie and Joe departed, Jackson reached into his leg pocket and pulled out another pair of socks, though these were used. He wrapped them around his neck and continued on his rounds.

***

Christmas Eve, 1944

Christmas Eve morning was crisp and clear as Gilmore, Rufus and Spiers walked along the line. Sergeant Taylor had been up most of the night and was catching any sleep he could. As they moved eastward, the first light began to appear through the woods. They moved to their right flank, which ran up against the railroad. All was quiet but everyone expected the Germans to attack at any time. Jackson moved back to the west where 3rd Platoon met 2nd Platoon. He saw the men still in their foxholes trying to get some sleep, each of them shivering in the ice cold air.

Rufus chuffed at Jackson. That meant he needed something, but Jackson wasn't clear. It was still early, a little before 0800 hours, with daylight coming in a little under 30 minutes. He led Rufus back to the foxhole while Freddie continued to walk the line. Rufus dove into the foxhole, and in a few quick seconds reappeared, with his tennis ball in his mouth. He tried to chuff at Jackson, but it came out like he had a lisp.

"No, Rufus, we're on duty. I'll play catch with you this afternoon." Rufus dropped the ball at his feet, then stared at

Jackson. "I said NO, Rufus. We have work to do." By this time, men were awaking and coming out of their foxholes. They saw Rufus push the tennis ball to Jackson's boots, the sit and stare. Several men chuckled at the standoff going on in front of them. Jackson turned to head back to the line, but Rufus was faster. He picked up his ball and outflanked his master, stopped just in front, and dropped the ball at Jackson's boots. Jackson had enough. He was miffed that Rufus decided he wanted to play ball and didn't understand why he wanted to play now. Jackson impatiently grabbed the ball, stuck it in his coat and moved toward the line. He turned to tell Rufus to heel, but Rufus sat on the ground, near their foxhole. *What is going on with him? He's never acted like this before, never really disobeyed me. Why now?*

Then, it all made sense. Jackson was driving Rufus extremely hard. Between night patrols, walking the line, both day and night, he was causing Rufus stress, something not anticipated by the K-9 Corps, or if it was there, they had not shared the information. Rufus was trying to deal with his stress in his own way--by playing ball. That thought struck Jackson hard. He felt ashamed of how he had treated Rufus, the best dog in the war, maybe the world.

He knelt in the snow, hugged Rufus with both arms, caressing his neck and ears. Rufus wagged his tail a few times but stopped shortly. "Okay boy, you deserve some fun. Ready to play?" He pulled out the tennis ball and showed it to Rufus, who stood quickly and tried to get the ball. "Hey! I throw it, you catch it and bring it back!" Rufus quivered with anticipation. Jackson saw the excitement in his eyes and was thankful for the strength and spirit in his dog. "Okay, go get it boy!" He hurled the ball to the east, Rufus tore out after it, dug it out of the snow quickly and dropped it at Jackson's boots. As always, he stopped and stared at Jackson, almost *daring* him to throw the ball. Jackson faked a throw but only fooled Rufus for a second. Again, he threw it to the east, careful to throw it toward the rear, Rufus sprinted the 90 feet to the ball, and the whole process started again.

By this time, 3rd Platoon was up and about, searching for K-rations or anything else to eat. The men watched Rufus run after the ball time after time, wondering where he found the strength, or even the desire to waste energy playing with a ball. Rufus saw the men, and after the next retrieval, he darted toward the men with the ball. He would drop the ball in front of a man, inviting him to throw it, but when anyone reached for it, Rufus quickly snatched it up and pranced away.

It was 0830 now, the Sun was up and shone brightly in the snow. Jackson knew it was time to get back to work, so he told Rufus. "Look, boy, I promise we'll play ball tonight, okay? Now, last throw. Got it? LAST THROW." Rufus just stared at the ball in Jackson's hand, seemingly refusing to accept that this was the last throw. But in his mind, Rufus knew Jackson meant it and would obey. Jackson turned to the west, raised his arm and let loose. Rufus took off, then realized he had been tricked. He whipped around and chuffed at Jackson. Gilmore laughed, turned back to the east and let loose the ball on a high arching flight, traveling nearly 150 feet. Rufus took off. Tracking the ball in flight. Rufus was only 30 feet away when the ball hit the ground, but this time with a BANGGGGG!!!! An artillery round hit where the tennis ball had landed, knocking Rufus to the ground and covering him with dirt and snow. He raised his head in alarm, looking directly at Jackson, as if saying, *What the heck was that?*

Jackson knew what it was, an attack on the east flank. "Incoming! Get in your hole! Let's go! Rufus! HEEL! But Rufus was already on his way and within seconds he was beside Jackson in his foxhole. Only a few more artillery and mortar rounds hit near 3rd Platoon. German machine-gun fire began firing at the same time. A sniper fired one shot and hit Corporal 'Smokey' Gordon in his left shoulder, then ripped through his right shoulder. Smokey fell to the ground in his foxhole, unmoving. Sergeant Rader was there first and administered care. Smokey would be paralyzed for quite a while but would recuperate at hospital in England. He would later return to his family in Mississippi and Louisiana, would live a good life but suffered from years of pain.

The withering machine-gun fire continued, but Easy, initially caught flat-footed, answered the German assault. It was obvious the Germans were trying to move the line south toward

Bastogne, attacking the right flank and head on from the north. But Easy Company took the fight to the Germans, who they caught out in the open field. After a furious gun fight, the Germans retreated, leaving nearly 40 fellow German soldiers dead in the open field.

Later that day, as Jackson continued to check the lines and escort men to the outer posts (with Rufus, of course), he returned to his foxhole for some rest. Freddie had scrounged up more coffee which was percolating upon a small fire. He opened a K-ration and poured a tin of beef stew into a bowl and fed Rufus. It wasn't much but it had to do for now. Suddenly he heard his name called loudly. "Sergeant Gilmore! Sergeant Gilmore! You have a package! Sergeant Gilmore!"

Jackson hurried out of the foxhole with Rufus at his side. The man calling him was a corporal from division. "I'm Staff Sergeant Gilmore, Corporal. What do you have?" The Corporal looked at Jackson, back to the package. "Sorry, Staff Sergeant, I'm looking for Tech Sergeant Rufus Gilmore. Got a package for him, special delivery." Gilmore laughed and pointed to Rufus. "This is Sergeant Rufus Gilmore, Corporal. What do you have?" The Corporal turned over a large box which had been part of the air drop on December 23, then departed quickly, not wanting to spend an extra second on the line.

Back in the foxhole, Jackson opened the box and was happily surprised. In the box was a week's worth of food for Rufus, including horse meat, tins of eggs and rice, a blanket, a first aid kit specifically for K-9s, a new bowl, boxes of cereal, and powdered milk. A note was enclosed.

To: T/Sgt Rufus Gilmore and Staff Sergeant Jackson Gilmore
Easy Company, 2nd Battalion, 506th PIR

Hope you boys are giving the Krauts hell. Keep your heads (and tails) down, we'll see you in a few days. Hope these supplies help Good ole' Rufus.
Regards,
Staff Sergeant Kenneth Jones, QM Corps

Jackson smiled at the note. Good ole Sergeant Jones, who he met at Ramsbury while looking for a ride to Holland. Once again, a soldier had gone out of his way to help the best dog in the Army.

***

Christmas Day, 1944

Easy Company woke before sunrise to the sounds of artillery and tank fire to the southwest, but nothing near them. It turned out the Germans tried another route into Bastogne, almost the same attack as Easy Company had withstood on Christmas Eve morning. This time the 502nd PIR, the 327th Glider Infantry, and the 463rd Parachute Field Artillery stood in the enemy's way. But also waiting for the Germans was the 705th Tank Destroyer Battalion. After the attack was over, it was noted that 18 German tanks attempted to break the line, and 18 German tanks had been destroyed. The German 115th Panzergrenadier Regiment, two battalions of the 77th Panzergrenadier Regiment, supported by artillery from the 26th Volksgrenadier Division had attacked the defenders, failed miserably, losing tanks and infantry, with only a small contingent left able to fall back.

The 101st and units of the 10th Armored Division had held the town against multiple attacks from every direction. The news of the surrounded division captured the hearts and souls of Americans and Europeans alike. The War Department released the name of the division surrounded in Bastogne, and the 101st Airborne Division became known as the 'The Battered Bastards of the Bastion of Bastogne.'

Courage, friendship, good training, and good leadership up and down the chain of command allowed the disparate units to fight together as a team despite short of ammunition, artillery, and tanks. Men volunteered for dangerous missions. Negro truck drivers, caught in the battle, volunteered to serve on artillery gun crews. Pathfinders parachuted into Bastogne to allow vital supplies to be dropped with precision. The Battle of Bastogne proved to be decisive in the war, it allowed Allied forces to regroup, re-arm, and attack, denying the Germans to take the Port of Antwerp.

The men of Easy Company tried to relax on Christmas Day, but the threat of a German attack kept them uneasy. The outposts were still manned, making for a cold and lonely Christmas. Freddie gave Jackson ear muffs he made from rabbit pelts. Jackson gave Freddie his hunting gloves. Rufus got a heated can of horse meat and warm milk. There were no further attacks that day.

The men walked around to try to warm up and keep trench foot from setting in. Jackson looked over the men and noted a couple of younger replacements who appeared close to the breaking point. After talking to them, he sent them back to Regiment CP to warm up and get a hot meal. They would only be off the line for a couple of hours, but that short time helped immensely. After a hot meal and time by a fire, the men were ready to return to the line and join the fellas. This occurred quite often. A man would near his breaking point, but just a few hours off the line and a hot meal, and he would be ready to go back to the line with his friends.

***

December 26, 1944

The Germans attempted another attack on the western side of Bastogne, but it was repelled by American forces. German and Allied air attacks occurred throughout the day but stopped before early afternoon. By 1500 hours, elements of the 4th Armored Division were four miles southwest of Bastogne. C-47s overflew them bound for Bastogne, which caused Lieutenant Colonel Creighton Abrams, commanding the 37th Tank Battalion, and Lieutenant Colonel George Jaques, commanding the 53rd Armored Infantry Battalion, to make a run for the besieged town. By 1700 hours, the first tank of the 37th Tank Battalion drove into Bastogne and were met by men of the 326th Airborne Engineer Battalion.

Though much hard fighting was to come, the siege of Bastogne was over and signaled the beginning of the end of the German Army in the Ardennes. Supplies came in by trucks and the men were finally outfitted with proper equipment, food, ammunition, and clothing, though winter boots were still in short supply.

Easy Company saw little action over the next few days, with most of the men expecting to return to Mourmelon. But higher powers needed the men of the 101st and 82nd Airborne Divisions. What was to come would be the bloodiest test that Easy Company would endure.

***

12

DARKNESS

January 1945
Bastogne

    Easy Company, along with 2nd Battalion, was relieved of holding the line on January 2 by 1st Battalion. The line began just a third of a mile south of Foy, ran southeast to the Foy-Bizory Road, then south for half a mile to the railroad line. Instead of going into reserve, 2nd Battalion attacked across the Foy-Bizory Road into the Bois Jaques. The Germans fought hard, but 2nd Battalion was able to push them back, extending the line now along the Foy-Mageret Road.
    Rufus was held back, along with Jackson. They knew where the Germans were dug in, so no scouts were needed. Instead, Jackson moved with 3rd Platoon, along the right flank, next to the 501st PIR on their right. But once they worked their way into the woods, the snow and trees deafened all noise to the point that men were soon separated from their platoon or squad. Rufus helped. He would listen, smell, then march through the snow until he found a lost trooper and got him pointed in the right direction. This happened several times until the platoon was back in a good formation to attack.
    Machine-gun fire hit Easy Company with no warning. The men counter-attacked, and Army artillery whizzed over their heads to assault the German force. The Germans countered with

artillery fire but aimed at Easy instead of the artillery battery. Rufus and Jackson hid behind a tree, other men did the same, finding cover any way they could. An artillery round exploded high in a tree next to Jackson. The explosion rocked them both, the savage blast overwhelming their senses. Both laid as low as they could for protection. For the first time Jackson could remember, Rufus whined. Jackson wrapped him in his arms and pulled him under his chest. A few more rounds hit but none as close as the first. As fast as it started, the barrage ended.

Jackson stood, but Rufus remained in place, not raising his head. "It's okay, boy, it's over. C'mon." Rufus slowly raised his head, his eyes wide with shock. He finally rose and stood next to Jackson, Heel position. *That's better, maybe he was just shook up from the blast*, he thought, but a sense of concern stayed with him. He'd watch Rufus closely and keep him near.

2nd Battalion resumed the attack but faced fierce machine-gun fire. American artillery fired salvos, but the Germans returned it round for round. Easy Company took several casualties, though none were from 3rd Platoon. By late afternoon they had pushed the Germans well back to the north. The men hunkered down for the night, digging foxholes and covering them with any branches they could find. It was bitterly cold, new snow fell and made it extremely difficult to move by foot.

Freddie and Jackson dug a deep foxhole but only large enough for them and Rufus. Freddie, good with his hatchet, cut branches large enough to provide a little bit of cover. No fire tonight, they ate K-rations while Rufus had cold meat, rice, and water. After dinner, Jackson checked on 3rd Platoon, checked in with Lieutenant Batson, who was eating a sandwich (*where did he find a sandwich?*), and Sergeant Taylor. Outposts were set along the line, stretching from the 502nd on Easy's left flank, to the 501st on their right. Rufus remained at his side, never leaving Heel position. Even when they visited the men, Rufus remained at heel, no longer jumping into foxholes to see the men.

The night was long and cold. Sundown occurred before 1700 hours and dawn didn't break until after 0800 the next morning. The Germans shelled the woods a few times during the night, but no one was hurt. When the shelling started, Rufus began shaking. This had never happened before, *never*. Jackson held him close, Freddie helped, and between them they settled Rufus down. But Jackson was worried. *Have I put Rufus in too much danger? Is he too scared to perform?* Jackson had valid concerns. He decided to keep Rufus close from now on, maybe try to play fetch if it seemed safe.

After a cold breakfast of K-rations, the rest of the day was quiet. Jackson and Rufus made rounds, talked to men, helped the fellas with whatever they needed. Rufus seemed his old self, happy to see the fellas, even jumping into foxholes again with Mize and Parker. Then, the order came down from battalion: Easy 2nd and 3rd Platoons were to pull back from advanced positions and return to their old position overlooking Foy.

When they arrived, it was easy to see the large shell holes all along the foxholes. Tree bursts had felled large branches, which, luckily, the men could use for cover. The fellas jumped into their foxholes like they were returning home. Freddie got to their foxhole first and was glad to see 1st Battalion hadn't done any damage or stolen blankets.

Men were still settling in when the Germans opened up. Jackson was with Rufus, helping the men get settled in along the line. Artillery shells from Foy began hitting, men dove into foxholes, not caring who it belonged to. Jackson made a run for his foxhole, Rufus running a little ahead. Freddie opened the blanket and they jumped down into cover. Rufus started shaking again, but his head was up, and he was alert. The sound was deafening and shook the men to their core. A shell burst in a tree, throwing large chunks and branches down on them. Jackson fell back with Rufus under him. Freddie was hit by a branch, but not bad. Then it stopped. The forest became eerily quiet. Then, calls for medic came from all through the woods.

Joe Toye was one of the men who called for help. A shell had exploded just above and to his side, badly mangling his right leg and peppering his torso and arms with shrapnel. Staff Sergeant "Wild Bill" Guarnere heard Joe calling for help and ran to Toye's aid. Sergeant Lipton came out of his foxhole and told everyone to stay down. "Stay in your foxholes! Stay in your foxholes! Those crazy SOBs are just waiting for you to come out into the open to blast you again!"

Jackson leapt out of his foxhole and ran toward the sound of men calling for help. After a split second of indecision, Rufus quickly followed. Guarnere had Joe Toye and was pulling him to safety when the Germans opened fire again. They had planned well, expecting the Americans to come out in the open to help the wounded. A shell burst over Guarnere and Toye, and Guarnere went down with a badly mangled leg. As suddenly as it began, the shelling stopped. Doc Roe made it to the wounded men first and began treating their wounds. Toye and Guarnere were taken to the Battalion Aid Station, and later, both went on to England for surgery. Both lost their right leg, and both returned home. The war was over for them.

Jackson was only 40 feet away when Guarnere went down. He and Rufus fell to the ground but weren't hit by shrapnel. But they were close enough to the burst to see and feel the concussion. Rufus approached Toye and Guarnere slowly, staying behind Gilmore. As other medics came to help, Jackson decided to leave and let them work. He tracked down the other NCOs and they reported losses across the line. Lieutenant Buck Compton had walked back to the aid station after seeing his two friends, Guarnere and Toye, get hit. Other losses were listed but none were as bad as what Buck witnessed.

Rufus stayed glued to Gilmore's side the entire time out of the foxhole.

***

The next few days were quiet, and Jackson was relieved to see Rufus return to his old self. They played fetch a few times with no further explosions interrupting the game. No attacks along the line held by the 506th occurred for several days, allowing the men to recover a bit and fortify their foxholes. In Berlin, Adolf Hitler, on January 8, ordered the withdrawal of his Army on the western tip of the 'Bulge,' officially ending all dreams of German tanks across the Meuse River and into Antwerp.

Easy Company and the 506th had cleared the woods east of Foy. On January 9, they were ordered to clear the woods west of Foy. Jackson was relieved to see Rufus ready to go to work, taking the lead in the woods, through deep snow. A few Germans provided resistance, and a replacement private was killed. But soon the woods were clear, and they dug foxholes in the snow-covered, ground as best they could.

Gilmore was tired to his bones. He moved continuously between 3rd Platoon men, encouraging the replacements who arrived only a few days earlier. The look in their eyes made Jackson turn away. He saw fear, fear of the unknown, and fear of dying. He turned away, not wanting any of their fear rubbing off on him and Rufus. The Army was sending replacements to the airborne division as fast as possible. But the airborne units were different than regular Army units. The Army's position was to leave companies on the line for long lengths of time, sending replacements as needed to fill in for casualties. The airborne did things different. They continued to fight without replacements, complementing each other by reassigning platoons to strengthen lines. Once pulled off the line and back to garrison, replacements were assigned. At Bastogne, replacements for all units were sent.

That evening, more snow fell, further decreasing the men's morale. The cold was more than most men could endure but endure they did. They continued to change wet socks for almost-dry socks. Most men had trench foot and tried to treat it as best they could. Jackson avoided it by switching wet socks for dry socks every four hours. He had enough socks to swap out, thanks to his mother's Christmas gift. Rufus appeared to weather the cold well. His paws were in good shape, Jackson took time every hour to check them and clean crusted ice from between his claws. And he fed Rufus more often. He knew he was burning calories, so he tried to give him as much meat and rice as he could.

The Germans attacked on January 10 at 0230. German artillery nearly overwhelmed the 506th. During the early morning attack, Jackson and Rufus were along the MLR (Main Line of Resistance), far from their foxhole. They had just repulsed a small combat patrol attack along the line and were checking on the men. 3rd Platoon didn't lose a man, but several were injured. Jackson and Freddie helped the medics clean up wounds and helped men who could walk to jeeps, where they were carried to the Battalion Aid Station.

The morning of January 10 brought only severe cold for the fellas. The temperature never rose about freezing and reached as low as fifteen degrees below zero. The men stayed mostly in their foxholes, only getting up when called upon. Jackson was making rounds when he saw men bringing cut logs into their area. It turned out to be men from the 326th Airborne Engineer Battalion, the unit Eugene had served with. He thought about stopping the men and asking what happened to his brother, but ultimately decided now was not the best time to do that. Still, he appreciated the help and made a note to follow up.

Suddenly (that word again that describes surprise in battle), German artillery rained down on Easy Company. Caught in the open, Jackson and Rufus took off to the south. Jackson looked to his left and saw Freddie running toward their foxhole, only a few yards ahead. To his right he saw First Sergeant Lipton dive into a foxhole partially covered by logs cut by the 326th. Rufus ran alongside him. Rounds exploded everywhere, above them in trees, on all sides. A round hit in front of them, but far enough away that they only felt the concussion, which was almost as bad as taking shrapnel. Freddie slid into the foxhole first, with Jackson and Rufus close behind.

The artillery barrage seemed to go on forever. Trees exploded, sending splinters and large chunks of trees hurtling toward the fellas, now deadly missiles. A shell hit close to their foxhole. The explosion sucked the air out of their lungs, incapacitating them for a moment. Unable to breathe, they nearly passed out. The concussion rattled their ears and sinuses, making their senses useless. Rufus felt all these effects, and not understanding, leapt out of the foxhole and *ran toward the artillery fire.*

Jackson jumped up and ran after Rufus, screaming at him to stop. Rufus either didn't hear or refused to follow orders. Rufus closed on the front line, running at breakneck speed, focused only on what was in front of him. A paratrooper came from their right and tackled Rufus, they went down, but the man held onto Rufus' collar and harness, capturing him. Jackson arrived a few seconds later, and was surprised to see Sergeant Greg Maher, from H Company. Jackson made a snap decision. "Let's go! This way!" Maher grabbed Rufus, threw him over his shoulder and ran with Jackson. Artillery rounds burst everywhere. As they ran to the rear, they saw men waving and calling them to get in their foxhole. Jackson saw Freddie ahead and decided to try to make it. In only a few seconds they dove into the foxhole, just as a round hit 30 feet behind and above them in a tree.

Then, the barrage stopped. Freddie threw the blanket over the foxhole to close it up. Rufus was panting wildly, almost hyperventilating. Jackson quickly attached a leash and handed it to Freddie. They were crowded, but that actually increased the sense of safety for them all, including Rufus. As Jackson talked softly to him, rubbing his fur, Rufus slowly calmed himself, until he laid his head on Jackson's lap, closed his eyes, and rested. Jackson decided he wouldn't move unless it was an emergency.

With Rufus asleep, Gilmore had time to talk to Maher. "Where'd you come from? It looked like you just appeared out of nowhere!" Greg laughed but turned serious. "I'm back in H Company. We're in reserve just a few hundred yards back. I was walking to see I Company on your right when the attack started and had just dived into a foxhole when I saw Rufus. If he had been a little ahead of me, I never would have caught him."

Maher told him what he'd been doing. "Back in Mourmelon, I was asked if I wanted to join the Pathfinders. I figured why not? I'd get to be the first one into combat and set up the beacons for the C-47s to guide on. Then I could start killing Germans before you slackers arrived." Jackson laughed and thanked him for saving Rufus. "I think he's had too much. He was fine in combat, doing some good work. But the artillery attacks we've been through the last few day...well, it's been a lot. We have some rounds land close, a couple in the trees, it's been too much. Heck, I saw some paratroopers just get up out of their foxholes and start walking to the rear. Nothing I could do, so I let 'em walk.

"But I think Rufus will bounce back. He just needs to rest and get the attack behind him. You'll see, Ole Rufus will be just fine." He rubbed his fur gently, Rufus never woke, even snored a little. It was as if he accepted that Jackson would keep him safe and surrendered.

Maher said he would find them again and departed. Freddie left to check on the platoon while Jackson continued to comfort Rufus. Thirty minutes later, Freddie returned with bad news. "Muck and Penkala took a round directly in their foxhole. Nothing's left of them. A few other guys got wounded but nothing the aid station can't fix. We were lucky it wasn't worse." Gilmore thought of the men, all good soldiers, Toccoa men he had known since August 1942. Don Malarky was best friends with Skip Muck, he knew Malarky would be devastated by the loss of his friend and would talk to him later when Rufus was well.

The next two days were quiet, no more artillery attacks. Easy Company performed combat patrols along their front, but Jackson held Rufus back. He told Lieutenant Batson about his concern for Rufus, and Batson agreed, keep him in reserve, let him recover. On January 12, Easy Company was told they would lead the attack on Foy the next day. They were relieved on the line and formed up to the south of the small village, almost exactly where they had dug in weeks ago.

***

The attack on Foy started at 0900 on January 13. Easy Company would lead the assault, with I Company on their flank and H Company in reserve. Jackson stood with Rufus at the edge of the woods overlooking Foy. 3rd Platoon was in front of them. Freddie was ready to go, he carried a Thompson machine gun today instead of his M-1. Easy had about 200 yards of open field in front of them before they reached the village. Large haystacks and scattered trees were the only cover until they reached the town.

Freddie shook hands with Jackson and gave Rufus a good rub.

"I'll see you in a little bit. Don't get worked up and think you need to join us, we'll be fine. See ya at the first coffee shop on the right." Freddie laughed and joined his squad as they got ready to jump off.

At 0900 hours, Winters gave the order to execute the attack. Easy Company moved out in a line across the field. Covering fire opened up and the men sprinted down the sloped field, 1st Platoon on the left, 2nd Platoon in the middle, and 3rd Platoon on the right. Freddie took off in a sprint, moving ahead of the other men. German machine-gun fire poured from buildings, along with sporadic artillery and mortars. 1st Platoon peeled off to the left chasing Germans hiding in shacks. 2nd Platoon continued to race toward Foy, along with 3rd Platoon slightly ahead on the right. Freddie arrived at a small farm building on the outskirts of the town, broke a window and lobbed a grenade inside. Just as the door opened, the grenade exploded, sending two Germans to the ground. Freddie unloaded on them quickly, cleared the building and came out just as his men were stopping in the field. *What the hell are they doing! They'll get creamed there!* He hollered to them. "C'mon! Get moving down here! Let's go!!!"

Then he saw and heard Lipton giving the order to fall back. The rest of 3rd Platoon moved behind any cover they could find, but there wasn't much. Freddie was enraged. *Why did they stop?* He turned back to the front and fired his Tommy gun into the buildings. He jumped back behind the shack, reloaded, and looked for his squad. He found Parker and Hall, hunkered down behind a small hay wagon. He wanted to yell at them to join him, but they were focused on Lipton, now trapped behind a large haystack.

Freddie waited a moment, saw some men attacking on the left, *probably 1st Platoon*, he thought, *but where are they going?* He started shooting again, hoping to provide a little cover for 1st Platoon. A mortar hit near him, knocking him down and slammed shrapnel into his right leg, then machine-gun rounds found him and hit him in his left thigh. Freddie jerked backward from the force of the hits. He didn't move for a brief moment, then he tried to roll over and pull himself to cover.

Jackson watched in horror as the Germans continued to aim at Freddie. Luckily, he had fallen back behind the shack just enough that no rounds could hit him. Then mortar rounds began falling around him. Jackson unshouldered his rifle and nearly took off running but held back. In the next instant, he saw Rufus sprinting down the field, his leash flying behind him. Jackson was stunned. He took off running after Rufus, yelling at him to stop. He looked to his left and saw another paratrooper running down the middle of the field, an officer. It looked like Lieutenant Speirs from Dog Company, but he didn't have time to think what it meant.

"Rufus! RUFUS! GET BACK HERE!" Someone called out from the edge of the woods. It was Colonel Sink. Rufus did stop, looked back at Sink, chuffed once, and sprinted ahead. The pause allowed Jackson to gain on him a little, now only about 40 yards behind his dog. No one shot at Rufus, either they were amazed to see a dog sprinting toward them, or they didn't want to hurt him. Either way, Rufus arrived at Freddie safely. Jackson didn't care, he was just thankful.

Rufus grabbed Freddie's jacket in his teeth and began dragging him to safety. It was slow, but little by little he pulled his friend to safety. Machine-gun rounds hit the ground around them, then walked up and hit Rufus in his left thigh. About a dozen rounds stitched across his hind leg, disintegrating the bone and destroying the muscle and tissue. Shocked by the blow from the powerful machine-gun, Rufus laid on the ground, stunned. But after only the smallest of moments, he stood up again, on three legs, and tried to pull Freddie further into cover.

Jackson slid into them, grabbed Freddie and pulled him behind the shack. He went to grab Rufus, but as he did, machine-gun rounds stitched his lower left leg, his ankle and foot. At least five rounds tore into his flesh and bones, one round hit him in his shoulder, a final round pierced his helmet and exited out the left side. He went down hard from the hits and didn't move.

Blackness surrounded him. His vision was blurring, going black, and he knew he was dead. He tried to call for Rufus, but no sounds left his mouth. Just as Jackson was giving in to unconsciousness, a large hand grabbed his jacket and pulled him to safety. That was all he saw as he blacked out.

***

Nothing. There was no sound, no light, no sensation of anything. He was dead. Is this what death is like? Nothing? Then he heard a sound, very low, but a sound. He tried to open his eyes, no luck. He tried to breathe but didn't know how. He tried to open his eyes again, they flickered, a small amount of light crept in, then a warm feeling came across him, and he fell again into darkness.

***

January 15, 1945
Belgium

Jackson awoke the afternoon of January 15. He had been unconscious for two days. His wounds had been treated, bullets and bits of shrapnel removed. His head was wrapped in a large bandage around his forehead, where a bullet had pierced his helmet but ricocheted to the side of his head and only creased his temple. However, the force of the bullet had caused a concussion and knocked him unconscious.

He tried to talk, but his voice was raspy and barely discernable. A nurse stopped to care for him. "Well Sergeant Gilmore, welcome back to the living! Here, you need to drink this, slowly." She held a cup for Jackson to drink water. At first, he only sipped at it, but soon he drank it all and asked for more. The nurse gave him a little more, then stopped. "That's enough for now. You rest and the surgeon will be by in a little bit to see you."

"Wait…my dog, Rufus, where is he? Is he alright?" He was scared to know the truth, but he needed to know. Then he was ashamed of himself for not asking about Freddie.

"He's fine, Sergeant, he's recovering the same as you, except he's been awake since yesterday. I'm sure he misses you. After the surgeon sees you, I'll see if I can get him in here, does that sound alright? Good, now get some rest."

Gilmore had no intention of going to sleep, he needed answers. But he really was tired and decided a nap wouldn't hurt.

He woke up that evening, hungry. He was fed a light supper. Even though he was starving, he could only eat a little bit before he was full, and tired again. But he asked to see the surgeon before he fell asleep. A nurse returned about 15 minutes later with the doctor, a tall, trim man of about 40 years of age, receding hairline, glasses, but a friendly face. "Hello Sergeant Gilmore, I'm Doctor Howard, I operated on you when you were brought in. I want to talk to you about your wounds. First, how are you feeling? You've had a tough time, I'd say."

Jackson wanted to ask about Rufus (and Freddie), but he waited. "I feel okay sir, just tired and sore. When can I get out of here? I'd like to join my unit in Belgium as soon as possible." The doctor took off his glasses and moved closer to the bed. "Son, I have bad news. You won't be joining your unit again. When you heal up a bit more, we're transferring you to a convalescent hospital in England."

The doctor walked to the foot of the bed. He looked over a clipboard with Jackson's medical chart. "What do you mean I won't go back to my unit? What's wrong?" Howard set the clipboard back on its hook and sat on the edge of the bed. "Son, you received a lot of injuries. You were shot seven times in your left leg, in your left shoulder, bullet fragments from all wounds had to be cleaned. The bullet that hit your forehead caused a concussion and some brain swelling, but we got it under control yesterday."

Slowly, Doctor Howard continued. "These injuries alone will keep you in convalescence for a while. The bullets that tore into your leg caused a tremendous amount of trauma to your lower leg. Your tibia and fibula were shredded. The muscles and tendons were torn off and detached."

He let Jackson digest all that. He looked with intense apprehension, but softly said, "Go on, sir, continue."

"Son, we tried to save your foot, but the damage was to

intense. I removed the bone and tissue about five inches above your ankle."

Jackson's ears were burning, ringing. *I lost my foot. I lost my foot.* The news hit him hard, but he didn't flinch, he didn't cry. "Sir, do you know if my dog Rufus is okay, and my friend, Freddie Spiers? They were hurt with me; I'd like to know if they're okay."

The doctor nodded, "Your dog is here, and he is fine. Your friend is more than likely at another hospital, but we'll see if we can find him." He cleared his throat. "About your dog…he is a very determined animal. He was awake when he was brought into the field hospital and obviously looking for you. You were unconscious, but he found you and it was all we could do to keep him from running to you. We sedated him, cleaned up his wound, and he's resting comfortably. But, well…his injuries were traumatic as well. He received several large wounds to his leg, similar to you. His left hind leg was attached by only a tendon, the muscle was destroyed, the bone atomized. We removed his leg, cleaned up the area and closed him up. He'll be fine soon, ready to chase rabbits in no time."

"Could I see him, sir? I sure miss him and want to check on him." The doctor would check and see if Rufus could be moved. "But it will probably be tomorrow. So, you do what the nurses say, take your meds, and we'll do our best to keep any infections from setting in. I'll check on you tomorrow and we can talk about convalescence." With that he was gone.

***

Rufus was awake. He had received penicillin and pain medication, plus injections for rabies, distemper, and other canine illnesses. His stump was bandaged around his haunch, but he didn't chew at it. He was focused on one thing – finding Jackson. He remembered running to Freddie, his other master, pulling him away from the bad people, but then he got hurt, and didn't know what happened. He knew his leg was missing, but he didn't care, he could find Jackson with only three legs. He needed to find him, but his bed was in a cage. He laid down and waited.

***

The next day Jackson felt better. The morphine wore off and he felt a dull pain in his left leg. His shoulder hurt but not too bad. He was hungry, and when breakfast came, he ate everything he was served. He tried to look at his leg but the blanket was secured over his legs. He wanted to see Rufus.

He stopped an orderly, told him what he wanted, and waited. The nurse who tended to him last night came to see him. Nurse Lunsford was tall for a woman, slim, brown-blonde hair, and a pretty smile. She appeared to be a few years older than him, he thought. But if he could have looked in a mirror, he wouldn't have thought that. War aged him, he looked like a man in his late-30s instead of the 24 years he was.

"I have good news," Nurse Lunsford said with a lovely smile. "The doctor said we could move Rufus over here to be with you. We need to do a little rearranging is all, so be patient and Rufus will be here in no time." 'In no time' turned out to be six hours. It was afternoon when they rolled Rufus' cage into the ward and placed it a few feet from his right side. Rufus was standing in his cage, tail wagging, and when he heard Jackson speak, he let out a loud "BAROOOO!!!" A nurse dropped her instrument tray, adding to the disruption. Anyone who could sit up did, looking for the commotion. Jackson gave Rufus the sign for silence, then the SIT command. Rufus did both immediately, impressing the staff around them.

Jackson thought for a moment, then turned to the head nurse. "You can let Rufus out of his cage now. Since he's with me, he'll stay here and do whatever I tell him to do. Please?" The nurse considered it, but waivered. "I'll check with the administrator, but don't get your hopes up." Rufus stared at Jackson intently. "Hang in there, boy, I'll get you out of there in no time."

'In no time' took 2 days.

***

February 7, 1945
Camberley, Surrey, England

    The weather was milder in the English countryside than Jackson had survived in Belgium, but the temperature was only a little above freezing. But Jackson thought it was just fine, compared to Bastogne. His wounds had healed enough that he could be pushed along in a wheelchair. The cold air felt good after being stuffed in a crowded ward with other patients. It was almost a month since he lost his foot, the staff of the 10th Convalescent Hospital had an excellent convalescent program for him to learn to cope with a missing limb, and how to use a prosthetic foot. Rufus was already up on his legs, walking alongside the wheelchair. The orderly took them to an outdoor exercise area, where other soldiers were performing assorted calisthenics. Two men were boxing, or at least sparring with one another.

    Jackson was told he could relax here before they went inside for rehabilitation. He let Rufus roam among the men, making sure he didn't get in there way. He looked down at his legs, pulled up the blanket to see the stump of his left leg, now with only a small dressing under a wool sock. He covered it up, not wanting to see it anymore. He didn't know how to go on from here. He knew thousands of veterans were in the same shape or worse as him. That didn't help because it wasn't about his injury, it was about letting his men down. He was supposed to be there through the end of the war, making sure others didn't get hurt. He let them down.

    Letting his head fall in shame, tears of hurt, of shame, streamed down his face, nearly freezing to his face in the cold morning air. He didn't care if anyone saw him. *This isn't about me, it's about my men, and how I let them down. It's not about me. It's not about my leg. It's not about me!*

    Rufus suddenly appeared. He had been playing with a few of the other men in wheelchairs, then moved on to check out the perimeter, small bushes and trees lined the property. He quickly pulled his head out of a bush and made a beeline for Jackson. He didn't see Rufus as he approached, his head still down, but felt something fall in his lap. It was an old, dirty tennis ball. Gilmore grabbed it and threw it away as far as he could. Rufus took off, three legs propelling him nearly as fast as his four legs could. He returned the ball and placed it in Jackson's lap. This time Jackson looked up at Rufus.

"No! No playing! Just leave me alone!" He hurled the ball again, and Rufus took off after it. The other soldiers started to watch Rufus run. They were amazed at how fast he could run on three legs, grab the ball and fetch it to Jackson. Each time, he would drop the ball in Jackson's lap, sit and stare directly into his eyes. Jackson, still crying, threw the ball as far as he could while sitting in the wheelchair. He watched Rufus take off chasing the ball, not caring that he lost a leg. It was then that he saw the other men watching and laughing at Rufus' antics. Rufus arrived again, and went through his routine—fetch, drop in lap, sit, and stare.

This time Jackson held the ball. He looked at a few of men watching, then waved them over. Four men walked over. One had a noticeable limp, the others appeared fine. Later he learned they had been hit in their arms, chest, and abdomen with 88mm artillery, and were almost ready to return to combat after three months of rehabilitation. Jackson introduced Rufus to each man, allowing Rufus to shake each man's hand. He asked if anyone wanted to toss a few to Rufus. They all did, so they took turns. Rufus didn't care, he just wanted to chase the ball. After one of the men made a good, long, toss, Rufus returned, panting, placed the ball in Jackson's lap, sat, and stared.

"He sure is single-minded, that's for sure!" one of the men said. His name was Larry Taggart, a staff sergeant in the 10th Armored Division. Taggart was the man with a limp. He had been hit in December when the Germans made their push through the Ardennes.

The men asked about Rufus, and Jackson told them the entire story, meeting in New Jersey, training at Camp Toccoa, jump school, and jumping into Normandy and Holland. Finally, he told them about Bastogne, the horrendous artillery attacks, and how Rufus ran to save Freddie at Foy. They were amazed at what he had done. But they were also inspired by Rufus' ability to overlook his missing leg and go on with work and life.

    Taggart watched Gilmore as he talked about his dog. He saw the pride and love Jackson had for Rufus, but as he watched Rufus run after the ball, he saw the sadness felt by the soldier. It was obvious that Gilmore had much more rehabilitation to do than his dog. What he didn't understand was Jackson's sadness was for Rufus and his men, not himself. The cold finally became unbearable, so Jackson asked for help to return to the ward. An orderly caught up to them and took over. Jackson promised to bring Rufus again to play with the fellas.

***

13

LEARNING TO WALK

February 8, 1945
Camberley, Surrey, England

Shortly after breakfast, Jackson had therapy for his shoulder and then strength training. He learned to walk with crutches and a primitive prosthetic, just good enough to allow him to feel the pressure on his leg while walking. *I'm getting better every day,* he thought, *I may be out of here in a few weeks and go home!* The Army had other plans.

After lunch, Jackson and Rufus were in the lounge, visiting with Taggart. Taggart had fought hard in the Ardennes, but the Germans were too much. But he was ready to get back to his unit. His limp was caused by several shrapnel fragments that penetrated his thigh and hamstring. Taggart figured a few more days and he would bust out, go AWOL and get back to his unit, wherever they were. Few men trusted the Repot Depot.

A rumor had been floating across the men the last few days. Some said the hospital was closing and all the men would be sent to Repot Depot, healed or not. Another rumor was that the hospital was deploying to France, and the men would be transferred. With no control in the matter, the men just gossiped about it while smoking cigarettes in the lounge.

The lounge and wards slowly seemed to fill up with MPs. They were going to each patient, giving them orders, it appeared.

But what orders? A squad of MPs entered the lounge, led by First Sergeant McKay. He came directly to Jackson, handed him orders. "Sergeant Gilmore, I have orders to take ownership of your K-9. We're taking him to the train station tomorrow where he will be loaded up and sent to Liverpool, there to board a ship for New York. You are ordered to the 107th General Hospital in Kington. You will depart tomorrow morning at 0800 hours with a group of patients making the same trip."

Jackson was stunned. *Why are they doing this? They can't split us up!* "Hold up Sergeant! Me and my dog are a K-9 unit provided by the Quartermaster Corps. QM policy is that splitting up a K-9 unit is prohibited. We are required to stay together. So he'll stay with me and go to Kington." He thought he had them stumped.

"These orders supersede anything the Quartermasters put out. This hospital is moving to France, beginning tomorrow. All you men will be given orders for another hospital, so you will be taken care of. For now, wait for your orders, follow instructions, and you'll be fine."

McKay nodded to his men, two of whom approached Rufus and attached a heavy leash. Rufus growled but quickly cut if off. Jackson grabbed the hand of the man with the leash and squeezed. "Let go of his hand, Sergeant. Don't make me repeat it because it will only end up bad for you. Now let go!" Jackson slowly let go, the man took hold of Rufus and led him out of the lounge.

Jackson was enraged. "You can't do this! You don't have the authority! He's my dog! He needs me! HE NEEDS ME!" Jackson's head went back, and a loud wail left his throat. "DAMMIT! I NEED HIM! YOU HERE ME? I NEED HIM!!"

Taggart put his hand on Jackson's shoulder just as he collapsed forward, nearly falling out of his wheelchair. Everyone was stunned by the happenings. Jackson was openly sobbing as several men came to offer support and sympathy. An officer with his right leg in a cast watched from across the room. He stubbed out his cigarette, wheeled out of the lounge and to the nurse's desk. He asked a question, an orderly pointed him down another hall, and he left.

***

Train Station, Camberley, England

It was a little before 0800 hours when the Army MP jeep and truck pulled up to the train depot. Six men, along with First Sergeant McKay, jumped out and began unloading. They didn't notice the British jeep and Leyland Retriever parked with their rear facing the depot. As the MPs exited the truck, so did eight British Paratroopers, while a British Captain and staff sergeant, both wearing paratrooper jump wings, exited the jeep.

The MPs continued to unload Rufus, a cage, and two bags of supplies. McKay took the leash and control of Rufus. As they turned to enter the depot, Captain Smythe stepped forward a few paces and blocked the path to the depot. McKay, confused by the delay, stopped. He recognized the officer rank and quickly saluted, not waiting for a return salute from the Brit. "Morning sir, what can I do for you?"

"Good morning, Yanks. I'm Captain Smythe, and I've been ordered to take ownership of the dog you have. So let's make this easy, old chap, and hand me the leash."

McKay didn't understand what was going on, but he knew better than to disobey his orders. "I don't believe I can do that, Captain. My orders are to put the animal on the train, and that's what I'll do. So, unless you and your men want to end up in the stockade, you'll move aside and let me get on with my business!"

Smythe allowed a slow smile to escape but hid it quickly. He raised his left hand and made a 'come here' movement. His paratroopers raised their rifles, pointed expertly at McKay. "As I was saying, I'll take the leash, Sergeant." McKay looked at the paratroopers and had no doubt of their determination. Without a word, he reached forward and placed the leash in Captain Smythe's hand.

"Thank you, Yanks, for a splendid morning, now off you go. Leave the cage and supplies, thank you very much."

***

Jackson was forced to get up in the morning. He had no desire to go anywhere, too devastated over the loss of his best friend to care about anything. Once dressed for cold weather, he was given a breakfast of orange juice and a couple of biscuits with ham. He threw them away, untouched. The convoy to Kington was preparing to load, and Jackson was helped into a truck bed, along with his wheelchair and small bag of possessions. But before the convoy could move, a group of British paratroopers pulled up to the front, blocking the trucks. A British officer, a Major wearing paratrooper wings, stepped out of a British staff car just a few moments after Captain Smythe was confronting Sergeant McKay at the train depot. Another paratrooper, a Company Sergeant Major, stepped out of the car with the Major. The Major nodded to the Sergeant Major, who whistled loudly, which was followed by eight British paratroopers exiting the truck and formed up loosely behind him. Sergeant Major Loughty stood silent in front of his men, his large mustache hiding his mouth.

Major Harcourt stood tall and straight and appeared to not suffer fools or exaggerations. His voice was loud and rumbled across the convoy. "My name is Major Richard Harcourt. I have orders to deliver to Staff Sergeant Jackson Gilmore. Would you please present him to me? Staff Sergeant Gilmore, please come forward." The soldiers and staff were too startled to do much, but the orderly who helped Jackson into the truck quickly helped him to the ground, wheeled him to the Major, then departed.

Jackson looked at the Major, his uniform magnificent in the morning son, his awards and jump wings proudly displayed across his chest. Jackson stood up from his wheelchair and saluted, maintaining his balance without a crutch. "Staff Sergeant Gilmore reporting as ordered, Sir." He didn't know what this was about and really didn't care. He would care very soon.

"Sergeant Gilmore, I have orders to escort you to Queen Alexandra Military Hospital in London for treatment. Another team has already retrieved your dog, they will meet us at hospital. Now, as quick as possible, let's load you up and get you to your dog." Jackson was stunned. He quickly grabbed his crutches and stumbled to the truck. "Wait, Sergeant, we'll help you into the car." Harcourt yelled over his shoulder, just as the hospital administrator came charging forward. Jackson saw this and knew they had to hurry to make their escape.

Doctor Hill was stomping toward Major Harcourt, his white lab coat streaming behind him. His face was red, his glasses nearly steamed up from his anger. "What's going on here? Who are you men and why have you stopped our movement? By God I want answers, now!" Harcourt smiled and quietly handed a copy of the orders to the administrator, who glanced over them quickly.

"Why, these are British orders, not American! You have no authority to take an American soldier from this facility!"

Harcourt quietly responded. "Sir, we have *every* right to escort this soldier to another facility. You will see that the papers are in order, run them up your chain of command, you will find they are approved at the *highest level*. But we're not waiting, we have our orders and will follow them to the letter. With that, I offer you good day, sir." Harcourt performed a perfect about face, waved his arm in a small circle above his head, and before the administrator could say a word, they were gone.

***

The 30-mile trip took over an hour to get from Camberley to Queen Alexandra Military Hospital. Jackson had a thousand questions to ask, but Major Harcourt would only provide a few details. He was forced to sit in anguish, but finally realized there was nothing he could do but wait. At least the staff car was warm. He tried to get more details, but it was difficult. Either the Major didn't know, or he wasn't telling.

The ride was uneventful, but when they reached London, Jackson was overwhelmed by the size of the city. He enjoyed the chance to see the historical city, especially the ride along River Thames. When they reached the hospital, a small group of British and American officers were waiting. Jackson saw Rufus, on a leash held by a British enlisted man. The driver took them past the main entrance, where Rufus was, and into a parking lot across the road. Jackson couldn't get out of the car fast enough. When he was finally on the pavement, the Sergeant Major handed him his crutch. "Here, go get your dog, laddie," the Sergeant Major said, in a thick Scottish brogue.

Jackson thanked him and hurried toward the front of the hospital. Rufus saw him and almost pulled the leash out from the paratrooper's hand. Captain Smythe saw this, got the man's attention. He mouthed 'Let him go to his mate.' The Sergeant knelt by Rufus, rubbed him one last time, and said "Here you go boy, go see your master." He unhooked Rufus, and he was gone in a flash. Jackson saw him running, all three legs churning. He dropped his crutch and knelt. Bad move. Rufus plowed into him, bowling him over. Astonished, the bystanders began to run to Jackson to assist him. But Jackson was fine, he grabbed Rufus by his neck and held him close.

"I'm okay boy, I'm okay. I'll never let anyone take you away from me again. NEVER." He hugged Rufus as he received slobbers across his neck and face. Major Harcourt and Sergeant Major Loughty arrived and faced Captain Smythe. Smythe was his executive officer of the airborne battalion from which the men had been selected to assist with the 'relocation' of Rufus and Gilmore. He watched the unseemly act of emotion, asked "How long have they been apart, Smythe?" Captain Smythe allowed a minute smile across his face, then covered it. "Why, I believe about 20 hours, in total, sir." Harcourt watched the joyful reunion a bit longer, then shook his head. "Hmmmf. That's quite a show of affection to be apart for less than a day."

Sergeant Major Loughty watched with amusement. Harcourt added, "Yanks. I'll never understand them." Sergeant Major Loughty added, "But God Bless them, sir."

Harcourt agreed. "Quite so. Yes, God Bless them all."

***

April 1945
Queen Alexandra Military Hospital, London

The weather was perfect, a mild 70 degrees, partly cloudy skies and a soft breeze. Staff Sergeant Gilmore was walking his K-9 partner along the sidewalks of London. He wore his winter service uniform even though the weather was mild, as the Army had made it policy that the winter uniform would be worn throughout the year. His trousers covered where his leg attached to a prosthetic ankle and foot. The joint was primitive, but effective; he could walk, though he needed a cane for additional support. An orderly walked silently behind him, giving him privacy but close enough to be there if Jackson needed help.

Rufus walked beside him, in Heel position. Rufus' gait was different now, but he learned to walk in Heel position with three legs without difficulty. Jackson remained amazed at how easily Rufus accepted his injury and shook it off and moved on. He remembered all the attacks, gun fights, mortars, and machine-guns they had faced together. The only time Rufus seemed to be affected was the horrendous shelling they survived at Bastogne. *What animal could go through that unaffected? What man could?* He thought. He was right. Each man who made it through Bastogne carried what he went through in himself. Jackson thought he handled it well, but he also had come to realize that he depended on Rufus more than the other way around.

He came back to the present, looked at Rufus. Rufus walked with his funny three-legged gait without thinking. Jackson had a slight limp, caused by the connection of human flesh to a metal and plastic joint. A new prosthetic was promised when he returned home. He was ready now. A thought occurred to him; if he had not lost his foot, and the doctors saved it, his rehabilitation would be much longer, probably over a year. But by starting with a stump, which healed extremely well, no infections, he was ready to go home in four months after his injury.

A cry brought him back to the street. A beautiful young woman in a blue uniform had stopped in front of Rufus. "What a beautiful dog! May I pet him?" Rufus didn't wait for Jackson, he nuzzled the woman, rubbed against her, and nearly lost his balance. "Oh my, he is a friendly lad! What's his name?"

"Rufus. Tech Sergeant Rufus, actually." He looked at her again. She had short, dark hair under her blue garrison cap, and wore wings over her left breast pocket. Her jacket was pressed and clean, as was her blue skirt. Just then, another woman in uniform joined the first, then a third, all in the same uniform. They lavished praise on Rufus, rubbing his thick fur as his shortened tail wagged furiously. Jackson recognized that Rufus had been around only men for most of the past three years. One of the ladies finally asked Jackson his name and what he does in the Army.

"Staff Sergeant Jackson Gilmore, ma'am. Rufus and I are a K-9 unit in the 101st Airborne Division. We're going through rehabilitation at hospital down the street." More questions came. He gave them the short story, explaining how Rufus had been injured, and finally lost his leg. "What a brave lad he is!" said the first WAAF who had seen Rufus. She continued to rub him along his head and neck, Rufus just closed his eyes.

The WAAFs (Women's Auxiliary Air Force) were together, taking lunch in a nearby café. "It was so nice to meet you, Staff Sergeant. If you are still around this weekend, you should drop by here." She handed him a card with an address and dance hall information. "We host dances for the many soldiers and airmen here, helps keep them out of trouble, if you know what I mean."

He knew what she meant. Since arriving in England, American soldiers would try to get to London to enjoy the city's nightlife, and the ladies. Soldiers would return to garrison and have to be treated for venereal diseases. Jackson didn't much care for that kind of entertainment, but he thought the dance would be nice. He thanked the women as they departed, and decided it was time to head back to the hospital. He watched the beautiful women walk away as a faint hint of perfume lingered in the air. A thought struck him. *I've been gone a long time. Boy, do I need to get home. Rufus needs to get home too.*

He decided he would push to go home. Now.

When he returned, a letter awaited him. He was shocked when

he read it. Prime Minister Churchill would be coming to the hospital for dinner with Jackson. Tonight. 6:00pm. Jackson scrambled.

He stopped a nurse and asked for help. He didn't know how to act at a formal dinner, he needed training. The nurse sent him to the dining hall and told him she would be there in a few minutes. When she arrived, she laid out a dinner setting. She showed him how to select which spoon for soup, which fork for the main course, how to turn the fork upside down when eating, and so on. He understood but was nervous.

He brushed his wool jacket until he had it as neat as possible. He gave Rufus a bath, brushed his fur until it had a beautiful sheen to it. His leg wound had healed perfectly, his fur had grown long and covered the wound. He didn't have a harness for him to wear, so he only wore a collar. Once dressed, they were ready. A few of the British nurses and doctors went with him to the front of the hospital to await for Churchill's car to arrive. They all gave him advice on what to say, what not to say, how to act, all good things to know.

The PMs car arrived, an assistant jumped out of the left front seat and opened the rear door. Churchill appeared with a cigar in his mouth, waved to all the hospital staff, but focused on Jackson and Rufus. Jackson was standing at attention, Rufus at heel position. But as soon as Rufus saw Churchill, his tail started wagging. The PM shook hands with the hospital administrator and his staff, and finally stood in front of Jackson. Gilmore saluted while Rufus rose to attention. Churchill raised his right arm, stuck his cigar in his mouth, saluted, and grabbed his cigar with his hand on the way down.

"Hello Sergeant, it's very good to see you and Rufus in one piece. Well, mostly, I'm told. Shall we go inside?" Churchill's chief of staff, a full colonel, followed them at a respectful distance, but close enough to hear if Churchill needed anything. A special room had been set up for the PM's visit. A small dining table had been set in a staff dining room, which also doubled as a reading room for staff and patients, as the walls were covered in shelves full of books. Churchill lit another cigar as they were seated.

As the dinner was served, The Prime Minister carried the conversation, discussing the state of the war, the Battle for Berlin, what the world would look like post-war, and about the loss of his good friend, Franklin D. Roosevelt. President Roosevelt had passed on April 12, and Churchill still mourned quietly. Churchill's chief of staff remained mostly quiet but did throw out a comment here and there. After dinner, they moved to another room, where Churchill and the Colonel both smoked cigars while waiting for Brandy to be served. Jackson, normally a teetotaler, decided he could use a drink.

Churchill asked him about the day he was wounded at Foy. Jackson started in Bastogne, detailing what they went through, how Rufus became disoriented by the terrific shelling they survived. That was why they stayed back during the initial attack on Foy. "My buddy went down, and when Rufus saw that, he took off to save him. I ran as fast I could but there was no way I could catch Rufus. He was hit badly before I could reach them. I was hit before I could move him to safety. I still don't know what happened after that."

Churchill looked at his chief of staff, Colonel O'Neill, who nodded. The Colonel would send a message requesting the field report of the incident. But Gilmore had a question. "Sir, how did I get here?" He didn't know how he was moved to the British hospital, but it felt just like the other times when someone intervened in his and Rufus' path.

Churchill smiled and blew out a large amount of smoke. "I assumed you came over on a troop ship or airplane, Sergeant." Before Jackson could say he meant 'get to the hospital,' Churchill winked at him as he stood. "I know what you meant son, just having a little fun with you. Colonel O'Neill, could you please explain how Sergeant Gilmore and Rufus ended up here?"

O'Neill was happy to explain. "The PM received a call from General Eisenhower on February 8. He had a request of great importance that needed to get to the PM as quickly as possible. It seemed that a Lieutenant Colonel at Camberley witnessed how your dog was taken so rudely. He is a member of the 101st Division, the 501st Parachute Infantry Regiment, and had been wounded at Bastogne by artillery. He put a call through to General Taylor's headquarters, at that time, in the Ruhr Valley in the town of Glehn. Taylor immediately called Ike, who had his chief of staff call me. I informed the PM of the events which had transpired, he immediately ordered me to get both of you out of that hospital and into one of ours. I thought the best men to do this job were paratroopers. And here we all are."

The story amazed him. Gilmore had lost count of the times someone had intervened to help him. No, help *Rufus*. Now, once again, Prime Minister Churchill had intervened on his behalf. He had to ask. "Sir? Can you tell me why? I mean, you got me out of a pickle, that's for sure, but why? I'm just a soldier who has a dog for a partner, nothing special. Well, Rufus is special, but not me."

Churchill turned from the books he was reviewing along the wall and sat down next to Jackson. He started rubbing Rufus along his neck and back. "From the day I saw you and Rufus jump from an airplane, then sprint across the field, outrunning everyone else, I was very interested in the both of you. Your spirit was greatly welcomed, as well as the rest of our brave boys. I received reports on your whereabouts and activities and became more impressed. I did not receive any reports out of Bastogne, of course, but soon learned of both of your wounds at Foy. But when Colonel O'Neill told me of your predicament, I had to act. This animal's heart and courage have been a bright spot in this dark, dark world."

Jackson agreed. "But sir, he was just doing his job. If he acted on his own, it was to protect me, or Freddie. He didn't know the Germans were bad, he just knew they were trying to hurt me." Churchill smiled. "Well lad, doesn't that make what he did all the more special?"

***

14

HOME

May 1945
In Transit

The flight across the Atlantic was long and uneventful. Churchill made his personal transport available to take Jackson and Rufus home. A few British Army officers and civilians accompanied them. The first leg took them to Newfoundland, where Jackson and Rufus had spent a few days on the way to England. From there they flew direct to New York and set down at LaGuardia Airport during mid-morning hours.

Mail had caught up to Jackson a few days before he departed for home. A letter from Freddie caught him up. Spiers was fine, his leg had healed just fine, though he was still recovering, and probably wouldn't be released until June. He wrote of what happened after they were all hit.

> *After I went down, I lost consciousness, until I felt somebody pulling me to safety. It was Rufus! Then Rufus got hit, and I just laid there, unable to move. I think I passed out again, but then I saw you pulling me to safety. And that's all I saw. Next thing I knew I woke up in a field hospital. Johnny Martin told me what happened. A big guy from H Company, Sergeant Greg Maher, broke out of reserve and raced down the hill not far behind you. He saw you get hit, grabbed you and Rufus and pulled you behind the barn. When he came back*

for me, he was hit several times in his leg but didn't go down. He pulled me to safety too. Johnny said he picked up my Thompson and sprayed the Germans that were out of their hide. About then, Easy Company picked up the attack again. Maher ran down the road into Foy and killed a sniper and a machine-gunner. But then several Germans ranged in on him and he went down. After the battle, Johnny said they counted 17 rounds in his legs and torso. But he never quit. Major Winters nominated Maher for the Medal of Honor, Sink approved, and General Taylor sent it up to SHAEF.

Jackson took Rufus down the steps to the tarmac, where he was greeted by an Army Private, who would drive them to Camp Shanks. Another soldier arrived with his wheelchair and bags, and they were on their way. At Camp Shanks, he was provided temporary quarters for a technical sergeant. As Rufus was an E-7, he deserved a better room. After settling in, the first thing he did was call his mother. He had written her, told her about his wounds, and that he was coming home soon.

The call was emotional for both of them, as it should be. His mother cried for her son's losses, but also for his safe return. He told her he would try to get home soonest, but he was still in the Army, and they dictated his schedule. He told her he would call again soon and would write every day.

The next morning, they reported to the admin building. There he received his schedule:

Report to:
- Elberon, New Jersey for 'demilitarization' of Rufus (One week)
- Military Hospital, Nashville, Tennessee – prosthetic fitting (One month)
- Release from Active Duty
- VA Hospital – prosthetic adjustments

He would be home for good in five weeks.

***

Tennessee

"Momma! He's home! He's HOME!" Penny ran into the kitchen holding a letter from Jackson. Now fifteen years old, she had shed her awkwardness, her hair was a shiny red, pulled back into a pigtail, her face clear and beautiful. Her mother suspected Penny was excited that both Rufus *and* Jackson were home.

The letter from Jackson told her about Rufus, how brave he was, and how he lost his leg. He asked her to not be sad because Rufus was fine, he didn't know it was missing. He would visit her when he got home. The letter said nothing of giving Rufus back to Penny.

***

He travelled by train to New Jersey. With frequent stops, the 85-mile trip took over four hours. But Jackson didn't mind, he enjoyed looking at the countryside, with Rufus sitting at his side. Soldiers and airmen filled a quarter of the train, returning home like him, or reporting to another base. *This trip is silly*, he thought. Rufus was already 'demilitarized.' Jackson had made some important decisions about the care and feeding of Rufus, and he would prove it.

When he arrived at Elberon, he and Rufus disembarked and waited for their baggage. He figured he'd either have to call or catch a ride to Mrs. Erlanger's home. Before he could retrieve his luggage, he heard his name called. He couldn't believe who it was! "First Sergeant Sellers! I didn't expect to see you here!" They shook hands, then hugged. Rufus got in on the welcome too, weaving in and out of Seller's and Gilmore's legs. Clyde gave Rufus a good welcome too. "C'mon, I've got a truck waiting to take us to the kennels."

Waiting at Mrs. Erlanger's was none other than Henry Stoecker. After a joyous reunion, they went to Henry's office to settle in from the trip. Henry told Jackson how he ended up in New Jersey. "The Army directed that all returning K-9 units to be 'demilitarized,' or detrained. I was placed in charge of the training and requirements. I've been looking for your name to come across my desk, and it finally did. Thanks to the Dogs for Defense program, K-9s are returning to a normal life. We've been sending the returning units to the War Dog Training Centers to allow the dogs to return to homes instead of being locked in an Army kennel somewhere. Once the dog has completed training and given a clean bill of health, his owners are contacted if they noted they wanted the dog upon his return. I requested for you and Rufus to come here so I could review the detraining."

Jackson didn't think much detraining would be needed and said as much. "You'll be surprised at how much he's already adjusted to being home. But I'll be honest. I departed from our training pretty quickly. When I saw how the fellas reacted to Rufus, I knew they needed to be as close to him as I am. So, I allowed them to pet Rufus, allowed a few close friends to see to him and feed him. You saw how the men reacted to him in Kentucky. It's been that way for three years. In garrison, in town, in combat."

Gilmore had more to say. "Rufus learned the difference between children and adults, and never snapped at or bit a child. I left it up to Rufus to decide if a soldier was a friend, or someone to avoid. He never thought a German was a friend," he said with a chuckle. "I almost never put him on leash. In fact, the only time he was on leash during combat was at Foy, and that was to make sure he didn't run into the fight. But he did it anyway, to save our best friend."

Henry nodded his head. "You know Jackson, you may have just changed the way we train K-9s. Maybe dogs could be more than what we trained them to do. Rufus proved he can become part of a unit, and not just a K-9 that only answers to one soldier. I think I'll make some suggestions."

The next day, Henry observed Rufus playing, meeting strange men and strange dogs, new scents. He showed very little aggression. Everyone and every dog he met, he wanted to be friends. At Henry's order, a strange man attempted to hurt Jackson. Rufus blocked the man, pushing him away, growling and barking. But he never attempted to hurt the man. Later, when a man wearing padding attacked Jackson, getting him in a choke hold, Jackson hollered in protest. Rufus attacked the man violently, biting his protected arm and trying to drag him down. But as soon as Jackson was free, he let go and stayed between the man and his master.

After three days, Rufus was declared detrained, a ceremony was held where Rufus stood at attention while he received a certificate of faithful service and was honorably discharged. Jackson stood at attention in his service uniform (summer dress), so proud of Rufus. Rufus not only served with distinction, his actions and interaction with so many different people, in battle, in garrison, proved that he would transform the nature of K-9 training. Henry Stoeker would make sure of that, utilizing First Sergeant Sellers to lead the new training, once approved, of course.

After a day of rest and relaxation, except for throwing a tennis ball a hundred times to Rufus, they packed up for a ride to the train depot. Clyde drove them in an Army truck, with Rufus sitting between them. Clyde drove the big truck with one arm, shifting with his right arm while driving with his left leg on the steering wheel. It looked dangerous, but Clyde had it down to a science. "The Army is sending me to a prosthetics maker in Ohio in a couple of weeks. Some companies have made some big improvements lately, and more are coming. When you get fitted, be sure to keep coming back every year to see what the VA has. It will only get better."

Sellers told Gilmore he was moving to North Carolina to take over as the head trainer at the War Dog Training Center near Camp Mackall. He was in line to be the First Sergeant for the entire center upon his arrival and take over as the senior enlisted of the training center. "You know Jackson, if it wasn't for you and Rufus, I don't think I would be here where I am. I gave up back in England, I thought I didn't have anything left to give the Army, even less what I could do for my family. But your belief in me and help from Henry...."

He choked up a little, then got it together. "Without you and Henry's belief in me, I probably would have come home and took disability, and never tried to work." He rubbed Rufus with his right hand, driving with his knee. "Ole Rufus helped me most. He gave me cheer when I had nothing. My heart and soul were black, but your kindness, and Rufus' love pulled me out of it. I'll never be able to repay you." Clyde looked at Jackson, his eyes telling him more than words what Clyde was feeling. Jackson looked away, embarrassed by the raw emotion. Rufus sensed the sentiment, reached and licked Jackson across his face, then did the same to Clyde, making him laugh and turn away and almost drive off the road. After Clyde got control, they burst out laughing. Clyde would be just fine.

***

June 1945
Greensburg, Tennessee - Home

The train took forever to get to Greensburg. It was only a few hours ride from Nashville, but to Jackson, it was an eternity. He had spent two weeks at the Nashville Military Hospital, where the Army had specialist in prosthetics helping the returning veterans. Jackson remained on active duty until the end of June, his orders telling him that he would be free to return home as soon as he completed his fitting in Nashville. The doctors were impressed with how clean his wound had healed. The prosthetic technicians studied his wound, took exacting measurements, and fit him with another temporary foot which was an improvement over the one he wore. He was ordered home and to come back in two weeks to receive his new prosthetic.

***

The entire town (almost 400 citizens) turned out to greet Jackson and Rufus. The train stopped, a few folks got off before them, but when Jackson stepped to the door to disembark, the cheers overwhelmed him. Rufus took a step back as well. Then his mother was hugging him, then his dad, and friends. Rufus was squeezed out by all the people, but Jackson saw it and pulled him close. He moved off the train and onto the depot boarding platform where there was more room. With all the attention and hugs, he almost lost his garrison cap, so he took it off and tucked it in his belt.

Finally, the crowd pulled back enough to give his mother room to hold her son again. Her black, silky hair was grayer than when he left, but it was beautiful under a large cartwheel hat, her blue dress immaculate and shiny. Jackson hugged her tightly, and finally, cried for Eugene. Faye instinctively knew he cried for his brother and cried with him. The crowd quieted out of respect for the family, shooshes going through the throng. "I'm sorry, Momma, I'm so sorry. I didn't know where Eugene was that day, but it turns out we were only a mile or two apart. I could have taken my squad and protected him."

His mother looked up at her baby boy, held his face in her hands. "There's nothing you could have done, baby, nothing. We'll talk about your brother when we get home. Now, dry your face and say something to everyone who came to welcome you home."

The train whistle blew loudly as it departed the depot, people moved back from the tracks, and Jackson took advantage of the small disruption to move Rufus to a less crowded area. After the train departed, the crowd turned to Jackson again. He stood on the steps leading into the train station so he could see everyone. Someone yelled "Speech! Speech!" followed by cheers and hand claps. He wasn't prepared but had to say something. His mother caught his eye, and with a nod from her, he had strength.

"I want to thank all of you who came out today to welcome me and Rufus home. It feels like I've been away for a hundred years, it's hard to believe it's only been a little over three years since I left to fight the Germans. We went through some tough training, some tough times. But when we finished a battle, or stopped the enemy from pushing through the line, we looked at each other, thankful that the man next to us was a paratrooper."

The crowd cheered loudly at that. In December 1944, everyone knew that the 101st Airborne Division fought bravely at

Bastogne. Thanks to locals who contacted newspapers, it was announced that one of Greensburg's own was fighting bravely in Bastogne. AP news articles were carried by local papers, where the journalists wrote of hometown heroes. Jackson was the last man to consider himself a hero. But he considered Rufus a hero. And Freddie, and Maher. And many, many others.

"We fought hard everywhere we went. Ole Rufus here was a real hero, he saved my life many times, and saved the lives of many paratroopers. He got wounded more times than I did. And when he lost his leg, he…he…"

Emotions overwhelmed him. Someone shouted "Take your Time, Jackson! It's okay, your home now buddy!" Others spoke up, reassuring him. Finally, he was ready to speak again. He raised his hand and the crowd quieted. "When he lost his leg, he was knocked back from the force, nearly knocked out. Instead of lying there, he jumped up and went back to dragging Freddie to safety. He cares more about the life of a paratrooper than his own life. He never received a medal because the Army refuses to assign a medal designed for men to a dog."

He took a deep breath. "Anyway, it sure is nice to be home, it was swell to see all of you. I'm real tired now, so I think we need to go home. Thank you all." He stepped down as the town folk clapped him on his back, welcomed him home and cheered him on. Rufus stayed next to him without missing a step, figuratively speaking, of course.

***

Late June 1945

He did not want to do this. He almost told his dad to stop the truck and turn around for home. They travelled down a dusty dirt road toward a small farming community in middle Tennessee, only two hours away from Greensburg. Rufus rode in the middle, having already had his fill of wind and smells with his head out the window. It was already hot in the mid-morning, but they knew it would only get hotter. Jackson was hot in his summer dress uniform. Gene, Jackson's father, drove about 30 miles per hour, and slowed even more when a vehicle approached, so as not to throw too much dirt in the air.

They were going to meet Penny, Rufus' true owner. When she had donated Rufus, she had checked the box to return him to her at the end of his service. Jackson had received a letter from Henry Stoeker, reminding him of his responsibility, no matter how hard it would be. Rufus was released from service at Mrs. Erlanger's kennel in May, over a month ago. Secretly, he hoped to keep Rufus, explaining that Rufus would need a lot of care and tending to because of his wounds.

They arrived just before lunch time, as planned. The whole family was there to greet them. Jim and Marilyn, Penny, and Jimmie, also dressed in summer dress uniform, now wearing sergeant stripes. Rufus was dressed in his jump harness, with his rank and jump wings sewn in the middle. On the left side, he wore two medals: a purple heart and a bronze star. Jackson had given them to Rufus to wear. *He deserves them more than anyone, including myself,* Jackson thought. Rufus saw Penny, who wore a green skirt and a white sleeveless shirt with small frilly collars. Her hair was a beautiful, bright red, fashionably done under a small, green hat. She was beautiful. Rufus keened; he knew he was home.

Gene stopped the truck and turned it off. Dust settled quickly, and Jackson stepped out of the truck with Rufus on leash. He removed the leash, rubbed him on his head, and whispered "Okay boy, this is it. Go see your master, boy, go see Penny." Rufus looked excitedly at Jackson, then bolted to Penny. Rufus could still run fast on three legs, but when he reached Penny, instead of jumping on her, he hunkered down on his hindquarters and nuzzled her. He whined while he licked her face and neck, eliciting high-pitched laughter from Penny. After Rufus settled down, introductions were made, and the Gilmores were invited into the farm house. No one removed their shoes or boots.

Lunch was ready, Marilyn had cooked fried chicken, okra, black-eyed peas, green beans, cornbread, a homemade apple pie, and plenty of sweet tea. She asked about Mrs. Gilmore, Jackson's mother, who didn't make the trip. Gene apologized, giving Marilyn his wife's regards, but she had pressing duties with the newly founded town library. Rufus sat beside Jackson, but soon crawled over to Penny's feet, where he laid his head. Penny was filled with emotions, so happy that her dog was home, amazed at all the things he and Jackson had done, and so sad for both of their losses. But she was profoundly amazed at Rufus' outlook. His missing leg didn't faze him in the least bit.

After lunch and a piece of apple pie topped with homemade vanilla ice cream, they retired to the living room. Rufus sat on the floor while Penny went to her room upstairs, returning quickly with a large scrapbook. She placed it on the large, square coffee table and opened it. Inside were newspaper articles from all over the nation, New York, Saint Louis, Nashville, even San Francisco. The articles were ordered by date, beginning with Pearl Harbor. Marilyn had helped her at first, buying newspapers, asking friends to save articles of paratroopers, training, the 101st, the 506th, D-Day and so on. Soon Penny took over, riding her bike to neighbors, asking for any newspapers she could look through, taking old newspapers from the only drug store in town. Soon folks started saving newspapers for Penny. Marilyn also kept articles of Jimmie's travels and actions. He fought in Italy, came ashore at Omaha on D-Day, and fought across Europe until Germany's surrender. While Jackson wanted to see Jimmie's scrapbook, today was Penny's and Rufus' day.

Jackson sat on the floor, next to the coffee table and flipped through the scrapbook. Rufus and Penny sat on the floor also, Rufus between them. Both reached their arm up and rubbed the fur on his neck, sometimes touching hands and quickly withdrawing, only to do it again.

Jackson answered questions about each movement, battle, and jump he made during the war. He explained that Rufus never left his side, except when they were wounded and went into surgery. He told stories of Rufus' bravery, how he attacked Germans without pause, and how he had saved their friend Freddie. Penny even had articles from *The Stars and Stripes*. How she got them is a mystery. Jackson suspected Jimmie mailed them home to his sister. She was very proud of the photo of Jackson and Rufus at the hospital in England, where Rufus was covered in purple heart medals. Jackson provided the back story of how soldiers gave their medals to Rufus after hearing his story.

Jackson asked if he could take Rufus for a walk before they left. Penny quickly agreed and accompanied them on a walk around the farm. A breeze blew from the south, providing some comfort from the heat. Jackson had so much to say, but not sure where to start. "Penny, when I met Rufus, he didn't impress me, floppy ears and all. But after a few days of training, I knew he was special. When I volunteered for the Airborne, I knew Rufus wouldn't let me down. He took to parachuting like a duck to water. He absolutely loves it. If you ever get a chance to let him parachute, take it."

They continued to walk along a tree line, mostly in the shade. Rufus walked between them, stopping to smell something interesting here and there. "Something else that makes him special is his sense of compassion. I took him to a few hospitals to see buddies who were wounded, and he made everybody feel better. So, take him to see kids in hospitals if you can. They'll ask what happened to his leg, tell them the truth—he lost it saving a soldier's life."

Emotion swelled over Jackson. He choked up for a second but cleared his throat and wiped tears from his eyes.

"He doesn't take being left behind very well. He'll need to stay with you every day and night. He won't understand why you have to leave him to go to school, but after a few days he'll see that you come home each day. But your mom will probably have to watch him close the first few times you're gone."

Penny took all this in quietly. She was beginning to feel the weight of taking care of a war dog. Rufus had been on a great adventure; he had grown up to be a great war dog. But now he needed peace, and someone to love him and take care of him. She could do it. They made their way back to the farm house, where Gene was talking to Jim and Jimmie by the truck. Jackson stopped, turned to Penny, and handed her the leash. He kneeled by Rufus and attached the leash to his collar.

He couldn't stop himself from crying. Tears ran down his face uncontrollably. "I love you, boy," he whispered. "You take care of Penny, okay? I'll come see you real soon. But you belong here, with Penny. She loves you too, boy. It's OKAY." He hugged his dog one last time, stood and walked to the truck. Rufus, confused, pulled on the leash to follow Jackson. Penny, also in tears, just held the leash, but then kneeled down and wrapped her arms around Rufus.

"Let's go, Dad. Mister Jim, it was nice to meet you. Jimmie, I'm glad you made it home safe. Maybe we'll see y'all again sometime." They all shook hands, then Jackson slowly got in the truck and shut the door. He didn't look up. Rufus didn't understand, he just knew he would be separated from Jackson, so he barked his famous 'BAROOOO!' to get his attention. Jackson didn't look up. Gene drove off slowly to give Jackson time to take one last look. But he couldn't look. Before Gene turned onto the gravel road that led away, they heard Rufus.

"BAROOOO!!!"
"BAROOOO!!!"
"BAROOOO!!!"

And then Jackson broke down.

Not able to breathe, his body convulsing, he choked while deeply crying. About a mile from Penny's house, Gene pulled over. He put his hand on Jackson's shoulder, trying to comfort him. "You did good, son. I know how difficult that was, I know what Rufus means to you. He got you through the war and got you and a lot of other soldier's home. Be proud of what you and Rufus did." Gene patted his son's shoulder again, comforting him as best he could. Jackson settled down but continued to softly cry. "He means everything to me, Dad. I can't leave him here. He needs me, Dad, he needs me...."

Gene heard a soft rumble, looked into the rearview mirror. He saw dust flying up the road, someone was coming, fast, much faster than his 30 miles per hour. He rolled up his window so dust wouldn't fill up the cab. But when the truck got closer, it slowed, then pulled to a stop behind them. He recognized the driver, it was Jim. The passenger door opened, and Penny stood by the side of the road. She said something, then Rufus jumped to the road as well.

"Son, you need to look up," Gene said softly. When Jackson didn't move, he spoke a little louder, annunciating each word.

"Jackson. Look. Up."

This time he raised his head, saw where his dad was looking, so he turned to look out the back window. When he saw Rufus, he jumped out of the cab and ran to him. Penny unhooked the leash and Rufus ran to Jackson. It was only a few feet between them, but both of them seemed to run in slow motion. Once together, Rufus jumped into Jackson's arms, licking the tears from his face. He knelt and hugged his dog, looked at Penny, who was crying. "Thank you, Penny. Thank you."

Penny approached and hugged Rufus too. Through tears, she said, "He belongs with you, not me. He needs you as much as you need him. So, take him parachuting. Take him to hospitals, do all the things he needs to do, because he is a wonderful dog, a great dog. I'd like to come see him, one day, if that's okay."

Jackson, still choked up, tried to speak. "Of cour… of course you can come visit him Penny. Any time. Maybe I can bring him here to visit sometime. I promise to let you know how he's doing." He reached out and moved some stray hairs that had fallen to her face. "I promise."

After a quick goodbye, they loaded up and drove home. Rufus would be home.

***

EPILOGUE

1950
Franklin, Tennessee

The veterinary clinic was busy. Dogs, cats, even horses were waiting to be seen. Diplomas and certifications plastered the wall, along with photos of dogs. Some photos were from the war, of Easy Company, of Jackson and Freddie, of Rufus and Jackson. A glass-encased frame held a photo of Jackson and Beau. Two years earlier, Beau had passed at the age of 14. Rufus had taken to Beau quickly and they enjoyed their years together.

The veterinarian, Dr. Gail Harris, was very capable and good natured. The folks of Franklin depended on him to heal their pets and farm animals.

Jackson had gone back to Mississippi State College to complete his studies. This time, he was ready. He graduated from veterinary school with all A's and B's and found a clinic to start his business. Dr. Harris was getting ready to retire, but he needed to find someone to take over his patients. When Jackson wrote him, Dr. Harris invited him to visit. After a week of working together, he knew Jackson was the best man to take over the practice, one day. Dr. Harris still had a few years to go.

It was Friday afternoon; Dr. Gilmore was working on a dog with a laceration on his paw. Rufus, now 10 years old, lay asleep behind the front counter. Though still very active, Rufus had slowed down in the last five years. His naps were longer, his snores louder, but he still went where Jackson went. The bell over the door tinkled, letting them know someone was in the office. A soft voice asked, "Hello? Anyone here?" Rufus' floppy ears rose up when he heard the voice. He stood and looked around the corner, then let out a loud 'BAROOO!' That woke up the clinic, and three German Shepherd puppies came running out of the nursery. When they saw the young lady standing there, they scurried to her.

Jackson finished up with the dog, turned him over to his assistant, washed his hands and went to the office. Rufus ran into the surgical area where Jackson cleaned up, barked at him and ran to the front. *What has got into that dog?* He thought. He dried his hands and walked to the front. Kneeling among the puppies and Rufus was a young lady, beautiful red hair, deep green eyes. Penny. She laughed at the puppies, all with floppy ears like their father. She looked up with a smile and stood when she saw Jackson.

He walked to her slowly, not really believing she was there. He reached out and took her hand. She looked up at him, smiling.

Jackson took her other hand in his, they looked at each other, neither saying a word. Then he spoke.

"You finally made it."

***

They were married six months later, in Penny's home town. Rufus attended the wedding. They stayed in Franklin, where Jackson took over the clinic in 1954, when Dr. Harris retired. They took Rufus to hospitals where children were in treatment for varying things. Rufus cheered the kids up each visit. They all asked about his leg, and Jackson would tell the story of Foy.

A few times, Jackson and Rufus would jump from a small airplane into a field where school children of all ages waited for them to land. Once on the ground, he would gather the kids around him and Rufus, and would talk about overcoming problems in life. He told them how Rufus lost his leg but continued on without looking back. He told them that they could overcome anything in life, just by not giving up.

Rufus became famous, newspaper articles told of his hospital visits and jumps, and how the children were always excited to see him. When Rufus passed away in 1956, he was sixteen years old. Several hundred people, including Freddie, Smokey Gordon, Bradford Freeman, and other Easy Company men who lived within driving distance attended the funeral. Even Major Winters travelled all the way from Pennsylvania. But Rufus had sired several litters of floppy-eared shepherds, of which Jackson and Penny always kept at least one. They always named one of the puppies after their father, and later, when they sired litters, would take a puppy for themselves. In later years, Jackson and Penny attended Easy Company reunions, and Rufus went as well.

Rufus' lineage continues on today, through Rufus' sons and Penny and Jackson's son, Jackson, Jr. Their oldest son carried on the tradition for his parents, even now Jackson Jr. has one of Rufus' sons with him, floppy ears and all.

Sources

Rendezvous With Destiny: *A History of the 101ˢᵗ Airborne Division;* Rapport, Leonard and Northwood, Jr., Arthur.

Technical Manual for War Dogs, TM 10-396.

History of Dogs for Defense Downy, Fairfax.

Band of Brothers: E Company, 506ᵗʰ Regiment, 101ˢᵗ Airborne From Normandy to Hitler's Eagle's Nest; Stephen E. Ambrose.

History of the 101ˢᵗ Airborne Division: *Screaming Eagles – The First 50 Years;* Colonel Robert E. Jones.

Brothers in Battle, Best of Friends; William Guarnere and Edward Heffron.

The Road To Arnhem: *A Screaming Eagle in Holland;* Donald R. Burgett.

Call Of Duty; LT Lynn "Buck" Compton with Marcus Brotherton.

Beyond Band Of Brothers: The War Memoirs of Major Dick Winters; Major Dick Winters with Colonel Cole C. Kingseed.

The Supreme Commander: The War Years of Dwight D. Eisenhower; Stephen E. Ambrose.

Easy Company Soldier, SGT. Don Malarky with Bob Welch.

Shifty's War; Marcus Brotherton

Parachute Infantry: An American Paratroopers Memoir of D-Day and the Fall of the Third Reich; David Kenyon Webster.

The Filthy Thirteen; Richard Killbane and Jake McNiece.

Currahee!: A Screaming Eagle at Normandy; Donald R. Burgett.

Bridging Hell's Highway: The 326th Engineering Battalion During Operation Market Garden; John Sliz.

Fierce Valor: The True Story of Ronald Spiers And His Band Of Brothers; Jared Frederick and Erik Dorr.

A Company of Heroes; Marcus Brotherton

Normandy '44: *D-Day And The Battle For France*; James Holland.

Valiant Comrades: *A Story Of Our Dogs Of War*; Ruth Adams Knight.

The Siegfried Line Campaign; CMH Pub 7-7-1, Charles B. MacDonald

Web Sites:

506th PIR Scrapbook:
https://digicom.bpl.lib.me.us/ww_reg_his/47/

D-Day: State of Play:

http://www.6juin1944.com/

Easy Company:

http://www.easy506th.org/index.php

Camp Toccoa:

https://www.camptoccoaatcurrahee.org/

ACKNOWLEDGMENTS

I decided to write this story for two reasons: my love for dogs and my deep interest in Easy company. Over the last two or three years, I read as many biographies as I could find. When the idea hit me to write about a K-9 unit assigned to Easy, the story poured out of me.

Thanks, as always to my sisters, Diane and Bobbie Suzanne, and my good friend, Freddie Spiers. They encouraged me to keep writing, allowed me to bounce story lines off them, and listening to me go on and on about Rufus. My brother, Doug, also encouraged me and helped me along the way.

I've had two Rufus's in my life, both were extremely good boys. Rufus II was a German shepherd mixed with my Beagle, Lucy, so he did indeed have floppy ears.

I want to give a special thanks to Gordon Carrol, author of the Gil Mason series. Gordon gave me some incredibly smart tips and I hope they made this story better. And Athena, Gordon's eldest daughter, created the wonderful cover art. Athena, thank you so much for capturing Rufus!

ABOUT THE AUTHOR

David Oakes is the author of the Gilmore Clan series. Book one is Apollo Rising, the story of Astronaut Butch Gilmore, selected in the "New Nine" group in 1962. His exploits with Gus Grissom and others change the face of the Moon Race.

David was born in Jackson, Mississippi in 1960, but grew up in Louisiana, Iowa, and Missouri, before moving back to Mississippi in senior year of high school. He taught computer science and coached football and baseball at Picayune Memorial High School for three years begore enlisting in the Navy. He soon was accepted to Aviation Officer Candidate School and graduated as a "Three Bar" in 1989.

After graduating Naval Postgraduate School, he joined the Navy Reserves and accepted a systems integration position at U.S. Central Command. In 2000, he accepted a position as a senior system administrator at Stennis Space Center, where he works to this day.

His hobbies include building models, studying history, mostly World War II and all things space related, raising his dogs, and writing.

David can be reached at authorDavidOakes@gmail.com.

David R. Oakes

ALSO BY DAVID OAKES

Gilmore Clan Book I: Apollo Rising
Gilmore Clan Book 2: A dog For Easy Company

Blood Moon (Short Story)

A Dog For Easy Company

Made in the USA
Coppell, TX
21 May 2024

32609766R10176